By Mary Calmes

Acrobat
Again
Any Closer
With Cardeno C.: Control
With Poppy Dennison: Creature Feature
Floodgates
Frog
The Guardian
Heart of the Race
His Consort
Ice Around the Edges
Judgment
Just Desserts
Kairos
Lay It Down
Mine
Romanus • Chevalier
Romanus & Chevalier Anthology
The Servant
Steamroller
Still
Tales of the Curious Cookbook
Three Fates
What Can Be
Where You Lead
Wishing on a Blue Star
You Never Know

CHANGE OF HEART
Change of Heart • Trusted Bond • Honored Vow
Crucible of Fate • Forging the Future

Published by DREAMSPINNER PRESS
www.dreamspinnerpress.com

By MARY CALMES

L'ANGE
Old Loyalty, New Love • Fighting Instinct • Chosen Pride

MANGROVE STORIES
Blue Days • Quiet Nights • Sultry Sunset
Easy Evenings • Sleeping 'til Sunrise
Mangrove Stories Anthology

MARSHALS
All Kinds of Tied Down • Fit to Be Tied
Tied Up in Knots • Twisted and Tied

A MATTER OF TIME
A Matter of Time: Vol. 1 • A Matter of Time: Vol. 2
Bulletproof • But For You
Parting Shot • Piece of Cake

TIMING
Timing • After the Sunset • When the Dust Settles
Perfect Timing Anthology

THE VAULT
A Day Makes • Late in the Day

THE WARDER SERIES
His Hearth • Tooth & Nail • Heart in Hand
Sinnerman • Nexus • Cherish Your Name
Warders Volume One • Warders Volume Two

Published by DREAMSPINNER PRESS
www.dreamspinnerpress.com

HIS CONSORT

Mary Calmes

DREAMSPINNER PRESS

Published by
DREAMSPINNER PRESS

5032 Capital Circle SW, Suite 2, PMB# 279,
Tallahassee, FL 32305-7886 USA
www.dreamspinnerpress.com

His Consort
© 2018 Mary Calmes.
Cover Art

© 2018 Reese Dante.
http://www.reesedante.com
Cover content is for illustrative purposes only and any person depicted
on the cover is a model.

Mass Market Paperback ISBN: 978-1-64108-143-6
Trade Paperback ISBN: 978-1-64080-963-5
Digital ISBN: 978-1-64080-962-8
Library of Congress Control Number: 2018907625
Mass Market Paperback published November 2018
v. 1.0

Printed in the United States of America
∞
This paper meets the requirements of
ANSI/NISO Z39.48-1992 (Permanence of Paper).

Chapter One

I WASN'T thinking when I ran out of the cabin toward the scream, my father's rifle and the biggest flashlight I owned in my hands.

The snow was deep, up to my knees, but it was February in Washington, and as I trudged through it and around trees, ferns, and thick brush, I tried not to think of every horror movie about the woods I'd ever seen in my thirty-two years. Not that I was scared—I was a former Marine—but then I heard another shriek and increased my pace. I had to get there faster.

Unfortunately it had rained on top of the snow, and then the temperature dropped to freezing, so moving was like chiseling through shaved ice with my legs. I took a step and sank, took another and sank—getting anywhere quickly wasn't going to happen. The cold was trying to claw its way under my skin, so I zipped up my shearling-lined barn coat to try to keep it at bay.

What was going on, on the grounds of the estate owned by Mr. and Mrs. Rothschild? Ever since I arrived, I'd had questions.

The Rothschilds had contacted the company I worked for, Wild Wood Carpentry, after seeing pictures on the website of previous work I'd done. They were impressed and asked if I could come to their home and rebuild some built-in bookcases damaged in a fire. Money was no object, and they didn't need an estimate.

Wild Wood took care of the details. I left Bellingham in the north Cascade Mountains, near the Mount Baker Area in Whatcom County, and drove toward a town called Glacier. I was on a lonely stretch of 542 for a while and then turned off in the direction of Church Lake. It got a bit desolate after that, nothing in front of me or behind as far as I could see but snow and trees. When I finally saw the driveway appear out of nowhere, it was a bit of a relief.

The long, winding two-lane road led to a ten-foot-high wrought iron gate. The high-tech cameras and security system were a surprise, and I had to get out and stand in front of a video monitor while someone confirmed my identity. As I waited, I wondered why all of it was necessary. Why all the hoops to jump through in the middle of nowhere?

It was another ten minutes of driving before thick woods thinned and then cleared. Their house—if you could call it that—looked more like a fortress than a home.

What appeared to be a medieval stronghold from the outside gave off the same austere, museum-like quality once I crossed the threshold. It was as massive inside as out and just as frigid, if not more so: marble everywhere, ancient polished wood, enormous fireplaces in every room I walked through, and lots of gilded everything. I felt underdressed and looked down on by everyone who had the seeming misfortune of conversing with me. From the first day it felt like they didn't really want me there. And there were a lot of damn people walking around, pretending not to notice my presence: maids and other servants, a cook and his staff, but also a ton of other beautiful people sitting and standing around, not doing much of anything but artful lounging. But again, lots of movement too. It was like a small bustling village inside the thick walls. I wanted to ask what the deal was with the castle—were they fixing it up for a visit or something?—but I was there to do a job, not ask questions. So even though I was curious about the inhabitants of the house, I kept my mouth shut.

The lady of the house, Mrs. Rothschild, put me in a small cabin on their property a mile away from their front door for the duration of the job. I was fed two meals a day in the kitchen, in a nook close to the oven where it was warm, and then dinner was packed up for me every night before I left after nine to ten hours working on the bookcases. No one talked to me during the day except to bring me bottled water.

At the end of the fourth day, Mrs. Rothschild came to check on me, nodded, gave me a shadow of a smile and told me to continue.

"You're not at all what I thought you would be, Mr. Thorpe," she said. "You haven't been a bother in the least, and you don't smell at all like others of your kind."

I suspected the "others of my kind" comment referred to workmen she'd had in her home previously. Maybe those guys weren't that concerned about their body odor—more about getting in and out. It was a weird place, so I understood what might have driven them.

"I doubt my neighbors even know that you're at the cabin, as unobtrusive as you are."

That last comment had me thinking as I churned through the snow toward the scream that got me up off the couch, dressed quickly, and out into the night. No one knew I was out here. No one knew I was staying in the cabin except the Rothschilds, and if I didn't show up for work tomorrow, would they even check on me? Or would they just call someone to clean up the guest house?

It didn't matter. I wasn't going to turn back. I was going to find the source of the noise. I just really hoped I wasn't on my way to getting lost in the woods and ending up very dead. When I saw the light, I wasn't dodging trees anymore because they'd been cleared… and then I saw the bonfire.

It was huge, like the beach fires I'd attended during summers with friends, but instead of crackling away on wet sand, this one blazed upon cleared frozen ground. It was a touch strange and a touch surprising out there in the dark, but no more so than anything else about this place.

"Holy shit," I rasped, my voice going out, my breath heavy all of a sudden like a weight on my chest.

The second thing I noticed was all the people. A lot of fucking people. I kept getting surprised about the sheer number of bodies I'd seen on this trip. It was like… where were they keeping themselves, and why? Then the crowd parted, and none of that mattered anymore because I saw a boy, maybe seventeen, eighteen at the most, chained to what looked like a St. Andrew's Cross. He was bleeding from practically everywhere. His neck, chest, both wrists, both ankles, both thighs… and Mr. Rothschild, whom I had only ever seen in passing, was leaning down, moving in slow motion like it was a show—a grotesque spectacle—over the kid's groin, mouth open, a second away from biting down on the young man's penis. He could easily bite it off.

Jesus Christ.

Only years of training kept me from vomiting right there.

The worst part was everyone around the inner circle with Mr. Rothschild was so involved in torturing the poor kid they hadn't even noticed I was there. Even the twittering alarm of the folks actually looking at me didn't alert him.

In seconds I lifted my rifle, fired into the air, and then instantly braced it against my shoulder, ready to wing somebody if they didn't respond to my one and only demand.

"Everybody back the hell away from the boy!"

Nothing.

No response at all.

The only good thing that did happen was that Mr. Rothschild turned to face me instead of biting the kid's dick off.

"Did you fuckin' hear me?"

A chill crept up my back then on spider legs. Someone was coming up behind me. I did what I'd done for years in the Corps: I ducked and turned and put the muzzle of the rifle against the underside of the jaw of a man who clearly thought I was some yokel out there in the woods at two in the morning. He was good, I'd give him that. I hadn't heard him at all; his boots had not made the same sounds as they crunched through the snow as mine had earlier. But I'd been a Marine for years, fourteen, to be exact, and those reflexes never went away.

I wasn't prepared for his slow, cocky grin, but my relief was instant. No one who smiled like that was about to kill me.

When he spoke, his accent sounded like Italian and maybe German mixed up with some Scottish or Irish, definitely some kind of Gaelic there. Since Spanish was the language I studied in the Corps, I was just grateful he was speaking English.

"Did the prince conscript more guards? Are you one of them?" he asked.

An odd question that made no sense. "No, I—I just need to save the kid."

He slapped a hand over his heart. "This is my sacred duty as well."

That was very good news.

My breath rushed out, and I returned his smile. "Thank God," I said, turning back to the crowd, putting the gun to my shoulder again. Normally I would never have trusted anyone this quickly, but considering the insane situation I found myself in, I had to put my faith somewhere, and a man who also cared about the boy seemed a safe bet. "Move the fuck back!" I thundered to the crowd.

"You have no idea what you're doing!" Mr. Rothschild railed. Something was wrong with him. He was not in control of himself; his pupils were blown, his mouth was smeared in blood, and he was panting. He was very clearly having some sort of breakdown and needed help.

"Release the boy," I demanded because, whatever was wrong with the man paying me to fix the bookshelves in his upstairs library, he was not my foremost concern. The boy losing blood was.

"You don't understand!"

Oh, I was pretty damn sure I did. They had dressed the kid up in what looked like a gold silk karate *gi*, then opened his top to bare his chest and pulled down his pants. They were bleeding him dry for whatever freaky cult ritual bullshit they were doing, and I had only a moment to wonder how long they'd had him. Had he been in the house when I was? I felt remorse over the thought that I'd missed something. He already looked worse for wear, his lips blue and his skin gray, all of which I could easily see from my vantage point.

I took a step, and people surged forward until I put a bullet in the ground in front of them. "I'm ordering you to let him go!"

"You don't belong here!" a woman shrieked, and when I searched for the face the voice belonged to, I found Mrs. Rothschild. "Just leave now, Mr. Thorpe…. This is not your fight."

"You're killing him," I rasped as the guy beside me snarled.

I didn't want to turn and look at him because you never, ever took your eyes off the threat, but just a quick sideways glance told me he had armed himself with more than one knife.

"This boy is not human," Mrs. Rothschild yelled before gesturing at the man standing with me. "None of us are."

Whatever the fuck that meant.

"Mr. Thorpe," Mr. Rothschild pleaded, "things aren't at all what they appear to be."

What they appeared to be was something out of a book on medieval torture.

"I think it is exactly what it looks like," the man on my right growled, his voice garbled, guttural, almost more animal than human before he added, "I have others approaching. They will be here shortly. We shall part ways, but they will find me. We need only delay them."

His words were meant to soothe me, but *really*, the situation was far more dire. From the blood on everyone, it appeared they'd had a taste of the kid already, so I was guessing I needed to get him in my truck and to the hospital for a transfusion as fast as I could.

"Give me room," I roared, giving my command to the crowd, using the gun to gesture at them to move.

They didn't immediately fall back, and that made no sense because the gun I was pointing at them was a serious threat. I wondered vaguely if they were all hopped up on something, some drug that was dulling their senses.

As I advanced on them, ready to shoot, I knew I was dead if they attacked me. There were just too many. I hoped none of them had a death wish. I'd take out the first ones who lunged at me.

"Rothschild, move your people back!" I bellowed in the voice I used to project over gunfire in Afghanistan.

"You will bring down a plague on us if you persist with this delusion and alert him to our whereabouts."

Him.

Alert *him* to their whereabouts.

I had to wonder if maybe they didn't want *him* to know where *they* were because perhaps torturing kids was something *he* wouldn't approve of.

"If this creature doesn't die, it will be the end of us!"

But there was no *creature*, only a sweet-looking young man they were trying to kill—and still might manage to if I couldn't get things moving along with the negotiations. Even worse, Mr. Rothschild and his wife and all their people were between me and the boy, and short of shooting them, I had no idea what I was going to do.

If I got out of this, I was moving to New Orleans. Yes, the universe was trying to tell me something. Who was I not to listen?

I was saved from having to act by everyone starting to scream before they turned and ran.

Three guys blew by me—it was impressive how fast they moved in the snow, or over the snow, if I was seeing it right, which clearly I wasn't—but the point was, they looked badass, and that was what I wanted in reinforcements. I turned to my new friend standing there, hands behind his back, studying me.

"Do you belong to Varic?"

Weird question, even weirder timing, but then again, this whole night had become surreal. "I don't—" I lowered my gun and forgot about him as I raced over to the boy, concerned only with him. But that didn't stop me from being startled when I looked up and the guy was right there with me, like he somehow kept pace even though I didn't hear him move.

"Answer," he persisted. "Do you belong to Varic?"

I took a breath so I didn't yell at him. Who the fuck cared about anything but the kid? "I don't know who that is, yeah?" I said, concentrating on keeping my voice flat, without judgment. "Will you help me with him?"

He shook his head. "He would gut me if I paused to show either concern or compassion instead of punishing those who dared lay hands upon him."

"What?"

"If you would remain, I will loosen the chains when I return."

That made no sense. "I think I'll just get him off that thing now, all right?"

He graced me with that appealing smile of his again, a quirk of his mouth both wicked and warm. "You are human. I can smell the sweet scent of your blood from here. But you carry yourself like one of us… but also something different. What is your name?"

"Jason Thorpe," I told him as I looked over the several feet of chain wrapped around the boy's legs and each arm. It was like they thought he was the

Incredible Hulk or something instead of the ballet dancer he resembled. "Who're you?"

He gave a bigger smile this time, and I could have sworn I saw… but it was late and I was tired, and my adrenaline had spiked and was rapidly leaving me.

"I am Hadrian."

I waited a moment, noting the chiseled features, the deep umber brown of his skin, and the power in his frame until he lifted his left eyebrow like he was waiting. And then it hit me. "That's it? Just one name?"

He laughed.

"Like Beyoncé and Adele?"

"Yes," he said with a throaty chuckle. "Exactly like that."

I would have said something else, but my worry for the kid overrode my curiosity, and I got serious about the task of getting him loose.

"You should use both hands to free him," he suggested, "as no one will return to offer you peril."

"Thanks." I slung the rifle over my shoulder, glad I'd never taken the thick strap off, before going to work on getting the boy untangled.

"Name your clan," Hadrian continued.

Strangest conversation ever. "I don't know what you're—"

"What about the clan of your mate?"

"I don't—"

"Are you mated?"

He was so odd. "I—no, but we gotta get this kid outta here."

"I thought perhaps it was the scent of your mate I perceived, but… no. All I smell is you."

"Okay," I drew out because it was rude not to acknowledge the nice man who'd helped me, even though, sadly, he was nuts. "So I'm gonna get him some help."

I got a quick nod. "I suspect he will revive before you even have time to complete whatever it is you have planned, but I will leave him in your care until the time for me to collect him arrives, as I know you mean him no harm."

"Well, no, of course not, I wanna save him."

"But you did that already," he told me. "I did not know where to seek him. I was some distance away, up at the house, and then we traversed north toward the mountains, but he… he…. I was starting to turn just a bit mad—" He took a nervous breath that told me he'd been more than just a "bit" of anything. "—but then I felt… almost a… pulse, like a wave through the air that drew me back, and then I saw the fire and heard your yell, and I was rewarded with the sight of my precious quarry safe and sound."

"He's really not safe," I insisted, concerned for the boy and for the sanity of the nice man standing in front of me, because his mind was all over the place.

"Care for him well. Forgive me, but I must take my leave of you. I must needs gather the heads of this clan to take to my prince, as they have broken his law by attacking his vassal."

That, at least, made sense. They were in trouble, the Rothschilds and the others who'd participated, and Hadrian was going to round them up so they could see the prince and answer for their crimes. Heads would roll. "Sure," I agreed, starting on my task of unwinding the silver chains from the boy. When I glanced up a few moments later, Hadrian was gone. I pulled up the boy's pants and closed both sides of the gi, covering him as best I could. When his eyes slowly drifted open, I smiled wide.

"Hey there," I greeted him gently.

"Tell me you are not going to ask me how I am feeling?" he asked, much more sarcastic than I was anticipating given his current circumstances.

"No," I assured him, hand on the side of his neck to check his pulse.

"You show such care, and I am nothing more than a stranger," he murmured. "Thank you for your kindness and worry."

"Don't mention it," I said gruffly, scared for him but also touched that he was thanking me. "What's your name?"

"Tiago."

He looked like an angel with his blond hair and enormous sky-blue eyes and was, without a doubt, the prettiest, most delicate man I'd ever seen. "Well, Tiago, you're gonna be all right. I'm gonna make sure."

"I would be well regardless of you interceding on my behalf."

I didn't want to argue with him because I needed him calm.

"But they have the right of it, you know," he whispered as I lifted him gently off the cross and into my arms, the princess carry the gentlest way I knew to move him. "This situation is beyond your understanding."

"Then someone should have given me an itinerary of the activities that were going to occur while I was visiting," I replied softly, feeling how cold he was, terrified he was going to get hypothermia. "Because no one gets to hurt kids on my watch."

He sighed deeply. "I am not a child, I promise you."

"Barely legal, then," I amended, crushing him to my chest, trying to give him as much of my body heat as I could as I turned to head back to the cabin.

"This decision to help me may haunt you for the rest of your life."

"I'll worry about that once you're hooked up to an IV at the hospital."

He lifted himself, wrapping his arms around my neck, holding on tight.

"I'm sorry if I'm hurting you," I apologized as I trudged through the snow as quickly as I could. "I'm really trying to be—"

"No," he breathed, then swallowed hard. "You are much like a furnace…. I forget sometimes how warm humans are."

Humans?

If he forgot something about humans, then that made him… what? Though the question skittered through my mind, I couldn't hold on to it. At the moment, it didn't matter. The only important thing was to get him to my cabin.

I finally saw the lights up ahead but heard growling at the same time. Glancing to my right, I saw several men sprinting toward me. The running didn't scare me, but the speed did. They were in the same snow I was, but it didn't seem to be slowing them down in the least, just as it hadn't caused Hadrian or his men any extra effort.

"Shit," I croaked, moving as fast as I could toward the back door. "I thought he said no one was coming back."

But really, how could Hadrian have known how many people were out there?

Tiago purred in my arms. "You can put me down now, Jason Thorpe. I assure you I can stand against the others now."

"Not hardly," I admonished, reaching the door, then jostling him to open it with my right hand, and rushed through before kicking it shut behind me. Darting to the couch, I put him down, pivoted, and then ran back to the door to lock it before taking several steps back while yanking the gun off my shoulder to raise it and point at the door.

"What is your plan here, Jason?" Tiago asked. He sounded amused.

"I'm gonna protect you until they clear out and I can get us to my truck."

I heard him get off the couch and walk toward me.

"No," I said, sparing him a glance before turning back to cover the door. "Don't. You have to be careful you don't bleed out."

He moved in front of me, but I was scared of the people outside and of him dying, and I forgot to be gentle when I tried to push him back behind me. I gasped. Even though I had easily a hundred pounds of muscle on him, he didn't budge. "How're you doing—"

"I am hardly the curiosity here," he said, squinting, putting his hands on my face. "I should have been in need of some of your blood to be at full strength. I never expected those peasants to attack a member of the court, but somehow just being close to you… in your presence…. Jason, who are you?"

"Me?" I rasped, seeing the people collect around the back of the cabin. Why they weren't rushing the door, or the window, for that matter, I had no idea.

"Why do they hesitate? Why delay their entrance?" he questioned, sounding perplexed and fascinated at the same time, just as confused as I was.

Scared, I turned back to Tiago with some difficulty. He was still staring, studying me like I was some kind of alien creature.

"Why do these people fear you?" he asked, leaning closer. His nostrils flared like he was trying to catch some kind of scent off me.

"They don't," I answered, moving around him to stand beside the couch and look out at the tree line where more people appeared. "They don't have any reason to."

"No," he agreed, "they do not, and yet they press not for entry."

What he found interesting, I found a blessing. And… he talked funny. A lot like Hadrian, now that I thought about it. I wanted to ask if he knew what a contraction was, but maybe that was rude. It hit me, then, how long I'd actually been off active duty. Back on the line in Nangarhar province, on the ground with my unit, fighting alongside Afghan troops, any thoughts other than being alert and taking care of the guys around me were inconsequential. I wouldn't have even entertained something as inane as how someone spoke. But back in the world, as I'd been for a few years now, as honed as I once was, there were chinks in my armor now, which meant I could miss things.

Suddenly I was even more scared. If my training had slipped and only muscle memory remained, such as in the case of knowing Hadrian was there earlier, it meant someone could get the drop on me.

We had to get to my truck. Away from everyone was the only way I'd be sure Tiago was safe.

"Tell me who you are, Jason Thorpe."

"You've been using my name, but I don't remember telling—"

His smile was sweet, and he flushed, a soft pinking to his cheeks that was lovely. "I heard you say such to Hadrian."

I nodded as I pulled out my cell phone.

"What are you doing?"

"I'm gonna call the police."

He snatched the phone from my hand. "We cannot have that."

"We?"

"Yes."

"Who's we?"

"Just—you cannot call the authorities."

"And why is that?"

Crossing his arms, he tipped his head sideways as he regarded me. "There would be complications we frankly cannot abide."

"Again with the 'we'?"

He sighed. "Tell me, Jason, have you ever been to Malta?"

"No, I—who can't have complications?"

He took a quick breath. "Jason, for the last time, to whom do you belong?"

I shook my head. We didn't have time for this. "I don't belong to—"

"What is your clan name?"

"Thorpe," I told him, rushing around to grab the few things I had left out, plus the toiletries from the bathroom, then throwing them into the military duffel I still used while I traveled. "So since you seem to be standing up okay, do you think you can walk?"

"Of course," he said as though that was obvious.

"Great," I rushed out, thankful for his mobility, as it would make our exodus toward my truck parked out front that much easier.

Zipping up the duffel, I threw it over my shoulder with the rifle and darted back over to Tiago. Before he could say another word, I grabbed his arm and herded him toward the front door. I stopped him before opening it, then got the gun ready before I stepped through onto the porch. Checking around, even walking out a few steps to scan the overhang of the roof, I saw nothing and then gestured for Tiago.

"Jason?" he said softly, and I could have sworn I heard a hint of laughter. "I think perhaps your concern is currently misplaced."

"Well, I think you might be in shock," I informed him, thrilled that it looked like we were the only ones walking across the front yard. Even though he wasn't bleeding anymore, I was really scared he could still die. We reached my truck, and I unlocked the door and put him in the passenger seat as carefully as I could. Once I got the belt secured around him, I tossed the duffel in the bed and ran around to the driver's side, shoved the rifle onto the gun rack behind my seat, and got in. After locking the doors, even though I still saw no sign of anyone else, even Hadrian, I took my phone from him, then started the truck and sent up snow and mud as I gunned the engine hard to get to the road. I was going eighty by the time we were on the two-lane highway. I cranked up the heater as high as it would go and headed for the closest town I knew of. I wanted to get him to an ER as soon as possible.

"You know, I perhaps might have underestimated the volume of blood they apprehended."

No shit.

When I turned my chin to check on Tiago, he had either passed out or fallen asleep beside me. I checked for a pulse, found it beating strong and steady, and was finally able to breathe.

Chapter Two

I GREW calmer the farther away we got, even though I soon realized none of the small towns we were passing through—Glacier, Maple Falls, Kendall—had hospitals, only small clinics that were closed at that time of night. I drove like a bat out of hell after deciding I was better off just driving the kid back to Bellingham.

A half mile after passing a gas station, I nearly came out of my skin when icy-cold fingers wrapped around my wrist.

"Oh shit!" I yelled and struggled to get control of the truck because Tiago held the other hand in an iron grip.

"Where am I?"

"One sec," I bit off as the truck spun out in the middle of the road and came to a rocking stop, jolting us hard against our seat belts.

Once my heart was out of my throat and back in my chest, I asked as nicely as I could what the fuck he was doing.

"Did I catch you off guard?"

Understatement of the year.

He let go, and I drove the truck off the center divider, pulled over onto the dirt shoulder, and put it in Park.

It took me a few moments to get it together enough to talk to him because, for fuck's sake, after the night I'd had, I felt like one more thing was going to splinter me into a million pieces. I didn't have scares anymore; my life was steady nowadays, without the adrenaline rushes that came from life-and-death situations. I was out of practice.

Finally I took a breath and turned to face him. "So do you remember who I am?"

"Of course," he assured me, scowling. "I simply lost my bearings for a moment."

"Can you tell me what hap—"

"They bled me but did not drink because they feared that I carried him in my veins," he announced, his beautiful face lit up in happiness. "And of course I do. He has saved me countless times over the centuries with his precious blood, but nothing of his body could ever be unclean or—" He paused as if to cut off his ramble. "They are all superstitious fools."

"I'm sorry, what?" Who was *he*, and what superstitions? Centuries? I kept quiet, letting him talk, knowing shock when I heard it.

"When they learned to whom I belonged, their only thought was to drain enough of my blood that they could burn me alive so he would never know I had been there."

I gasped, horrified.

"As if that could ever happen," he scoffed, arrogant, voice dripping with conceit like it was the most ridiculous thing he'd ever said. "As though he would be unaware of my whereabouts at any given moment."

When you pulled people out of a combat situation or saved their lives, the first things that came out of their mouths weren't words of thanks, but a rant. Some of them were indignant, saying that whatever it was, they could have handled it. Others would just start talking about people in their lives and how they wouldn't have liked this or that. It was like the mind protected itself by way of speaking about something familiar and safe and strong. I was thinking normal equaled whoever "he" was for Tiago.

"As though I'm not precious to him."

"I'm sure you are," I soothed, reaching for his cheek, wanting to comfort him. I had no clue what he was talking about. "I'm so sorry. You must've been so scared." I could only imagine how much therapy he was going to need not to jump at his own shadow after being bound and attacked.

He made a noise filled with derision. "I assure you I was not frightened in the least."

But how could he not have been?

"I would have never allowed them to actually harm me."

I'd heard the same kind of bravado in war. Lots of guys I knew shrugged off the horrors, repressed them and ended up blindsided by a flood of emotion down the road. "I promise that you'll have time for your mind to heal once your body—"

"I am already close to full strength," he informed me, sounding more than a bit smug.

I really studied him, and I was amazed to see he was right. "I…. You looked like crap just a bit ago, but now you look much better."

He sighed deeply as he gazed at me. "Though I needed it not, your first thought was to save me, Jason Thorpe, and I thank you."

"Oh, you needed saving, all right. Your buddy Hadrian thought so too."

The inelegant snort was interesting. "Hadrian always believes the condition of the world to be far more dire than it appears. But what can one expect from the head of the *drek-kee*?"

"*Dre-kee*" made no sense to me. But what did make sense was Hadrian clearly cared for Tiago, and how lucky Tiago was. I had no one keeping tabs on me. My parents traveled constantly; my sister had her own life with family and friends in San Diego. We weren't connected. And a month ago, Eddie, one of my oldest friends, lost his battle with cancer. I was so very alone.

After the funeral I was in the kitchen helping clean up, and Eddie's wife, Rachel, surprised me by stepping in front of me and taking my hand.

"Rach?"

"Jason, honey, I need to tell you something, and I need you to let me get it out."

"Course."

She took a breath. "You have been such a wonderful—"

"Oh, no, sweetie, you don't have—"

"What did I say?" She pinned me with a look.

I needed to shut-up. "Sorry. G'head."

Her smile was watery. "Goodness, but the Lord did bless me with hardheaded men."

"Simple men," I corrected her.

She chuckled softly and straightened up, head back, eyes on me. "I need you to know from the bottom of my heart that I appreciate everything you did for Eddie and me, from building the ramp out front for his wheelchair to staying with us for six months to drive him to all his doctor's appointments while I was finishing up my residency, and then another four after that just to get us set up in our routine. I've been more than blessed," she said, her voice cracking, tears slipping down her cheeks before she wiped them roughly away, trying so hard to remain strong. "No one could have asked for a better friend, and I hope you know that he loved you like a brother."

I nodded, too choked up to even attempt any words.

"So—" She took another breath, quiet for a moment, composing herself. "—he left you something."

"What is this?" I asked, taking the large manila envelope she passed me.

"You remember Eddie's grandfather?"

"Destry Lane." I remembered all the stories about the old man Eddie used to tell me while we were out on endless patrols. His grandfather was indelibly linked to my time in Afghanistan just by the sheer number of anecdotes I could recall. "Man should've been a writer with a name like that."

"Oh, that's very good." She sighed because we both knew that was how Eddie began every memory of him. It was important I remembered.

"Eddie loved him so much."

"Yes, he did," she agreed, sniffling as she patted the envelope. "And he loved Eddie, which was why, in his will, he got his grandfather's favorite building, and why now that very same building is yours."

"I'm sorry, what?"

"Eddie wanted you to have it, to remember both him and his grandfather."

"Rachel," I said, tucking the envelope under my arm before taking her hands in mine. "Sweetie, I'm not about to forget your husband for the rest of my life, so please… you keep the building and—"

"No," she insisted, shaking her head. "This is what Eddie wanted, and I'll be damned if you get in the way of his wishes, Jason."

"Honey, you—"

"No," she said implacably, her face carrying so much sadness but strength as well. She was not about to bend on this. "He wanted this, and we both know that there was nothing, ever, that that man wanted that I didn't deliver."

It was true and went both ways. Theirs had been a love for the ages.

"So," she said, easing the envelope out from under my arm and putting it back in my hands. "This is what he wanted, this is what I want, and this is what his folks want."

"But you could go there and live and—"

"My life is here in Seattle, not somewhere I've never been."

"Then you could sell—"

She gasped. "Oooh, how pissed would he be at you for even suggesting such a thing?"

It was true; Eddie wouldn't have liked hearing the word *sell* in any sentence that had to do with his grandfather's building.

"Just suck it up, Thorpe," she ordered, almost growling at me. "Do what my dear sweet super-annoying husband wanted."

"Don't you think it should stay in the family?"

"Oh, honey, it is," she told me, leaning in to give me a hug. "You go live in the French Quarter, and I'll visit."

"Rachel, I don't deserve—"

"You so do," she argued, stepping back to look up into my face. "And it's time you start living your life, don't you think?"

"What're you talking about? I have a life."

"Eddie didn't seem to think so, and, I mean, he lived a lifetime since he left the Corps. You haven't done anything at all."

That wasn't quite true. I had work, but coming back to the world was hard for me, even though I knew reenlisting would have been just as bad. I'd started to develop what my captain called a God complex. There were situations I thought I could handle alone, and the chances I took became problematic. The last time, after I went missing for three days because I went out alone to save a little girl and her family—which I did—they told me I could either go home or face a court-martial. My heart was in the right place, but I didn't get to make the decisions about who I would help and when. I wasn't kicked out… not exactly. My record was beautiful, spotless, so I could have gone into law enforcement, but it wasn't for me.

I needed to take a step back from thinking I could save the world. I couldn't even save Eddie Clayton.

"He didn't need saving," Rachel said, wiping away my tears, making me realize I'd said that last part out loud. "He just needed us by his side, and guess what… that's exactly what he got. You and me."

I deflated because, yeah, she was right. Whatever Eddie wanted was always for the best.

"Just think how tickled he would be to know you were there in New Orleans."

She was right. He used to laugh at me as I bitched about the cold. After all those tours in Afghanistan, I'd gotten used to the heat. So really, if I lived, I'd pack up and go.

However, the "if" was big because, as usual, I'd gone somewhere I shouldn't have been, and now I was sitting in my truck with a stranger I'd just rescued.

No one who knew me would have been surprised. Eddie would have shaken his head as he often had, worried about my sanity. I had a real knack for rushing headfirst into things without thinking them through. But what were you supposed to do when faced with a life-or-death situation? Sit there and analyze it?

Hardly.

It was time for that change my best friend wanted for me.

Tiago furrowed his brows as he studied me. "Why are you sad?"

I cleared my throat, trying to get my voice to function as I worked through my epiphany. "I need to make a change and… I thought about it earlier, but I just realized how important it is that I don't wait another second."

"Oh?"

I shook my head, smiling at the same time. "Sorry. I'm in the middle of some weird existential crisis, and you were fighting for your life. Forgive me for being a selfish prick."

"I promise you that all your actions prove you to be the exact opposite of selfish."

"Yeah, but you don't wanna hear boring crap about me, and besides, I need to get you to the hospital so we can make sure that—"

"Stop," he ordered, not allowing me to put the truck in gear, slipping his hand around my wrist and holding tight. "I assure you that I will not expire in the next few moments, and I would love to hear all about you."

"Yeah, but you're—"

"Please, Jason. Everything about you is riveting. Just speak with me for a time."

My scoff was loud in the small space.

"Cross my heart."

I checked his face, and since he really seemed to be interested and did look pretty good with his color back, and because he was just sitting there waiting, I went ahead and rambled on. "So I'm about a minute and a half away from being the neighbor that no one notices is dead."

He shook his head. "No. Not at all. Believe me, I would notice."

I forced a smile. "That's sweet, but as soon as I get you taken care of—I'm in for a change."

"Oh yes, you are," he said, eyes widening.

"What's wrong?"

He appeared startled. "I had not taken notice before, but now... I can smell your blood," he said, aghast. "I thought you were one of... but you are human."

Smell my blood? Shit. Something new I hadn't considered. They'd drugged him. "Hey, lookit me."

"I am unable to do anything but," he declared, smiling slightly.

"No, I mean, open your eyes real big?"

"Whatever for?"

"Just—" I couldn't wait and took a gentle but firm hold of his face and, with my thumbs, moved the lids so I could check his pupils. Sure enough, they were enormous. "Oh man, what'd they give you?"

"The scent of your blood is really something," he insisted, slipping a still-icy hand around my wrist, brushing his thumb over my pulse point.

"Uh-huh," I agreed, a new concern in my head as I let go of him, put the truck in gear, and pulled off the shoulder and back out onto the road. I was flying down the highway, again, just as I had been earlier, and didn't care how fast I was going. If a cop stopped me—great! Whatever law enforcement pulled me over could give me an escort to the hospital, and once we were there, could take my statement at the same time. Two birds with one stone.

"Jason, why do you smell like that?"

"I just smell like me, kid."

"Yes, but there must be a reason."

Ignoring his ridiculous comment, wanting to keep him talking and calm, I asked, "So what were you doing with the Rothschilds that you ended up strapped to a cross?"

"Human," he repeated as though in a daze.

"Hey," I said loudly, wanting him to stay awake now, no more falling asleep. For all I knew, he had a concussion too. Just because I couldn't see any damage didn't mean there wasn't any. "Tell me what the hell was going on."

"I—it is a lengthy tale."

"Well, we have a long ride, so go ahead and start," I ordered, using the tone I used with new guys when they froze in battle. Somehow they thought because we went out on patrol with Afghan troops, they'd be safer. Nothing was further from the truth. Sadly, inevitably, they would end up hugging the wall, eyes glazed, mouths open, having just seen their buddy killed in front of them. My tone and volume got them moving again. Part power, part comfort, and they followed every time.

"The account concerns who I am," he said, the dazed expression still all over his face.

"Okay, I'll bite. Who are you?"

He preened, sitting up straight, flipping his hair out of his face. He was about to say something that made him feel good about himself. "I am Tiago Martín, the *rhah-jon* of the *drah-gore*'s court," he announced haughtily.

I waited for an explanation. That was two more words that meant nothing to me, even though he certainly was all puffed up about them.

He just sat there.

"Is there more?" I prodded gently.

He snapped his head sideways so he could glare at me. "I am the trusted counselor of the prince."

"Ah." Prince. Now we were getting somewhere. Between what I'd seen and heard at the Rothschilds', finding him trussed up like a sacrifice, the way those people all clustered in one place far away from town—isolated, self-sustaining with their own rules and leaders—all of that led to one conclusion.

He was part of a cult.

I was surprised it took me so long to figure it out, but again, I was out of practice with thinking on my feet, and in my defense, I had been woken from a sound sleep when I heard him screaming.

"You poor kid," I sighed.

"I beg your pardon?" He was indignant.

I glanced over at him, and he was glowering at me, not at all pleased with my sympathy. "What?"

"Please tell me that whoever keeps you has the good sense to tell you that their prince is called the *drah-gore*." He was terse, imperious, and each word was clipped.

Then the words sank in. What the hell was he talking about? "Keeps me?"

"They need to at least give you the generalities so you *know* your place."

My place? "Meaning?"

"You should address me with far more regard."

"I see." I was placating him. I couldn't get mad and tell him he was nuts. Clearly he'd been drugged, and I'd seen that they'd bit him or cut him, and maybe, initially, he'd been kidnapped. This could be a case of Stockholm syndrome and brainwashing…. God only knew what he'd suffered and for how long before I showed up. Certainly his brain had warped the truth of what was being done to him. He was probably really messed up. "So that word, *drah-gore*, is weird, huh? How're you spelling that?"

A deep, long-suffering sigh. "Give me your mobile."

"What? Why?"

"Just give it to me now."

I pulled it from the breast pocket of my coat, unlocked it with my thumb, and then passed it to him.

"I will type some words for you since your education is so horrendously lacking. I can assure you that when the prince finds out that you were not even told the basics, he will be sorely vexed."

"Vexed" was not a scary word. "Sure," I agreed, playing along, not wanting him wound up, not wanting his adrenaline to spike and get whatever drugs were in his system pumping any faster to his heart and head.

"Very well," Tiago said, typing into whatever app he'd opened on my phone. "This is what I am. Look at the word, I will watch the road."

He turned the screen so I could see he'd typed the word "rajan."

"And that's you?"

"That is my title, yes."

"It's a pretty word."

"It is," he agreed. "And there are many others, and you will need to know them all as they are of great importance."

"No doubt in my mind."

"Take heed," he admonished.

He had *drah-gore* as draugr and *drek-kee*—whatever it was he'd referred to earlier—as dreki, and he spelled out the word rekkr—"*reck-ur,*" which he said I should know because that's what Hadrian was.

"He's a good guy," I chimed in.

"He follows all the rules."

The way he said it, with an eye roll that I caught as I glanced at him, told me what he thought of that. "And why is that such a bad thing?"

He gave me a dismissive wave; evidently the subject of Hadrian was closed.

"So tell me what you do as the rajan."

"Well," he began, brightening, happy, it seemed, to talk about his place in the cult. "A rajan is quite similar to an ambassador. I always precede when meeting a new clan or when the prince has a question for a clan that needs answering."

"So you go somewhere, maybe take a gift, and make the introductions for your boss."

"Yes," he said, beaming at me, "precisely."

"But you have backup so nobody hurts you, and that's Hadrian."

"Yes, if I do not return within a set amount of time, the prince sends Hadrian, the rekkr—the leader of his dreki—after me."

So that was dreki. The prince's guard. "Which explains why he was looking for you."

"Precisely."

"Well, it's great that the prince sent him and all, but maybe you should just have them travel *with* you from now on."

"I—no! They are all animals. I could not possibly spend vast amounts of time with them."

The disgust he was trying to convey didn't come off as genuine. He was protesting a bit too much. I bet he was into one of the guys and, for whatever reason, didn't want to cop to it.

"You have a question?"

"No. I just think if you traveled with them, maybe you wouldn't get hurt."

"I assure you that I was far from hurt, only momentarily drained."

I shot him a look.

That put-upon sigh again. "I am sure it appeared quite catastrophic to your untrained eyes."

"Again, I'm gonna bring up the chains and the blood and the part where you were turning blue out there, and finally I'll come back around to Hadrian because he was concerned as well."

"It is his station! What do you expect?" Tiago retorted, his temper flaring. "He frets like an old woman."

Ah. So *Hadrian* was his guy. "I really liked him," I threw in, just so he'd know.

"I cannot possibly be expected to discuss Hadrian with—Jason," he said, wrapping his hand around my forearm again, holding tight. "I desire to know all about *you*."

Who cared about me? I was nobody; he was the one running from crazy cult people. I was going to say that, try to jog his brain into the real world and start pummeling him with questions, but I wasn't a trained psychiatrist, and I was thinking he would need one. Me trying to get any real answers out of him would be a total waste of time.

"Jason?"

"Yes," I said gently, still worried he was hurt more than he thought.

"Some strange aura surrounds you, something I cannot quite place, and… even though it is forbidden, I want to drink from you to see what you are. Would you allow that?"

Drink *from*? "You mean drink with," I corrected, grimacing. "I don't think that's a good idea right now. Even though you look and sound much better than you did, we still need to get you to the hospital," I advised.

"You are indeed odd."

I'd been called much worse.

"Jason."

"Yeah?"

"You—" He cleared his throat. "You feel no compulsion to do as I ask, do you."

I squinted at him. "No, because I know what you need, and that's to be seen by a doctor."

"I—"

"You were assaulted and God knows what else," I said sadly. "I'm thinking they must've drugged you, which is what accounts for your present condition and state of mind, but we won't know 'til we get you seen."

He murmured something under his breath.

"What was that?"

A quiet cough. "Normally all comply with my requests before those requests even turn into commands, but you… you are completely impervious to me."

"I'm not sure what you mean." I tried to soothe him, patting his chest gently. "I just wanna help you if you'll let me."

"But I do not need your help. What I need is to know what you are!"

The poor kid was a mess, and I was pretty sure he was still scared out of his mind. I needed to make him feel more secure. "Listen, I'm not gonna leave your side until we get this all figured out, all right?"

He seemed confused. "Jason, are you actually still worried about me, even after I told you who I am?"

"Of course."

"Extraordinary," he breathed.

"You're just a kid. You need someone to look out for you."

A moment of silence.

"Pardon me, what did you say?"

I groaned. "Sorry, sorry. Young man. I meant to say 'young man.'"

"For your edification, I am not a child!"

"Yeah, but—how old are you? Seventeen? Eighteen?"

"I am a millennium old," he intoned icily, trying to use a big voice on me.

I nodded, certain he felt ancient after the ordeal he'd been through. Even beyond that, he was still a teenager with all the drama and angst that came along with being that age. "I'm sure it feels like that sometimes, but—"

His laughter surprised me. When I glanced over, his smile, so big and bright, surprised me too. "Jason Thorpe," he sighed, "whatever under heaven are you?"

"I don't know what you're asking me."

"I know!" he half yelled in frustration. "I have never met nor seen nor even heard of anything such as you, and yet here you sit."

I concentrated on the road. If I focused on him and how me just being nice to him was such a revelation, it would make me sick. If basic human kindness and concern was this big a deal, I could only imagine how awful he'd been treated. I was betting his "prince," whoever the guy really was, wasn't so great after all.

"Jason, I am as healed by your proximity as I have ever been by blood, and all I want now is to taste of you so I might know if you are human, as I suspect, or something else altogether."

"I'm as human as you are, buddy."

He laughed again, more shrill this time, and I was certain he was actually deep in shock.

"Are you still cold?" I asked, pulling off the highway again, then taking off my coat once I'd put the truck into Park.

"No, I am not cold at all! Why on Earth would I be cold?"

But he had to be. I was, and he was tiny, with zero body fat. He had no natural insulation at all, and the karate gi thing wasn't doing anything for him. His hands, when he touched me, were still icy. I had the heater going full blast, but apparently it wasn't enough to warm him up. "Here, I wanna put this over you, all right?"

"Absolutely not. I have no need for your off-the-rack outerwear," he protested, face scrunched up like he'd bitten into a lemon. "What is the origin of this garment?"

"It's pleated corduroy, and would you just—here, lemme tuck it around you."

"I am not—I cannot be observed in this jacket! I only wear couture and… I would be the laughingstock of court should anyone see me!"

"I'm not gonna take a picture of you in it. I just want you to stay warm and—no, not halfway down your chest, put it up under your chin," I directed, using my coat to wrap him up like a burrito. "Now you just rest, all right? We'll be there soon."

"You are the most infuriating man! You are not listening to me at all," he grumbled, pouting, the epitome of a pissed-off kitten. He really couldn't have been any cuter. "I have slaughtered thousands."

"I'm sure you have," I said, brushing the golden waves of his hair out of his face before pulling the truck back out onto the road.

He growled, and I couldn't stifle my chuckle.

"For your information, the reason they bled me was because they feared me."

"Of course they did."

"You placate me, and I will not have it!"

I shouldn't have asked, but I had to know some details about the cult for when I eventually talked to the police. "So do you know, are the people you were with one giant group, or do they belong to different chapters, and there's a head of all of them?"

His groan of disgust was loud.

"What? I'm just trying to get it straight in my head."

"Your head will only be straight one way, and that will be when you speak to my prince," he informed me. "I will say this: had the Rothschilds not attacked me, they would have been owed a debt by my prince."

"And why's that?"

"Had you not been there among them, I would never have found you, and thus he, too, would be absent of your presence in his life."

"Who would be 'absent of my presence'?" I asked.

"My prince."

His prince again. Poor kid, they had him totally buying all this bullshit.

"Listen to me. You must—"

"Why don't you tell me about him?" I suggested, wanting him to stop working himself up. "I'd love to hear about your boss."

"He is not my boss," he insisted. "He is my lord."

"Sorry," I said, attempting to mollify him. "Go on."

"You will be his—of that I am sure—because you possess some innate power that healed me, and that sort of strength must only be meant for my prince. Of this I am certain."

I changed tactics. "So what were you doing up there? Just seeing if the Rothschilds wanted to join your clan thing?"

He rolled his eyes. "No. I was investigating charges leveled by a member of the Rothschilds' household that they were killing young men sent there from other clans."

"Oh my God." I was horrified, I jolted in my seat and veered in my lane, unable to control my reaction. Luckily there were no other cars around. "Why didn't whoever just call the police if they suspected something so horrible?"

"We handle these things ourselves," he explained. "That is the purview of the prince."

"I see. Then you were sent here by the prince, and when you arrived, they jumped you?"

"Basically yes."

"I heard you screaming," I said, remembering the high-pitched howl that reminded me of war. The memory had rousted me from sleep in an instant. "I got to you as quick as I could."

"I know, Jason, and I am well pleased."

I got choked up. The poor kid really needed a keeper. "You mentioned that they were superstitious?" I needed to change the subject before I offered to adopt him.

"Yes. They believed my blood tainted by the prince. They bit me many times but did not drink."

The drinking-his-blood part didn't surprise me. I'd seen the evidence myself. "Do you think it's true, then, what the people reported to you guys, that they were killing young men at their house?"

"I do, yes."

Something I heard earlier that night clicked into place. "So Hadrian's there now rounding up Mr. and Mrs. Rothschild and whoever else and taking them to see the prince?"

His wrinkled brow made him look confused. "Is that what he said he was doing?"

"He said he was gathering up the heads of the clan to take to the prince."

"Oh! Yes," Tiago replied, sounding like I'd cleared something up for him. Again, weird, but the whole night had been, so it was par for the course. "That's precisely what he's doing."

"How many young men did they say were killed?"

"Three."

"Jesus," I breathed, sickened by the thought. I forced my attention back to the road. "Tell me what happens now. Do you go to the police?"

"No, as I said, we address incidents of this excess ourselves."

"And you have the jurisdiction to do that?"

"The prince does, yes," he confirmed, "and therefore Hadrian."

"So the prince sends you out to investigate, you report back, and he acts?"

"In the normal way of things, yes, but not in this instance."

"Well, no," I agreed. "This time you getting jumped and then nearly killed basically answers any questions of guilt about the Rothschilds," I concluded, and at the same time, it hit me that this whole thing, with me being there, was nuts. Eddie was right. Weird shit always happened to me no matter where I was.

"Even had they not acted so stupidly," Tiago explained, "the prince would have divined the truth. He always does."

I could hear the respect and awe in his voice.

"He always makes the eminently wise decision," he added as an afterthought.

"Is that why you work for him? Because he's a good man?"

"I do not *work* for him, I *serve* him, and yes, he is a very good man."

As I thought about everything Tiago had said, I realized it wasn't really right, not based on his previous explanation of what he did. "But you don't really *serve* him, though, do you? You're more of an advisor, aren't you? More his friend?"

Tiago was quiet for so long I finally turned to check on him. The stunned look on his face told me perhaps I'd hit the nail on the head.

"T?"

Slow pan to me. "T?"

"Sorry," I amended quickly. "Tiago."

He moved his hand to my thigh. The touch was hesitant but tender. "I—no one has ever dared to show such familiarity toward me."

"Well, I promise I—"

"No, you misunderstand," he whispered. "It was surprisingly dear."

I grinned at him, and he flushed again before putting his face down in my jacket, inhaling deeply like he was steadying himself. I really felt sorry for the freak-out coming his way. Once his adrenaline burned off, he was in for quite the crash.

"Please continue."

"Tell me what you're thinking."

"I—" he began hoarsely, his voice bottoming out. "My prince has often insisted I am more than an emissary, but I—I never believed him."

"Maybe second-guessing him isn't such a good idea, huh?"

He fell quiet for several long breaths. "Perhaps."

"If he says you mean something more to him than as his ambassador, that he thinks of you as a friend—couldn't hurt to believe him."

He nodded slowly.

I really hoped some part of what he was telling me about the cult was positive. If the prince turned out to be a guy who was a true horror, that meant Tiago, in turn, would be even more screwed up for having put his faith in a monster. I was scared for him, and of the fallout—for his mind, his psyche—if what I was afraid was true actually was. But maybe there was someone above this prince of his.

"May I ask a question?"

"Certainly."

"Is the prince the supreme authority?"

"I do not understand your question."

"I mean, does he just decide on a sentence and carry it out, or are there more checks and balances in your cul—clan?" I corrected fast, hoping he missed the slip.

"Only him."

"Then does he get to decide whatever punishment he wants?"

"Yes."

"Anything?"

"Yes."

That was too much control for one person. Tiago needed out of this cult yesterday. "Does he say who lives or dies?"

"Of course."

"How? I don't understand. Why would you people give him that much power?"

"We *give* him nothing. He is the prince. He leads; we follow."

That was so much worse. "But people shouldn't blindly follow any—"

His long sigh interrupted me. "Herein lies the problem. You believe me to be speaking about *people*, and I am not. Were I, then you would be correct, as no one human in your world is allowed to mandate who lives or dies."

"How about the court system and—"

"I mean a single voice of judge, jury, and executioner."

"Absolutely not."

"But my prince does, as he rules over no one in the human world."

So we were back to this, to me being human and him being… not. "Human world?" I broached the subject even though I shouldn't have. I really needed to leave all of this to a qualified medical professional, but I was so curious about what had gone on at the Rothschilds'.

He ignored my question. "I am not speaking now of human laws, but of *our* laws. And even though your clan has been sorely negligent by ignoring your education in many areas—you know naught of the prince!—I can assure you that in our world, the prince is the lawmaker, charged with meting out justice when the laws are not followed."

"I don't understand any of this," I sighed, saddened just thinking about the shock the kid was in for. His whole world was going to come crashing down around him once he got a big dose of reality. I hoped he had a family somewhere, people who were missing him and still loved him. If not, maybe I could visit him in the hospital.

"I know you do not," he said, returning my attention to him. "Perhaps I might explain it all to you on the plane home to Malta."

"Sure, kid." Oh, he was so out of it. Now he was planning for both of us to escape to another country.

"I assure you I—"

"You need to be checked out and maybe stay a couple of days before you get on that plane home," I said, trying to appease him. I had no right to burst his bubble—that was for other people to do. What I could do was be his friend. "Do me a favor. Could you give me the names and phone numbers of any family I can contact?"

He shook his head. "There is only the prince. I lost my parents a lifetime ago."

"Oh, I'm so sorry," I said and reached out to pet him again, my hand in his hair, scratching his head for a second before I let him go.

"You have a very soft heart."

I grunted.

"You do. I know. I have met millions of people in my centuries."

"Yeah, well." I brushed him off. "I—"

"But more importantly, you are very pleasing to the eye."

My snort was self-deprecating, and the way he looked at me, as though stunned, made me choke out a laugh.

"No one is ever allowed to disbelieve my word!"

"I'm not. I just think it's funny that you complimented my heart and then had it take a back seat to what I look like. That's funny, don't you think?"

It amused me that he was trying to give me compliments on my appearance at all. Here he was, an angel who'd fallen to Earth, and on the other hand… there was me. I put the A in average. Brown hair, brown eyes, slightly tan skin from a Native American ancestor somewhere in the family tree, and muscles first built up in high school football as a free safety and then later, in the Corps, by carrying a pack that weighed more than some people and endless hours of weight training when not on patrol. Being a contractor made me even more bulky; I carried materials up and down ladders, swung a hammer, worked with power tools. So other than my body, which Tiago couldn't see, the rest of me was downright forgettable.

"You dare laugh at me?"

I scoffed. I couldn't help it. I had seen puppies scarier than him.

"You—"

"The kindness in your heart should be more important than anything, right?" I teased. "I mean, certainly more important than whatever the hell's on the outside."

"I should eviscerate you," he muttered.

I patted his knee. "I'm not trying to annoy you, I promise."

When he turned and I caught the glower, or what was supposed to be him all dark and deadly, I coughed to cover my chuckle.

"I swear to you that there are horrific accounts written about my wrath!"

"I have no doubt." He was getting loopier by the second. He was really adorable with his sharp elfin features, porcelain skin, enormous violet eyes, and full dark red lips. I would bet he drove all the boys and girls wild.

I returned my attention to the road, and after another few miles, when I checked, he was fast asleep.

Big and scary, my ass.

AN HOUR later I pulled into the St. Joseph Hospital parking lot in Bellingham, parked, and then took off my seat belt, ready to get out.

"Wait."

I was pleased to see Tiago awake, alert and staring at me.

"Let's go in, all right?" I said softly, gently. "They're nice here. This is where I came after I got hit by a drunk driver."

"You were—when was this?"

I dismissed the question. "Years ago, now c'mon," I said before I got out.

Strangely when I locked my door and turned to go around the truck to get him out, he was there beside me.

I jolted, couldn't hide it, and took a step back, my mind scrambling, tripping over itself, to justify his speed.

It was much too fast.

No one should have been able to do that, not with the laws of physics and all.

I should have seen him. It should have taken several moments to get around the truck, even scrambling as fast as I knew I could do it, considering my training. There was just no way.

And yet he'd done it.

I stood there and stared.

When he took a step forward, I took one back.

"*Now* you are afraid?" He sounded incredulous.

I took another step away from him. I wasn't scared, but I was… wary. There had to be an explanation, and I started cycling through options. Maybe I'd been hit with something too. Maybe the bonfire was full of weed I hadn't noticed and I'd been stoned this entire time. Perhaps what he was saying would have made sense if I were in my right mind. I didn't feel like I was out of it, but then what accounted for his movement? "I'm not sure" was all I could say because I really wasn't.

He rushed me and took my face in his hands, and most unnerving of all, his skin was still cold on mine. It focused my attention back on his welfare. He wasn't well, wasn't himself, and probably neither was I. Maybe my own crashing adrenaline was playing tricks on my mind. But I didn't matter. What was important was him and getting him inside to see a doctor.

I reached to move his hands. "Okay, let's—"

"Forgive me," he said with a wince but didn't let go. "But I need you to come with me, and I must gain your agreement before the others arrive."

"The others?" I said, latching on to his words.

"Hadrian and the dreki."

"Oh," I said. Now I understood what the holdup on seeing a doctor was. "Will you go into the ER if they're here? Are you scared?"

"No, I—"

"Because if you're more comfortable with your guys instead of me, I get it," I clarified for him. "That's completely understandable."

"I am not entering that facility, Jason."

I was still scared for him, knew he needed to be seen. "So what, then," I snapped, pulling free of his hands, scowling. "You let me waste my time driving you down here when you had no intention of going in?"

"I told you so," he asserted, taking another step closer.

"The hell you did!" I yelled, backpedaling from him, recoiling. "You need to—"

"Jason—"

"You're more hurt than you know."

"No!" he maintained, glaring at me. "I am not injured at all. That is not a concern at the moment. I only need gain your permission—for somehow I can do nothing without it—to take you with me."

"Tiago—"

"No," he snarled, and then he took a breath, visibly willing himself under control. "Agree now to accompany me!"

I put several more feet between us. "Listen—"

"No, you must listen," he rasped, and I saw it then, the pain in his eyes, and heard the frustration and pleading when he spoke. "I beg you. The dreki come even now, and the protocol resulting from an attack upon me is to deliver me to the prince immediately. They will not listen to reason, and only my prince will hear me, but I will not see him for days, and—if you agree, they will convey you as well, but without your accord, I will be forced to leave you, and then—"

"You're saying your own guys are going to kidnap you and take you home?"

"Not kidnap, but… yes," he conceded.

"Because they're worried about you, and they're going to take you to a safe place to get all checked out?"

"They have no fear for my present well-being, purely for my continued safety."

I couldn't have been more relieved.

Whatever the situation was, I'd misunderstood the role the prince played. Yes, he was apparently some high-ranking—if not the highest-ranking—person in the cult, but within the organization, one of the rules was his people stayed safe. I still worried for Tiago's long-term mental health in this situation, though my immediate concern was his physical health. What it sounded like to me was the prince would also be concerned, and therefore it fell to Hadrian to see to Tiago's safety. If the plan was to take Tiago home and get him rested and well, then who was I to argue? It didn't look like I was going to be successful in my attempts to get him into the hospital, so having Hadrian take custody of him seemed like the next best thing.

I saw him realize what he'd actually said to me, his reaction washing over his features, and something between awareness and dread filled his eyes. "No, no, no, Jason, listen to—"

"I'm still not sure about this prince of yours because of what you said earlier about him deciding who lives and dies, but I also know that you are really fuckin' out of it, so I'm not totally sure if you know what you're saying or not."

"Jason!"

"Hadrian seemed like a good guy, not really a brainwashed cult member—not that I've *met* any cult members, so I could be wrong on that front as well, but—"

"Jason, I beg of—"

"But," I said, lowering my voice, trying to soothe him, not mad anymore about him not going in because, as it turned out, he would be taken care of anyway. "I do appreciate that this prince of yours seems to really care about his people."

Two huge black SUVs came speeding into the parking lot, tires screeching, throwing up the water left on the ground from the snow that had fallen earlier in the evening.

"Jason," Tiago implored, moving too fast again, crowding me, hands on my chest as he stared into my eyes. "I need you to meet my prince. He will be ill that

I could not bring you with me and furious at himself for giving the order that the dreki listen to no one but him."

"I'm not going with you," I made clear, squeezing his shoulder as I stepped free. "But please take care of yourself. You take too many chances."

"I have never 'taken a chance' in my life!" he roared, and I couldn't help but smile.

The ridiculously big SUVs parked at each side of my truck. Hadrian was out of a passenger side door fast, and when he saw me, his eyebrows jumped, and he snapped his head up before I got a smile. "You yet still live?"

"Don't sound so shocked," I groused.

His laugh was deep and throaty, and I liked the sound. Then two men in black grabbed Tiago and pushed him into the back of one of the SUVs.

"Jason!" Tiago screamed as the door slammed shut and the SUV took off. Three men remained with Hadrian.

"You'll keep him safe, yeah?" I directed at Hadrian.

He put his hand over his heart, just as he'd done earlier. "I can do no less, Jason Thorpe."

"Good. He needs a keeper."

"Agreed."

I held out my hand to him. "Have a safe trip home."

The men around us appeared surprised, and I was clueless as to why.

Hadrian took a quick breath. "You would take my hand?"

If I'd met him at a bar, I'd take a lot more than that. Tall, dark, and handsome did not do him justice, and with that accent now warming his voice….

"Of course," I replied, shelving my interest, still holding out my hand. "C'mere."

He grabbed hold and squeezed tight, covering our joined hands with his other, smiling at me, his eyes crackling almost amber in the reflected glow of the overhead lights.

"You take care," I said, taking a step back when he let me go.

"And you, Jason Thorpe, the blessings of the goddess be upon you."

"Thank you," I said, genuinely pleased, appreciating all the kind words I could get.

As I watched them all get into the SUV, I wondered how long it would take me to get to New Orleans. I was so overdue for a change, and if this latest run-in with crazy had taught me anything, it was that life was to be seized, not trudged through.

It was time to join the land of the living.

Chapter Three

LIFE WAS different in the Quarter.

I loved the varied aromas of food cooking, the uneven and broken sidewalks, the sound of music anywhere you went, and the art everywhere you looked. I loved the crowds of people that, even at three in the morning, you could walk past, and others would smile and wave at you. And I was crazy about the addendum of haunted—or not—on the signs for apartments for rent.

I liked that anyone could have a second-line parade: just pick a route, get a permit, and find a band. I loved that if you wanted wild and crazy, you could walk down Bourbon Street; if you wanted things quieter, you went one street over either way.

New Orleans was so *different* that, even though I fell in love with it instantly, I still suffered quite the culture shock.

In the cold and snow of Washington, people
lived inside, separate from others. If you didn't have
friends or family to draw you out of your warm house
to a cozy restaurant or coffee shop or even their own
cheery homes… your life became so very insular. In
the Vieux Carré, people talked to me the first day I arrived. They reached out, and I went from being alone
to being part of a community.

It all started with my new home.

I went for a walk, looking at the neighborhood,
trying to get an idea about what kind of business
would fit, what I could do to make a living that would
make me happy in the small 750-square-foot space on
the 900 block of Royal Street. The building sat close
to the corner of St. Philip and Royal in the Quarter,
and I could open a shop on the bottom floor and live
on the second. Rachel hadn't mentioned that when she
gave me the deed, so I was pleasantly surprised as I
stood outside, staring up at the building that needed
work but had great bones.

"You look like you're contemplating your life."

I turned and found a woman, probably in her
midtwenties, all gorgeous dark brown skin with gold
undertones and a cascade of wine-colored curls that
fell to the middle of her back in tight spirals. Her bottomless brown eyes were even more alluring lined in
thick black kohl, and her lipstick matched the crimson
hair.

"I'm gonna open a shop," I explained. She looked
me up and down before her gaze collided with mine.

"That's great." She smiled slowly, and I was thoroughly enchanted by the stunning woman who made
the air snap, crackle, and pop around her. I could feel

the electricity flowing off her, whispering on my skin. "You need any help?"

"What can you do?" I asked, arms crossed, regarding her.

She mirrored me, except she put a finger under her chin. "I can match a person with a thing. I'm very good at it."

"I don't know what you mean."

"Well, let's say if there was a certain piece of art in your shop, I could sell it to whoever came in."

"Really."

"Yes," she said with authority and a nod, absolutely certain. "As long as that thing, whatever it is, is something they need."

"Or want."

"Isn't want just a hyped-up need?"

Made sense to me.

An hour later, over lunch at Acme Oyster House, Ode Reed had yet to stop talking.

"So we could sell consignment for people. Like a co-op."

She shook her head. "No. No co-op. Fuck that. We buy what we like, pay them a fair price, and we sell it at our own markup. That way we're being ethical, as in making the artists feel appreciated, but we make money on our end, and they don't have to handle the selling part that bums most creative people out."

"In what way?"

"If you made something from your soul and then had to convince someone to give you money for it, wouldn't that sort of kill your vibe?"

"But they're convincing us to buy it in the first place."

"No," she said with a shake of her head. "We're walking around looking for treasures, and once we sell a few things, artists and craftsmen will come to us."

I nodded. I could see it working like that, through good word of mouth.

"And for some artists, if we have an exclusive deal and everyone is in agreement, us and them, if we find them selling their stuff anywhere else in the Quarter—they're out."

"That seems fair."

"It does, right?" She smiled, and a man walking by our table plowed right into a wall. "Oh, you poor thing," she cooed, getting up to make sure he hadn't broken anything.

I watched him sputter an apology before stumbling away. As bespelled as I was, her business model sounded reasonable. Resale and then staples were what I had imagined; I just didn't think I'd find anyone to help me from the start. "Are you really here, or a figment of my imagination?"

Her laugh was as gorgeous as the rest of her, unexpected in how musical and resonant it was. "I promise you I am here and just as real as you," she trilled, slipping her hand into mine.

Holding it gently, I sighed deeply. "We need help to get that place fixed up."

"I have a lot of brothers."

"That's good because we're gonna need 'em."

And we did.

Her siblings helped out because I gave their sister a job, even though she could have worked for any of them. They were all in much better lines of work than me: one an electrical engineer, another a veterinarian,

another owned several car dealerships, and her oldest
brother owned a restaurant called Tau in the Quarter over
on Madison and Chartres. Ode was a wanderer, and her
mother, Josephine, was thrilled to meet me and even hap-
pier her child had seen me and decided to drop anchor.

"Thank God you came along, Jason," she told me
over dinner a week after I met Ode. "I wasn't ready to
have her sail out of my life just yet."

"Well, I don't know how long I'll keep her interest," I said honestly. "I'm not very exciting, and with
how fearless she is and scary smart, she can be anything she wants."

"I know," she agreed, smiling at me. "It's nice
that you see her so clearly."

"See and hear," I muttered.

"What was that?"

I grunted, and she chuckled.

"Tell me what you're thinking," she pressed.

"I have a theory that she thinks she needs to give
my life direction."

"Oh, absolutely," she agreed far too quickly.
"Without a doubt."

"Do you think so too?"

I got an eyebrow lift in answer.

"Well," I grumbled, "what am I supposed to do?
Say no to an angel?"

She patted my face with her warm, dry hand. "It's
good that you let her fuss over you. It makes her so
happy."

As if I had a choice. Once Ode picked you, it was
over.

"Leave him alone, Ma, he's mine!" Ode called
from the living room.

Josephine rolled her eyes heavenward and left us to figure out our lives.

Her youngest brother, Issa, didn't want to go to college and was giving their parents fits, so I put him to work finding treasures at artist co-ops, flea markets, and on his rambling walks around the Quarter. He found amazing crafts, from mercury glass to large-scale canvases to mosaics to installation pieces. He had an eye for quality, just like his sister had an eye on every customer who came through the door. She knew what they needed before they opened their mouths. Their sister, Kali, who came home from college at Notre Dame, worked for me whenever she was in town as well. Ode and Kali looked adorable together: Kali a younger, quirkier version of her sister, more pixie than Ode's earth goddess, same curls but not dyed red, and wearing huge oversized glasses.

A month later we officially opened the shop, and I named it Spark and Ember. Ode loved it because the words were the alpha and omega of fire, one to start and burn bright, the other to slowly subside to warmth. I was ridiculously pleased she liked the name, my heart now permanently set on making her happy.

Another six months after that, with spring and summer turning to fall, now September in the Vieux Carré, my circle of friends large, business booming, and everyone I met open and inviting, I felt as though I'd lived there forever. It was so good to have finally found the place I belonged.

A MONTH later, Ode was putting up Halloween decorations and trying to get me to see her side of a discussion/argument/issue we'd been having for a while.

"It makes sense," she insisted while she kept one eye on the young couple perusing the jewelry under the glass by the cash register. "Keeping the shop open later is a good business decision. I get so many calls and emails from people who saw something when they were window-shopping but couldn't get in because it was after six."

"Yeah, but it gets busy during the day a lot of times, and if I'm not here to help you, I—"

"Oh, for crissakes, J, I don't want you to work the night shift. I like seeing you first thing in the morning, and we both have to be here to talk to customers and decide what we wanna buy. Everybody's dying to be in here now because we blow out of things all the time."

We did. In the past several months, word got around that we had fair pricing, exceptional quality, and most of all, a phenomenal staff. I loved talking to people, so did Ode, and Issa's charm had plenty of people stopping by, hoping for a smile.

"It's 'cause your brother's so pretty." I waggled my eyebrows at her.

She rolled her eyes and turned around and sold the couple who'd been there the whole time a $3,600 wedding set, all conflict-free, ethical, made-in-the-lab diamonds that pleased the bride and thrilled her chemist husband.

"I have to call that designer and tell him we sold another set of his rings," Ode said after they left.

"You mean the last set," I corrected.

"This again?" she said irritably. "I thought we settled this."

"Clearly not, if you're still talking about it."

"But I told you—"

"And make sure you explain that because of how he treated you last time, we'll never sell another ring of his in this shop again."

She stared at me, arms crossed, waiting.

Shit. "What?"

"I know you didn't just try and talk over me."

I had, and it was something she didn't permit. Double shit. "Yeah, I—sorry."

She took a deep breath, let her shoulders fall, and a serene expression settled on her face as she uncrossed her arms before she gave me her attention again. "Now let's discuss."

"I'm not changing my mind," I stated, rock solid in my conviction.

"It's not your decision to make."

"The hell it isn't."

She arched one thick, perfectly shaped eyebrow for my benefit. "We have a deal, do we not?"

We did. She managed the store, I oversaw it, and since her taste was flawless, me butting into her area of expertise was a mistake. But this was different.

"Do you know how much the store makes when we—"

"I don't care what our commission is, and I don't care how sorry the man is. He was ignorant and he misjudged you, and he's lucky neither Issa or I heard it, or one of us would have laid his ass out."

"Really? You think going all Neanderthal on the man would have been the right choice?"

"I don't want anyone thinking they can come in here and throw their weight around and intimidate you."

"Oh, I was *so* not intimidated, and as for laying him out—I could do that myself, thank you."

I stopped inputting the order in the computer to give her my full attention. "He was a sexist pig."

"You only know that because I told you."

"And now that I know, you don't expect me to do anything about it?"

"I expect you to respect my decision when I tell you that I can fight my own battles and that I have my relationship with the man firmly under control."

"I just don't understand why you would wanna keep working with him. Why?"

"Because once he found out that I was the person in charge, he got down off his high horse and has been nothing but sorry ever since."

"Yeah, but you saw what he's really like."

"I don't care about any of that," she scoffed, making a face like I was ridiculous. "I only care that he makes beautiful jewelry that I negotiate an even better price on since he has to kiss my ring for acting the fool."

"He's a misogynist pig."

"Yes," she agreed.

"I think we send him a message that that's not okay."

"By showing him that we're not professional?" she asked, squinting. "I'm not sure how that does anything productive."

"It tells him that he's got to change his thinking if he wants to be in business since women run a lot of the world and apparently no one told him about it."

She chuckled.

"I don't care," I said implacably. "No one disrespects you in our store."

"Yeah, see, *our* store."

I shook my head at her.

"You can't run around trying to fight my battles for me," she explained, moving closer. "For one, I don't need you to do that because I'm a grown woman, and two, when I was done with him that day, he couldn't even speak, let alone give me any more crap. The only reason I told you about it was so that when you saw that his pricing was reduced, you'd understand why."

I grunted.

"I already won the battle, Jason. The man's been educated."

"He's got a crappy-ass attitude toward women."

"He does," she conceded, "but maybe I'm the first step in him seeing the light."

"Fine," I sighed, giving up. It was hard to be all pissed-off when she was thinking like a business owner and I just wanted to punch him. "It's your choice."

"I know it is," she concurred, reaching out and tapping my forehead with her fingertip. "You have to start thinking with this, not just your heart."

"I don't do that," I grumbled.

"Oh no? You wanna explain to me how the bottle cap earrings got in here?"

"No," I said, looking back at the computer screen. I had bought them from a girl on the street who gave me a sob story about needing money for college. I bought all fifteen pairs she had, and Ode came in the next morning and lost her mind. *"No trash in the store, Jason,"* she warned me.

She wasn't wrong. The same girl was in the same place when I walked by three days later. I was a sap, and Ode knew it.

"Look at me."

I raised my eyes.

"I appreciate you wanting to protect me, but if I need you, I'll ask, yeah? Trying to think for me makes you just as wrong as the pig jeweler."

"Well, that's fantastic."

She laughed at me and then went to help an elderly couple who wanted to talk about a large metal sculpture in the front window.

I was ringing people up on the iPad later when Ode bumped me. She was beaming at one of three men, passing him one of the shop cards and telling him that, yes, I was single. I had no idea why that bit of information was important, but I thanked them all for coming in and then went out back because I'd forgotten to water the cacti garden Issa had started.

"Oh dear God," she shouted before I made it all the way there.

I turned in the doorway. "What? Are you all right?"

"Did you not hear what I said?"

"When?"

"*When*?"

I shrugged. "Just tell me. You know I hate guessing."

"I told that man you were single right in front of your face."

"Yeah?"

"Ohmygod!"

I turned to go.

"Jason!"

After pivoting back to face her, I saw the bewildered expression on her face. "Why're you looking at me like that?"

"What does a man have to do to get your attention?"

I was lost.

"For God's sake, Jase, do you ever get laid?"

"You're a rude person, do you know that about yourself?"

"What did he have to do, draw you a map to his penis?"

"And crude. Did I mention that you're very crude as well?"

"Holy shit, he could not have been more obvious."

"Not true since I totally missed it!" I shot back, all in her face until I realized what just came out of my mouth.

"Uh-huh."

Crap.

She rushed down the short hall and stood there, hands on her hips, staring me down. "You are hot like the surface of the sun, and if you weren't gay, I'd have been all over you the second I met you. But Jesus, Jase, are you saving yourself for marriage?"

"I—"

"You might have to put out before that. I'm just saying."

I groaned loudly and left her to get the watering done. When I returned an hour later, she was smiling at a cute little family buying a set of coasters and some sage.

"Why do they need the sage?" I asked once they left.

"It's for the mom. After her in-laws visit, she always feels like their evil—as well as the smell of Ben-Gay—stays in her house."

"Ah."

"Hence the sage."

I made a face. "I hate it. It makes everything smell like Catholic mass."

"Oh, it does not," she griped.

I sat down at the computer behind the front counter to check invoices, and when she coughed, I didn't look up.

She coughed again.

"What?" I asked, my gaze meeting hers.

"You need to start dating. You're much too handsome to be sitting home every Friday."

"I don't sit home. I go out with friends." I said, horrified I was having the same conversation with yet another woman in my life. When Rachel had called to check in with me a week ago, she, too, was concerned over my lack of a love life.

"Not what I mean."

I let my head fall back as I moaned.

"See, that's a good noise. If you were making it between the sheets, I'd be happy. The first thing I noticed about you when you turned around the day we met was your gorgeous clear gray eyes."

"Awww." I waved her off, dismissing the compliment.

"I will kill you dead."

I chuckled.

"You don't even get it that women—and men—come in here all the time just to get a closer look at you."

"If you say so."

"Jason!"

"Ugh," I groaned.

"That guy the other day, the one in the teeny shorts, you remember him?"

"No," I said honestly.

"Well, I don't know how you missed him doing his stretches in front of the display case you were filling up, but he told me when you went into the back that you were built all strong and buff and beautiful and that your shoulders were made for holding on to in bed."

Really, my girl was adorable.

"He said it, not me!"

Sure he had. She was trying to give me compliments, and it was very sweet.

"Another lady told me that you were covered in the kind of bulgy muscles she loves, and what about that guy who fell over the candle display while checking out your ass?"

"That guy was an idiot." That irritated me, because *him* I could certainly recall. "We had glass everywhere, do you remember that?"

"Lord," she muttered under her breath.

"Are we done with—"

"Do you know what your best feature is, though?"

I winced. "Please don't say my personality."

She ignored me, plowing on. "It's those eyes of yours. They are just so pretty, and your deep laugh and those dimples, and that thick brown hair and that scruff that I normally hate but on you is so very, very sexy."

"Please go to lunch or something," I begged.

"No, I want to revisit the topic of keeping the shop open until at least ten."

"Ode, I—"

"We'll just try it for a couple weeks and see how we do, all right?"

Reasonable. If, like I thought, people just wanted to look after dark but not buy—we'd know that pretty quick.

"I'll hire someone, and we'll see how we do," she said cheerfully.

"But what if the later hours don't work?"

"It doesn't matter. We need another person in here anyway. Two, probably. I mean, what do we do if one of us actually wants to take a vacation?"

A valid argument.

"I'll get the job posted up on a few places like LinkedIn and Indeed and Monster, and then we can go through any résumés we get."

"Wait, we're not just gonna put up a Help Wanted sign in the window?"

Her eyes got huge. "You're not serious right now, are you?"

"I'd like to point out that you just walked up to me on the street."

"I know, and look how much trouble I am!"

"Yeah, but I mostly like you." Yes, she was a huge pain in the ass, but I loved her like the sister mine never was.

"Good," she said far too quickly. "Because the cutest guy just moved into my building."

"Oh God, please, no."

"Super, super cute."

"No," I pleaded. This was not the first blind date she'd suggested.

"I might have told him to come by the store tonight since we are going to be open late."

"That's just vile."

Evil grin, all teeth and dimples. "Yeah, I know."

She was incorrigible, but I adored her.

I CALLED her after the "cute" guy she'd sent over to meet me left the store a mere twenty minutes after coming in. It had seemed like an eternity.

"How old do you think I am?"

"What?" she asked. The club music on her end was deafening.

"How old," I reiterated, "do you think I am?"

Silence.

"Well?"

"I dunno, fifty?"

I groaned and hung up.

The man who'd come into my shop was in his midfifties, and while I enjoyed older men, he was much more interested in a notch on his bedpost than in taking me out for coffee. He even suggested we go to the back room and "get busy."

My phone rang as I watched a man limp past two of the four windows in front of the shop. "What?"

"No good, huh?"

"He wanted to fuck me in the stockroom," I informed her. "And while I've been known to be wild on occasion, I prefer to get a first name before I let someone have my ass."

"Shit," she groaned while I watched the man stagger forward and brace a hand on the glass.

"Hey, somebody's hurt outside. I'll talk to you tomorrow."

"What? No. Call the police," she entreated. "Don't go rushing out there to—"

I hung up, moved out from behind the front counter, and jogged over to the beautifully weathered antique leaded glass front door Issa and I had restored. It was heavy, so I opened it slowly and faced the man hunched over and panting.

"Hey, buddy, you all right?"

He lifted his eyes, and they were opaque, almost iridescent, not a color I'd ever seen before. He was sweating and shivering and seemed scared.

"I'm gonna go with you needing help," I mumbled to myself, moving quickly, getting an arm around his waist before I half carried, half dragged him into my shop. Once I had him inside, I helped him to the small love seat close to the indoor waterfall display near the back.

After I eased him down, I knelt so I could see his face. He was younger than me but not by much, maybe late twenties, with thick and coarse dirty-blond hair sticking up in tufts, a high, square forehead, a long, rangy body with clothes that looked like he'd slept in them. I was thinking he needed to eat.

When he lifted his eyes to mine, they were filling with color, and though still glazed, the deep brown was better than the sort of moonstone wash of a second ago.

"I'm Jason Thorpe," I said, keeping my tone gentle, coaxing. "Who're you?"

Thankfully the panting had subsided. "Cooke Slater," he answered, trying to smile but coming up with more of a grimace. "Who the hell are you?"

"I just told you," I said, chuckling and patting his knee. "Short-term memory is shot, huh?"

"No, I mean—" He took a deep breath and then straightened, lifting his ripped shirt.

A pale pink scar ran from his belly button to his left pectoral. It had to have been a vicious knife attack to leave something like that on his body as well as tearing up his shirt.

"Oh shit, did you just get out of the hospital or something?"

He stared at me, mouth open, looking just as confused as I felt.

"Should I take you there now?" I offered, needing to do *something* even as I heard my phone ring.

His movement, going from reclining one second to almost lunging at me the next, startled me. Because I was sort of waiting for some kind of response and was close, leaning toward him, when he came forward fast, I bounced up and took several steps backward. But he halted his own motion, freezing like he'd thought better of what he was doing.

It was weird and unexpected, and as I gave him room, I started to worry about what he might be on. "Are you tripping on X or something? Do you need to go to the ER?"

He fell back on the love seat, hugging himself tight, staring up at me like I might jump him at any moment.

"Cooke?"

"Man, who are you?" he asked, a trace of fear in his voice. "Or… what are you?"

I'd just crossed my arms, staring back at him, ignoring my phone ringing because I was trying to figure him out, when someone knocked loudly on the glass behind me. Turning, I saw four people of various ages, three women, one man with their eyes on me, the three women all crying, the guy looking like he might throw up.

"Could they—would it be okay if they came in?"

"Sure." I was bigger than all of them and trained to fight in close quarters. I could take them easily if things got dicey.

Once I opened the door, they raced across the room to Cooke and landed all over him. I smiled as he groaned under their added weight and hands all over him, checking him over. They gasped as they examined his scar, and they asked questions, one on top of the other, a barrage of sound until he finally yelled.

"Shut up!"

"How?" the guy demanded. "I still have your blood on me, but now you're healed? What the fuck happened? Did you find a *pee-bee* on the street to drink from?"

He shook his head and then looked up, and they all fell quiet, scrutinizing me. Then my phone rang again.

"Did your phone not ring?" Ode snapped after I answered.

"It might have. I wasn't paying attention."

"Liar."

"Yeah, okay, I just couldn't get to it."

"Couldn't or just didn't?"

"I was dealing with something," I explained.

"You're going to give me wrinkles before my time," she griped, exasperated. "You can't tell me there's someone hurt outside, hang up, and then not pick up the phone when I call to check on you. That's bullshit."

"But I didn't even yell like it was an emergency or something," I defended myself. "I just said I had to get off the phone."

"But what if you were just saying that because some guy had a gun pointed at your head and he was making you get off the phone or he'd shoot you?"

"Seriously?" I asked, deadpan.

"Yes, seriously!"

"I think you're watching too many cop shows again."

"Don't you dare belittle my concern for your welfare," she warned. "I'm not the one who didn't pick up his phone when I called back to check and make sure everything was fine."

"Why would you even do that? It's not like I can't take care of myself."

"I don't care that you think you're some badass. I had no idea who the hell was outside, now did I?"

Her argument was valid. "Yeah, all right."

"I don't need your permission to worry," she let me know, her tone all superior. "So now tell me, are you fine?"

And just like that, I felt bad. "I am."

"Are you sorry?"

"I really am."

She *hmphed* at me.

"Super-duper sorry."

"You scared me."

I knew I had, and it was terribly endearing and told me, as if I didn't know already, how much she loved me. It also made me realize if the roles were reversed, I would have been livid. "I won't do it again. I'll always pick up the phone."

"Yes, you will."

"Did you leave the club?"

"Of course I left, I'm halfway there."

I smiled into the phone. "Turn around, go back. I'm good."

"You swear?"

"I swear."

She grunted. "Don't ever do that to me again, you understand? My mother doesn't even not pick up the phone when I call."

"I thought me not being concerned on the phone would tell you I was fine," I pointed out.

"This goes back to the guy with the gun," she reminded me.

If this was an episode of whatever cop procedural she was watching at the time, then it would have all made sense. But that wasn't my takeaway. What was important was she loved me. "I swear to keep you on the line next time."

"See that you do," she said, her voice still rough with worry before she hung up.

Putting my phone in my pocket, I turned back to my guests and found them all crowded around me. It was a bit unnerving, but I wasn't scared. I felt safe inside the walls of my shop, protected, almost encased in a bubble of familial warmth. Maybe it was because it had belonged to my best friend's grandfather, maybe because Ode and I had imbued it with light and humor and happiness together and her family had blessed it with their care and compassion, guidance, and warmth. Maybe it was me, the strangeness that Tiago and Hadrian had both noted that I thought about from time to time. But for whatever reason, standing in the middle of my home, I just crossed my arms and endured them all looking me over like some kind of weird bug they'd never seen before.

"Tell me when you're all done."

They all gave me big smiles, and I realized they were younger than I thought, maybe around eighteen, nineteen, all pretty and wearing heavy eyeliner like goth club kids.

"Who are you?" Cooke asked.

"I told you already."

"No, really. Who?"

I leaned against the counter. "A few minutes ago, your friend there asked if you'd found a *pee-bee* to drink from. What is that?"

They exchanged furtive glances.

"It's okay." I gave him the out. "You don't have to tell me."

"No, no, I... I mean, I want to because—you healed me. I owe you something for that, if nothing else."

"I didn't do anything. It's not—"

"It is necessary, and just you bringing me into this amazing shop of yours and then letting the others come in and rest is way... more kindness than we've had in a long time."

"Good, I'm glad," I said, glancing at the others. "You guys can go sit down if you want. There's a love seat and some chairs over there." The furniture was clustered in the rear corner of the shop, and I had always found the area cozy.

They looked to where I pointed at the overstuffed piece of furniture that had a couple of chunky knitted blankets draped over one end, and moved en masse.

Poor kids, they were all, I was sure, emotionally exhausted from worrying about their friend.

When I turned back to Cooke, he was studying me again, but then he gestured to a stool beside the counter. I took a seat and waited.

"They're worried and scared," he told me.

"Yeah, I know. About you."

He shook his head. "No. About you."

"Me?"

"Yeah."

"I'm not the one who got jumped on the street," I reminded him. "Should we maybe be calling someone? Police or—"

"We can't call anyone." He was implacable, and it spurred a memory of another person not too long ago who had the same adamant reaction to my offer of a law enforcement summons.

"Why not?" I prodded, wondering and then dismissing the possibility just as fast that Cooke and Tiago could in any way be involved in the same cult on the opposite ends of the country.

"Because we handle things ourselves. We don't involve humans."

I shivered. The "human" part pretty much clinched it. "Why don't you involve us? Because the prince will take care of it?"

He scrunched up his face like he'd eaten a lemon. "Why the hell would the prince care what happens to us?"

Jesus. I was in over my head. "Could you just start—"

"So you *are* a vampyr, then. I thought so."

Oh man. "Is that what your cult is?" It was good to finally know. Now the whole bloodletting thing made sense. It explained people biting Tiago but not "drinking" from him because they thought his blood was cursed by the prince. It was very blockbuster summer movie and people who lived on the CW. From what I'd witnessed firsthand, though, it was not glamourous in the least.

"Could I just ask, though—if your organization is this big, how come I've never seen anything about it on CNN or *Dateline* or something?"

"What?" He was squinting at me.

"What?" I was confused.

"Organization?"

How had I lost him? "I'm just saying that no group with as many members as you guys must have could stay secret, but I looked after my first run-in with you guys, and I couldn't find anything on the net about a cult that had rituals with blood drinking beyond satanic ones or people who think they're vampires."

"I don't *think* I'm a vampyr. I know I am."

"Then your cult is, in fact, a vampire one."

"No."

I needed a drink. "But you just said—"

"We're not a cult of people who think we're vampyrs."

"Then what kind of cult are you?"

"Not a cult at all. We are *actual* vampyrs."

I didn't yell at him. What would that accomplish? I had to marvel at the brainwashing that went on and how it was done. "So are you guys born into the cult? Like that M. Night Shyamalan movie *The Village*? Is it like that?"

He scowled. "That movie's not about a cult."

"No, I know," I growled. "But are you guys raised believing—"

"It's not a cult!" he yelled. "We *are* vampyrs!"

I stood up and crossed my arms so I wouldn't grab him and shake him. I wondered how much time a psychiatrist—psychotherapist or whoever—would have to put in to get his mind right. If someone was told something their whole life, and they grew up and lived their whole life thinking what wasn't true actually was, how did that even get turned around?

In the Corps I saw lots of guys who grew up racist and slowly, over time, really started to *see* a person of another race for the first time in their life. Men who started out thinking something about black guys or white guys or whoever had their entire frame of reference altered when their lives were suddenly in another man's hands. But that was something they could experience. How did something you couldn't prove to begin with get changed?

"Do we need to go?" one of the girls asked, on her feet, her voice a frightened wobble as she looked from me to Cooke and back.

"No," I soothed, giving her a smile. "We're fine. I'm sorry if I scared you."

"Not you," she said, frowning at Cooke.

He groaned. "I didn't mean to yell."

She nodded and sat back down, sighing as she did, clearly relieved they wouldn't be expelled from my shop.

"Jason?" Cooke said hesitantly, "I didn't mean to—"

"You're saying a different word." Perhaps the first thing I could start with was to understand what was going on from his point of view. Instead of judging what I was pretty certain was a bad situation, maybe I should listen first.

"I'm sorry?"

"We're not saying the same thing."

"That's because you're saying 'vampire,' like Dracula or something, and I'm saying 'vampyr' as it really is."

It sounded like *vam-pier*. "Spell it."

"Think vampyr, with a *y* and an *r* and not an *i* and *r* and an *e*, and you've got it."

"I—what?"

He crossed his arms. "Are you or are you not a vampyr?"

"Oh no," I said quickly. "I'm not a member of your cult."

"I told you already, not a cult."

"Yes." I didn't want to fight, even though I was frustrated. I was getting no closer to figuring out what was going on with him, and thus Tiago and even Hadrian. They were all in it, but I had no real idea what "it" was.

"Who are you?"

"I told you already," I replied, sighing heavily.

"But you haven't told me *what* you are."

"I'm a human being, just like you."

He shook his head. "But I'm not human, and I don't think you are either."

Both he and Tiago, totally nuts. "How big is this cult? Can you tell me?" The part of my brain with all the military training wanted to know, needed to catalog the answers so I could better understand pre- cisely how it worked. "I won't ask how you got in or why—that's not my business—but I would like to know, like, is there a main location where you all go?" And then I remembered something. "Is it in Malta?"

His brow creased like he was trying to figure something out. "What's your deal?"

I'd pushed. "Sorry, I just want to get a few answers, if you can tell me. Or, I mean, if you're allowed to tell me."

"Who are you?"

Again with that, and I realized I wasn't going to get any information out of him. He, much like Tiago at the time, found *me* to be the curiosity. I wondered how they regarded regular people, our concern being so far out of their realm of understanding. It made me sad for both of them, but here, trying to get blood from a stone, wasn't doing me or Cooke any good. "You know what," I concluded with a sigh, "never mind, all right? Clearly you can't talk about this any more than he could, and I—"

He stopped me before I could get up, hand on my shoulder for a moment before he stepped around the counter to face me again. "Sorry. Just—I've never met one of… whatever you are before, and I'm a little freaked-out."

"Whatever I—what?"

"Sorry, sorry," he said quickly. "Just tell me—tell me what it is you wanna know."

"And *you're* freaked-out?" I was incredulous. "I'm confused about what I should be doing to help you, just like I didn't know what I should have done for him."

"Who?"

"Another member of your cult that I saved a while back," I explained. "I felt so bad that I didn't do more, but at the same time, I wasn't sure what that could have been."

"So we're not the first vampyrs you've met?"

"You mean you guys, right?"

"Yes."

"No," I answered. "I met some back in Washington where I used to live."

He nodded. "And they didn't convince you that we're not some big cult?"

"I—"

"How about I explain everything to you," he offered.

"Are you allowed to do that?"

"We are, to some people."

"Great." I huffed. "Talk to me."

"This might take a bit."

"I've got all night," I said cheerfully, urging him on. "G'head."

"All right."

I nodded. He exhaled.

I waited. He stared.

"Did you wanna start, maybe?" I nudged after taking a deep breath, worried he wasn't really going to give me the answers I was looking for. "Now?"

"Yeah, no, of course I can—okay, so… I'm a vampyr," he began softly, seriously.

"Yeah, you said that already."

"Listen," he pleaded, his voice gentle but firm. "And this time really *think* about the word and what you know and what you've seen."

I stilled, and it was everyone, not just me and Cooke, not just the others sitting behind me, but the entirety of the city, that held its collective breath.

I thought about Tiago and how he'd been shackled beside the bonfire, and all his cryptic words about his blood and his prince and his preternatural strength and surprising speed.

I thought about the fangs on Hadrian I assumed I'd imagined, and how agile he and his men were in the snow.

I thought about how, every now and then, here in New Orleans, I'd see odd things like people there one second, gone the next.

I thought about others on the street at night taking blood from each other's wrists. I told myself it was them sharing a needle, but I only ever saw teeth.

I thought about how I overheard strange words and names from people who came into the shop, glanced at me, and smiled.

All of it went through my head as I got up and walked around my little store, pacing, running everything through my logical brain, looking for something other than the obvious to make sense.

Vampyr.

As crazy as it sounded, the single-word explanation helped make sense of other things that had not. It wasn't a cult. They were *actually* vampyrs.

And now, finally, I could listen and hear the truth. I crossed the shop quickly and stopped in front of Cooke and stared.

"Are you all right?"

I nodded. I just wished I had some way to get in contact with Tiago and Hadrian, especially Tiago, so I could apologize for not realizing what he'd been trying to tell me.

"I know you probably don't believe me, and if I showed you my teeth, you'd say they were fake or filed or whatever, but that's what I am. Just so we've got that part straight."

"No," I said so he knew I was listening, just as he'd asked. "I believe you. Please go on."

He checked my face, his brows furrowed like he was worried. "Really?"

"Yeah," I whispered, my throat dry and my voice in and out.

"Interesting. The last guy I came clean with had problems from the jump, but it seems like you're all right."

I stayed quiet, letting him get himself together.

"Diving right in, then. Vampyrs as a whole are called *nori-ah* and—"

"Could you write these down for me?" I asked, smiling to myself, remembering Tiago putting things in my phone that he quickly erased. "I need to have them for reference."

"You sure you're all right?" he asked suspiciously, looking at me the way people did when they thought you were crazy. "Because you're acting sort of odd."

I bet I was. "Yeah, I know, sorry. Just—I'm fine."

"You believe me, then?"

"I do."

"Just like that?"

"Thing is," I said, taking a breath, "it's not *just* like that, right? I've been working stuff out in my head for a while now, so yeah… I'm wrapping my brain around the word 'vampyr.'"

"I know. I've told other humans, and they always look just like you do right now. Kinda shell-shocked, like your brain is ready to explode."

"Did you know about vampyrs before you became one?"

He squinted. "Became one? I was born one."

"*Born* one?"

"Yeah," he replied with a quick huff of breath. "It's not like in the movies. No one gets bitten and becomes a vampyr. You're either born one or not."

"I just thought—"

"That you'd get bitten and grow fangs and the whole deal."

"Yes."

"No," he said flatly.

"But you have fangs or no?"

He opened his mouth and lifted his top lip so I could see canines that were a bit longer than mine, more pronounced, and beside them, a smaller set that looked exactly the same but sharper.

"You have two sets of canines?"

"Yeah," he said, moving his fingers. "And I don't have any grinding surfaces on my molars like you do."

"Why not?"

"Why would I need to grind anything?"

"So you don't eat at all?"

"No."

"Just blood."

"Well, I drink water, and in my case, bourbon," he said with a smirk, "but all my nutrients come from blood."

I gestured at him. "Lemme feel your teeth."

"Gross," he said, face twisted in horror. "Like I want your disgusting fingers in my mouth."

"Yeah, all right," I acquiesced because, really, if the shoe was on the other foot, I wouldn't want his fingers in my mouth either.

"I can see your mind working," he said, chuckling, clearly enjoying this conversation with me.

"Sorry, I'm just wondering about your teeth."

"What about them?"

"They're all sharp? Even your molars?"

"Of course. They're all made for piercing, cutting, even shearing if need be," he answered logically.

"And the extra set of canines are called what?"

"Supernumerary teeth. And just so you know, a lot of humans have them as well."

"No shit."

"No shit. But in humans they're just weird extra teeth that come in randomly. Some people have extra incisors or molars, and some even have the canines like us."

It was fascinating. There had to be a whole evolution of being a vampyr, and that in turn filled my mind with more questions. "Can I ask something else?"

"Course," he sighed, tipping his head as he regarded me.

"Why don't vampyrs come out?"

He snorted a laugh.

"Shit, you know what I mean."

"But we have, haven't we?"

"What are you talking about?"

"People talk about vampyrs all the time," he pointed out, leaning on the counter.

"Yeah, but not like as something real."

"Maybe, maybe not. I think you'd have to take a poll to really know that for sure."

"Gimme a break. No one thinks vampyrs are real."

"But you say vampyr, and everyone knows what that is, right?"

"Sure."

"*Vampyr* is part of the lexicon, like *egg* or *car* or *lamp*. It's a thing you know."

"Sure," I conceded. "I'll give you that. But what if a vampyr wanted others to know you all were really real and not just something in books and movies?"

He shrugged. "I think that person would need to consider how old vampyrs actually are and that we are everywhere, in everything, from the bottom to the top, and then make an informed decision."

"I'm not following."

"So let's say you're some young idealistic no-body and you've fallen head over heels for some human, and you want the whole wide world to know."

"You're sounding very cynical right now," I commented. The way his voice rose told me he didn't think too much of love. "What happened to you?"

"Don't get me started on how fucked-up love is, man. The girl I followed here from Seattle dumped me for a rich human lawyer who set her up with a house in the Garden District and bought her a tricked-out Mercedes. Love is for brain-dead idiots."

"I see. So, jilted party of one, can you go on?"

"Fine," he grumbled. "So my bet is that our guy who wants to tell the world about vampyrs is dead before anyone has the time to even check out his story. We're taught from the time we're little that humans are fine in small doses—we evolved from humans, after all—but to be known as real is a death sentence."

I nodded. "That makes sense."

"And the internet is insane. Who can tell what's real or not?"

He had a point.

"Right this second I bet you can go on YouTube and find a ton of videos from people who thought they saw a vampyr or who are vampyrs or God knows what else."

"You said God. You still believe in God?"

"Of course. I'm Episcopalian, man."

"Huh."

"Let's face it: there are a billion things in the world scarier than vampyrs, and everyday people on the street don't have time to deal with the supernatural. They have enough to do just to take care of their families and put food on the table."

He was not wrong. Who had time to believe in things that went bump in the night when you had to go to work in the morning, pick up the kids from school, make dinner, and pay the rent? Most people would go for what made more sense, just like I had. A cult instead of a mythological creature? Absolutely.

"So yeah, no one's outing anyone. We keep quiet, and no one's the wiser."

"Then you just live in plain sight, but nobody knows—or more importantly—believes."

"Yes."

"And you all, I mean, vampyrs, you're fine with that?"

"If it's something you're raised with, the secrecy, you don't question it."

At least that made sense. "I have to ask. Where do vampyrs come from?"

He shrugged. "I don't know exactly because we go to school just like you, with you, but we're the kids with weird allergies that don't eat anything at lunch."

"Really? During the day?"

He rolled his eyes. He obviously thought I was the biggest dork on the planet. Then he shook his head with so much judgment. When he finally spoke, he sounded very aggrieved. "Seriously, do not believe everything you see in movies. It's total shit."

"So what you're saying is that vampyrs evolved from humans, you're just not up enough on your own history to know when and where."

"That was bitchy and judgmental."

"I'm just sayin'."

"Well, the *when* was during the Late Bronze Age, the *where* would be originally eastern Europe, but later, all over, traveling with humans and settling all over the world."

"You don't seem to care a lot about this."

"Do you think about ancient history every day? I mean, if you're not a historian, if that's not your job, wouldn't going to work be farther up on your to-do list?"

I smiled. "So you're a practical vampyr."

"I'm a practical *person*," he informed me snidely, smirking for good measure. "The only difference between me and everyone else you know is that I drink blood to stay alive."

"Okay," I said, chuckling at his indignant, defiant expression, like what the hell was I thinking? "But your history, it has to be written down somewhere."

"I'm sure it is, and I have no doubt that if you were granted an audience with the king or the queen or even the prince, that any one of them could tell you and maybe even show you some big superserious etched carving done in solid gold or some shit, or maybe just an extremely informative and well-researched PowerPoint presentation, but for those of us out here in the world—the fuck do we care?"

Had he even taken a breath while venting at me? I wasn't sure, but I could see his point. What did knowing about the evolution of homo sapiens—if you even believed in evolution—do for the average person on the street? Still, I was disappointed I couldn't get the whole story.

"Is that it?" he prompted.

I'd hoped he could fill in so much more. "No, not at all."

He nodded, and I glanced at the others just to see if maybe any of them had a different take on things or had anything to add. They had all passed out.

"They seem exhausted."

"It's a fight for your life out there, man. It's nice to be in here where it's safe."

"What'd you mean? Safe in here how? And why aren't you safe outside?"

He shook his head. "I have no clue why it feels like it does in here, but I think it has something to do with you."

Back to this. "I'm not a vampyr, I promise you."

"And I believe you, but you're not just human either."

"That makes no sense."

He shrugged. "I have no idea what to say to you."

We were getting nowhere, and I still had a billion questions. "Then in the meantime, could you give me the rundown of everything you do know?"

"Oh, sure, why not," he said sarcastically.

"Are you gonna be an ass?"

"You don't know me yet. This could be me in a fan-fucking-tastic mood."

I snorted, which drew a smile from him. "Could you do me a favor, though?"

"Hit me."

"If there are any weird words, would you write those down?"

"I don't—"

"It'd make things a lot easier. It's how my mind works, I gotta see it."

"Sure. Whatever," he agreed, a bit disgruntled, and took the pen and paper I passed him. "Okay, so I'm gonna start with the *nori-ah*"—he scrawled "noreia" as he spoke—"because that's all of us as a race. With vampyrs, how old your family is, is directly related to how much wealth, status, and privilege you have."

"Technically that's people too. I mean, old money and new money and no money."

"Exactly," he agreed. "So there are the *pee-bee*s—as in purebloods—who have only ever bred with other vampyrs, and they've got ancestors that go back to the Iron Age or before, and their fancy name is *row-genus*." He wrote down "roginus." "You can't miss them; they have sticks firmly wedged up their asses."

"Got it."

"Right. And then you have vampyrs like me with no lineage, regular folks, vampyrs who mixed with humans, and like the slang for roginus is PBs, for us, everyone says 'made.' Like you're just made, no big deal, nothing special—which is most of us—but the real term is *ee-cee-knee*."

"That's not fair," I said, repeating iceni silently after he wrote it down. "Money or breeding or whatever counts for crap in the real world. It's who you are and what you do with your life."

He smirked. "Yeah, I know, oh champion of the common man, but I'm trying to get through Vampyr 101 over here."

"Wow," I retorted, scowling. "You're really a dick."

"I was stabbed earlier," he reminded me. "Not having the best night."

"Yeah, all right, I'll give you that."

He made his eyes huge for a second, like *Wow!* and I laughed.

"Now above the purebloods are the nobility, who have titles, and I've only seen a few in my life. One time outside a club I couldn't get in when I lived in New York one summer with my cousins, and then again when I went to Europe after high school for a month. They're called the *deh-nee*"—"dene" was what he wrote—"and they run with celebrities, and that's crazy old money."

"I think I'm missing the difference between the purebloods and the nobility."

"It's the elite mating with the elite, like one royal house mating with another one. Think of it like in the old days how a prince could only marry a princess."

"Oh, I see."

"Yeah, that's some serious shit."

"And that's all?"

"No. The last is the very top of the food chain, and those are the descendants of the first vampyr king, Ascalon. That's the royal line: the king, the queen, and the prince. They're the *day-see-uhn*,"—dacian—"and don't ask me anything about them, because I have no fuckin' clue. No one I've ever met has seen any of them."

But *I* had met two men who saw the prince on a regular basis. "All right, so, calling you all the 'made' is probably what gave rise to the whole legend about being able to 'make' vampyrs, don't you think?"

"Maybe," he said. I could tell he could not care less.

"This isn't fascinating to you?"

"This is ancient history you're talking about. Who gives a crap?"

"You should care."

He made a derisive noise.

"Do you all get along?"

"Who?"

"Like you and the PBs?"

"Us and them, you mean?"

I grunted. "I think that answered my question right there."

"Yeah, it's not good."

"I'm so sorry."

"It is what it is. They hate us on general principle, and we feel the same about them. Mostly we all stay clear of each other, but if you're a made vampyr walking alone at night, like I had to earlier, you might get jumped and killed."

"It's that bad?" I was horrified. It was a war zone right there where I lived, and I'd had no idea people were dying.

"Hell yeah. And that's a shitty way to go because they kill you and send your fangs and a finger to whoever knows you. The rest is just burned."

"That's horrible."

"Yeah, but you can't have vampyrs in the news with our weird teeth and strange cell structure," he apprised me.

I had no idea what to say in response, too shocked and dismayed by what he'd just said. It had to be terrifying for the individual being killed and heart-wrenching for their families.

"So yeah, it's dangerous out there."

"They kill you, you kill them just because you can."

"Absolutely."

I studied him.

"You wanna ask, so g'head."

"Have you killed any purebloods?"

"Yes."

I would have asked something more, but I stopped myself because it wasn't right for me to ask him to implicate himself, and beyond that, I had no frame of reference for the struggles of vampyrs. In human terms, having been to war, having seen carnage up close, I could take a side, try to help, make a difference, but this was a reality he understood and I didn't. "What happened tonight?"

"I was meeting my friends and the party was a block away, but I got to the end of my street over there on Ursulines and Chartres, and I turned a corner, and they were there, waiting on me."

"Why?" I asked, angry for him that this was his reality, what he dealt with every day.

"I have no idea," he said but glanced away. He knew exactly why he got grabbed; he just didn't want to say.

"So they just jumped you and tried to slice you up."

"There was no trying. They did a pretty good job, but my friends came looking for me, and since there were only a couple of PBs and four of my friends, they stopped carving me up and bailed when they heard my buddies yelling."

"Jesus."

"Like I said, it's bad out there if you're a vampyr, which is why, on both sides, we try and never go out alone."

"That's crazy to hate others just like you. I mean, you're all vampyrs, it's just a class distinction and money you're talking about," I said vehemently, having seen this over and over again at home and abroad.

His grunt was judgmental.

"What?"

"As though humans are any different," he sighed. "It's exactly the same."

He was not wrong. Apparently humans and vampyrs had a lot more in common than simply an ancestor. "I have more questions."

"Go for it," he said, smiling. "This isn't as bad as I thought it was gonna be."

"Thanks a lot."

His shrug told me he could not have cared less if he offended me.

"I want to know about humans now. How do they fit into the vampyr world?"

"Pureblood vampyrs only have children with other vampyrs, but made vampyrs—"

"No, I got that part. I want to know what other ways humans fit in."

"Well, there are vampyrs in both groups, PBs and made, who don't follow the rules where humans are concerned."

"How so?"

"They drink them dry and kill them," he explained. "And that's bad."

That's bad? "*That's bad*?" I said incredulously, getting louder, astounded that he could say something so appalling and horrendous as though it were the most mundane, everyday occurrence.

"Jason—"

"Are you screwing with me!"

"Why're you yelling?" he had the gall to ask.

"*That's bad*?" I intoned dramatically. "Seriously?"

"It's a law that you don't do it."

"I think I like this law," I said dramatically as he cracked a grin.

"Humans are off-limits unless you're married or mated to one."

"And how do you prove that?"

"With a marriage license or a mating ceremony," he explained, "both of which have paperwork that's filed either at city hall or with the leader of your community."

"And if you drink from someone outside of marriage?"

"Don't get caught."

He made it sound like drinking blood from humans was like using a recreational drug. "Now what if you kill a human?"

"Then you're dead."

"Who carries that sentence out?"

"Either the head of the PBs or the head of the made vampyrs," he explained. "Whatever type you are, they do it."

I absorbed what he said, thinking back to Washington.

"If you fuck up like that, either drink from a human outside a covenant bond—that's the marriage or mating—or kill a human, you're called a *foe-more-ee*." Cooke added "fomori" to the list he was making. "Usually anyplace you go, you'll find both roginus and iceni and their leaders. Here in New Orleans, Niko Gann is in charge of the made vampyrs, and the Diallo family—the ruling pureblood clan of the city—is run by Benny Diallo."

I nodded, listening, wondering how in the world all of this existed outside of what I'd known all my life. I was trying to take it all in; I'd have my own private freak-out as I went over everything in my head later. Now was the moment to learn all I could.

I briefly checked on the others, still dead to the world. Were they vampyrs too? "Is there anywhere I can find out this stuff on my own?"

"Check out *The Law of Ascalon*. It's a book of rules. You can buy it online or check it out at the library. I have a copy if you wanna borrow it."

"You can find a vampyr book in the library?"

He shrugged. "Well, yeah. I mean, to anyone but us, it reads like a piece of fiction. It's the vampyr laws all written down, and we're all supposed to follow them."

"And so if you don't, then you're considered a fomori?"

"No," he said scornfully. "You think every law is punishable by death?"

"Like I would know," I snapped.

"Well, it's not like that," he assured me. "We're not so rigid that every slight transgression means you're dead meat. Only drinking from a human who you're not bound to makes you fomori, which means you're done."

The way he said fomori, drawing the word out, using it like the word *heretic*, told me what a huge deal it was. There was nothing worse in his book. "And everyone has to follow the same rules?"

"You mean like purebloods and—"

"Yeah."

"Of course," he asserted. "Across the board certain things are finite."

The night I met Tiago, when he said who he was and how important he was—if the prince was at the top of the food chain, did Tiago have to follow all the laws or was he untouchable? "And what about the rajan?"

He scowled.

"What?"

"The rajan. The counselor of the prince?"

"Yeah."

"What about it?" He sighed, looking pained.

"It?"

"Well, I can't say he or she 'cause I don't know who the current rajan is."

Interesting. "Why not?"

"Why don't I know who the rajan is?"

"Yes."

"Why would I?"

"Because you should know, shouldn't you?"

"I guess, but I'd have to go to what Madagascar or—"

"Malta," I corrected.

"Oh yeah, that's right," he said, "Malta. Madagascar, Macao, Mozambique, I get all the M countries mixed up. But so yeah, since the king's court is on the other side of the planet and I'm not independently wealthy, I'm thinking I won't be running into the rajan anytime soon."

"But—"

"And how do you know about the rajan anyway?"

"Tell me about the prince," I said, ignoring his question. "What's he called?"

He started at the top and went down the list. The title of the king was the boria; the queen, the mavia; and the prince, the draugr. The court was in Malta, though apparently the Maedoc family had purchased a Greek island and the queen had moved there. She and the king were *not* close.

"I guess if you're married for thousands of years, it's hard to keep that old spark alive," Cooke said, snickering.

I would suspect so. "I thought vampyrs liked darkness. Why would Greece be good?"

"The sunlight and garlic and not being able to see your own reflection—that's all crap."

My preconceived notions were getting blown all to hell.

"But one of the things that is true is that for us, the older you get, the stronger you are, and drinking blood slows down our aging process."

"By how much? How long a life does metabolizing only blood get you?"

"I dunno, but I've met guys who are eighty who look twenty-five."

"Then the immortal part is true."

"You're not immortal if you can be killed."

"How long do vampyrs live on average?"

"That depends on your line too. The stronger the genes, the stronger you are."

I smiled.

"What's with the happy?"

"Nothing. I—This is just so interesting."

"If you say so," he said with a shrug.

"So how old are you?" I asked, excited.

"Sixty-one."

"Wow. You look damn good for a senior citizen."

"Aww, gee, thanks."

"And what about Benny Diallo?" I wanted to gauge the age of vampyrs versus their places in the world. Like, would I be talking to people who had been born centuries before me, or just a few years? "Do you know how old he is?"

"I think he's like a hundred, hundred and two."

"What about the prince?"

"I've heard the prince fought in the crusades so if he was of age by then, that puts him well over a thousand."

"Holy shit."

"Well said," he teased.

"So it's safe to say that there's no preset time for how long a vampyr can live."

"Again, it's genetics. The king's life can probably go on indefinitely. I'll maybe see two hundred if I don't get killed walking home."

"I wonder what a thousand-year-old vampyr is capable of?" I mused, ignoring his obvious fishing for concern.

"Anything he wants would be my guess," Cooke said. "Okay, so now you. Explain to me what you are."

"I don't get your question."

He gestured at himself.

"You lost me."

"I was losing blood, then suddenly I find this place—find you—and now I'm all healed up," he said pointedly, staring at me. "So tell me... what the hell are you?"

"I'm not anything special, I swear. I'm just a guy."

He shook his head. "You're not just 'anything.' Are you a pureblood?"

"I told you already. I'm human, not a vampyr."

"Yeah, I can smell your blood like sharks do in water, and if you were a vampyr, I wouldn't be able to."

"See? Then you know I'm human."

"Yeah, but then how are you doing this?"

"Doing what, the healing?"

"Yeah."

"I have no idea."

"Man, this is a mindfuck."

It most certainly was. All of it. From when I had first met Tiago and Hadrian to Cooke nearly collapsing on my doorstep, all of it, all of them, had made me doubt my sanity, only to realize there wasn't a thing wrong with me all along. My perceptions, what

I observed, all of it was valid. I had to stop doubting myself.

We were silent a moment. "I've met one of the prince's guards," I threw out.

His eyes got big and round. "Are you fucking with me?"

"No. Why?"

"That's amazing. Do they shift into wolves, or are they more like part men, part wolves and walk on two feet?"

"What're you talking about?" I couldn't go from vampyrs to werewolves—that was asking too much. One paradigm shift per lifetime was more than enough.

"They call the prince's guards the wolves of the house of Maedoc; I just assumed they were werewolves or something."

"Have you ever seen a werewolf?"

"No."

"You just assume there is such a thing?"

"That's ancient shit I have no idea about."

"Well, I hate to burst your bubble, but there were no werewolves, just guys."

"Really?"

I nodded.

"That's disappointing," he said and then abruptly jolted.

"Jesus, what's wrong with you?" I asked, concerned, because watching him almost jump out of his skin, hearing him catch his breath, studying the way he was now shifting back and forth from one foot to the other, was unsettling.

He tipped his head at the front windows, and outside loomed five guys in suits, looking in at us.

"The guy right there by your door, he's the one who cut me."

I made a decision. "Then lemme go see what he wants," I said gently, getting up, wanting to see if I could help the situation while resolute in the knowledge I would let no harm come to my new friend.

"No, wait, you gotta listen."

"It's gonna be fine," I promised, walking around Cooke and heading for the door.

"They'll kill us all if you let them in!" he yelled, and he must have startled the others because everyone was shouting at once, their voices layering, pleading with me, one of the girls shrieking, absolutely frantic.

"Stop," I ordered. "You're all safe with me," I stated before unlocking the door and leaning out.

The closest man actually snarled and lunged at me, but he hit an invisible wall between us. He bounced back into the man at his shoulder, who caught him and helped him regain his balance.

None of the others moved, and they didn't look mad anymore, more startled and wary.

"Hey," I greeted.

"Who the fuck are you?" the first guy asked.

"I'm Jason Thorpe. I own this shop. Who're you?"

"Garrett Spencer," he said, glaring at me.

I met his gaze, held it, didn't look away, holding my ground, waiting for him to make some kind of move.

After a moment he glanced sideways and then back to me. By the huff of breath and the anger rolling off him, I understood he was both annoyed and hesitant. He wasn't afraid of me, but he wasn't sure of the situation either. And so we stood, watchful and ready, also wary, two gunslingers in the street, each waiting for the other to twitch.

"Did you wanna come in?" I offered. Something had to give. Vampyr or not, I wasn't afraid. Maybe I should have been—I'd seen both Tiago and Hadrian move—but I was also a big believer in fate.

I was supposed to be at that cabin in the middle of nowhere to help save Tiago, just as I was meant to be here now to intercede on behalf of Cooke. For whatever reason that had not yet made itself clear to me, I had been ushered into the new (technically old) world of vampyrs. I had a part to play; I just had to figure out what that was. But while the reason escaped me, understanding dynamics seemed like the best way to start.

"Do you want to come inside?" I repeated to the vampyr standing in front of me.

He gave me a curt nod, begrudging, brows furrowed, lips in a tight line, jaw clenched, really not happy to find himself here. He stepped inside, the others following close behind, and when I turned, Cooke's friends were up from the love seat and clustered around him.

In my shop, ten of them plus me, gathered together, they eyed each other up, and once that was done, all attention was on me.

In that strange, quiet moment, I instinctively understood I was supposed to do something—an opportunity I didn't want to miss.

"So what can we do for you all?" I asked.

He didn't answer.

"Sir?"

"Garrett," he corrected.

I offered him another welcoming smile. "Garrett."

"I don't know."

"What do you mean, you don't know?"

"I mean that outside on the sidewalk, I wanted to get in here, kill him—kill all of them," he said, gesturing at Cooke and his friends. "But... I don't know, because now wanting that seems strange, like that wasn't me, even though of course it was, 'cause that's one of the things I do for my boss...." He glanced around the room. "Somebody else say somethin'."

The rest of the men who came in with him—vampyrs, men, it was hard to make a distinction between human and other—glanced among themselves and then back at me.

No one spoke, no one threatened, they waited instead, and after a few long minutes, that got really awkward. Cooke finally looked at me and turned his palms up.

"What?" I asked.

"I dunno, what?" he snapped. "What are you wanting here?"

"Yeah," Garrett said, tipping his chin toward Cooke. "Answer."

It couldn't hurt to ask. "Well, don't you all think that we have an opportunity here, right now, to air some grievances? And then maybe try and figure out where we could go from here that might not include homicide?"

Silence.

"Wouldn't it be nice if we could make the Quarter a place where both pureblood vampyrs and made vampyrs could all feel safe?"

I got a lot of scoffing, some snickering, and a bit of swearing. Apparently this war between the upper and lower class was not something to be fixed overnight. I understood the hostility and resentment ran deep and poisoned everything. Casting aside hundreds, maybe even thousands, of years of bad blood wasn't going to just miraculously happen. They were all carrying around ancient grievances none of them had a hand in creating. Programmed to judge and fear and hate, they just wouldn't see with new eyes.

"Maybe we could start with a small fix and work up to a big one?" I suggested because a journey of a thousand steps and all that.

I expected more of the same—snide comments and profanity—but none came, and I was happily surprised.

"How are you doing this?" Garrett asked, his eyes narrowed, studying me.

"Doing what?"

Cooke cleared his throat, and Garrett turned to look at him. "It's weird, right? It's like we should all be calm in here or something."

Garrett nodded. "Yes. Why? Do you know?"

They were talking, just them, finding common ground in the oddity I was.

Cooke shook his head. "No, but it's felt like that since I walked in here, and it still hasn't changed even with"—he tipped his head at Garrett and his men—"you all, and I'm not scared."

"Yeah," Garrett agreed. "Me neither."

Cooke lifted his brows, and he was trying to hide his astonishment over what was just said. "You guys—you worry about us too?"

"Everyone has the same fears when they're out alone," Garrett said quickly, trying to sound nonchalant but clearly failing, with how sharply his breath caught.

Their gazes met, held, and then both turned back to me. Clearly they were waiting, again, for me to do or say something.

They would stand there all night, frozen, it seemed, in anticipation.

Whatever was happening, it was of my making. I was the spider, and they were caught in my web, so that now, in my shop, everyone felt safe, protected. Even the guys who normally intimidated others were scared, or they wouldn't have started threatening people to begin with. It was a self-fulfilling prophecy: people were on guard, it put others on theirs, and round and round and round until somebody snapped and blood and death reigned.

But here I had an opening for peace.

Maybe.

Hopefully.

I just had to see how far my reach could actually go. I needed to start small.

It turned out Garrett worked for Benny Diallo, and Cooke was tight with Niko Gann, so they had inherent issues right up front.

"I would love to see if maybe Mr. Diallo and Mr. Gann could come to the shop and sit down and talk with me about calling a truce."

The irritation on Garrett's face told me he wanted to say it would be a cold day in hell before that happened, but instead he said, "I'll ask him, all right?"

"Thank you," I said sincerely before turning to Cooke. "And I need you to speak to Mr. Gann as soon as possible, okay?"

Cooke nodded hesitantly.

"Excellent," I sighed, pleased with both men, because even though they had barely agreed to my terms, they still *had*, in fact, agreed. Smiling, I returned my focus to Garrett. "In the meantime, what can we do about the animosity between you and my friend Cooke here?"

"Cooke there," he scoffed, "almost died tonight—"

"Died?" I asked, feigning confusion. "From what?"

"From what?" Garrett retorted. "Are you kidding? I ripped a hole in his abdomen as big as the Grand Canyon!"

"What's he talking about?" I projected as much innocence as I could, and when I turned to Cooke, he snickered and then smiled lazily, lifting his shirt to show nothing but freckled skin over tight, wiry muscle. Even the pale pink healing mark was gone.

Garrett was stunned to silence.

The men with him blinked, openmouthed.

I cleared my throat and drew everyone's attention. "Since clearly Cooke is a lot stronger than you thought—can we get back to figuring out the source of the trouble?" I asked patiently.

"Yes," Garrett said, arms crossed, scowling at Cooke.

The issue was easy enough to understand. As Garrett explained, if he'd told Cooke once, he'd told him a thousand times: don't work the sidewalk in front of his restaurant. Cooke was a street musician with enough of a following to make it hard on certain businesses.

I shot Cooke a look.

"What?"

"How many times did he ask?"

He had to think.

"That's really not helping," I informed my new friend.

Cooke shrugged.

"I can't have them outside my restaurant," Garrett explained sincerely. "I have a nice, steady clientele, but I'm going to start losing them if they have to keep asking people who reek of patchouli to get the hell out of the way just so they can get inside."

It was a valid point. Cooke and his band impacted Garrett's ability to make money for his family.

"But he gets to come at me with a fuckin' saber?" Cooke asked, horrified.

Also a legitimate point.

"And we need a place to go that will draw people at night," Cooke countered.

The solution hit me.

"You know what?" I said brightly, "I think I can help."

Chapter Four

THE NEXT evening Cooke and his crew serenaded people in front of my store, and after a month, they still came on the nights they weren't playing a club. With their CDs in the store and playing there at night, they picked up enough buzz to book some gigs.

Ode hired a girl named Leni to work in the store who, after a week, revealed to me she was a made vampyr. She gave off a hippie vibe and knew everything about the oils we sold and the different stones and all the Egyptian talismans, and like Ode, could seemingly read people and tell at a glance what they truly needed. I liked her and her long flowing blonde hair, big blue eyes, and freckles. Amazingly Ode—who normally didn't like people right away (I was an exception)—and Leni became fast friends, the force of nature and the vampyr. When they walked around together, traffic came to a screeching halt.

Then once we realized the night shift was profitable, Ode hired two more people: a clean-cut college kid named Farraday Biel, and Benny Diallo's little sister, Joy, whose name embodied her spirit. I wasn't sure how she would do working with Leni and having Cooke in and out of the store all the time, but unlike many of the other purebloods, she did not, as Cooke informed me, have a stick up her ass.

Despite his newfound fame, Cooke still stopped by to visit and kept me company at night when I covered the store.

"It's November," he groused, turning the fan on the counter to face him as he flipped through a magazine. "Why is it still hot?"

"It's New Orleans," I reminded him, "not Boston."

He grunted.

"You could move."

"Oh hell no. This is the first place I've ever lived where the PBs and made get along. I'm never leaving."

I pivoted to look at him, surprised by the words. I knew from talking to him, and now others, that the struggle between the classes was ongoing. What I hadn't known was me being there was influencing the bigger population. "What do you mean?"

"I mean that because of you, we all get along. Everybody knows, PB or made, that if they have an issue, they can come here, and you'll sit them down and iron out whatever the issue is. I mean, both Benny and Niko actually come and see you on a regular basis, and everybody walks the streets together without any bloodshed! It's fuckin' amazing."

Benny would sit above me on the stairs that led up to my apartment while I sat below and sideways, looking up at him, and Niko leaned against the side of the building smoking a cigarette. We ironed out so many small things that might have snowballed. And while I was more at ease with Niko because Benny was a bit more standoffish, I respected them both.

It matched up with what Leni had offered by way of explanation one night after both men left.

"It's funny," she said, leaning against the side of the building, arms crossed, staring at me. "Everyone thinks that it's the store that's somehow imbued with magical properties, but how in the world could that be the case?"

I smiled. "Maybe it's built over some mysterious vortex of power."

She snorted a laugh. "Yeah, okay."

"Who knows." I sighed, looking up at the cloudy night sky. "Whatever it is, it is peaceful, though, isn't it?"

"It is," she agreed, "because of you. It's like in *Charlotte's Web*."

I couldn't help squinting at her. "I'm sorry?"

"People in the book were all, *Wow, that pig is amazing*, but really, a spider that could spell? When I was little, I was, like, they should have still made Wilbur into bacon and figured out how to extend Charlotte's life."

"I do see your point," I said, chuckling. "But it would have been a very different book."

"My point is that vampyrs come into the store, and they're always in awe over how at peace they feel, how unafraid, and they chalk that up to the building, to being inside the store, even though you're walking around right in front of them."

"I don't—"

"The building has been here forever, but guess what. You haven't."

I shrugged.

"I mean, seriously, connect the dots, yeah?"

"*Jase*." Cooke looked bored.

"Sorry. I was thinking about something Leni said the other day."

"Something about how great you are for the community, and if you decide to move somewhere—any-where—that we're all coming too?"

"Sure," I teased. "No. That wasn't quite it. She was just putting a theory out there about how it's me and not the store."

"Which is exactly my point," he said, grinning. "You're the anomaly, right? Not the store."

"Well, apparently you and Leni are in agreement."

"I would like for us to be in agreement about a whole lotta other things."

"Hands off my staff," I said flatly. "I've seen how you treat women."

He rolled his eyes.

"And I think all this newfound peace is a result of Benny and Niko being open to working together and nothing else."

"Don't kid yourself. Those guys feel it like the rest of us. We're all compelled to do what you want, for whatever fuckin' reason, and it just so happens that you're using your power for good and not evil."

I groaned. "I have no powers," I grumbled. "Just because the Quarter is a magical place doesn't mean I am."

"Just keep using your power for good."

"Absolutely," I said sarcastically.

"Nobody likes a smartass," he assured me, looking up from the magazine.

I scoffed. "I dunno, people seem to like you."

He flipped me off before returning to the pictures of clothes he wanted. "I would still love to know how you're gettin' everyone to sit around and sing 'Kumbaya' together."

It had been an… interesting month. With so many noreia landing on my doorstep, I had even more people to talk to and ask questions. Happily the sanctity of human life was universal, and most human and vampyr interaction was not scary in the slightest.

But one point kept bothering me.

There were humans who knew all about vampyrs and would allow them to tap a vein without the benefit of a bond. They were called fuillin, blood-givers, and it was done in a variety of ways. Some humans were part of a vampyr's entourage. Some were "kept" humans; they belonged to that particular vampyr, involving collars or lockets. The problem was that keeping a fuillin in any capacity was, by decree of the king, illegal. Even when the human was more than willing, or even if said vampyr and human were madly in love, it was breaking the law.

Humans could not regenerate blood at the same speed a vampyr could, so the laws protected them from becoming human juice boxes, the kind sucked dry and crumpled up. If mated, in theory, the human trusted the vampyr not to kill them. The law came into play with unmated humans, protecting them from being preyed upon and protecting vampyrs from accidents that would lead to interaction with human law enforcement, the results of which could be catastrophic.

The law served everyone well, vampyr and human alike. But I saw problems concerning free will. How was it fair for the law to say who a human could love and in what way? Why did the law get a say in a vampyr's bedroom about who they could take blood from and when? If both parties were consenting adults, what was the harm? And why was the onus all on the vampyr?

"Your brain is running," Cooke said absently, yawning before closing the magazine. "What's your question?"

"How did you know I had another question?"

He snorted loudly. "Whatever. Just ask me already."

"That night when you said that you were going to feed off me, you would have fed off me only to be killed later?"

"I wouldn't have."

"But you said you would."

"But I wouldn't have," Cooke explained.

"But again, you *said* you were going to," I insisted, wanting to get to the crux of the matter without him arguing.

He growled. "I wouldn't have, all right?"

"Then why say it?"

"Man, I was so fuckin' out of it before you healed me. I've never been in pain like that. It messed with my head."

"So you're saying there's no way you would ever drink from me, regardless of the situation?"

"That's right."

"You're so lying right now."

"Oh hell no," he said implacably. "I refuse to ever be labeled as a fomori."

"Because drinking blood from anyone else but another vampyr or your human mate is forbidden, right?"

"That's right."

"But what if nobody ever sees you? Can't you just lie?"

"I guess you could, but supposedly the PBs can smell it. Niko says that Benny can, so I guess it's true."

"*They* could lie."

"They could, but the prince can tell exactly what you are from drinking your blood."

"Really?"

"I heard he does when those cases are brought to him, but otherwise no."

"And so he, what, just pops in from Malta to be a vampyr blood test?"

"No, you gotta go to him."

"Do people actually do that?"

He shook his head. "I dunno. Maybe. I guess you either care or you don't, you either follow the commandments of the king or you don't. Simple as that."

"Then if you just follow the laws or don't, what's the upside of being a follower?"

"The prince can send the dreki."

"I think your prince wields far too much power," I said to him, just as I had to Tiago.

"But someone has to be the bad guy. There has to be a scourge."

"Big word," I said sarcastically. "Did you read it somewhere?"

"Fuck. You."

I laughed as I punched him gently in the shoulder.

"Owww," he complained.

"Tell me why."

"Why *what*?" He was still irritated.

"Why does there have to be a bad guy?"

"Because without rules, there's chaos, idiot."

It sounded suspiciously like dogma, which was why, initially, I'd thought that all of this was about a cult.

"I prefer to live by *The Laws of Ascalon* and not roll the dice with my life," Cooke said.

It was too arbitrary. "I think that by your king putting limits on who vampyrs can drink from, that he's also trying to put limits on who his people can love."

"What are you talking about?"

"It shouldn't be any of the king's business who you want to love or sleep with or do anything else with. His laws should extend to not hurting anyone, and that's all."

"Why?"

"Because he's not God," I explained, remembering what my CO used to say to me whenever I went off and took chances. "He can't save everyone, even from themselves."

"I'm not following you."

"The king shouldn't be allowed to choose what's right for everyone. He can't save everyone from poor choices—which is what he's trying to do. He has to let them live their lives for themselves."

"And then, what, drinking blood becomes a choice that any vampyr can make?"

"With consent, why not?"

"I think you open yourself up to all kinds of problems if everyone can take blood from whoever they want, whenever they feel like it."

"I think it makes sense," I argued. "As long as the person is old enough to give proper consent, and as long as no one is getting hurt, I say go for it."

"You have this idea in your head about drinking blood, fueled by bad movies and trashy novels, that somehow makes it out to be more than just taking sustenance."

"I have no idea, but I do know that vampyrs should be able to enjoy it and make it part of the whole seduction process if they want."

"Oh, for crissakes, Jase, it would be like you falling in love with a cheeseburger!"

"I have been very close to a few cheeseburgers in my day. The first one I had when I got back from Iraq, I could've married."

He groaned, loud and dire: I was too annoying for words.

"What?"

"I don't get people and food," he muttered. "It's weird."

"You'd get it if you ever had great gumbo," I said, grinning as I left the desk and checked the deadbolts on the back door.

We walked through the shop and I set the alarm, then we walked out, and I locked the door behind us. "Hey, I'm feeling like coffee, so I'm gonna run over to—"

The honk of a car horn turned us to the street, and there in the back seat of a silver Cadillac Escalade sat Garrett Spencer.

"Holy shit," I greeted, walking to the curb and leaning on the door, smiling. "What're you doin' away from Blue Moon?" It was his newest club over on Bourbon Street, a big mixing place for vampyrs and humans. Blue Moon served blood in wineglasses—very over-the-top bad B movie—and handed out tiny glass vials of "vampyr blood"—actually a drop of X dissolved in corn syrup and red food coloring—for fifty bucks a pop. It was one of several drugs being dealt to humans there. "I didn't know you could leave your new baby unattended to visit the lowly who aren't good enough to get in."

"If you want to come to the club—"

"Oh no, no, you had the little opening and then the big one—twice was enough, believe me."

He growled.

I continued ribbing him. "And, by the way, real original name you picked there."

"No one but you would even think to give me this much shit."

"So everyone gives you less shit?"

"You know, I imagine my hands around your neck sometimes."

I couldn't control my snicker.

"I've made more money in a week than you'll make in your lifetime," he railed.

"You have a club full of posers," I countered. "It *does not* incorporate the NOLA vibe at all. Both you and that club belong in Los Angeles."

He flipped me off.

I stepped back from the car. "I'm getting coffee. I'll catch you—"

"No." He stopped me, reaching out, taking hold of my wrist. "I need you to come with me over to Benny's house."

I waited for the reason, staring at his hand.

"What?" he said, letting go of me.

I lifted my gaze and met his. "I have never been invited to Benny's house, and he even told me once that he doesn't have humans in his home."

"Yeah, but—"

"I think he's worried I'm not housetrained." I cackled, took a step back, and turned to go.

"Wait."

I did because blowing people off, even if they weren't technically human, was still rude.

Garrett took a breath. "Things have changed. We have a visitor who has requested an audience with you to correspond with us welcoming him to our city."

"And what visitor is that?"

Garrett's deep brown eyes met mine. "The draugr, our prince, has arrived in New Orleans."

Chapter Five

I INSISTED Cooke join me and was surprised when Garrett shrugged instead of muttering something derogatory about mongrels. As a rule, he never missed an opportunity to point out the differences between purebloods and everyone else, but instead he just changed seats to make room for us.

Hand clasping the roof of the truck, I bent over to peer in at Garrett. "I'm gonna run upstairs and change, all right?"

He shook his head.

"Really? You think I should meet your prince in jeans and a Henley?"

"You look fine," he insisted, waving me inside. "Just get in the truck."

"Are you sick?" I asked as I squeezed past the folded rear passenger seat to settle into the third row. Cooke lifted the seat and sat in it.

"No," Garrett snapped. "Why?"

I shrugged and leaned forward between their two seats. "You're normally not this accommodating."

Instead of saying anything more, he rolled down the window and breathed in the fragrant night air always thick with jasmine. Cooke turned his head and lifted his eyebrows, as confused as I was about how nonconfrontational Garrett was behaving.

The trip to Benny's home on Third Street near Coliseum took only fifteen minutes the way David, Garrett's driver, navigated the roads.

"Holy shit," Cooke said, leaning out the window, "lookit all the damn cars."

They lined both sides of the street near Benny's home, and while we stopped at the enormous wrought iron gate, I could see high-end vehicles cluttered the long circular driveway as well.

Once through, David drove us to the entrance, and Benny Diallo himself opened the door for Cooke.

"Mr. Diallo!" Cooke greeted Benny enthusiastically, even though I knew, from seeing them interact when he came by my shop, Benny scared him. "How are you, sir?"

"Good," he replied curtly but then smiled at me as I climbed out. Garrett came around the side of the truck to join us. "How are you, Jason?"

"Fine," I answered slowly, unsure, because he was normally more familiar with me. He usually called me Jase, not Jason, and the change seemed out of character, cold, soulless.

"Excellent. Shall we go inside?"

He was being too civil, robotic, and it tripped my weirdness meter. Air that was moving a moment ago had stilled. The ever-present breeze was gone, and the air felt heavy, almost smothering. My skin felt tight, and I was cold, which in seventy-three-degree weather was impossible. But I'd had these feelings before, and I knew what it meant. Even though I was outside, I was good and trapped.

"Jason?"

This must be how a mouse felt, cornered in a room by an owl or a cat.

"We should go in."

They were stronger than me, faster, and even though I had a rapport with some of these men, my first thought was for my father's rifle, under my bed in a locked gun safe, and how it would even the odds a bit. My military-issue knife, my sidearm… anything would have helped me with the adrenaline settling in. I could grapple with the best of them—I'd excelled at close-quarter combat tactics—but these were vampyrs standing outside in the cool night air, and if they all came at me at once, I'd be toast. I surveyed the driveway, the gazebo that stood in a grove of magnolia and willow oaks with hydrangeas and azaleas, and recognized outrunning them was never going to work.

I began edging away toward the SUV. I needed to leave.

"Jason?"

I pointed to the front door. "I'm not going in there," I explained. "I'm not sure why I got in the car, and for that, I apologize, but I'm human, and the idea of being the lone snack in that house is *not* appealing."

"You know better than that," Benny retorted, the icy behavior now freezing his tone. He was clearly disgusted with my fear. "You've been told the law. No one's going to hurt you. Humans are the safe ones, not the other way around."

But the savagery in his voice was in no way comforting.

He took a step forward, appearing threatening to me, and I moved around the SUV, putting it between us. I wasn't scared, but I could feel myself slipping into combat mode, getting ready to defend myself. His smile was slow, slightly sinister, and affirmed my feeling that he knew what he was doing, purposely trying to intimidate me. More vampyrs than I had initially noticed fanned out around us, and the hair stood up on the back of my neck.

Cooke took a step forward, but Benny reached out and took hold of his arm. "Remember where your loyalties lie," he said, and Cooke froze in place.

I didn't feel betrayed. We were friends, yes, but Benny was not only forging a new alliance with his leader, but was easily the most powerful vampyr in New Orleans. One didn't argue with the man in charge, especially over a guy who could very well be lunch.

"Get the fuck back," I warned two vampyrs closing in. I got smug, cocky smiles as they kept moving, not giving a damn who I was.

Something was wrong—my "mojo" wasn't working—and when I glanced at Cooke, he looked as confused as I felt. Why weren't these vampyrs responding as the others had?

"Jason Thorpe!"

The vampyrs who seemed intimidating moments before quickly moved back, hands up.

Hadrian descended the steps from the house, and an immense wave of relief came over me. He was as tall as I remembered, six five to my own six feet, broad shouldered, his teeth very white, as he smiled and the contrast to his deeply tanned skin was noticeable and appealing. He looked tremendously capable, and watching him come closer, I exhaled my fear. I'd been holding my breath.

The vampyrs took more steps back, making certain Hadrian was crystal clear on the fact that they were not threatening me. Hadrian's guards stood at the top of the stairs, six in total, three men and three women.

Hadrian didn't spare Benny, Garrett, Cooke, or any of the others a second glance, he just walked up to me, hand extended, wearing the grin I knew, mischievous and friendly.

"Hey," I managed to get out, clasping the offered hand, holding tight.

He furrowed his brows instantly. "I smell fear on you. Why are you in distress?"

I tipped my head at the vampyrs around us. "I just didn't wanna be dinner, ya know?"

He scowled, glanced around at the others and back at me. "It is forbidden for any to take the blood of a human, and albeit I know there are those who partake," he said, shooting Benny and Garrett a disdainful look, a hint of revulsion on him, "I can assure you that you are, without question, secure in my presence."

"Yeah, but you were surprised when you saw me alive at the hospital that time," I reminded him.

"Because you were not with me, and thus I was not responsible for your safety."

"So you plan to stick around this time?"

He squinted like he wasn't following.

"You ditched me last time, as you recall."

"I had hunting to do," he admitted. "But I left you with Tiago for company, certain that once he recovered his strength, he would protect you."

"It's a good story." I sighed, calming, my adrenaline rush subsiding.

"The truth always is," he agreed. "However, allow me to assure you," he continued ominously while narrowing his eyes, "should any attempt even to touch you while you are under my care—their lives will be forfeit to me."

The way everyone was looking at him, respectfully, not moving, just waiting, watchful, let me know that being under his care was a serious thing. "Thank you."

He gave me a slight tilt of his head before he took gentle hold of my bicep. "Now come inside. The prince would speak to you."

"Is Tiago in there too?"

"He is."

"Oh, that's great. I've been wanting to talk to both you and him, but I had no idea how to get in touch."

Hadrian eased me forward before letting go of my arm, and I walked beside him, keeping pace, not glancing at Cooke. I hadn't expected him to take my side over Benny's, but still, it hurt.

Shaking it off, I concentrated on Hadrian. "It's really good to see you."

"And you as well, Jason," he admitted. "I had hoped our paths would cross once more."

It was a nice thing to say, and the feeling came through in the tenor of his voice. I knew he meant it just as much as I did. "So this is weird, but the Rothschilds went ahead and paid in full for the job in their library, even though I never finished?" We climbed the stairs to the front door. "Did you do that?"

"No, I did not, but neither am I surprised."

"How come?" I smiled at Hadrian's people as we reached them, who gave me the same, plus a few nods, in return.

"The Rothschilds are no more, Jason," he said. "And Tiago compensated your company to make certain no loose ends remained."

"You mean they're dead," I stated just so we were clear, making sure "no more" meant the same thing to vampyrs as it did to humans.

"Just so," he affirmed, walking in front of me through an arched door easily twelve feet high that looked like it belonged in *The Lord of the Rings*, all thick burnished oak.

"Everyone?" I asked, laser focused on him, on his words, how bored he sounded, as though this conversation was completely beneath him, utterly inconsequential.

He nodded.

"But that's—"

"Is this house not lovely?" he asked, not subtle in the least.

I would not be so easily distracted. "I'm sure there were innocents among the—"

"Oh no, you misunderstand. Of the family, only those who held sway were purged," Hadrian informed me. "We are not monsters."

I met his gold-flecked cognac eyes. "You can't simply pass judgment on—"

"The prince may, and does," he instructed flatly. "Now, I invite you to please admire the chandelier."

I opened my mouth to say more, but he pointed up, and when I looked, I was momentarily stunned into silence. Up until that point in my life, I had never been in a home with murals on the ceilings and a crystal chandelier that belonged in *The Phantom of the Opera*.

"Holy shit," I gasped.

He chuckled. "If you designate this impressive, wait until you see the castle my prince calls home."

I scoffed, still taking in the gorgeous artwork above my head.

"Laugh now, human."

The walls held works just as notable: enormous paintings, some portraits, a few lush studies of still life, and landscapes rendered in stunning detail. I could walk the halls for days; taking it all in, though at the moment, with people crowding around us, moving anywhere in the house was a struggle.

"Attend," Hadrian ordered, and I followed, careful not to bump into anyone as we snaked our way through the crowd.

The ceilings in the Greek-revival mansion were high in every room, at least thirteen feet. The floors were all wood, and I was certain the crown molding and millwork and medallions surely dated from the original build, which Hadrian said was in the 1860s.

As we stood in the great room, I noticed Hadrian had an earpiece in, and he was quietly checking with his men.

"You may walk freely through the home and be assured no harm will be offered you," Hadrian said without looking at me. "Tiago is about, but he has much to attend to, and you will be called when the prince is ready to receive you."

"So you're saying beat it, you can't talk to me anymore 'cause you're workin'."

He grunted.

"Is that a yes?"

"Indeed."

I weighed his earlier words.

"I assure you that no one here is ignorant of the truth that you abide under the personal protection of the rekkr."

"And that's a big deal?"

He turned his head and focused on me. "It is."

The ego on him made me chuckle, but I took him at his word and left his side, confident to explore on my own.

Upstairs had a terrace and downstairs a patio with a pool. In total it had to be something like twelve thousand square feet, with nine bedrooms, several drawing rooms, a study, and a library I slipped inside of to take a look around.

It was one of those rooms out of a movie, adorned with chandeliers, heavy brocade drapes, and crushed velvet and leather furniture. It smelled like citrus and beeswax and an underlying sandalwood and musk I wanted to inhale. The imagined history of the house and that irresistible smell utterly mesmerized me.

"Are you impressed with Benny's home?" Niko asked, suddenly there beside me, smiling as he offered me a snifter of brandy.

"Yeah, his home is stunning," I admitted, thoroughly impressed. I shook my head at the alcohol. "That you can keep. I never developed a taste for the hard stuff."

He chuckled. "Beer, then?"

"Sometimes," I said quickly. "But I think I should stay clearheaded tonight, yeah?"

He stepped in front of me, barring my path. "Cooke came and told me what happened outside. Are you still scared?"

I took a step back. "I wasn't scared. I was thinking I was going to have to fight my way free, though, and that leaves you sort of keyed up and watchful."

"And now you don't trust me either?"

"It's not about trust. It's more that I shouldn't get comfortable or let down my guard and forget that you're not human. It's not a smart thing. It's not what I was trained to do."

"And yet now here you are, inside and unharmed. Perhaps you overreacted."

"Or perhaps something would have happened if Hadrian hadn't showed up," I suggested, studying his concerned expression. "I can't say what could have been, but what I do know is that after this, I won't be accepting any invites from anyone who isn't a friend."

"Am I your friend?"

"No," I answered honestly. "But I trust you a helluva lot more than I do Benny, that's for sure. Tonight was very eye-opening."

"He's a pureblood vampyr, Jason. You're a human. He has little to no use for you. He puts up with your interference because it's brought a truce to the community, nothing more."

"And you don't feel the same about me?"

"You've helped us all a great deal," he said, putting a hand on my shoulder and squeezing gently. "My people aren't being slaughtered in the streets anymore. I'm nothing but grateful."

It was nice to hear. "Okay, so, let's go have coffee or something soon."

He smiled and nodded. "Good," he said, taking a breath. "Now tell me, what do you really think of Benny's home? I want to know."

"It's beautiful, and I'd love to spend some time here to take it all in, but I'm also very glad I don't live here."

"And why is that?"

"It would be like living in a museum."

He grunted. "I know you mean that sarcastically, but you're honestly not impressed with the trappings of wealth, are you?"

"I don't—"

"I mean that you'll go back to your little store and your tiny apartment and still be happy and not once think how unfair it is that Benny has all this."

"Of course not. Why would I?"

He shook his head. "Some of us want more and don't want to lose what we already have."

"Then some of us should work harder to get whatever the hell we want."

He scowled.

"What? You were talking in generalities, but I get it. Benny has a lot of stuff, and I don't know if it's because he comes from old money, or if it's new money he's made. But I don't care because it's not mine. If you want to be rich like this, Niko, then go get it."

He was staring at me like he was missing something and trying to figure it out.

"The only gift I've ever received is that building," I told him. "I've worked for everything else. I figure as a vampyr, you've got nothing but time to make all your dreams come true. What's a hundred years to you?"

"Maybe I want my riches now."

"I've seen what you drive, heard about where you live," I said, taking a step back, needing space from another powerful vampyr. I was tense, it was obvious, and going home was a good idea. I would need to find Hadrian and tell him I'd have to see Tiago and meet his prince another time. "I think you're probably plenty rich. You just want more."

"Is that so?"

"Yeah, I think it is."

"You're fascinating to me," Niko said, taking a step forward, closer. "You would make a powerful ally if I could trust you… or bind you to me."

Bind.

I'd heard that term before and I knew what it entailed.

He wanted to bind me to him with blood. He wanted to drink from me on a regular basis. He wanted me to feed him, and in return, I'd be protected from anyone wanting to do me harm. I knew several made vampyrs who had that arrangement with a pureblood. But I wasn't a vampyr, so that was *not* going to happen. I wasn't about to offer a vein to any vampyr.

Annoyed at myself for being alone with him, I went to move, but he grabbed my bicep tight. It was jolting because I didn't expect it. He'd never shown me a hint of his power before.

"Niko?" Even though I was concerned—he could snap my neck in a second if he wanted—no one put their hands on me without permission. "Lemme go. Now."

He searched my face. "I'm tempted to lie to Tiago and tell him that I couldn't find you, because I fear what will happen when you meet the prince."

"I could just leave," I suggested. Why not? What was the real harm in not meeting the prince? Hopefully Tiago would still come and find me at my shop.

"I'm not sure that you can," he said, brows furrowed, considering me before he released his grip enough that I could ease free.

"I can," I promised, then turned and headed for the front door.

But Hadrian barred my exit—not intentionally, since he stood in a circle of gorgeous women, all of whom could have been supermodels—but he was there, and if I tried to sneak past him, he'd grab me and take me to Tiago. Before he spotted me, I doubled back and slipped by Benny, who muttered a halting apology before asking me where I was going, but more beautiful women stopped him. I moved as quickly as possible to the first parlor.

In the antique-laden room, I found people sipping what was probably blood, and then I passed through to the second parlor, where I smelled sex before I realized I was walking through an orgy. Vampyrs didn't have a lot of issues about their personal space or, apparently, letting others see them fuck. Cooke once tried to explain it to me as a display of possessiveness and power, but I didn't really get it.

After closing the double doors behind me, I bolted across another sitting room and found an exit, but once I stepped through, I wasn't outside. It was a gorgeous conservatory with a chaise, an armchair, and a small table. I could imagine how nice it would be to have the windows open and a cool breeze blowing through. It would be so quiet and relaxing.

I realized then what I'd said to Niko was wrong. If this was what wealth could provide, I could learn to covet as well.

Three sides of the room were made of glass. I was sure that in the sunshine, it was stunning, but it was beautiful in the moonlight as well. The night-blooming jasmine, wisteria, magnolia, tea rose, and hyacinth filled the room with an amazing layered scent, one on top of the other, mysterious and inviting at the same time.

I shouldn't have stopped to admire any part of the scene in front of me. Not the artistry of the planted and pruned flowers, not the intoxicating smell, and definitely not the man standing in the doorway to the garden. I had a clear path to another door, but I hesitated when he turned his head to look at me.

"Hi," I whispered. Beyond that, my voice deserted me.

He moved forward, hands in the pockets of his black suit pants, and I had a moment to appreciate how well the matching jacket encased his broad shoulders and tapered to a narrow waist. His hair fell just above his shoulders, brushed straight back. What would it look like in the morning before he styled it, tousled and in his face?

It struck me that I knew him, that we'd met somewhere before, but I dredged my memory for his name and couldn't find one. My breath caught as he stopped only a few feet away and held out his hand.

I took it without hesitation. "This is gonna sound lame, but… do I know you?"

"Do you feel as though you do?" he asked, and whoa, did I like the sound of his voice, gravelly and low, smooth and decadent. I *trembled*. Jesus, I had never had a reaction to anyone like this anytime in my life.

I nodded, and he took the final step into my personal space. I could smell him: that same sandalwood from earlier, and musk along with wood smoldering in a fireplace, pipe tobacco, incense, and bergamot. I breathed him in, wanting more, and I fought an urge to press my face to the side of this neck.

"You have caught my scent many times in this house tonight," he said, still holding my hand. He leaned in and inhaled me as I had him, and a wisp of a smile curled his full dusky lips.

"Have I?"

He nodded. "It calls to many."

"Oh, it does, does it?" He was very full of himself, and yes, for good reason, but still. A bit of humility went a long way. And as I'd never been a fan of being quite that conceited, I felt the spell breaking.

"This ride is not for the faint of heart."

It was a staggeringly bad line. "Well, then, I don't want to waste your time," I conceded because all of my life, I'd been out of my depth with smooth operators like him. "You have a good night," I bid, easing my hand free.

"Wait," he insisted. He took my hand back and held on, but not tight. It wasn't jarring or alarming, not at all what Niko's grip had been. This was gentle, coaxing. "Forgive me, I didn't realize."

I didn't encounter deep green eyes on a black-haired man every day and found myself unable to stop staring. "Realize what?"

"That you were speaking from your heart. I can see the sincerity in your eyes."

"Now that sounds like a line," I teased, grinning.

He stepped closer, crowding me, his sudden smile making an already gorgeous man utterly mesmerizing. "And yet not, because it's true. Your reaction to me is refreshingly open and honest. So again, forgive me for being glib."

"Done," I assured him, slipping my hand from his.

"Have you been here all night? Because... I don't know how I could have missed you."

"Man, you're just one pickup line after another, huh?" I was trying to keep things light, flirty, being charming because I wanted to impress him, keep his interest so he'd keep looking at me with those gorgeous eyes. I wanted to soak up every drop of his attention.

"No, I—" He stopped for a moment. "Oh, that's true, isn't it. That's terrible," he said, chuckling, and I felt myself decompress. He was real. Anyone who could laugh at themselves was good by me.

I gestured at him. "If I looked like you, I'd be making with the cheesy lines too 'cause who cares when you look like you do?"

He tipped his head, his smile wicked, as if he knew what his effect was on me. "I think that was a line as well."

"Yeah, all right, we'll call that even, then," I said, clapping him on the shoulder.

His breath caught. I liked that I'd caused it.

"So were you on your way out?" he ventured.

"I was."

"Why?" He touched my wrist, turning it gently to trace his fingers over the veins in my forearm. "You should stay here and talk to me."

"Should I?"

"Yes." He was adamant, but the tone of his voice enticed me, alluring, and I felt drugged and sluggish. When my eyes drifted closed, I didn't think it was weird, didn't open them, just let whatever was happening happen.

It was like being in the ocean and the lazy rise and fall of the waves. When he released my wrist and took hold of my hips, I couldn't contain my sigh.

"You should stay," he suggested, a warm puff of his breath on my throat. I finally found the strength to reopen my eyes. "I'm Varic Maedoc, the draugr, prince of the noreia. Who are you?"

I had a name, but it was stuck on the tip of my tongue.

"You're not a vampyr," he concluded, studying me. "I can smell your blood."

"No, not a vampyr," I agreed, barely able to speak, wanting so badly to lean into him that my muscles hurt.

"You smell so good," he whispered. When his lips touched my neck, and then his teeth, I shuddered under his hands, a flush of heat rolling through me. "I want to taste you. Give me permission."

I had thought I would never allow any vampyr to have my blood, but now I couldn't remember anything I ever wanted more. He could have all of me, if that was what he wanted. Everything was his for the taking. "Yes, good, you have *all* the permission."

His chuckle was filthy, seductive, and so fucking hot. He pressed against me, his cock hard inside his dress pants, and the urge to be under him overwhelmed me.

I would beg, if need be.

"Give me your name," he murmured, no bite to the words, just a request.

"Jason Thorpe," I answered breathlessly, and recognition and surprise flickered across his face. "You asked to see me."

"Jason—" His voice faltered, then he inhaled and began again. "Yes, I did, and now I need to do so much more than merely see you," he declared, slipping his hand around the side of my neck, easing me forward.

A burst of laughter broke the spell, so loud and jarring, like nails on a chalkboard, as five beautiful young men poured into the room. I pulled free, embarrassed about other people seeing me so vulnerable and exposed.

They were hard to look at in their designer clothes, with their flawless skin and perfect bodies. It was a lot of beauty to take in all at once. "We're here for your pleasure, my prince," a platinum blond announced, laughing and tossing a tube of lubricant to Varic. "And, of course, ours," he finished with a wanton leer.

I didn't think. I was far too mortified, just moved as more people filled the conservatory—all there, I was certain, to service the prince. All of them were vampyrs, all more than I could ever be, utterly breathtaking.

I charged for the door leading to the garden, burst out into the night, and ran, needing to put as much distance as possible between me and the player prince.

I was so much more than embarrassed. The ground swallowing me up would be preferable to living through that interaction again. I was thirty-two years old, for fuck's sake, not some stupid teenager with a raging boner. So why in the hell had I thought the prince of all the goddamn vampyrs would want anything more to do with me than a quick bang or draining drink? What the ever-loving fuck was I thinking?

I was crushed.

"This is what happens when you don't get laid regularly," I told myself, stepping around one of the magnolia trees, realizing I was near the gazebo I'd noted on my way in. "You end up confusing vampyr princes with the charming ones."

When I closed my eyes, he probably laughed at me, thinking about how pathetic I was, how needy and ridiculous. I looked older than all his pretty boys, older than him, and still I'd…. Christ.

Varic Maedoc had Abercrombie & Fitch models to screw. In comparison I was that leering old guy at the club, trying to pick up a hot young stud.

I shuddered, thinking about what I must have looked like, standing so close, his hands on my hips….

Horrible.

I wanted to go home, needed to talk to—

Wait.

What did I see? What moved?

Something wasn't right, and it gave me pause. I stopped, took a breath, released it slowly, and then checked my surroundings.

There was a man in a Kevlar vest thirty yards away from me, skulking toward the house, holding a high-powered rifle. Then another man, and another and another…. All carrying guns.

What the hell?

I thought about Hadrian and Niko and Cooke, and even Benny. I thought about Tiago. I knew he was in the house somewhere too. My pulse spiked and my adrenaline kicked in. I was in full battle mode in seconds.

I had to save them.

Quietly, carefully, hoping the men weren't actual military, or vampyrs who were military, I moved behind the one closest to me and grabbed him around the neck, used my bicep like a vise to cut off his airflow, and dropped him at my feet, unconscious.

Not military. Anyone with training could have gotten me off them even with the element of surprise. I would have still put him down, but he could have shouted to the others. People were noisy in real life; only James Bond knocked people out without a sound. And he normally killed them, which wasn't my objective.

I took the Heckler & Koch G36 assault rifle, sprinted to the next guy, and took him out with the butt of the gun. He went down hard, face-first, and I took his weapon and shoved it through the lattice work under the gazebo.

Unfortunately when I stood up, someone shot at me, grazed my left bicep, and I had to scramble around the gazebo to get to cover. It was really stupid and hurt like hell. I hadn't been shot at in years, but instantly I was back on the battlefield and pissed that I'd been so careless.

It seemed to be the theme of the night.

The good news was I could hear shouts and yelling from the house; the bad news was the invaders began firing as they ran forward.

I had no choice. They were shooting at unarmed civilians, and vampyrs or not, there were women and men inside who came for a party and nothing more.

I shot the closest guy in the leg, and he went down fast, but I was momentarily stunned as I watched a few vampyrs exit the house in a blur of speed before someone shot up the willow tree beside me, snapping me out of it just in time for me to be caught in a flying tackle. I was driven against the side of a cypress tree so hard that, for a second, I was certain my attacker had snapped my spine.

"Here!" the man called before he used his hand to wrench my head sideways, baring the side of my neck. "I have him!"

I struggled as hard as I could, but he was inhumanly strong. And it hit me—of course I understood why. I was fighting with a vampyr.

"I'm going to rip out your throat," he snarled.

No matter how well trained I could have been, how many grappling tactics I might know or how capable I was, there was no way out of the grip he had me in. He had leverage and strength on his side.

I was dead.

A hand appeared on his face, cupping his jaw, and the crack that followed was loud. No mistaking the sound of a neck being snapped.

His eyes widened and then emptied of life in quick succession, and as he dropped from sight, I was faced with Hadrian.

"Hey," I rasped, catching my breath, shivering with the kind of fear that'd been ratcheted up as high as it could go in anticipation of death.

"How many?" he asked curtly.

Without Hadrian coming to my rescue, that guy would have had me. In a fight between man and vampyr, there was no contest.

"Jason," he barked.

"Ten, I think, and I'm pretty sure some are human and—"

"I care not what they—"

"Yeah, sorry," I babbled, out of it, recovering from my close call. "I think there's ten, though there could be more of them closer to the house that I didn't see. I shot one, knocked out two, and"—I lifted my left arm so he could see—"got shot in the process 'cause I'm a dumbass that forgot my training."

He nodded, his eyes locked with mine. "You did a fine job. Now remain here until I return, yes?"

I smiled. There was no way I was sitting the rest of this out. He had no idea who I was, and yes, I was rusty and clearly no help where vampyrs were concerned, but I was still an asset. "Yeah, no, not staying here. Former Marine, and even though I fucked up a little, I'll bet I'm better trained than you."

"I fought for King Henry in the War of the Roses," he countered. "Your training versus mine is debatable."

"Oh yeah? Lots of guns in your day there, buddy?"

He scowled. "We are a thousand times faster than you. My men and I will dispose of the others and then question the ones you left for us."

"I can do—"

"No, you have done enough."

I was going to argue, but he disappeared. In front of me one second, gone the next, and in that moment, I gave myself a reality check. I knew he was right. I was out of my depth, and I'd been playing at something I didn't understand. I'd been lured into thinking I was more important than I was, but I was only an anomaly, no more necessary to the vampyrs than any other human with blood in their veins. If the events of the night had taught me anything, it was I didn't belong in the vampyr world.

Running back to the gazebo, I shoved the gun I'd been carrying through the lattice with the other to keep it out of the action and then darted to the edge of the property. The gate was locked, so I scaled it, up and over, and when I dropped on the other side, I looked back at all the lights in the house as people streamed out. Odd movement caught my eye, and I turned my head to see a man all in black drop from the brick wall halfway down the street.

"Hey!" I yelled.

He took one look at me and bolted.

In retrospect, yelling was stupid. I should have just run up on him, but I'd given away the element of surprise. Because why should I suddenly start being smart when the whole night was a clusterfuck of idiocy?

He wasn't a vampyr, or I would have lost him immediately. He was a man like me, and he ran down the sidewalk like I was the devil behind him.

We crossed streets, both of us almost getting hit in traffic, but it was later in the evening and, out of the Quarter, the sidewalks weren't filled. He couldn't get away. I wouldn't let him. Even if I wasn't going to be part of the vampyr world anymore, at least I could get Benny and Niko some answers. Someone had come for one of them or the prince. My money was on the latter, and whoever planned the assault needed to be dragged into the light.

The problem was my legs, which started out churning beneath me, eating up the sidewalk, were burning with fatigue. My breathing was shortening, my stomach tying itself in knots, and my arms were no longer my own, instead like weights, heavy and spongy at the same time.

I had no idea how he was running so fast for so long. I was in shape, thanks to the Marine Corps and every-other-day trips to the gym where I lifted weights and swam. But I had never done cardio like this, and so I was relieved and thankful enough to send a quick word up to my maker when I saw my quarry run to and crouch on the other side of a parked truck.

I ducked behind a building and waited a moment before checking to see him jimmy the lock on the parked delivery truck and climb into the cab. I darted across the street, wishing I had a gun to pull to make him stop. I ran to the driver's side, reached up, grabbed the door, and flung it open to find… nothing.

"The fuck," I gasped, ready to throw up, the chase having taken every drop of strength and adrenaline out of me.

"Idiot," someone behind me said before everything went black.

Chapter Six

I GROANED as I came to on the ground. If I was going to chase people down, I really needed a gun to make them stop.

"Stupid," I muttered as I sat up. My head was pounding, my left arm throbbing, though no longer bleeding, and the rest of me was covered in dirt and water.

Worst night in a long time.

I got to my feet with some effort, and when my phone buzzed in my back pocket, I answered after seeing Ode's name on the display.

"Where are you?" she asked, sounding worried.

"I'm not sure," I replied, wincing as I tried to move my right foot and realized I'd rolled my ankle. "So stupid."

"What is?"

"Nothing."

"Well, Cooke called me, all freaked-out," she said. "You guys went to a party, and he lost you after there was some kind of trouble."

I grunted.

"Are you all right?"

"I'm fine," I lied, limping away from the truck, thrilled that my captain couldn't see me now. He would have been horrified I'd allowed myself to get jumped from behind. I could visualize the look of disappointment. "I'm just embarrassed."

"Why embarrassed?"

So I told her about the prince, without the part about *who* and *what* he really was, but I told her about his fuck buddies and how I couldn't compete.

"Where are you?" she snapped when I was done, and I couldn't tell if she was worried or annoyed or what.

"I told you, I don't know."

"Well, walk to the fuckin' corner and read me the damn signs!"

Bingo. She was pissed. I should have known. "Why're you mad at me?" I growled.

"Because you're a damn idiot," she snarled. "You are gorgeous and—"

"Sweetheart—"

"Don't you dare try an' placate me! I don't have to kiss your ass; we're friends, for heaven's sake!"

"No, I—"

"I think I'm gonna beat you when I see you."

I groaned. "It'll be easy."

"Why?" Deflated, anger gone, she was breathless in an instant. "Why easy?"

"I got grazed by a bullet, and somebody knocked me out."

"What?" Her voice faltered, sounding suddenly very young.

"Oh no, honey, I'm fine. I just need to get home and get cleaned up, and I need to lie down."

"Are you to a corner yet?"

I wasn't, but wonder of wonders, I saw a cab. I yelled for it, and the driver pulled over.

"I'll meet you there," Ode told me. "At your place."

"It's okay. I don't need—"

"See you soon," she said brusquely before hanging up.

I didn't try to call her back; I wouldn't win. I got comfortable in the back seat and finally took a breath.

"You look like shit, man," the cabbie said.

I had no doubt.

WHEN I got out of the cab, Ode and Kali stood waiting, visibly horrified upon seeing me.

"Ohmygod, he needs to go to the hospital," Kali insisted, wincing as I draped an arm over her shoulder so they could help me up to my apartment.

It was small, the same 750 square feet in the store, but cozy and warm. It had a Franklin stove for if it ever got cold—I hadn't used it yet—windows in every room, original hardwood floors, cream-colored walls except for the aqua kitchen, and the most comfortable furniture on the planet. I truly loved it. In the summer when I had friends over, many of them would sit out on the steps and talk and drink into the wee hours of the morning. Walking in, I was so happy to be there I almost cried.

Ode made me strip and get into the shower while Kali went through my medicine cabinet looking for supplies.

"I'm showering in here," I grumbled. "Could you get out?"

"You can't see through that curtain, so shut up," she snapped. I knew it was because she was worried about me. She was a younger, kinder version of her older sister—normally gentler and sweeter—but even though we weren't quite as close, it was a near thing.

Everyone was in a bad mood.

Kali apparently didn't find what she wanted, muttered under her breath, and left moments later. I stayed under the warm water for a while, the heat feeling really good on my muscles. Once I changed into sweats and a T-shirt, I walked out to the couch and collapsed beside Ode.

"You gonna wrap my arm?" I asked, turning to her, only then realizing she was crying. "Sweetie, what's wrong?"

"What's wrong?" she yelled, leaping to her feet. She whirled around and faced me, hands on her hips, clearly livid. "Are you kidding me right now?"

"Honey—"

"Who shot at you?"

"Yeah, who shot at you?" Kali echoed.

"I don't know, I was chasing some guy away from the party and—"

"The party where the guy didn't want you," Ode stated.

I groaned loudly. "Thanks for that."

"Who doesn't want you?" Kali asked, visibly puzzled.

"You sound like her hype man," I said to Kali, trying not to smile.

Both grabbed pillows off the couch and smacked me.

"Ow," I groused. I was really ready to go to sleep. "How 'bout you guys go away now?"

"Jason Thorpe, you are hereby strictly forbidden from going on any dates or going to any parties without my express permission," Ode declared.

I grunted.

"I'm sorry, what was that?"

"I just think maybe since you have shitty taste in dates for me, perhaps you shouldn't get a say in my love life."

Kali crossed her arms and lifted her brows over the top of her glasses, watching her sister.

"Oh, never mind," Ode muttered, dismissing her sister's judgment with an imperious wave of her hand.

"He wanted to do me in the back of the store," I told Kali, just to stir the pot.

"And you picked this man for him?" Kali questioned Ode, voice dripping with derision.

"You shut up," Ode said, pointing at Kali, "and you shut up," she said, pointing at me. "And now I gotta call the police because shots fired in the Quarter is a serious thing."

"No," I corrected. "It was down by Third Street and Coliseum."

"Baby, that's a nice neighborhood. Whose house were you at?"

"Benny Diallo's. He's a businessman or something."

"Huh. Well, I ain't heard of him, but now we really have to call because what the ever-loving *fuck* is goin' on?"

Kali's eyes got huge and round, and Ode groaned loudly. "Girl," Kali warned, "if your mother catches you swearing, you are a dead woman."

Ode pointed back at me. "It's him! He swears, and I pick that shit up."

"Mmm-hmmm," Kali mumbled, not buying a word of it, her raised eyebrow clearly conveying her disbelief.

"And for the record, she's *our* mother, not just mine."

"She'll be *your* mother when she kills you, 'cause I won't help her hide the body."

"Well, I appreciate the solidarity."

"Could you two get out now?" I asked hopefully.

"Not yet," Ode singsonged.

I groaned and fell over sideways on the couch. At the same time, I heard someone climbing my stairs. I looked at Ode in horror because at this time of night, and both girls there with me, there was only one person they would have called.

"Oh yes," she said in that superior, smirking tone she used sometimes as the door opened and Josephine walked into my apartment.

I gestured at her. "You shouldn't have woken your mom."

"As if they wouldn't," Josephine chided, her scowl dark. She crossed the room to me, and Kali took her medical bag for her. As a registered nurse, she was always prepared. "Now sit up so I can look at you."

It was grueling. She checked me out better than any doctor ever had, wrapped my arm, checked my head, determined I might have a slight concussion but mostly worried that I hadn't eaten dinner, and it was now well after midnight. She called Issa then, who arrived fifteen minutes later carrying two reusable shopping bags filled with food. He'd brought all the leftovers he could scrounge.

I thoroughly enjoyed the bustle in my kitchen: Josephine saying again, as she always did, how cute it was, how she liked the layout and color, and then making judgmental mom clucking sounds about my empty refrigerator. The sounds of pots clanking, the sizzle of oil in a pan, and then amazingly delicious smells wafting from one room to the next made my stomach growl. Issa passed me one of the wireless PS4 controllers so we could at least get some *Borderlands* in before food was ready.

"Man, now I'm hungry," Issa told me.

"It's your mother's food. It's like crack."

"You see," Josephine said, standing in the doorway, "I told you, you needed to eat." She was always right.

"Yes, ma'am."

It turned out my night wasn't so crappy after all. I was glad that in the midst of family Ode forgot about the police… because how was I supposed to explain vampyrs to the NOPD?

THE NEXT morning I woke up sore and didn't want to get out of bed. Ode called me and told me to stay there. I didn't even realize I'd nodded off until she woke me to eat lunch down in the shop.

I felt better by the afternoon, which turned out to be good because Leni called to tell me her mother insisted she go with her to meet the prince, who was receiving people at Garrett's new club, the one I'd been teasing him about the night before, which was closed to the public for the occasion.

"Yeah, no worries," I assured her, my stomach clenching as I finally let my mind wander back to the prince. I could live the rest of my life without laying eyes on him again, and I hoped Leni would have a better time. "I'll cover the store; you go pay your respects."

"I guess it was supposed to be at Benny Diallo's mansion, but there was some kind of trouble there last night, so they moved him to a new location."

"Good," I told her. "You be careful."

"I will, thank you, Jason. Love you." She always signed off that way.

"You know," Ode said as she was getting ready to leave, grabbing her giant rucksack that passed for a purse, "I was kidding that time."

"What're you talking about?"

"When you asked me how old you are, and I was teasing you and said, I dunno, fifty? You know that was a joke, right?"

I grinned because I knew that already.

"I know how old you are, and just because the guy you met last night prefers 'em young doesn't make you a fossil."

"No, I know."

"I don't think you do. I think you think thirty-two is ancient, and I'm telling you that men—and women—just start to get interesting after thirty."

"Well, thank you, dear."

She leaned up to kiss me, and I bent down and gave her my cheek.

"I adore you, you know," she said in reassurance.

I did.

Once she was gone, I made some Earl Grey tea and realized it had started raining. That didn't change the foot traffic up and down the street, and people still wandered in and out. I had about ten customers in the store looking at books, essential oils, and candles, and a few regulars checking on what new jewelry Ode had put out on display when I saw Tiago outside the front window.

I rushed to the open door and outside and, without stopping, charged up and grabbed him in a bear hug.

"Jason," he gasped as I squeezed tight, face down in his shoulder, so delighted to see him.

"Thank you for coming," I sighed into his hair before slowly releasing him, smiling wide. "I didn't wanna miss you, but I couldn't go back to the house."

"No, of course not," he said solemnly, his smile bemused, clearly not sure what to do with me. "I thought perhaps, if you wanted, we might exchange numbers."

"That would be perfect," I confirmed, turning to go back into the store. "I've wanted to talk to you so many times, but I had no clue how to get in touch and—"

"Wait, where are you going?"

"Oh," I said, reaching for his bicep to give it a squeeze. "I'm the only one here right now, so I gotta get back inside, but please come with me so we can talk."

"I have Aziel here with me, a member of the dreki," Tiago said quickly. "Is he allowed as well?"

"Of course," I said, smiling over at Aziel as he got out of the driver's side of a nearby car. I recognized him from last night. "Come on."

People stood at the cash register, waiting for me, and I apologized as I walked over to ring them up.

After they left, I had to open one of the display cases to show another customer a freshwater-pearl-and-blue-topaz necklace. She bought it, and once I cashed her out, I gave Tiago my attention. "Let's do the number thing now before something else happens."

We leaned on the counter with our phones out.

"Why were you just standing out there? Why didn't you just come in?"

"I could not enter until you invited me in," he commented.

I nodded as I created a new contact.

"Aziel said he saw you last night when Niko was holding you, and that you could not free yourself until he let you go."

"I know," I answered absently, typing in his name. I looked up at him. "That was so weird, like my vampyr juju short-circuited or something."

He snapped his head up. "Your what?"

I grimaced. "Yeah, I'm an ass, and I need to apologize to you."

"To me?" I nodded. "For what?"

"I know so much about vampyrs now, and I'm so sorry I wasn't really listening that night at the Roth-schilds'." I sighed, feeling like total crap. "I was blind, and I was trying so hard to make sure you were taken care of, but I also needed everything to fit into some reasonable frame of reference that my brain could process."

He nodded, reaching for my wrist and squeezing for a moment, reassuring me, offering comfort and understanding.

"I just didn't understand then," I said as he let me go.

"You have nothing for which to apologize. You acted on what you knew, and never forget, you heard me scream and came running."

That reminded me. "Why were you screaming?"

"What do you mean?"

"I mean, you weren't actually in any danger. That makes no sense."

"It still hurt," he deadpanned.

He was such a smartass, and I couldn't help smiling at him.

"Also, I am bound as rajan to test any clan leaders who attempt to do me harm."

"I see. So you were screaming your head off—"

"I would not characterize what I was doing as—"

"—to see if Mr. or Mrs. Rothschild or anyone else there would take pity on you and step up and do the right thing."

"Yes."

Aziel cleared his throat expectantly, and we looked at him. He had his arms crossed and seemed to be waiting for Tiago to say something more.

"Fine," Tiago snapped, turning back to me. "I also might have been slightly concerned about my blood loss," he confessed, not meeting my eyes, chin up imperiously.

"Slightly?" Aziel repeated.

"Hadrian resorted to feeding me once I was on the plane," Tiago huffed, glancing at me and then quickly away.

"So it was actually good I got you out of there."

He paused before saying, "It was not, perhaps... done in error."

The man-child always had to be right. He wouldn't admit to a weakness or that maybe he'd been in over his head. Not him. Not ever. "Tell me, how old are you really?"

"I was born during the French Revolution, in seventeen ninety-two."

"Holy shit." I was in awe. "That's awesome."

"Thank you," he said, beaming.

"It must be so crazy for you to see all the advances in science and medicine and—"

"Oh yes, thrilling," he replied, forcing a smile but clearly bored out of his mind. "Good stuff, that."

He wanted to talk about something else, not my awe at his long life. "What do you want to discuss, mighty rajan?"

"I have killed others for far less disrespect."

"Oh, I know, you told me."

"Jason."

"Don't like people being snide, huh?"

"Jason," he warned, voice rising.

"Fine. What do you want to talk about?"

"Your vampyr 'juju,' as you have so quaintly named it."

"G'head."

"Well, after I was informed of your interaction with Niko Gann, I asked the prince for his thoughts concerning your inability to break free of Gann last night, and he replied."

"And?"

Tiago cleared his throat. "The prince seems to think you are a *mah-tahn*, so—"

"Spell it."

He gave me a brilliant smile. "I admire such about you, your desire to get things right. Not only say them, but know them."

"I learned a lot of other words from a guy I know."

"Cooke Slater?"

"Yeah. How'd you know?"

"After your heroics, accompanied by your disappearing act," he said, shooting me a clearly unhappy glare, "and because the prince is confined to our new quarters, he had no choice but to speak to everyone here who knows you to try to obtain some answers."

I was at a loss. "Why're you pissed at me? I saved your ass last night."

"Yes, I know. You saved us *all* last night," he whispered harshly, his voice dropping, I was certain, because he wanted to yell at me but wouldn't do that in front of any customers. "And then you left!"

"I chased a guy for like six blocks or something," I told him. "And then he got the drop on me and knocked me out."

He gasped, sharp. "You were hurt?"

"Am hurt," I corrected, touching my left bicep. "I got grazed by a bullet and hit in the head," I griped. "So cut me just a little slack here, will ya?"

He wrapped his hand around my wrist. "I had no idea you were a superhero in disguise."

I snorted. "Not so much, but I thought if I could catch that guy, then maybe Hadrian could question him and figure out who tried to hurt you all."

"That makes sense."

"Did you get any answers from the guys I knocked out?"

"We—no," he disclosed, sounding sad, his face creasing in disappointment. "They all preferred to die instead of speak to Hadrian."

It wasn't my place to offer any judgment. "That's too bad" was all I said.

"Yes, it is," he agreed, "but what is not sad is that you, again, saved us all. Had you not alerted us to the presence of armed men on the grounds, they might have killed many of us on their way to assassinate the prince."

"Is that who you think they were after?"

"Of course," Aziel interjected. "Who else but the prince? Whenever he leaves his home, his safety is at risk."

"Is that the same for the king and queen?"

Tiago replied, "It would be, but the king never leaves Malta, and the queen never strays from her island. Only the prince travels, which is why he holds such sway over the law."

"Makes sense. He's the one actually in contact with the outside world."

"Precisely." He offered me a small smile. "At the royal court, all is the same, as it has been for centuries. Only the prince brings life and movement to their dark world."

I coughed. Holy crap, was that laying it on thick.

Tiago scowled. "You have something to say?"

"Life and movement to their dark world." I snickered. "Kinda dramatic, don't you think?"

"I have a burning desire to murder you at this moment."

I cackled and excused myself to talk to a customer who was waving at me, leaving Tiago with Aziel at the counter. Once I was done explaining about all the benefits of peppermint oil, I returned to Tiago, got his number, and had him spell "matan" for me.

"So what is that?"

"I know not all, as he did not have the chance to explain to me his thoughts, but he did say that the power I spoke to him about—that others also reported—had to do with what you think of as yours."

I tried parsing his words for a moment. "Nope, I don't get what you just said."

"For example, the night you saved me, the reason the Rothschild clan could not rush into the cabin was because you thought of it as yours."

"But it wasn't my house."

"Yes, but it was where you resided in the interim, so somehow, in how you thought of it, it was, in fact, yours."

"Okay."

"Just as when we were in your truck. I had no power there because, again, you were in *your* truck, which belongs to you."

"So the prince, he thinks that if I was here in my shop, and Niko tried to grab me, that he wouldn't've been able to?"

"Correct."

"What about when we were in the parking lot of the hospital?"

"It was *your* hospital," he emphasized. "You said you stayed there when you were hit by the drunk driver. Do you recall telling me that?"

"I do."

"That is how it works for a matan. They keep control as long as they are in a place where they feel safe, a place that is theirs, or…"

"Or?" I asked when I realized he had no intention of finishing his sentence.

"Or if their mate is present."

"Interesting."

"Agreed. Apparently once a matan finds their mate, wherever their mate is, whether at home or not, the matan has that same power."

"You're saying that if I had a mate and he was at that party, Niko wouldn't have been able to touch me."

"Yes."

"Because my mate would give me power?"

"No. It sounded like the opposite, like the matan gives the mate power, and then the mate acts…. Perhaps like a battery, I cannot guess. When the prince was explaining, it was confusing because he was talking in generalities and not specifics."

"Why?"

"Because you were not present, thus he was only guessing."

"I see," I said because we were getting into an area where I didn't want to proceed. I wasn't stupid. Tiago had an agenda, and I wasn't missing it with hints like "generalities" and "only guessing." He wanted me and his prince in the same room.

He stared at me, expectant, and arched one of his brows in exaggerated question.

I played dumb because, again, I already knew what it was. "Just ask me already, whatever it is."

"Will you see the prince?"

"No," I said flatly, ready, not even having to think about it.

"Why did you grimace before you answered?"

"Did I?"

"Yes, you did."

Aziel nodded. "You did."

"Sorry?"

Tiago released a frustrated huff. "He wants to see you."

"I'm thinking he has enough people to see without adding me."

"What does that mean?" Tiago snapped, frustrated, not used to having anyone turn him down.

I shook my head, *so* not wanting to get into it with Tiago, who thought the sun rose and set on his prince.

"Varic Maedoc is the prince of the noreia, and he has requested your presence above all others," Aziel pointed out. "Who are you to not obey his summons?"

"How about not a vampyr," I replied with a shrug. "Doesn't that get me off the hook?"

"No," Aziel insisted, and the way he was scowling at me, I understood he had no idea how I was even being given a choice to start with.

"I'd rather not," I told them.

"Fine," Tiago granted, "would you meet *me* at the penthouse after you close this little shop of yours this evening?"

"Little shop?" I asked pointedly.

"Oh, you know, it is terribly quaint, but really, is this not beneath you?"

He was a pompous ass. Anything less than Versailles he found low-rent. "I love this store, you conceited piece of crap."

"When was the last time it was cleaned?" he asked with a shiver of revulsion, running a finger across the glass case he stood next to, the disgusted look on his face making me smile.

Such a snob. "Go away," I teased before I left to help another customer.

The shop was slammed then; maybe it was the rain or all the inviting twinkling lights in the display windows or the mix of candles Ode lit before she left, but I was running around busier than a one-armed paper hanger.

"Could you just ring people up?" I pleaded to Tiago. The horror on his face made me laugh. It turned out working the sales on my iPad was too much for him, but he could unlock display cases and pull things out for people to look at up close, and he had a vast knowledge of stones, precious and not.

Aziel also proved helpful, taking tags off different items, wrapping them in tissue paper, and putting them in bags. He wrote down the charges for me, one piece of paper per customer, and between the two of us, we moved through a line of patrons quickly. I really appreciated his help and told him so over and over.

"You owe me no thanks; it is I who owes you all."

"I just appreciate you helping me with—"

"You saved my prince," he explained, his tone crisp, matter-of-fact. "I am forever in your debt."

"Thank you anyway," I told him. I was betting guards in the service of the prince didn't get much thanks on a daily basis.

His sheepish smile charmed me.

"Clearly I missed my calling, and instead of being the rajan, I should have gone into retail!" Tiago thundered when I checked on him.

"Being snarky isn't helping anything," I pointed out. He grunted loudly, and I laughed, because really, it was like pissing off a bunny. "You are really so fuckin' cute."

"I had nearly forgotten how infuriating you are."

I ignored that. "Nice job selling the pricey stuff over there," I continued. "I like how you steered people away from the amethyst and topaz to the sapphires and diamonds."

"Please," he muttered disdainfully. "Amethyst?"

"You're such a snob," I teased again. It was adorable, the things his conceit extended to.

"And if I am?"

"If? There's no *if*, Tiago."

The pouting was too much. I tousled his golden waves before leaning in to give him a quick hug. He was like the little brother I never had.

"Stop that," he protested, pushing me away, smacking at my hands. "You are far too vexing for words."

"Yeah, but you came to see me."

"I am aware," he grumbled, glaring. "And Lord knows why."

I shrugged. "Maybe you like me."

He gave a long sigh before fixing his attention on me seriously. "You have the purest heart I have ever encountered," he rushed out. "You saved me. You saved everyone at the house last night and gave not one thought for your own safety. You are utterly selfless."

"No, I just do what I can to help."

"It is far more than that."

I needed to change the subject. "So tell me more about—"

"The prince can answer all your questions. You could come with me now to see him. What do you say?"

"Yeah, no thank you," I said. I checked around for customers, and upon finding none, walked to the front of the store, flipped the sign from Open to Closed, and locked the door. "You guys wanna go get a drink?"

"No, we do not want to go for a drink; we want you to come to the penthouse with us to see the prince!"

What was I supposed to say? I crossed the room back toward him, leaned on the counter, and met his gaze. "Let's put it this way: if I live to be a thousand, I will still be embarrassed about what happened last night."

"When?"

"I don't wanna—"

"He spoke of a misunderstanding with his courtiers, but they have since been dismissed, sent home. They were on the first plane to Malta this morning."

"Yeah, but—"

"He ordered them from court as well," Aziel added, "which is unprecedented."

"They were told to not be in attendance when he returns," Tiago confirmed.

I studied him, the solemn expression on his face, the weight of his stare, the placidity of his tone. No more playful banter, just him being serious, letting me know what he was about to say was important.

"You ran from him, and I realize it was fortunate you did because it put you in a position to see what no one else could have. But at this very moment, instead of receiving the vampyrs of this city in his normally calm and regal manner, my draugr is pacing his private quarters like a tiger in a cage, waiting until he may leave to come and see you."

I shook my head. That was total crap, and I was pissed at myself for even caring. If I was so important, he could have made time for a visit. As it was, I had not seen or heard from the prince, and really, why would I? He had no real interest in me. "I've been here all day, so I know he—"

"You do not understand," Tiago insisted. "He must live by certain rules, precautions and safety protocols that are finite. And yes, he is very strong—the chances that he could be killed are infinitesimal—but still… just that chance makes his life not his own in so many ways. He is so much to so many. We cannot lose him. Just the thought is—"

"Unimaginable," Aziel chimed in. "He's the draugr, our prince, our heart."

"Yes," Tiago echoed. "The king and queen are beloved fixtures—they are our sovereign rulers—but the prince, he is the lifeblood of our race. The attack you prevented last night… we are *all* forever in your debt."

"Well, you don't have to be, that's what I was trained to do."

"Still, we are grateful," he imparted, stepping close into my personal space. "Yet I must insist that you accompany me."

"I don't think I can do that."

"You must give him another chance! It's unheard of that someone like you—of your station—would be able to deny him," Aziel interjected, sounding almost angry.

Tiago pointed at the door, and Aziel huffed a breath before walking over to stand there.

"He's mad at me, and I get it." I sighed, because I did. "I think Aziel just wants to make me go."

"I suspect so, but that is not what I desire, and neither does the prince. He wants you to choose to see him."

"But that turned into a total shitshow the last time."

"Yes," he allowed, then bit his bottom lip. "But you misread him, or the situation. I was not in attendance, so I cannot speak to what occurred. All I do know is that when I finally reached him after the attack was over, the courtiers were all on their knees, heads down, forbidden to even regard him. I have never seen him that angry, and I have known him for over two centuries."

"If I go with you, he'll tell me what a matan is?"

"He will," Tiago said, smiling, hope infusing his face. "He will explain everything."

But I wasn't a glutton for punishment. "Lemme think about it, okay? How long are you guys gonna be in town?"

He deflated, realizing I wasn't going with him right then. "I have no idea."

"I promise to think about it."

He sighed heavily, dramatically, and when I grinned at him, after a moment he gave me one back. Apparently he did like me just a bit, and as it turned out, that was enough.

"He's receiving vampyrs at Garrett's club, right?"

His face brightened, as did his eyes, and the smile I got could give the sun a run for its money. "He is."

"So if I show up with you and he never gets around to me, that counts, yeah?"

"It would," he agreed. "But Jason, you have to understand that there is no one Varic wants to speak with more than you."

"I'm going because you asked me," I said, knowing it was halfway true. Because I didn't want to disappoint Tiago, and I did still feel bad about treating him like he was a nut job who needed extensive therapy when I first met him. But also, against my better judgment, there was the lure of the prince. He was beautiful and sexy, and while denying what I wanted to others was easy, I couldn't lie to myself. Being under him, his hands all over me, feeling him inside and out—I couldn't get the desire out of my head.

"I care not *why* you attend," Tiago sighed happily, interrupting my treasonous thoughts, still beaming at me. "Only that you do."

I grunted because if I answered, he would have been able to tell the truth from my voice that wasn't there. I could hardly breathe. Talking was off the table.

"Now," he said, looking me up and down before wincing. "What do you have to wear?"

Chapter Seven

TIAGO WAS surprised. I was pretty sure I knew why. He'd expected a different kind of club on Bourbon Street. Standing outside of the blue neon–lit techno monstrosity, he was stunned, and it showed on his face, the open mouth and wide eyes.

"You were thinking a jazz club, right? Or swing dance or even blues?"

"I—with a name like Blue Moon, I…. Varic must despise this."

"Why?" I asked as Aziel led the way inside, a doorman in Hugo Boss having opened the velvet rope the moment he saw Tiago walking toward him.

"He wants to talk to you, and this will render that nigh impossible."

A short hallway led from the front door to another doorman, this one in Prada—Ode had opened up my fashion world and was always taking me to try on suits—who was checking IDs, and a cashier, a stunning blonde woman in a Saint Laurent tuxedo who would have collected a cover charge from me if I wasn't with Tiago.

Once we stepped into the club, a wall of music assaulted us, the techno beat so loud and pounding that I could feel it in my chest. I leaned in close to Tiago and told him that I would go up on the balcony, get a beer, and stand along the railing.

"You have been here before," he said against my ear.

I nodded, patted his shoulder, and then began making my way through the teeming mob.

Snaking my way up the stairs, smiling, making apologies, the whole "excuse me, pardon me" every other second, I finally got to the second floor and made my way to the bar. Once I had my Abita Imperial Stout in hand, I made my way to the railing and looked out over the dance floor below me.

I could see everything but no one in particular; of course I could see the bottle service area where the prince had to be. While half of me really wanted to go down there and talk to him, the rest of me wasn't up for it.

"Jason."

I turned to see Niko with two others. "Hey," I greeted him over the throbbing, pounding music.

He smiled and put a hand on my shoulder as he leaned in close so he could be heard. "I think I have to leave soon. I'm getting a terrible headache."

"You're giving creatures of the night a bad name."

His laughter looked good on him, infusing his face with ease. "I'm a creature of the morning. I have meetings early, but I'm glad I ran into you before I left."

"How long have you been here?"

He groaned. "At least twenty minutes." He was really not a fan of the club, and something about the grimace of pain made me feel better about the night before.

"I wanted to apologize," he said, arm around my shoulders now because we had to be that close so I could hear him. "I misspoke last night and scared you with what I said about the binding. I didn't mean to suggest anything untoward, it's just that you've already done so much for the community, and I was worried that with his wealth Benny could have influenced you unfairly."

Niko had been feeling me out, trying to see where my alliance was when it wasn't with either the purebloods or the made vampyrs, but with both. He was worried, maybe even scared, seeing my influence over others, and he didn't want that to shift from something balanced to something that was not.

It was funny how things became clear once they were explained. Patterns emerged, truths became evident, and dots suddenly connected.

"You don't have to worry about me," I promised. "I would never take anyone's side over the other's. I know how important it is to be fair."

He nodded.

"Not that I think I'm doing anything special or that *I* am anything special. I was telling Cooke the other day that the peace in the Quarter is because of you and Benny, nothing else."

"And yet we've been here for a while, he and I, and this is the first truce we've ever had." He squeezed my shoulders. "You must take some credit, Jason, because I know the truth. Without you, things would go right back to how they were."

"Which wasn't good for anyone," I commented. All I'd ever heard was horror story after horror story.

"Of course not," he agreed, leaning away. "Now I really need to go before I get a migraine."

"Vampyrs can get migraines?"

He squinted at me. "When we go for coffee, I'll explain the not-so-vast difference between our two species."

I smiled as he gave me a head tip before leaving, two of his men trialing after him. As I watched him descend, seeing him do the same thing I had coming up the stairs, I felt so much better about him. He'd not only made the effort to come over and apologize, but then reminded me we had a standing date for coffee. I understood why his people were so loyal. He actually worried about them enough to confront me about my plans and my alliances.

My phone buzzed in my pocket, and when I pulled it from the breast pocket of my suit jacket, I saw a text from Tiago. He told me to make my way to the bottle service area.

I turned from the railing to find myself face-to-face with a stunning man. Seeing his platinum-blond hair, it took me only a moment to place him. I was looking at the same courtier from the night before. All on a plane home, my ass.

"You're like a bitch in heat, aren't you, human?"

Oh, he was charming. "Get out of my way," I said, feeling my face get hot. I was embarrassed all over again because, really, if you had guys who looked like him around, what did you need with regular mortals?

He grabbed hold of my bicep when I moved to step around him, and luckily it wasn't the one I'd been shot in, or I would have decked him. "If you're here for a fuck and suck, you're out of your league, human. The prince doesn't drink from filth."

Yanking my arm free, I moved through the crowd, put my half-empty beer bottle on a table I passed and made my way to the stairs. Halfway down, I saw Aziel and decided to join him. But when he looked up, he didn't see me. Even when I waved, he missed me. And then I had the weirdest thought. Tiago told me that Aziel saw Niko holding on to me the night before. Since Aziel worked for Hadrian, shouldn't he have walked over to investigate? Checked that I was all right?

It was strange.

I wasn't sure what to make of a guard—who Hadrian must have told to be on the lookout for me—not, in fact, looking out for me.

All my life, I'd trusted my gut, so when he finally saw me and waved, I forced a smile but turned left at the bottom of the stairs instead of heading right toward him.

A man stepped in front of me, tall, in a black suit, but there were so many people around us I got jostled into him instead of stopping my forward momentum.

I opened my mouth to apologize, but he grabbed me so fast I didn't get a chance. One second I was facing him, the next he took hold of my throat hard, painfully, and when I went to pull back to twist loose, instantly he tightened his grip, cutting off my air.

I grabbed hold of his wrist in both my hands, but his grasp was immovable. When he took a step back, moving me with him under the stairs toward the hallway that led out the back, my training kicked in. Using my left hand, I pressed his wrist down against my collarbone, holding tight, and with my right, I found his elbow and rolled him sideways. Because his wrist was locked, I had the leverage. Once he was doubled over, I kicked him in the face. If he'd been a normal man, I would have had him on the floor, but he was a vampyr, so he moved faster than I could counter and twisted free, facing me a moment later. But I wasn't at his mercy anymore and readied myself, fists raised, prepared to defend myself.

But he wasn't looking at me anymore. His vision was caught on something behind me. Whatever it was, he made the decision to turn and run. As I watched him disappear down the hall, I felt a hand on my back.

Rounding fast, ready to fight again if this was the second wave, I was relieved to find Hadrian instead.

I tried to smile but couldn't quite manage it and watched as one woman and one man moved by us in pursuit of my attacker. Since it was just as loud downstairs as it was upstairs, I moved forward, and he bent toward me, his ear close to my lips.

"We should go with your guards to find out who that guy was," I said adamantly, remembering another oddity from the night before when the guy who grabbed me yelled to the others that he had me. "There's something weird going on."

"I agree," he acknowledged, his voice just loud enough to carry over the driving beat of the music. "But first we need to see the prince," he directed, sliding his hand up to my shoulders as he turned me slowly around before easing me forward. "Come."

I stopped moving. "I don't think that's necessary."

"I disagree," he said with a smile, pressing firmly but gently to get me moving again.

Turning, stepping sideways into someone I had to apologize to, I got my eyes back on Hadrian in seconds. "I just want to go home," I almost yelled, trying to be heard.

"After you see the prince and I explain what transpired, I will escort you," he shouted back. "But you must see him before you leave."

"I don't need to be escorted," I argued, trying to move around him. "I can walk home from here just fine."

"But the prince has requested your presence and now I must report to him this incident or be in breach of my duty."

Rubbing my throat, staring at him, I realized it wasn't worth it to stand there and do the whole back-and-forth thing with him when we could just have a two-minute conversation with the prince and be done.

"I wanna leave as soon as you tell him what happened."

"Of course."

Letting out a deep breath, I gestured forward. His smile, in response, was warm.

I followed closely after him, and when we reached the steps, Tiago met us. I leaned in close so he could hear me.

"You lied to me."

His eyes widened. "I would never."

"You told me all the courtiers went home. I just saw one."

"What? Where?"

I pointed up toward the balcony.

Tiago moved around in front of Hadrian, forcing Hadrian to stop. "I thought all the courtiers were dismissed."

"It was my understanding that they did as commanded."

"Apparently not. It is your job to glean the truth, rekkr," he said haughtily.

"I know my place, rajan. Perhaps you should mind yours."

If I hadn't known better, if I hadn't heard them speak of each other before, I would have drawn a completely different conclusion. But I knew posturing when I saw and heard it. Something was going on with them, and their long drawn-out use of each other's titles as well as the cutting civility was straight out of a romantic comedy.

"Where's the prince?" I asked Tiago.

He didn't answer, turning on his heel, making a show of it, then striding purposefully off on his way toward the stairs, I was sure.

Hadrian watched him a moment, visibly torn between his duty and following the man who clearly gave him fits.

"Go, I'll tell the prince what happened," I assured him.

He nodded and rushed after Tiago.

I watched him go before another hand appeared on my arm. When I turned, I found a woman dressed in a finely tailored suit holding out her hand, gesturing to where I needed to go. Another of Hadrian's guards.

I did as prodded, walking around several tables on my way to the very back and through a gossamer curtain that led to a short hall, which then opened up into a room that overlooked Bourbon Street.

It was noisy outside too but so much better than being inside the club. The balcony was private, featuring several tables crowded with talking people, no one looking at me, in rapt conversation between themselves. The area was covered by a canopy on three sides, the fourth allowing a view of the revelers in the street below.

The prince was standing, waiting away from the tables just inside a doorway to another short hallway. It probably led to another exit, or to offices. I had been to the club only two other times, invited by Garrett to the soft opening and then to the grand one. I had not investigated the entire space on either visit, and I had no idea of the layout beyond the main areas. What I did realize, though, was the prince was in the space that could be considered farthest away from the music and still be in the club. Tiago was right; the prince was not a fan of Garrett's monster dance club.

I stood there, unsure whether I was supposed to sit down at one of the tables or walk over to him. I had no idea what was expected when you addressed vampyr royalty. Deciding I should give him his space, let him walk over if he wanted, not intrude, I went to take a seat overlooking the sprawling crowd, but he cleared his throat when I was halfway there. When I met his gaze and felt a tightening in my chest, and when he lifted his hand, the excitement that washed over me made it hard, for a moment, to breathe.

Nervously I walked by the tables until I reached him.

"Your highness," I said because, this time, I was certain from the start who stood in front of me.

"Don't call me that."

"Oh, okay. What would you prefer?"

"Varic," he murmured, his gaze locked with mine. "Call me by my name."

"Varic it is, then," I said, sounding lame to my ears.

He stood quietly, staring at me, and I felt the weight of his stare like a caress and wondered if it was real or a fanciful flight of my imagination. Either way, the silence was an unbearable vacuum I rushed to fill.

"I'm sorry I didn't walk right over here. I knew you'd asked to see me, but I wasn't sure if that was okay to do or if there was some protocol about that," I rambled. I wanted to stop talking but apparently was unable to. "That's why I was gonna go sit down until you called me, but then you gestured me over here, so I came."

He nodded, not having any trouble staying quiet.

"Have you spent your whole night talking to people here to see you?"

"I have, yes. And there are still so many more to meet."

That was my cue. "Well, then, I'll let you get to it," I said, torn between wanting to stand right there for as long as he'd let me and needing to run before I embarrassed myself any further.

"Wait," he ordered, but it sounded more like a request. "What happened?"

The rough rumble of his voice did crazy things to my ability to focus on anything but his mouth. "I'm sorry?"

"To your neck," he said, stepping closer, lifting his hand toward me only to drop it back to his side. "Your throat is red."

It would be bruised by the next day, I was sure. "I dunno what was going on, but some guy grabbed me right before I came back here. I got away, but I'm pretty sure he would have tried again. Hadrian showed up and sent a couple guards after him when he ran."

He was obviously listening but didn't comment.

"I wonder if he was working with the guy I chased last night. And when he saw me here, maybe he thought I'd seen him, too, even though I never got a good look at anyone but the guy I was after."

"Perhaps."

My brain always looked for logical reasons for strange occurrences—cult instead of vampyrs, for example. "I bet that's why he attacked me," I said, standing my ground as Varic moved closer. "He probably didn't want me to be able to tell you that I saw him during the attack last night, didn't want me to put him at the scene."

"That makes sense, if that's what happened," he agreed, his voice hoarse and low. He inhaled deeply. "But we'll know very soon."

"How will we?"

He stepped around me, putting himself in my way, barring my escape, and I liked it, the subtle movement that telegraphed his desire that I remain. "Hadrian will find him, as you said. And we'll get to the bottom of his mystery."

"Well, he's with Tiago at the moment, looking for the courtier."

"I'm sorry?"

He didn't need to put on an act for me. It wasn't necessary, and I found my equanimity in that moment and took a step back, putting space between us. "The one you had stay."

His brows creased. "You're mistaken."

"No, I just talked to him."

"I have no doubt you spoke to someone, but not a courtier."

The hell I didn't. I saw the man with my own eyes. Maybe Varic sent the others home, but the hottest one of all, the only one with a speaking part the night before, had remained for his pleasure. "It's none of my business," I said gruffly. "I don't—you're the prince, so you can do whatever you want, so… I get it."

"I assure you that no one remained."

The scowl I got was still sexy as hell, and it convinced me he meant what he said. "Then he didn't listen to you," I informed him.

Varic looked away at the wall but not really, instead thinking about something, eyes distant, running through events in his head and working out what he knew.

"I should probably—"

"Jason," he said then, taking hold of my elbow, holding me still. "I need you to stay here while I go find Hadrian."

"Actually I need to go home," I told him. "But it was good to see you again."

"No," he said flatly, almost growling, his composure slipping for a second. He crowded me so I had to move sideways or be knocked back into the wall. "I need to know that you're—would you allow me to have a car take you to the penthouse where I'm staying?"

"That's not necessary, I know you're busy. You've already taken more time seeing me than I know you have."

"I have all the time in the world for you," he made known. "Now please, don't make a beggar of a prince."

I smiled at the line, and he arched a brow in return. "You got a whole book of those, huh?"

He made a contented noise, like a lion's rumbling growl of satisfaction. I was a fan.

"You're full of some cheesy lines."

"I hadn't thought so, but apparently you bring it out in me."

It was nice to hear. Really his romance game was on point. "Listen," I said, and I took a breath. "If you have time before you leave, maybe we can—"

"No," he said sternly, the change in tone giving me whiplash. "You may either remain here with me and leave when I do, or go now to the penthouse and await my return. Which would you prefer?"

"Neither one of those works for me because I need to go home, and let's face it, you just don't really have the time to do anything but meet your subjects."

"You don't know anything," he rasped, which I would have rebutted, but voices behind us preceded a group of people who entered and hurried over to him. Apparently it was their turn to meet and greet him.

I was bumped and pushed out of the way until five and then ten people stood between us. It happened fast, and I took the opportunity to bolt even as I heard him yell first an order for everyone to be still, and then my name.

I pretended I didn't hear him call for me. I was already at the hallway, and I dodged more people walking in, and then I was in the main club, the music back to being all I heard, the push of it against me almost welcome because it cleared my head completely.

Once I was outside, I took a deep breath and got my bearings, then turned to head up Toulouse to Royal, happy to be off my least favorite street in the Quarter.

Chapter Eight

I MET Ode, my friend Brandon and his wife, Claudia, and my friend Liam and his husband, Cole, at Katie's over on Iberville and had brunch just like every Sunday. The food was great, as were the bottomless drinks, and by the time we left, I'd had four Bloody Marys, which was two more than usual as I told Ode all about my latest interaction with Varic.

"You need to stop making yourself available for that man," she cautioned. "Where's your pride?"

Gone, apparently, where the prince was concerned.

"Just say no from now on."

It was very good advice.

Ode had her normal three mimosas that morning, but since neither of us worked on Sunday, it was fine. Normally the six of us meandered through the Quarter or walked over to Jackson Square to the park to look at the artwork hanging on the fences, but this week Ode had a family thing, and everyone else had somewhere to be as well. Since they all ditched me, I strolled on my own through the streets.

I enjoyed the Quarter alone or in a group, but now and then the idea of having someone in my life tugged at my heart. Not that I did anything proactive about that, so I had no one to blame but myself. Still, between the last effects of the alcohol and the solitude, a bit of loneliness clung to me.

"Jason."

I saw Hadrian down the sidewalk ahead of me, standing on the curb in a dark navy suit and black wingtips. He was the last person I needed to see at the moment, after having just recounted to Ode how seeing his boss turned me inside out. I turned around to walk the other way.

"Jason!"

I wasn't surprised to see him right there when I turned around.

"I hope nobody saw you do your Flash impersonation."

He squinted. "Pardon me?"

Superhero references were lost on him.

"You look very serious," I commented, noting the purse of his lips, the clench of his jaw, and the lack of glint in his normally warm brown eyes. He had not run into me by accident; he'd been looking because he had business with me.

"What I am is annoyed," he warned. "My prince has invited you to meet with him, and yet you stay away."

Invited or insisted? I wasn't sure the prince knew the difference, and I was betting Hadrian, as his rekkr, didn't get the distinction either. "I went last night as I was asked."

"And then you left, which was not what he wanted."

"He has a lot to do and—"

"You need not explain his duties to me; I am well aware of what those include. What I am trying to explain now is what the prince requires, and that is your presence."

"Yeah, I don't—"

"It is unacceptable that you refrain from accepting his invitation," he explained through almost gritted teeth, clearly ready to grab me and throw me into a car. "Therefore I must insist that you accompany me now so that I may deliver you safely unto him."

My eyebrows shot up as I looked at him because, holy shitballs, who talked like that? He must really be steamed to lapse that far back in time in his speech patterns. I had to figure out what century he was from.

He scowled.

"*Unto him*?" I repeated sarcastically. "Really?"

He exhaled sharply. "I was born during the reign of Caesar Augustus, so at times my vocabulary slides between time periods. For that I apologize."

He was *so* not. "That was so not an apology!" I snorted a laugh. "Dude!"

"As though one needs diction lessons from the Americas," he replied snidely.

I bit my lip so I wouldn't laugh. "Well, I'm *really* not coming now. You insulted my whole continent, you dick."

He rubbed the bridge of his nose. I was clearly dancing a tango on his last nerve. "Get into the car before I *put* you in the car."

It was fun poking the bear; I got why Tiago liked it. "Born when Rome was still in full swing. That's kind of awesome."

"I do not care to speak of—"

"I bet cell phones were tough to get your head around, huh?"

Any serene expression on his face was long gone. I was driving him nuts.

"Shit, I'm sorry, but—"

"Jason." Hadrian crowded me, his voice guttural but even. "I want to give you a choice, but my prince—he entrusts me above all others with keeping him safe. Do you understand?"

"I do, but—"

"And right now he is climbing the walls, and by tonight, I fear he will cease to listen, which will render me unable to perform that which he charged me to do, and if I am no longer able to serve him, then—"

"*Fine*," I conceded, needing to put Hadrian out of his misery. I'd been a soldier too. I understood about sworn duty. "I'll go for you, all right?"

He put his hand over his heart, right there in the middle of the sidewalk, and pledged, "I swear I will let no harm come to you, and if your desire is to depart after you have spoken with the prince, I will not allow any other to curtail you."

"Even the prince?"

He changed instantly. Coldness washed over me as his eyes turned flat. I was second-guessing a man he loved, on the razor's edge of an insult that couldn't be taken back. I was pushing my luck, and I would have felt exactly the same if anyone ever had the balls to disrespect my old CO. It was a shitty thing to do, and if I wasn't completely sober moments before, I certainly was now. I needed to be far more careful with my words.

When he took a breath, I rushed out an apology. "I'm so sorry. I didn't mean to insinuate that he would—"

"Were you a vampyr, I would take your head, but I know you do not understand what you just implied."

"I really am sorry," I entreated. "It won't ever happen again."

"Hear me now," Hadrian began, his tone measured. "The prince would keep no one against their will. It is not in him to do so. He would never deny anyone their liberty."

I nodded, feeling like absolute crap for overstepping. I would have felt better if he hit me, but I was scared he might actually kill me.

"Do you believe what I say?"

"I do," I affirmed, and even if it was a lie—which it wasn't—I would have said it anyway because I wanted things back to normal between us.

"Thus?"

"Okay. Let's go."

The relief that seemed to flood him, from the drop of his shoulders to the quick release of breath, made me smile. It was like I'd made his whole day, and he smiled and gestured to the car parked halfway down the street. "I will never forget this."

I doubted I would either. Seeing the prince had been nothing if not memorable.

I STAYED silent on the short drive to the very edge of the Garden District and Uptown. Seeing the cars lining the 2700 block of St. Charles Avenue didn't surprise me. All the vampyrs in the city would, of course, want to see the prince before he left.

Hadrian explained on our elevator ride up that the two-story penthouse had a wrap-around terrace on the first floor and a large private patio off the master bedroom on the second, along with other details of the building.

"I'm sure it's great," I murmured, my buzz wearing off in the face of seeing the prince again. I felt itchy, didn't want to be there. The idea that I'd made a mistake was pressing in on me.

The elevator opened directly into the living room, which had far too many people crowded in it. According to Hadrian, the penthouse was about nine thousand square feet smaller than Benny Diallo's sumptuous mansion, so Hadrian and I and two more of his guys had to gently push and say "excuse me" every few seconds as we made our way out to the terrace. I staked out a place on the rail, and Hadrian asked me what I wanted to drink.

"Just a bottle of water, if you have it."

"Certainly," he obliged, smiling before he left me.

I closed my eyes and enjoyed the cool breeze on my face. People thought it was always warm in New Orleans, but in the fall, the nights got chilly, tumbling into the low fifties. That temperature didn't used to be sweater weather for me, but I had acclimated fast. Today, as it had rained earlier and stayed overcast, was on the cold side if you were a human. It was funny, but just thinking about something as inane as the weather calmed me with every passing second. It would be fine. I could be cordial for a few minutes and then excuse myself. I worked in retail, for crissakes. If I could deal with the public, I could deal with anything.

"Jason?"

Cooke stood a few feet away, looking a little pale and hesitant.

Crap. I should have known he'd be upset, the two sides of him warring because he could still remember what being scared and hunted was like. He couldn't very well stand up for me when the truce between the vampyr classes was still so new.

"It's fine, we're fine," I contended, needing to clear the air between us even though I still felt betrayed by him siding with Benny instead of me. "I get it. You're a vampyr first and foremost, no two ways about it."

He moved quickly, beside me in seconds, his hand on my shoulder. "I'm your friend, and I should have—I've just never been put in—"

"Really," I tried to mollify, "it's okay. I forgive you already."

He looked stressed and worried, and I had to relieve that because, at the end of the day, we were friends.

"Just do me a favor, all right?" I said, needing to put us both back on solid ground.

"Yes, whatever, just tell—"

"Don't stop coming by the store. Don't stop playing out front. You don't need to plan on disappearing because that won't help anything."

He moved his hand from my shoulder and slid it down my back as he leaned on me, and even though I didn't want to be that close to him, still a bit frayed around the edges, I let him be.

"Move."

We both straightened from our lean on the railing to face Hadrian, standing there all scary and glowering at Cooke.

"You should not—" He stopped talking to Cooke and turned his attention to me. "The prince has requested to see you upstairs on the balcony, if that would be agreeable to you."

"Sure," I said, ready to follow him.

He choked out a breath. "Would you take your jacket off for me, please?"

"What? Why?"

He rubbed the back of his neck, clearly uncomfortable.

For heaven's sake. "Uh, maybe you can't feel it since you're a vampyr and all of you guys are always freezing," I explained, a bit annoyed with everyone trying to give me orders. "But it's a little cold out here, and if I'm going upstairs and then right back outside, I kinda need this."

He sighed deeply. "Yes, I am certain you do, but unfortunately, as your jacket now smells like Mr. Slater, and since the prince gave specific orders that no one but the rajan, myself, or my men be allowed to touch you, it would not bode well for Mr. Slater were my prince to catch his scent on any of your clothing."

That was insane. I didn't belong to him, I wasn't his to put demands on, and he certainly wasn't allowed a say in who could or couldn't touch me. "But Cooke didn't know that the—"

"Which is a fair and logical argument that would perhaps allow him to retain his head," Hadrian said flatly. "Or perhaps not. That would depend greatly on the mood of my prince."

"And you would do, what, just come down here and cut off my buddy's head?"

At this point Cooke gagged behind me.

Hadrian glared at me. "You are missing again that I am the sword of the prince, his rekkr. Whatever his command, I would see that carried out."

"That's nuts. Do you get that that's nuts?"

He lifted one eyebrow in question.

"Not the following orders part, of course I get that, but the chopping off Cooke's head because he touched my jacket part."

"It is really the most simple of decrees."

"But me and Cooke have been friends for—"

"Perhaps we might stop having a discussion about this, and you could be so kind as to give me your jacket," Hadrian said, his tone strained, feigning calm—ready, I was sure, to murder me and Cooke right there, even though he'd plastered on a fake smile.

I glanced over my shoulder at Cooke. His eyes were wide, and he opened and closed his mouth like a fish. He was scared, and I would be too. Hadrian did not come off all patient and soothing; he came off like a badass who could rip out your spine with his bare hands. Pissing him off seemed more than a bit counterproductive. "Sure," I agreed. I turned back to Hadrian, slipped my leather racing jacket off, and handed it to him. "We all good now?"

"Your sarcasm is not lost on me," Hadrian said before draping my jacket over his arm and then pivoting to lead.

I pointed at Cooke. "You can hug me after he goes home."

"And if you leave with him?" Cooke asked.

"That isn't gonna happen, no worries."

"He's already this possessive, Jase. I think maybe you're in trouble here."

"I don't even know him. You're—"

"Jason," Hadrian said sharply.

I gave Cooke a quick wave and followed Hadrian, who cleared the way through the crowd in the living room to the stairs where people stood waiting, and then up to the second floor. The main room featured a chandelier, just like downstairs, the same high ceilings, and a balcony that looked out over the first floor. It was beautiful but still crowded.

Hadrian led me through an amazing door—not a sliding glass one at all, but instead a giant pivoting window—and out onto the patio empty except for a grouping of furniture sheltered by several large plants that blocked the sightlines from neighboring buildings and a clear view otherwise. A second door at the far end of the patio led back into the house. As predicted, I was cold.

"I will bring you a blanket."

"It's fine. I won't be here that long," I said, even as a slight tremble ran through me as my body tried to acclimate to the temperature. Downstairs, the temperature in the condo had to be set on frostbite. Upstairs, the air had to be set on arctic.

"Jason," Hadrian began. "Perhaps you should wait inside—"

"I'll be fine," I muttered while I walked to the railing. "Let's just get this over with."

I didn't check to see if he left, just looked out at the buildings, waiting for whatever would happen next. I didn't expect something warm to drape over my back. It was an oversized cardigan, and after I turned, sliding my arms into the sleeves before wrapping it around me, all I saw was green.

Again, I had no idea eyes came in that shade of deep, dark forest green framed by long, thick raven-wing lashes.

"Thank you for coming."

I didn't say Hadrian hadn't give me much of a choice, because standing there with him, I could feel how much my body enjoyed his proximity, even if my head was confused over my excitement. "Sure," I said, glancing away at the skyline for a moment to get myself in check. I needed to calm down.

"Jason."

I looked back at him, and he gave me a slight smile. "I don't—there are not many things in my closet that will fit you, but blessedly I found at least one."

"Thank you."

He nodded, and it sank in that even though he was only an inch or so taller, we were built very differently.

I had always been thick and bulky, covered in hard, hewn muscle. Varic's musculature looked like the kind built in the gym. I bet he had six-pack abs under his clothes, because he was all coiled power, more toned and sculpted, sleek and elegant. He was classically built, an aristocrat, and so everything fit him like it did the models in magazines.

With his physique, the mane of glossy black hair, the alluring green eyes, and his carved features, I'd never seen a more breathtaking man.

"I'll give it back before I go," I promised, forcing a smile.

"I'm sorry?"

"The sweater," I reminded him.

"No, that's… fine," he whispered, crossing his arms and then quickly uncrossing them before dragging a hand through his hair. It was almost like he was nervous… but why would he be?

I took a breath. "So did you figure out who tried to attack you the other night?"

"No, not—not yet," he answered, coming closer to the railing. "But I have a working theory."

"We should probably move, huh?"

"Pardon?"

"Out of the line of fire," I explained, walking over to the furniture behind the plants where the skyline blocked out. He stayed right there beside me, and when I sat, he took the chaise in front of me, sitting at the very end, only a couple feet separating us. "I just don't think, with someone out to get you, that you should make yourself an easy target. A sniper could take you out fast from over there."

He nodded. "I appreciate the concern, but at my age, the only way to kill me is beheading. Even fire won't work anymore."

"Really?" I asked, intrigued and illogically excited. How often did someone tell you they were basically bulletproof?

"Yes," he said slowly, drawing out the word, seemingly unsure why I was pleased.

"What about being blown up?"

"No."

"Drowning?"

He shook his head.

"No?" I waited for him to nod. "Wow. So deep-sea diving, you can just go without a SCUBA tank?"

"I wouldn't because it would be painful. But were I thrown in the ocean with weights attached, I wouldn't drown."

"Holy crap, that's awesome. You're like Wolverine."

"Not quite, but—"

"What if you got pushed off something high?"

"No. I'd land on my feet."

"Seriously?"

He nodded.

"What if someone knocked you out and then cut out your heart?"

His eyes widened comically, and I had to chuckle. "These are getting more elaborate as the questions progress."

"Yeah, I'm sorry about that."

"No, no, they're reasonable inquiries. Knocking me out would present a problem in and of itself, and if I ever were unconscious, the second I was cut, I would wake."

I nodded. "Good to know."

"And as I said, even a shot to the head would not prove fatal."

"You're speaking from experience," I said gravely, the question-and-answer session coming to an abrupt halt as I was struck by the thought of him being hurt. Already, that fast, the thought of a world without him was painful.

"I am."

"Someone shot you in the head?"

"With a high-powered rifle, yes."

I was stunned. "What happened?"

"Well, it hurt, of course," he teased, giving me a shy smile, "but the bullet stopped before it entered my brain and then had only to be removed."

"So that fast, it got lodged in your skull?"

"Yes."

"That's amazing."

He kept his gaze steady on mine.

"You know," I said awkwardly, feeling the need to fill the silence, "I'm sure there are scientists out there who would love to study your kind to see how your genetics work."

"I would agree. I'm sure there are."

"We have to make sure they never get their hands on any of you."

"Why do you say that?"

I shook my head. "That's a zombie outbreak movie just waiting to happen."

He laughed, and the sound—deep, husky, sincere—plucked a chord of painful yearning in my chest. I liked being the guy who made him laugh.

"You know that whole thing with the bullet not going in deep would have been really handy during my last tour," I reasoned, grinning. "I still have scars from where different medics had to dig out bullets and shrapnel."

"That reminds me. I understand you were hurt the other night, saving me."

"Well, apparently you didn't need saving, did you?"

"No, but my people did, and in saving them, you saved me as well."

"It's not a big deal, just a graze. And my friend Ode, her mom's a nurse, so she fixed me right up."

He remained quiet, staring at me.

"And I got fed too," I added, rambling.

"Yes. Being fed is… good," he agreed, his voice gravelly and low. "But tell me, are you hungry now?"

"No, I just had brunch not too long ago."

"Is there anything I can get you?"

"Well, Hadrian was supposed to bring me some water, but I think he forgot when he saw me talking to my buddy Cooke."

"Mr. Slater, yes, I saw him as well," he said, his voice suddenly rough, thick with something I couldn't place.

"We have to…." I wasn't sure what I wanted to say about my friend. "…sort of redefine our relationship, I guess. I think I got spoiled meeting Tiago and Hadrian first."

"Spoiled? How so?"

"Well, the two of them do whatever they want, and the only person they have to report to is you," I explained, looking into all that green, only to turn away, not wanting to be pulled in again. I needed to stand up, but I was worried it'd be rude. "But why do I care?"

"Why do you care about what?"

I had to get out of there. What the hell was the point of hanging around talking to the vampyr prince, getting to know him, maybe even ending up liking him? It was an exercise in futility, and there were ridiculous rules I already knew I couldn't abide, so why did I care if he thought I was rude? I'd be walking out of his life now or later, same outcome on the horizon. It was frustrating just thinking about it, so I stood and walked toward the door but stopped abruptly, remembering his sweater. When I turned around to take it off and give it to him, he was right there.

"Man, that vampyr speed is really not fair."

"You didn't finish your thought," he said, lifting his hand toward my face, but he let it slowly drop back to his side.

I took a breath, wanting to explain at least this to him because he was the one who could make changes. "Cooke wanted to help me the other night, but he couldn't because he couldn't challenge Benny's authority."

"And how is that different from Tiago and Hadrian?" He took a deep breath, and he closed his eyes for a moment as if he was concentrating on keeping himself still. "They too could not challenge my word."

"But they would if they felt you were being unfair."

"And how would you know that?"

"Because of who they are," I explained. "They're strong, and they think for themselves, and if I was in trouble, they would defy you if they needed to."

"They would not. They are both unquestionably and unwaveringly loyal."

"Yeah, but if you went crazy and ended up hurting others… they would stop you."

"They would act to protect me from myself, yes."

"And you'd expect it of them because they're not just your minions, but men you respect."

"Yes," he said flatly. "Because if one rules by fear, that wears off. If you rule by intimidation or even love, all that can change. Mutual respect is the only path to being a kind and just leader."

"There, see?" I sighed, gesturing at him. "That's what I meant when I said I was spoiled. Cooke can't be who he should because the guy in charge doesn't believe in him or respect him. How's he ever supposed to become the best version of himself that way?"

"Perhaps I need to speak to both Niko Gann and Benny Diallo about how they treat their people and what they can do better."

I nodded. "I think that would be great, though it's probably happening all over and not just here."

"I would agree."

"This could help a lot of your vampyrs."

"Yes, good," he said gruffly, touching the hem of the cardigan and then the zipper pull, as I hadn't pulled it off yet. "Now that we've figured that out, let's talk about you."

I realized that while he did mean it—he did want to help and make things better—at the moment, looking at the way he had eased closer but wasn't crowding me, he was completely distracted by me. "Could I ask you something?"

He lifted his gaze from his hands and met mine. "Anything."

I smiled big. "Could you tell me where vampyrs come from?"

His grin could lure any man to his bed, as salacious and seductive as it was. His eyes glinted, his lip curled at the corner, and he lifted one brow in invitation. "Well, Jason, when two people love each other—"

"Stop," I said, trying unsuccessfully not to laugh. "Just tell me, please. No one in my circle has any clue."

"All right," he said, voice like honey, leaning on the doorframe, arms crossed, looking very relaxed. "You want to hear about the first vampyrs."

"Yes."

"Well, then, by any chance do you know what a berserker is?"

I had to think. "Maybe? They were Vikings, right, that went nuts in battle and killed everybody?"

"They were Norse, yes, but they go back centuries before the Vikings, and there were different cults for different animals, like wolves or bears or boars, anything that would have been around back then that hunters would kill and gatherers had to be protected from."

"Tiago called Hadrian a wolf once, and when I first mentioned Hadrian to Cooke, he thought he was a werewolf or something."

"That's because the strongest of the hunters became like a pack themselves, having learned how to work together like the wolves."

"That makes sense," I agreed. I could imagine Bronze-Age humans looking at apex predators and thinking the hunting style made a lot of sense. "And now the dreki are called the wolves of the house of Maedoc, right?"

"Yes," he sighed, a hint of a smile on his lips. "Who told you that?"

"Tiago. He's had to endure a lot of questions, and he's been mostly patient about answering them."

"Tiago has?" He seemed surprised.

"Yeah. I think I bring out the best in him."

"I suspect in everyone."

So nice of him to say that. "So the dreki are called wolves because back in the day, they hunted well together?"

"Yes, but again, that's only something they're called. It's a holdover from an early belief in hunting magic."

"Hunting magic?"

"In prehistoric times, if you wanted to be as successful a hunter as the wolves, then you prayed to that animal, and the belief was that you would become like them during a hunt."

"I think I saw a show about this on the Discovery Channel."

He chuckled. "No doubt."

"Sorry. Please go on."

"Well, you have these people," he said, levering off the door and moving toward me again, "these hunters hunting, providing for their families, but there were always wars, always hunger, and pretty soon, they can't hunt for food anymore. Something has to give."

"And that's when they started drinking blood?" I asked as he reached me.

He smiled before stepping in close, his breath warm on my cheek. "This is evolution, right? You can't simply acquire a trait because you need it. Things don't work that way."

I knew that. "Right. Then what happened?"

"I'm getting there," he teased, leaning in, which made my breath catch inadvertently.

Jesus.

I was trying really hard not to get comfortable with him, but it was difficult. He was a very easy man to talk to, and his full attention made my heart beat faster, no matter what had happened the other night.

"When the hunters brought back less and less game and everyone had to subsist on smaller and smaller amounts of food, over time, the blood of the animal became just as important as anything else."

"If we're talking evolution, then eventually someone was born with a mutation that allowed them to metabolize the blood as everything they needed."

"Exactly. We don't know how long it took to be passed down. This is all thousands of years ago. But what we do know is that the blood-drinkers had an advantage in that environment, and it was passed down generationally. Then, of course, there was a horrific winter or a famine or a plague—again, we have no idea—but because of that disaster, those who couldn't just drink blood died. And what started out as a mutation became the rule."

"What about the berserkers?"

"Well, by the time of the Vikings, there were the stories about the berserkers who chewed on their shields with their long teeth," he said, arching a rakish brow for me in case I missed the teeth part, "and they fought without any armor. And it's also recorded that they *tasted* blood, but of course we know that 'tasting' was actually 'drinking.' And when they fought, they used their teeth as much as their swords."

"So vampyrs, then."

"Yes."

"And what the historians are calling a *frenzy* is actually vampyrs killing each other and humans, drinking blood in the process."

"Far too much blood, yes. It wasn't an induced trance, or drugs or alcohol, or anything else that people have assumed down through the centuries that caused the savagery in battle—but purely bloodlust."

"Too much of it spilled in one place."

"Yes."

"And is that when the laws were enacted?"

"Yes, very good," he praised, returning his hands to the hem of the sweater, then the T-shirt underneath. It was gentle, a small, subtle movement, the slightest tug, but I felt every twitch of his fingers.

I took a breath, so grateful to finally learn the whole story, knowing he was the only one who could have filled in the blanks for me. Listening to him, I could see the history in my mind, having always preferred to be told a good story than anything else. "Thank you so much for explaining. I really appreciate it."

"It's my pleasure," he said, lifting his eyes to mine. "It's good to be asked."

"The hiding in plain sight that you all do is amazing to me."

He gave the slightest tip of his head. "More people than you would guess know all about vampyrs."

"I was in the military. I know how secrets work."

"I'm sure you do," he agreed as he removed his fingers from the cardigan to slip them over mine, tentatively, as if seeing what I would allow. "Jason—"

Sidestepping, I moved into the doorway, ready to go. As interested as I was, as ready to be whatever he wanted as long as I could get into his bed, I was still worried I would get too attached, which would do nothing good for me. Getting out of there was the safest move. "I have a lot of other questions, but I know you have a lot of people to see, so maybe I can come back another—"

"No, don't go," he coaxed and commanded at the same time, his tone like a fist in a velvet glove. "Stay."

The silky tone, his eyes half-open, a trace of smile on those full lips…. He knew how seductive he was, how tempting, how utterly decadent and beautiful. I desperately wanted to give in, but I had to be smart. I had to use my head, not my heart.

"I should let you—"

"You were embarrassed by the others that night," he rushed out, "because you thought I was not as be-spelled as you were."

I met his gaze, all that rich, beckoning emerald, and faced the humiliation that had been eating away at my heart for the past couple of days. "Think an awful lot of yourself, huh?"

"Yes," he said implacably, no mistake there, but I would have known he was lying if he said anything else. Varic breathed out self-confidence and radiat-ed a pulse of magnetism that made it impossible to take your eyes off him. From the way he walked and carried himself, the tilt of his head, and his piercing stare… you knew he was in absolute control of his many charms. He was utterly lethal in his beauty and presence. "But make no mistake; I was just as frac-tured as you were when we were interrupted because I *too* was utterly bewitched."

I tried to tell if he was lying, tried to read him, but I couldn't. All I saw when I looked at him was something I wanted, something I craved. Because yes, I was eaten up with lust but also something more, something forbidden and tempting at the same time.

He moved slowly, fluidly, hand on my wrist, turn-ing it to stroke his thumb over the underside gently, soothing me, the urge to flee draining from my heart, ebbing, the surrender of a vicious wave retreating from a battered shore, leaving me calm as its intensity drained away.

After a moment he released me and stepped in closer. He slid his hands under the sweater to my hips, and he curled his fingers into the belt loops of my jeans.

"Forgive me for allowing that disruption," he whispered hoarsely in my ear. "Those men meant nothing, mean nothing, and you will never lay eyes on them again, even the one who disobeyed me, not ever."

"But you fucked them, all of them," I said because it hurt—like he'd cheated on me, which was ludicrous and so unlike me because I'd never been controlling or jealous, but still—it felt like trying to choke down a rotting piece of meat. I couldn't swallow it, couldn't let this go. "Earlier that day you did. You screwed all of them."

"I did," he admitted. He pressed a kiss to first my ear and then right below before moving lower to where my neck and shoulder joined. "But I will never take another again, I swear on your life, which is the most precious of my possessions."

"I don't belong to you," I advised weakly as he kissed along my jaw. But even as I said the words, they didn't ring true because belonging to him sounded heavenly.

"Oh, you most certainly do," he said, his voice thick and growly when he spoke. "You're so very mine."

The scent of his skin, the sound of his voice, the touch of his lips, and the clutch of his hands were utterly devastating. I was drowning in my own desire for him.

"Invite me in," he demanded, but it was wrapped in his sultry, silvery voice, all heat and seduction and hunger. "Now."

I shoved him off because I still could and had to. I didn't give myself away, never had, and it was vital he knew that before things combusted between us. The shocked look on his face was priceless. I guessed not many, if any, guys stopped him once he got started.

"This'll probably sound stupid to you, but anything I allow has to mean something," I said, meeting his gaze and holding it. "So if this is just—"

"I can barely breathe," he whispered, inhaling fast, swallowing hard, almost as if he were about to be sick. "My hands are shaking, and I can't make it stop. Look at them."

I took them in mine, feeling how cold they were, his skin almost icy. "You make me nervous too."

"Oh no, I'm not nervous," he clarified, easing from my grasp, only to step forward, into me, pressing a kiss to my cheek as he slipped his hand around my neck. "I'm just afraid of hurting you if you try to leave me again."

The dark confession was slightly twisted and a bit scary, yet it dragged a sound up from my chest that was all yearning and desperation.

"You need me. You want me, I can feel it," he growled, sliding his hands up under my T-shirt to my skin. "That wasn't a fluke the other night, and you weren't the only one out of their depth. Now give... in."

I couldn't say no to him. I didn't want to, didn't feel like I should. My gut said yes, jump, try, chase down what you need, don't let it go. It was like watching a fiery sunset drowning in a deep, velvety night sky. I just wanted to give up and give in. And since I couldn't imagine saying anything else, I voiced the only answer I could. "Please."

"You're mine," he husked, and only then did I realize where his mouth was, his teeth pressed to my throat for a moment before the bite.

Logically I knew what was going to happen, but I still tensed at the first puncture. Not that I was scared, it wasn't that, but I'd never been bitten before, and then right on the heels of that new sensation came pain, overwhelming, searing. I fought for my balance when my knees went weak, and I became light-headed enough that I was afraid I would pass out. I thought about telling him to stop, because I needed to know if this was how it was supposed to feel, if the pain ever abated, or if this was how it always was. Everything cycled through my mind, and I started to worry I'd hyperventilate... until he started to drink.

Holy... God.

Why would any human willingly feed a vampyr? I had made plans to go to some of the clubs around town just to ask, but in the end thought better of it because, really, it was none of my business. Those people were clearly masochists who were into pain, and it wasn't my place to judge.

But now I knew better. Now I knew why.

It felt like *sex*.

Like the good kind of sex everybody wanted, the kind where you could feel your body melding with the other person, where you felt like one thing, one soul, one open beating heart.

I closed my eyes, and tears ran from under my lashes, down my cheeks. My gasp, my breathing filled my ears. The pull of his bite, the suction, made me press against him, my back bowing as I fisted my hands in his shirt.

It was exquisite. Feeding a vampyr had to be the greatest high in the world. No drug could be as good as this, nothing could compare to the rightness of having him take my blood to sustain him. I could nourish him; I could be everything to him. It was almost too much to bear, and I shuddered in his arms as he clutched me tight, one hand cupping the back of my head, holding me still, the other on the small of my back, pressing me against him.

When he slid his fangs free and licked over the bite, I realized I was painfully hard, my clothes far too tight, my skin hot.

"Tell me yes," he demanded, loosening my belt before opening the top button and lowering my zipper. "Because I must have the words."

"And if I say no?" I asked, opening my eyes to slits, needing to know about his control, that he'd never lose himself, that he had complete mastery of his desire at all times. It was imperative because he was stronger than me and could make me do as he pleased without my permission. But even as the thought came into my head, I discarded it because watching him go to his knees in front of me was the hottest thing I'd ever seen.

"Then it's no," he said thickly as he jerked down my jeans and underwear with one hand and wrapped the other around my cock when it bounced free.

Just seeing his fingers on my skin almost made me come, and when he licked over the head, I cried out his name.

"Declare yourself to me!" he snarled, his eyes going black, the emerald bleeding to onyx in a heartbeat that was more than blown pupils.

I was past thinking, past speaking; all I wanted, needed, craved, desired, was him all over me. "I don't—"

"You're mine! Swear it now."

There was nothing else to do; no other choice even made sense. He was the only thing that mattered.

"Jason!" he rasped, pleading with me, the ache in his voice as rich as a peat whiskey.

"Yours," I whispered, but he heard it nonetheless.

He swallowed me to the back of his throat in one seamless movement, and I thought I would die right there. Then he eased back and did it again.

"Varic," I chanted, one hand in all that gorgeous silky black hair, the other braced flat on the glass door behind me as he sucked and laved, taking all of me until I was wet and dripping. "I can't…. It's too much," I begged, nothing in the world better than him taking control, his dominance as big a turn-on as his hot mouth.

When he dragged his fangs along the top of my shaft, to the edge of pain but not over, his tongue flat along the underside, then slid his fingers through saliva to grip my balls, I lost it. The orgasm boiled through me, convulsing, twisting before the burst of euphoria that came with sweet release.

He swallowed it all, drank me down, and when I couldn't bear it a second longer, oversensitized physically and visually, I tugged on his shoulder.

My cock slipped from between his pillowy lips, and he stood, rising until he was looking down from those couple of inches he had on me.

I had to say something, tell him he was already the most ravenous lover I'd ever had, that I was in his hands, his to do with as he pleased, ready for whatever came next, but he bent and kissed me, and I tasted myself on his tongue. He mauled my mouth, the kiss grinding and deep, claiming and hungry. I couldn't get enough of him. I wanted more.

I wrapped my arms around his neck and held him tight as he palmed my still thickened cock. Even the tender contact sent an arc of electricity through me.

With his other hand, he cupped the back of my head before he yanked hard, broke the kiss, and exposed my throat.

"I have your blood and cum both on my tongue, Jason Thorpe."

Yes, he did, and his words, nearly snarled, made me shudder in his hands. "What else may I have?"

I wasn't sure there was a limit, and that was terrifying. I could easily see how people died accidentally while feeding a vampyr. The high was something to be chased, coveted, and combined with the ego stroking of being another's whole world in that moment—you were their nourishment, their lifeblood—all of it swirled together into a soaring, blinding rush.

Always I'd been strong enough not to succumb to addictions, especially when I was still active military. The pills some guys took to stay awake or go to sleep, the drinking they did to forget—none of that was me.

But this, with Varic… this was something else entirely, and I saw the spiral it might become and didn't care.

"Jason. Tell me what I may have of you." His voice sounded like poured honey and drew words from my throat.

"All of me," I got out before I took control and kissed him. I tasted and explored, catching on his fangs, rubbing my tongue over his before I deepened the kiss and melted against him.

He clutched me so tight I could barely breathe, and I gasped as he went to his knees again. My jeans were still pooled around my ankles, and he eased off my right shoe, a white Converse, and slipped my foot free before lifting my leg over his left shoulder. I watched him through narrowed eyes as he licked over my length before nuzzling my thigh. When he bit me, my cock came to immediate attention, thickening fast as he gorged on my blood.

I could feel myself becoming something new in that very moment. I was changing and staying the same, instantaneously, inexorably. I wouldn't be able to walk away from him after this. The connection was powerful, a living and breathing thing between us, a tether as vital as one forged over years. It went beyond me; he was holding on to me as hard as I held on to him, and for once, I wasn't guessing or hoping. I knew.

I knew it like I knew myself, like my own skin, my own face.

It was the blood.

My blood was inside of him, and I could feel his joy as he ingested what made me *me*.

"Varic," I moaned hoarsely as he licked over the bite and then the head of my cock.

It would be an endless cycle of pleasure, and I was ready.

He rose and slid the zippered cardigan from my shoulders, letting it drop to the floor. He manhandled me out of the other leg of my jeans and pushed me through the second door into the bedroom, where I stumbled forward and toppled over onto the king-size bed.

He fell on me, pinning me under him, his groin pressed to my bare ass. It felt illicit, him fully clothed, me half-naked, and I felt like spoils of war.

"I'm going to take you now because it's my pleasure to have my consort however and whenever I choose," he said, dragging my T-shirt over my head so he could smooth his hand over my bared back. "Do you understand?"

I did, and I wanted to tell him that whatever he wanted, I wanted, that he didn't have to ask my permission. I'd given it once. I was already his. "I can't just—"

"You can. You will," he said, yanking the T-shirt from around my wrists and tossing it away. I was naked now, and when I looked over my shoulder, his smile was decidedly carnal. "Now get on your hands and knees."

I did it, moving bonelessly because his voice tripped a tumbler in my chest. It was so strange, as if I'd been in limbo, waiting, everything happening on the outside and nothing on the inside until he woke me up.

I was kindling and he the match. We got close and ignited.

"It's too—fast," I gasped, trying to make sense of who I was… until his hands spread my cheeks and his tongue was in my ass.

I couldn't… think.

He was voracious. No one had ever wanted all of me before, never wanted to taste me inside and out.

"Varic," I rasped, my breathing ragged as he licked and nibbled. He stopped to blow on my saliva-covered hole, the chill on my skin eliciting a needy moan.

"Imagine my dilemma, Jason," he began, his voice a velvet rumble as he rose from the bed, only to return in seconds. "I find a strong, virile, beautiful man who I see and want instantly, the craving like nothing that's ever happened to me before, only to find out that he's human."

"And you hate humans."

"I don't hate them," he soothed. The snap of a lid told me he'd retrieved a tube of lubricant. "I have no feeling for them one way or another because I purposely stay clear. Your kind doesn't live long enough to interest me."

I would have said something in defense of my humanity, but he chose that moment to slide two lube-coated fingers into my ass, and my brain shut off.

"But you, above all others, do more than interest me," he confessed. He added a third finger, screwed them inside, and muscles already softened from the rimming, relaxed even more as he stroked down my spine with his free hand. "I'm enthralled, and since that's never happened before, I have no recourse but to take you until my heart tells me that you've surrendered your soul up to me."

It was the best plan I'd ever heard. "Good. Make me surrender."

He bit me then on my hip, but there was no pain, just bliss and a feeling of finding what had been missing, like I was becoming whole.

"Did that hurt?" he asked, releasing his hold.

"No," I managed to get out.

"Would you care if it did?"

"No."

When he bit me again, on the other, it wasn't discomfort that made me gasp, but the drops of blood hitting the down comforter, the wine-colored splatters a stark contrast to the pristine ivory.

He moved to my side, over my ribs, marking me, biting but not drinking, not sucking at them, instead letting them seep blood he licked from his fingers.

It should have been sick, gross, or disgusting, but it was anything but.

"You know it's against the law for me to drink from a human, and I'm the prince, I'm the champion of those laws, but… human or not, forbidden or not, for the first time in the long history of my life, desire takes precedence over all else. And do you know why?"

I hoped I knew, because already I wanted more from him. Another time just like this, and another and another. I needed to be the one and only person in his bed, and the reason was simple.

I wanted to be his mate.

"Jason?" he said as he bit into my shoulder, and I jolted under him. It was so good, feeling him drink, and I knew all the blood should have scared me, but instead my concentration centered on pushing back onto him, wanting to fuck myself on his fingers.

When he withdrew them, only then did I cry out.

"I've broken a sacred law to have you, but my paramount concern is not that," he ground out as he pressed against my entrance, notching there as he plastered his chest to my back. "The duration of your lifetime cannot possibly quench my thirst for you, my mate… my consort."

The words, his words, his actions, the heated thundering want between us was overpowering, and I wasn't sure how to sate my mind, body, and soul all at once until he bit into the side of my neck and shoved himself in to the hilt at the exact same moment.

"Varic!" I howled. He stayed still, drinking from me but letting my body get used to the long, hard, thick length of him buried in my ass.

He slipped his left hand under me to my belly, sliding lower, mapping skin, and then reached my cock. He curled his fingers around me, and he squeezed and tugged, working my shaft until I was leaking on his fingers.

When he slipped his fangs free and laved the bite, I begged. "Please, Varic, move. Just move."

"Tell me how you like it," he asked as he slowly withdrew, only to press back inside, pushing deeper, filling me up as my muscles clenched around him. "Shall I be gentle or not?"

"Not," I whined, the word crawling out of my throat before I could curtail the aching sound. "Do it hard. I wanna feel you tomorrow."

"I'll still be inside you tomorrow," he promised and pulled out slowly, retreating, letting me feel the slide before driving in, harder, faster, and then again and again, his body beginning an ancient rhythm, one carried in genetic memory, timeless, endless, as I begged him for more.

"This is why they keep attacking you," he snarled, his voice feral, the sultry purr gone, replaced by something far more primal. "They knew everything would change once I had you."

I couldn't process the words. Me? They attacked me? Yes, at the club, that man had tried to grab me for whatever reason, but the first time? At Benny's house? That made no sense. I was nothing, no one. I had been a soldier, was now a shop owner, easily lost in a sea of people.

Until now.

In this moment I was extraordinary because Varic Maedoc *had* to have me, and I luxuriated in the feeling and let it fill me even as he shoved my face down onto the mattress and held me there.

Ass in the air, the new position slid him over my core, and the drag combined with the pounding and pressure and his heat sent me flying. The orgasm rushed over me before I was even aware I was caught in the wave.

"Oh yes, so tight, so hot," he moaned as my muscles clamped around him, my entire body rigid with my release.

He followed me seconds later, pulsing inside my clasping channel. His grip in my hair and on my hip was so tight that even as I trembled with aftershocks beneath him, legs shaking with fatigue, cock spent, I couldn't sink down onto the bed.

He continued to grind his hips against me until he finally stilled, heaving for breath, before he released my hair and lifted me up and sideways, just enough so that when he collapsed across my back, still balls-deep in my ass, he didn't drive me down into my own cum.

"That was considerate of you," I croaked, arms and legs splayed under him.

"That's me," he said, chuckling, and eased tenderly free of my body. His hand stayed in my hair for a moment before he rubbed the spot where he'd held me.

"Don't worry about it." I yawned, sated and exhausted, my body replete and my soul settled in my skin. "I'm good."

"You're not," he advised. "That graze on your arm has bled through the bandage, you're dehydrated, and you have to eat, and I need to give you a vitamin B shot."

I grunted, turning my head so I could see him. My smile was huge.

"Humans have tricky upkeep."

I laughed softly, so very happy in that moment that I felt anything was possible.

"Whatever can you possibly find funny about this situation?" He stroked my hair again and traced over my right eyebrow.

"You never even took off your suit." I snickered, trying hard to keep my eyes open.

"It couldn't be helped," he informed me, his tone matter-of-fact. "My consort is far too tempting for me to waste time with getting undressed."

"Is that right?"

"Yes." He kept petting me. "He's also quite vocal and demanding."

"Oh yeah?"

"Yes, he's very loud." He sighed as he bent and kissed my temple and my eyebrow, the tip of my nose, and then gently, with those firm but supple lips of his, took my mouth.

I had been ravaged, and now he lay close, still touching me, kissing over my shoulders, and worshipping me with every brush of his lips. It was like a dream.

"I like you screaming my name," he confessed, kissing me again before checking me over, pressing his hand to my forehead and gently prodding some of the bites he put on me. "I need to get you that water. You look flushed."

"Just a few minutes more of this."

"Any more of this, and you'll fall asleep."

I had no idea why he made that sound like a bad thing when falling asleep in his bed with him giving me every drop of his attention sounded like heaven to me.

"My consort," he whispered as he stared at me. "Mine."

I wanted to say yes, all his, for however long he desired, but I could feel myself fading, my body sinking down into the bed. No more words were happening.

I passed out within seconds.

Chapter Nine

MY EYELIDS fluttered open, and the first thing I saw was Varic outside on the patio, pacing back and forth as he yelled on the phone.

He was dressed differently than before: a pair of tight-fitting olive pants and a white T-shirt that clung to his muscular chest and hard, ridged abs. Neither piece of clothing left anything to the imagination, making it easy to see the long, lean, chiseled lines of him and know how beautiful he was.

When I tried to sit up, everything went dark for a moment, and I blinked several times to try to clear the patches.

"You need to eat," Tiago said as he walked into the room with a tray of food. Hadrian followed right behind him, carrying another tray of drinks, a pitcher of ice water, orange juice, and what looked like iced tea and several bottles of Gatorade.

I tried again to make myself vertical and lost my balance. One of Hadrian's guys who had entered unnoticed behind him reached for my arm.

"No!" came the sharp command.

As I righted myself, I looked out at Varic, who was shaking his head. He didn't look mad, he wasn't glaring, but what he wanted was conveyed easily enough. No touchy.

"Who, then?" Tiago called over to him as he put the tray down in front of me and Hadrian deposited his on the nightstand to my right.

"You." Varic clipped the word. "And Hadrian. That's all."

Tiago nodded and waved Hadrian's men off, and Varic smiled at me, hesitating a moment before returning first to his conversation and then his walk, the latter taking him out of my line of vision.

I pulled the sheet higher up into my lap as Tiago removed the domed lids covering the food. It smelled amazing, the steak, the mounds of mashed potatoes, and the pile of steamed vegetables. I grabbed the utensils and immediately started in on the meat. Normally I would have cared that I was naked while everyone else was not, but I was too hungry to care.

"Yes, eat every scrap," Tiago ordered, and I returned my wandering attention to him, watching him pick up a small wicker trash can and walk to the chest of drawers, where he picked up several syringes. "You need more iron."

"What is all that?" I asked between bites.

"This is vitamin B12, B9, and B6." He dropped each syringe into the trash. "And this is vitamin A, and this one is the first dose of iron that you had this evening."

"And he gave those all to me?"

"Yes, he did, all in the arse, three on one cheek, two in the other."

I chuckled, going back to my steak. "I figured. He said he would."

He put down the trash can and took a seat at the foot of the mattress. "And you care not?"

I chewed and swallowed another piece of filet. "They're vitamins, and I think he was kinda worried that he depleted me, and most of all," I said with a shrug, "I trust him."

"Even after he shared you with others?" he asked, his face scrunching up,

I looked up at him, surprised. "What're you talking about?"

"Well, it is one matter to have an orgy with you as the buffet, but he should not have let them take so much blood," Tiago snapped, his tone full of judgment. He was clearly disappointed. "You should see your neck and back and sides. When I walked in here earlier tonight, I thought, for a moment, that you were dead."

"Would've died happy," I said, smiling between bites of fluffy, creamy, whipped potatoes. They were amazing.

"Is that right?"

I nodded.

"And what happened to you never coming over here, and how much you hated the courtiers and how the prince clearly had no real interest in you?"

I stopped eating, thinking about everything I'd said, how much I'd protested and how angry and humiliated I'd been. But it was hard, when you were happy, to dredge up the bad. "Yeah, I'm sorry about that, it was childish. I got my feelings hurt, and I thought something that wasn't true. I was just confused."

"Oh?"

I went back to hoovering down the steak, then the vegetables, and finally the potatoes again.

Hadrian poured me a tall glass of water and told me to hydrate. "If you do not drink some water, the next time the doctor comes by, he shall have no choice but to hook you up to an IV."

"That won't be necessary. I'll hydrate."

"Jason."

I looked over at Tiago.

"Tell me what you were confused about?"

I picked up the bowl of peach cobbler from the tray. "I thought he wasn't serious."

"You thought who was not serious? The prince?"

I nodded, smiling around the food in my mouth.

"That is disgusting. Define serious."

I took a bite, fell madly in love with a new favorite dessert, and then took the glass of milk Hadrian passed me. For a man whose job it was to protect and kill, he was on top of the beverage service.

"Jason?"

"Sorry," I obliged, laughing, swallowing quickly before giving him my attention. "After the night when we were interrupted at Benny's house, I thought that he was just some player. I thought he liked fucking pretty boys and that I could never mean anything to him."

"But now?"

"Tiago," Hadrian warned, bristling.

"*Sta 'zitto!*" Tiago barked, then turned back to me. "Jason?"

"He called me his mate, his consort."

I was finishing up the phenomenal peach pie and so didn't notice no one was talking until I replaced the plate on the tray, drank the milk, and wadded up the cloth napkin.

When I looked at Tiago, I saw he'd turned ashen.

"Oh shit, are you all right?"

He seemed to be having trouble breathing. He started to pant and pressed his hand to his heart. "I thought when we first got—I was certain once he met you, he would know what you were, and that of course when he saw how beautiful you are, that he would want you, but—" He looked quickly around the room and then up at Hadrian. "What happened!"

Hadrian didn't say a word, but the two men locked eyes, wildflower blue and brandy, and slowly Tiago rose, mouth open, utterly gobsmacked.

"You assumed," Hadrian finally said, indicating me with a wave of his hand. "But if you used your beast and not your eyes, you would know the truth."

"I am not a wolf like you!" Tiago shouted before pounding on Hadrian's chest with his fist.

Hadrian grabbed him tight, hands on his biceps, and shook him. Hard. "We are exactly the same! You insist because my family always served as guardians and yours as cup bearers that you are so much better than I, but that is a lie," he said raggedly, yanking him forward, looming over Tiago until there were only inches separating them. "We were all made the same way, all share the same lineage. It was only the path of our families that diverged."

Tiago gazed up at him with absolute naked want, and if Hadrian missed that, he was an idiot. It was very romantic—the gruff, strong man who needed a gentle presence in his life, and the spoiled snot who loved being protected and adored.

Hadrian asked for the room to be cleared, and his men complied at once. When the door closed behind the last one—Aziel, as it turned out—he bent closer until he and Tiago shared breath.

"You take me to your bed, allow no other there, have made certain I know that were I stupid enough to touch another, that you will *geld* me—and yet in public I am treated like your servant, and you rage against my ancestry that, again, is the same as yours."

Tiago squirmed in Hadrian's hold, but Hadrian just tightened his grip.

"I am done with this, do you understand?"

The way Tiago caught his breath was very telling.

"No, not with—" Hadrian growled in frustration. "—you. I shall never be done with you… but I am through being treated as though I am not your heart, because we both know that to be a lie."

"I—"

"Stop!"

Tiago pouted again, and based on Hadrian's sudden smile, he was as charmed by it as I was.

"We are all descendants of the same blood, no matter from what place in the hierarchy our lines descend, so stop this, tell the prince whom you love, and truly be his friend and shelter the man who is his chosen consort."

Hadrian loosened his arms, and Tiago turned to me before Hadrian wrapped him up again. He looked so very young as Hadrian kissed the top of his head and held him close. When Tiago nuzzled Hadrian's chest, I had to smile. He was a handful; I didn't envy Hadrian in the least.

"Forgive me," Tiago whispered, looking very contrite as he faced me. "I thought—I have never known Varic to bed a lover alone, and there was so much blood and so many bites... I... assumed."

I understood about assumptions. I'd made them about Varic myself. And had been so very wrong. "I understand."

"But even the little I know about you should have pointed me to the truth," he said, swallowing hard. "You do not seem to me the kind of man who would allow himself to be shared or would share his lover with others."

"No, I'm really not, though if you're into that, more power to you. It's just not me. I'm way too possessive."

"As am I," he confessed, flushing slightly, "as you heard."

"I did hear," I teased.

He nodded. "I should have thought about how upset you were over the courtiers and gleaned the truth from that."

It was true. Just the thought of Varic putting his mouth or hands or any part of him on anyone else made me queasy.

"And Hadrian has the right of it. Now that I have been standing here, not just looking at you but breathing you in, I can smell the change in your scent."

"Oh yeah?"

"You smell like him, like Varic."

"He marked you," Hadrian added, giving Tiago another squeeze, "in all ways as his, and you are the first and only."

I liked hearing that. Yes, it was fast, and yes, we were going to have to talk about a lot of things, but the fact that he was compelled to show others I belonged to him was a great big turn-on.

"I have never known him to be possessive of anyone," Tiago informed me, "until now."

"He has broken the law," Hadrian conceded, "and I worry for what that means."

I did too.

I was still mulling it over when Varic rushed into the room and over to the bed, taking a seat beside me and putting his hand on my head.

"What're you doing?"

"My temperature seems to have acclimated to yours for the moment, so I'm checking to see if you're running a fever, but you're not."

"Explain that again?"

"Has it truly?" Hadrian asked, awed, as he and Tiago came closer.

Varic put his right hand on the back of my neck and offered his left to Hadrian, who took it firmly in his and made a choked sound before he smiled.

"You are warm! How are you warm?"

"Jason's blood."

Tiago was next, taking Varic's hand in both of his. "But how is—the blood of a human cannot change ours. It is not... this is unprecedented."

"I know."

"Then how? Does this have anything to do with him being a matan?"

"I'd like to know this part too," I chimed in, smiling at him.

"Well, everyone," he began playfully, smiling at me, "a matan is two things. First he, or she, is a human vampyr, and second, that person is a conduit of power for those of the royal line."

Hadrian instantly grinned, and Tiago eyed me fearfully.

"A human vampyr," Hadrian repeated, disbelieving. "There is no such thing."

"There is. They're called matans, and here one sits."

"Such stories," Tiago hissed. "Tell us the truth."

"I am," Varic said irritably, glaring. "Jason is a human vampyr."

Tiago fell silent, and when Hadrian put a hand on his back, he didn't snarl at him as I'd seen him do just a bit ago.

Not that I was focusing all my energy on Tiago, because I was too involved in having a nervous breakdown.

A vampyr.

Me.

Just thinking it made no sense! There was no way. How could that even be possible? How did a regular person walk through their life not knowing something like that?

"How can I be a vampyr?" I said to Varic, which was impressive because I had to take several breaths so I didn't yell at him to talk faster, to explain my whole life in an instant.

He turned on the bed to face me and took my hands in his. "A matan is the offspring of a vampyr and a human."

"Yeah, but so is a made vampyr."

"There's a specific difference," he insisted. "A made vampyr is a vampyr as in they drink blood for nourishment, have the double canines, the extended lifespan, and all the other traits of my kind."

"Like the speed and the strength."

"Yes."

"And a matan is what?"

"Human," he said flatly. "A matan is a human."

"Meaning…."

"Meaning they eat and drink, have all the human frailties, can catch all the diseases that we cannot, and have a miniscule lifespan."

"Go on."

"Well, I've never met a matan until you, but there are records of vampyrs who bred with humans, and the recessive gene, not the dominant one, was what appeared in the offspring."

"So instead of a made vampyr coming from a human and a vampyr, instead a human was born."

"A matan. Yes."

"Why doesn't that happen more of the time?"

"It's a random, unpredictable mutation, but because the vampyr gene is so much stronger in a union of a vampyr and human, most of the time, you'll get a vampyr."

"But not every single time," I said, studying him, memorizing every detail of his face.

"No." He leaned in to kiss me. It was just a quick press of his mouth to mine, but I felt a pulse of arousal tumble through me and leave me flushed. Not that I was going to jump him, but the connection was there, powerful and living, between us. I did need to focus on his words, though, and not on the tornado of new feelings whipping around inside of me.

And speaking of his words….

"I have an off-topic question."

"Please."

"Tiago and Hadrian, both of them speak more properly than you. Like, there aren't any contractions, no *don't* or *I'm*. It's all *I am* and *the prince is* whatever, but never *the prince's*."

"And you want to know why I don't speak the same?"

"Yeah," I said, smiling because he could follow my drifting mind. That was nice. Already he could, and really, it warmed me all over. "And why doesn't Aziel sound the same as Hadrian?"

"For many, it depends on their age. Aziel, for instance, is a mere two hundred years old."

To be alive that long was just a drop in the bucket for Varic. Crazy.

"As I am the prince of my kind," he continued his explanation, "I therefore need to be able to communicate in many different languages, and I must also express myself using far more modern speech patterns. If I sound odd, I'll be perceived as such."

It was all very logical. "How many languages do you speak?"

"Only sixty at the moment."

The number was staggering. "What was the hardest?"

"Mandarin," he said with a chuckle. "But I've become quite fluent in it over the past three hundred years."

He was so casual about the passage of time. It had to be nothing to him. His life was endless, as far as he knew. I hoped mine would be a bit longer than usual just so I would have more of it to spend with him.

"So," I began, getting back on track with our earlier conversation, "you think that somewhere in my very human ancestral line, that there was a matan, a human vampyr, and that gene got passed down to me."

"I do, yes. It's the only thing that accounts for your power."

"Which is what, exactly?"

"That's what I was asking my parents about, and they—"

"Was that to whom you were speaking earlier?" Tiago asked, sounding interested.

"Yes."

"You had both of them on the phone?" Tiago questioned, his tone lowering, sounding both surprised and worried.

"Yes," Varic snapped.

"And they spoke to one another?" Hadrian asked tentatively. "Or just to you?"

"They haven't spoken to each other in twenty-three years," Varic retorted. "Did you expect that would change merely because I had a question?"

"No," Tiago conceded with a tip of his head. "But I do think them even talking to you at the same time is a crack in the ice."

"I agree," Hadrian chimed in. "There was a time your mother would have hung up the moment she heard the voice of the king on the line."

Varic grunted, and I couldn't tell if he agreed.

"What happened with them?" I asked.

He sighed deeply, let go of my hands, and rolled off the bed. "My father has a few courtesans, and—"

Tiago scoffed, and Hadrian started coughing.

Varic let out a long, annoyed sigh. "My father has *many* courtesans—as is his right," he emphasized, glaring at Tiago and Hadrian for a moment before turning back to me, "and my mother has her courtiers, the difference being that my mother doesn't sleep with hers. They're her retinue, her friends."

"So your mother's mad because he cheated on her?"

"No," Varic, Tiago, and Hadrian said at the same time.

"Then I don't get it."

"My mother's not mad. She's hurt because my father continues to father offspring with his courtesans."

"Your father is thousands of years old. How many children are we talking about?"

No one spoke, and I realized, as each one of them stood there, brows furrowed, heads tipped, Varic with his arms crossed, that they were counting.

"Are you kidding?" I awed.

Varic glanced over at Tiago. "Are there thirty now?"

"No," Tiago assured him, but he didn't sound all that convincing.

"Lady Geneva gave birth in July, and Lady Elaine in September," Hadrian said dryly. "The count is thirty-three, my prince."

Varic returned his attention to me. "Thirty-three."

"Holy shit," I breathed. "Your father has thirty-three children? His harem can populate a small town somewhere!"

Varic nodded. "It's true."

"I get why your mother would be pissed, though. She probably feels like she lost him."

"Perhaps."

"Is she worried that one of your father's other children could take your place in the line of succession?"

He shook his head. "No. I'm my father's only living child with his queen. No one can challenge me."

"Only *living*?" I repeated, because I'd heard his sadness.

"Yes."

"Did you have a brother or a sister?"

"A brother. Cassius," Varic answered softly. "He died in the Siege of Jerusalem during the First Crusade."

"I'm so sorry," I said softly, gesturing for him to come to me.

He met my gaze for a moment before climbing back onto the bed and tackling me down into the pillows. He pinned me under him, a heavy thigh between my legs and his face against the side of my neck.

"You have a soft heart to be the consort of a draugr," he said gruffly, kissing under my ear.

I wrapped my arms around him as I heard the door close. "Hadrian and Tiago bailed on us. I think the hugging makes them nervous."

"I think they know I just want to lie here with you," he said, nuzzling his face deeper into the crook of my neck.

I turned my head away from him, offering my throat, my blood, knowing this was what I was supposed to do, feeling it inside without question.

No one would believe me. They'd think I was crazy in lust, in thrall to this man, all hopped up on endorphins and drowning in what was new and urgent, but that wasn't how I felt. Everything was suddenly complete because of him, because of Varic, as if I'd been missing something all my life that was now in place and whole and living. It was strange and amazing at the same time, like a filter had been removed from my sight and I could see everything as it truly was.

"What are you doing?" he asked, the raspy purr sending a throb of arousal rolling through my frame, causing me to break out in goose bumps.

"I want to comfort you."

"You're holding me," he murmured, his breath warm on my skin. "I'm comforted."

"Please."

"You need to let the food and water and vitamins do their work. I can't have you weak, and I hardly ever drink blood anymore. Today was the first time in over a century that—"

I couldn't contain my choked gasp and turned my head to look at him.

"What's wrong?" he asked, worried, trying to lift off me so he could check me over, but I took his face in my hands, stilling his motion.

"You don't—you didn't drink from the courtiers?"

His brow furrowed as he held my gaze. "Of course not!" He sounded appalled. "I only drink from the dene, the nobility. A courtier's blood could never sustain me. Even a pureblood courtier's could not."

I was thrilled with this turn of events. He didn't drink from them; he only drank from me. I was special; I was his. I was above any courtier, any other vampyr on the planet because Varic Maedoc only took *my* blood. I was his mate, his consort, so I alone fed him. He could not have made me feel any more special if he tried.

"And now, of course, I will drink from no one but you, as you are my consort, my mate."

"Why?"

"Why?" he asked, and I heard the anger infuse his voice, the bristling reminding me this was a prince I was in bed with. He wasn't used to having anyone question him. I bet having me around would be a bit of an adjustment for him, and I was really looking forward to breaking him into the wonderful world of humanity. "Don't you want me to feed from you?"

Before he got himself all in a twist thinking I didn't plan on him drinking from me for the rest of my life, I put my hand on his cheek to soothe him. "Of course I do," I rushed out and saw him visibly calm, his shoulders relaxing, his body settling back over mine. "I just want to know how my blood will be able to nourish you."

"Oh, well, I claimed you," he explained, clearing his throat, having gone from righteous indignation back to calm in seconds. "I made you my own."

"How?"

"When I bit you and didn't drink, basically wounding you, your body automatically responded by changing so you could heal yourself, which, in turn, will sustain me when I drink."

"And that just happens?"

"There's more technical terms, I'm certain, like when a foreign agent attacks your blood, antibodies are created in response to fight what is perceived as an infection. That's what this is. It's not magic. It's simple biology."

"And this happens every time?"

"When a royal takes a mate, claims them, yes."

"Is that what happened when your father mated with your mother?"

He made a face. "Could we not speak of my parents mating?"

Even vampyrs apparently got grossed out thinking about their folks in bed. "You know what I mean."

"Yes, of course. He changed her blood to make her his own."

"And could that have happened if I was human?"

"You *are* human."

"I mean *all* human."

"No. I would have never attempted such a joining."

"But you did it because you knew I was a matan."

"I did it because I was driven to, and that pull, that need, would not have been present were you merely human."

I chuckled. "Merely human."

"Don't tease the prince of the vampyrs," he scolded.

"Oh yes, sir," I baited, smiling wide.

"It's fortunate I find you so beguiling."

I smiled and had to wonder if I was glowing. Just looking at him, talking to him, hearing his voice made me ridiculously, stupidly happy. I was falling so hard, so fast, and I was a smart guy. I knew great sex, the best sex, didn't equal love, but damn if it didn't feel like that. "You know, the claiming is amazing, if you think about it. That's all chemical, and it's like you left a fingerprint in my blood just for you."

"That's it exactly."

"So what if someone else were to drink from me?"

He shifted his weight, moving sideways enough so he could slip his hand under the sheet separating us, down over my flat belly and lower until he took hold of my cock that had been lazily thickening with his closeness. "You're my consort. *My. Consort.* My own. No vampyr in the world would ever presume to even touch you without my express permission. It would be—" He shivered like he was imagining his reaction if someone tried. "—forbidden," he finished with deadly intent.

It was a rush. I couldn't explain it, because it wasn't jealousy. It was more finite, more life and death. And he didn't say if I thought to feed another, because already he knew better. I couldn't even see beyond him; he was what the sun rose and set on. But if someone else decided they might want to taste the particular vintage I was—the draugr wasn't having it, and I could have crowed with how desired that made me feel. He was crazy possessive, but not in a way that scared me or gave me pause. He was perfect for me.

"It was a question," I whispered, lifting to kiss along the underside of his jaw. "I was just wondering if I could poison other vampyrs with my blood now or something."

"No." He quieted, stroking my length. He slid his thumb over the end. "In fact, the opposite is true. Your blood is changed now from what it was just hours ago.

It's thicker, richer, sweeter—reformed to sustain a royal."

"Oh." I teased him, pushing up into his fist, lifting my hips the little I could from the mattress with my thighs trapped under his granite weight. "So is it like crack now? Will all the other vampyrs wanna drink of me?"

He laughed, and I felt the low, sensual chuckle as much as I heard it. It reverberated through me, eliciting a decadent moan in response.

"Don't tease or I'll have you chained to my bed," he growled, and even though he was being playful, I heard the trace of threat in his voice.

"Like you'd have to chain me." I sighed, letting him hear my submission and be comforted. He was used to giving orders, used to telling, but I was different, and he'd realize that quickly. I was on board with what he wanted, ready, willing, and able. He didn't have to make demands; I'd already happily be wherever he wanted me. I wrapped my arms around his neck and drew him down to me.

"You're not—I took too much before, and now that your blood is just mine, made for me, if you offer and then change your—"

"I won't," I murmured, lifting for a kiss as he melted over me.

I opened for him, and he swept his tongue inside possessively, all his languor evaporating in a conflagration of touch as he mauled my mouth, sucking on my lips, nibbling before he broke the kiss and touched his teeth to the side of my neck. The bite and the first long draw made me gasp.

It felt so much better the second time. He wasn't just drinking from me, he was savoring, relishing, and

I felt the tremble in his muscular frame. The pull was different, hotter, slower, an undulating current he made dance in my veins racing through my entire body.

I held him tighter, wanting him to take more, but he licked over the bite instead. I opened my mouth to protest, but he reclaimed my mouth, letting me taste my own blood on his tongue.

"Jason," he gasped, sounding desperate, almost pleading as he broke the kiss so he could sit back on his haunches and reach under the pillow for the lube he'd stashed there.

"Let me help you," I urged, my voice at a dangerous timbre. I needed him almost savagely but moved deliberately so I didn't tear at his clothes.

He stilled, closing his eyes, breathing through his nose as I unhooked and unzipped him. Then I let my hands fall away, back beside the pillow, as his eyes, now all that gorgeous glittering onyx, popped open.

"They're beautiful when they're green," I told him as he roughly pulled out his long, thick, uncut cock and slathered it with lube from head to base. "But there's something really hot about the black."

"It scares many," he said, his voice gravelly, almost ominous, sending a thrill of anticipation sizzling over my skin.

"It makes me think about sex," I confessed hoarsely as he ripped away the sheet, and I lifted my knees, letting my feet drag across the mattress to rest on his muscular thighs.

"You make me think about sex," he said in return and settled a hand under my knee. He lifted my left leg, kissed my inner thigh, and then rested it on his shoulder as he curled forward, pressing the wide head of his cock against my tender opening.

"Varic," I rasped, trying to get him to move, to just fucking take me, squirming under him to get closer.

He wouldn't be rushed and sank slowly into my body. The sheer size of him caused a stretch and burn that ached and sent prickles of heat to my cock in rapid, unrelenting succession.

"Varic, please," I implored, my breathing rough, starting and stopping. I slipped my hands under the headboard to hold on. "I won't break. You won't hurt me."

But he wasn't listening, instead staying careful, concentrating, sweat beading on his forehead as he rode my body tenderly, drawing out each slow press inside and long retreat.

"Look at me."

He wouldn't.

"Varic!"

Black pools flicked to my face, and I reached up and cupped his cheek. He leaned into my palm, turned his head, and kissed it before again pressing his flesh back into mine.

"I like this side of you, this tender, loving man." I moaned as he filled me again, deep, buried to the hilt. My legs stayed over his shoulders as he rolled his hips, rocking inside of me. "But right this second, I think you're scared of hurting me, so you need to show me your beast."

He swallowed hard, never stopping, and I moved my hand from his cheek and slipped my thumb into his mouth and pressed it to his canine, scraped it over the razor-sharp end and quickly drew blood.

Instantly he was sucking, and I pulled my hand back and let it fall to my chest as I bared my throat for my lover.

He attacked, and I yelled in triumph, craving all that he was with nothing held back. If I couldn't feed his hunger, quench his thirst, sate him in every way he could possibly want or need, I would have to leave him. This was a vampyr prince in my arms, and to be his true consort, I had to be everything to him. His fangs locked in my throat. He thrust inside me, snapping his hips fast, ramming deep and hard as he took long pulls from my vein in an endless loop of ravening hunger. He was so powerful. It was the rutting that I craved, the pounding now delivered as he unleashed himself, combined with his trust that if I told him I wanted something, it *was* the truth. That was enough to make my body tighten around him.

"Varic," I moaned hoarsely, and he slid his fangs free, laved the wound, and then turned my head so we were eye to eye.

"You're going to be tempted at some point to think that my interest in you lies in what you are, and not who you are," he said, panting, his voice catching. "There may be others who attempt to instill in you fear due to my many conquests over the centuries, as though the past could ever matter more than the present, more than now."

If he only knew how much I agreed with that.

"And finally," he whispered, his eyelids fluttering for a moment as he slid his hand over my shoulder as leverage, bracing so he could jerk inside of me, slower now but just as deep, my dick trapped between us, rubbing against his abs. "Wait," he said, moving inside me, adjusting for the angle he wanted. He grabbed a pillow and shoved it under my ass so that when he pushed in again, it was a long, smooth stroke that pegged my gland and made me cry out his name.

"Oh yes," he crowed, slipping his hand over my forehead, pushing my hair back before he kissed me again, sucking on my tongue, and ground into me.

I came apart under him, his possession, his domination, all that I craved, almost too much to bear.

I slid my legs, anchored on his shoulders, down his arms to drape my knees over his elbows. He held me open and made me his.

I came hard, spurting over his chest, lost, broken into a million flying pieces. He'd woken me to the joys of pleasure and pain, longing and release, and being lost and then found. In that moment he was all there was.

Wrapping his arms under and around me, he broke the kiss to bury his face in the juncture of my neck and shoulder and howled against my skin as he came.

I was branded as his, inside and out.

His touch ignited an electrical tempest between us. It stole everything from me: my breath, my thoughts. And I was afraid I would lose my heart completely. Stupid because it was already his. When I was able to draw air back into my starved lungs, I let my head tilt, resting against his, thankful he'd held me close and given me shelter in the passionate storm we'd made together.

After long minutes he lifted his head, kissed me wet and sloppy, laughed softly into my hair, and lifted off me slowly and with infinite care. We were covered

in cum and sweat, sticky in places and slick in others.
The air was thick with moisture and sex. He surprised
me when he nuzzled the side of my neck before collapsing on top of me again, content, it seemed, to lie
right there.

"I must smell rank." I grinned, lifting my hand
and burying it in his sweaty hair, combing my fingers
through the long strands before tightening my hold for
a moment.

"You smell good, you taste good, you feel good."
He sighed and moved off me enough so he could rock
me gently to my side and spoon around me. "I have no
complaints."

This was the life right here, having Varic plastered to my back, not caring for a second about anything but skin on skin.

"I was trying to tell you something, but your body
distracted me."

"And what was that?" I drawled lazily.

"There will be those at court, and perhaps even
here, who will tell you that, were you not a matan, I
would not have claimed you as my consort, and their
words might make you doubt me, or, worse, yourself
and your feelings."

I remained quiet. I'd be a fool if I said that fear
could never haunt me. Was it *who* I was, or *what* I was
that gave me value?

"I need you to remember something very important if you ever hear any of that."

"Yes?"

"I didn't know what you looked like."

It took me a moment. "What are you talking
about?"

"When Tiago first told me about you, he said you were handsome—but nothing else, no description. He was far more interested in what you could possibly be."

"He did have a rough time back in Washington."

He grunted.

"I'm still lost."

"Friday night I asked for you to be brought to the Diallo house so I could talk to you and perhaps figure out what you were, and help you if I could."

"You have a good heart."

"At times, yes, at others, no, but I'll accept the compliment," he said, pressing his face to my nape, inhaling deeply.

"I can't possibly smell that good."

"You have no idea."

I had to concentrate on his words. The sound of him, rough and husky, sounding like sex and heat, made me shiver. "Finish what you were saying."

"Well, as I said, I asked for you to be brought to the house, and I was waiting for either Niko or Benny to escort you in, maybe even Hadrian or Tiago. But no one came, and I got tired of waiting and was going to return to the party to search for you, but I was distracted by the beautiful grounds of Benny's home."

"It is lovely."

"It is," he agreed. "I can barely wait to show you my many homes."

I smiled as he kissed my shoulder, his arms tightening around me, snuggling close.

"But yes, you came in, and I had no clue who you were."

"No, you didn't," I agreed, remembering.

"And yet after only moments of speaking and re-alizing, mistakenly, that you were not a vampyr, I still wanted to drink from you and have you in my bed."

"Which proves what?" I asked.

"That I had no idea you were you, Jason Thorpe, and could not guess you to be a matan. That call came the next day." He yawned softly. "So always remem-ber I wanted you first, before all else, as a man."

I locked the words away for safekeeping.

Chapter Ten

I HAD to go home, shower, and change. Varic was supposed to meet Benny Diallo and Niko Gann at Benny's club, the Tombs, over on Bourbon Street, but he didn't want to go without me, so instead he followed me home. And because Varic never traveled without protection, I had Tiago, Hadrian, and the rest of Hadrian's guards tromping up the narrow stairs to my apartment.

I unlocked the front door that led directly into the living room, entered, and Varic followed me.

"So it's kind of messy, but—what's going on?" I asked as soon as I noticed they hadn't followed.

Tiago cleared his throat. "We cannot enter until you invite us."

I turned to ask Varic a question, but he was gone, now in the kitchen. "Yeah, of course." I said to Tiago. "Come on in."

The others entered quickly. It was a lot of height and width in my small apartment where the men were concerned. All Varic's male dreki stood at over six feet and were built like defensive linemen, except for Hadrian, who had more of a swimmer's build. The women were more varied, one tall and lithe, another short and compact, and still another in between. What was the same across the board was that all of them looked like people you didn't want to mess with. Maybe it was the tailored black suits.

Walking into the kitchen, I found Varic striding back through the short hallway that led to the bathroom and farther on to my bedroom.

"These are the smallest living quarters I've ever been in," he remarked in awe.

I leaned on the counter and watched him walk through my apartment to the front door, turn, cross the living room again, then into the kitchen, passing me, and back down the hall again.

"What is he doing?" I asked Tiago.

"He has never been inside an apartment," he informed me.

"What do you mean?"

"I mean, yours is the first apartment he has ever visited," Tiago reiterated. "He is the prince of the noreia. His mother owns an island in Greece. He has his own wing in the royal villa in Valletta."

"And?"

"And," Tiago repeated, "this is modest for him."

"This is a very small space for him," Hadrian echoed, coughing. "For all of us."

I stared. "You're being serious?"

"I am sure he finds it quaint… and a bit claustrophobic," Tiago explained.

"You know," I called down the hall to Varic as he walked out of my bedroom, "there are some places in the world that have microapartments that are, like, a hundred and sixty square feet total. This would be a palace in many countries."

The look on his face was priceless. He was utterly dumbfounded.

"What? How big are your quarters in your home?"

"Your home would fit inside my closet."

That had to be an exaggeration, to tease me, so I walked over and took his hand in mine. "So you're saying you don't want to move in here with me?"

"No!" He sounded horrified. "I want you to move in with me."

I sucked in a breath. Playful had become serious fast.

"Did I scare you with that?" Varic asked. "Because from the look on your face, I'm going to say I did."

"No, I just want to hear what you're thinking."

"Normally," he began, taking my other hand as well and facing me, "as the prince's consort, you wouldn't have a choice where you would live. You would bide at a place of my choosing. But as you were not raised as a vampyr, you had no idea that your life was no longer your own before you allowed me to take your blood. Because of all of that, and because you identify as human, you have choices that no other member of the noreia does."

"So even though I'm your consort, you won't make me move to Malta."

"No, I won't."

"And if I don't go with you, who will you drink from?"

"I don't need to drink blood often, you know that. I told you how long I can go without feeding," he explained, squeezing my hand.

The last time before me was a century ago. It meant I could go the rest of my life without his fangs in me again. "But you claimed me and changed my blood," I reminded him, as if either of us had forgotten. "Don't you need it more now?"

"I drink from you because I want to, and for no other reason."

It sounded good, him wanting my blood. But him *needing* it would have been far more comforting. *Need* implied something he *had* to have. A want was controllable. I was like dessert. He could go without that.

Everything I thought I knew changed in that moment.

He wasn't bound to me for blood, and because I'd thought he was, because he'd made me his, a shiver of dread licked down my spine. "So you could just go back to Malta and not need to see me," I concluded, making sure he couldn't hear the crack in my voice as I came to terms with the size of the mess I was in.

"Yes," he said flatly. He eased his hand from mine and walked around me to stand at the kitchen sink. He looked out the small window there onto the street below.

I was in so much trouble. I'd fallen so far so fast, and just like that, I realized my heart didn't belong to me anymore. It was his. It was Varic's. I was already too far gone to walk away and could only hope to God he felt the same.

I heard the others leave the apartment then, quickly, closing the door behind them. It was considerate of them not to want to intrude.

And then I thought about us in bed.

I thought about how his eyes looked when he watched me, all soft and warm. I thought about how his voice sounded, all possessive and dark, when he said I belonged to him. Mostly I thought about how he held me and didn't let go.

This was not a man who wanted to fly away from me.

"Hey."

He didn't give me his attention, seemingly riveted by whatever he was looking at.

"I would love to see your home."

Slowly he turned to look at me, those dark green eyes filled with worry while he clenched his square jaw tight.

"I really would."

His exhale was slow, measured, as he turned to face me. "Earlier this evening you heard me yelling on the phone."

I nodded.

"As you know, I was speaking to my parents, and after my mother hung up, my father and I were talking, and at first, he was very angry."

"Oh?"

"He doesn't know how to feel."

"About what?" He tipped his head expectantly, like I should know. "About me?"

"Yes."

"How come?"

"Because he's thrilled that you're a matan… and horrified at the same time."

"Why?"

He crossed his arms, looking at me. "A matan, once mated, amplifies the power of the mate. You make me stronger in every way."

"Do I have to be with you for it to happen?"

He squinted. "No. You're not some sort of ring of power."

"You made a *Lord of the Rings* reference," I said playfully. "Nice."

"I haven't been living under a rock," he said, glaring.

"Stop, I'm teasing you," I said, leaning in to place soft kisses along his jaw. "Now tell me how you power up if I don't have to be there with you."

"Through the claiming and having your blood in me," he answered, slipping his hands up my chest, over my collarbone, and higher to each side of my neck. "I drink from you, your blood mixes with mine, matan and royal, and I'm changed, just as I changed you."

"And my power is what?" I asked, gazing into all that green as he held me, content, it seemed, to do so.

"There's a barrier you have in your home or anyplace else that is yours, which is where the mythos about a vampyr having to be invited in stems from."

"That's why the others couldn't just follow me in here just a few minutes ago."

"Yes."

"But you could."

"You're my mate," he said like it was obvious. "I can follow you anywhere."

I loved that he was so matter-of-fact and a little indignant with my questions, like *How are you missing something so basic?* It made my heart swell that he took us being together for granted, as though we were two sides of the same coin. I was the other half of him. It was an irrefutable fact. Our mating was innate, organic, and part of who he was. It was overwhelming to be faced with such absolute faith in something so utterly new. He didn't have the same questions I did about our bond because they never occurred to him. Not the part that was me, because clearly I'd given him a scare just a moment ago, but the part that was his understanding, his part of us, he wholeheartedly accepted. As the prince, he'd made his claim, and it was therefore indelible in his mind. I just needed to find the same bearings. I had to believe that I was as necessary to him as he'd become to me.

I needed to move the topic away from "us" so my brain wouldn't run down a rabbit hole of self-doubt. I couldn't fit him into any frame of reference for the rest of my life because I was in a fantastical place, a realm outside of everything I knew about the natural order of the world. "And getting others to talk to each other and not fight?" I threw out.

"That's a byproduct of the barrier. You don't want strife or pain around you, so no one will be allowed to harm themselves, or you, or anyone else in your presence," he answered, verifying something remarkable and surreal as though it were commonplace.

"I sound so cool, like a superhero."

He scowled. "Try and remain a bit more grounded. Your power only works on vampyrs; you're not the human whisperer."

I laughed. "Lookit you, being funny."

More scowling.

"Oh man, I am cool," I said, waggling my eyebrows.

"You're the exact opposite," he said, smiling as he chuckled, gesturing for me to join him.

When I stepped in close, he wrapped his arms around me and hugged me. And even though it was already one in a long line of many—he'd been hugging me all night—I gave him my weight and leaned, soaking up the feel of him, his warmth and his scent. I could be held like this forever.

Never in my life had a lover been all over me outside the bedroom. It was new and uncharted territory. I had missed out on cuddling, on being held. I'd gone into the service straight out of high school. There was sex for years, bent over in bathroom stalls, behind buildings, and in the back seats of cars. I was never on furlough long enough to meet anyone serious, and nothing was safe anywhere I was stationed. I'd never had a boyfriend, and I hadn't missed it, figuring that when I was ready, settled down, I'd meet someone.

It never happened until, out of the blue, I found not only the man of my dreams, but one who wasn't even supposed to exist.

My life no longer fell into parameters that fit other peoples' lives, but really, it never had. What was normal anymore, and who judged that? My life was about to become a wild, complicated ride, and I didn't care what it looked like from the outside, only how I felt on the inside.

"Tell me, your parents," I said as he let me go and leaned on the counter again. "How did you leave it with them?"

"My mother is elated that I have a consort, because she was worried about me not being grounded for so long."

"She sounds like a mom."

"You'll love her, and I'll be lucky if I get you back from her," he grumbled.

"And your father?"

"He too was worried about me not settling down," he said, and the affection he held for his mother drained out of his voice. "Which is hypocritical coming from him, don't you think? He thinks because he's married but lives with his many courtesans that he can lecture me about fidelity? It's ridiculous."

"He sounds like every other parent on the planet," I appeased him. "Great advice, but maybe not so much self-reflection."

"Yes," he muttered. "And also we had a disagreement about the law."

"Explain."

"He immediately amended the law regarding fomori to include only the prohibition of killing humans, not drinking from those who are unmated," he told me. "He said it was hypocritical to not do so immediately."

"And you said?"

"I said that there should be consequences for me as well."

"Death is a pretty severe consequence," I whispered, my heart in my throat.

"Not death," he assured me, touching my cheek. "It couldn't be, as you turned out to be a matan and my consort, which basically cancels out the punishment of death. You can't identify a matan unless blood is ingested."

"I see. That's tricky."

He nodded. "But I told him that I should still be punished."

"And he said?"

"That the draugr is *not* a commoner and will therefore not be punished like one." I suspected those were his father's *exact* words.

"He loves you."

"I got snobbery and class distinction from that, but you heard love?"

"Very clearly," I assured him.

His grunt told me he wasn't convinced.

"And so?" I prodded.

"He changed the law as he saw fit, and now it stands going forward. The new law was posted to the website and—"

"You have a website?"

"Of course there's a website," he snapped, scowling. "This is the twenty-first century, where we have the internet and mass email and everything else."

I couldn't stifle my laughter. He looked so indignant.

"Think of us as a huge conglomerate with millions of members."

"What if someone misses the update and kills someone over the offense of drinking?"

He shook his head. "There are far too many people with the app on their phones with updates. I can't imagine anyone missed it, even in some backwoods burb."

My brows lifted. "There's an *app*?"

Palms up, looking at me expectantly, the message clear as day in body and expression, the *Are you kidding?* more than implied. "Of course."

"Please tell me that it's called, like, *Fang News* or something," I said, egging him on, grinning like a crazy person. "Are you guys on Twitter too?"

"You can be utterly infuriating at times," he said irritably. "Are you aware of this fact?"

I waggled my eyebrows, and he threw up his hands in disgust.

I stopped chuckling and got serious. "So you said the ban on killing humans remains?"

"Of course. Always."

I exhaled sharply. "Your father's amazing."

He shook his head. "He's the king of the noreia and can do as he sees fit. And though it helps if he also has the backing of the council, keeping everyone happy, he doesn't need them to enact new law."

"Pretend I'm not a vampyr, so I don't know anything."

"You're such a smartass," he told me. "You should have warned me about that up front."

"You should have asked Tiago. He knew."

He crossed his arms, scowling at me, which I found terribly endearing. Yes, I asked more questions than anyone else in his life, and he answered for no other reason than he liked me.

I couldn't stifle my chuckle. "Just go on about the council, because you haven't mentioned them before. I thought your father was just this all-powerful king."

"He is, but all things go more smoothly if, before he does something, he consults my mother and the council and everyone gets to weigh in."

"So if he wanted to make a law, then he'd convene this council, invite your mother, and everybody would talk about it first."

"Yes."

"And what do you do?"

"I make sure all the laws are followed."

"How do you police everyone?"

"Laws are handled by individual leaders of individual cities across the world. I travel, I see my subjects, and I investigate defilers of the law."

"Basically your mother and father and the council, they make the laws and you enforce them."

"Yes. Unless I disagree with them. At which point the noble families send one person who has the proxy for that family, and we vote again."

"How many times has that happened?"

"Never."

"And who's on the council?"

"Five members selected by each of us—my father, my mother, and me—to oversee the laws and the administration of them, either in changes to the law or hearing cases where members of the noreia are to be punished, exiled, or put to death."

"That seems pretty fair."

"It's tedious and time consuming, but it works."

"I interrupted before you could finish, so tell me what else was amended in the law."

"It now states that every human, in every case of blood drinking, must give explicit permission before a vampyr may drink from them."

"I think that's perfect."

He grunted.

"I have to tell you, I know you have issues with your old man, but I like the way he does things. He's quick and decisive."

"And a cheat."

"How so?" I asked.

"He backdated the law to yesterday."

It was too good.

"Stop laughing."

"He's awesome. He didn't want you to get in trouble, so he made it so you wouldn't. I think that's great looking out."

"You don't see what a poor precedent this sets? That any law can be treated with so much disrespect? That he can change something so cavalierly and indiscriminately on a whim without the full support of the council?"

"I suspect that normally he doesn't do that, right?"

He was quiet, which told me I was correct.

"I bet he usually gives things a lot of thought and does accept input from your mother and the council, but this time was different, and really had to be because you were involved."

"That doesn't make it right."

"I love that you're arguing about something that benefits you."

"Which is my point."

"But the amendment to the law, was it a whim like you said, or was it a long time coming?" I asked. "Because I suspect that a lot of people wanted to see that law ratified. It's like I told Cooke a while back—the king should not be able to tell his people who to love, and loving a vampyr requires blood."

"Jason—"

"I want you to feed on me when we're in bed. I do. I'm addicted to it already."

"Are you?" he husked, eyes riveted on me.

"I am. And if I am after just a few hours, people who have been together for years probably can't separate the bloodletting from the sex. So… I think your father might have made a choice based on you, but I'll bet you there are thousands of requests cluttering up his inbox and his secretary's desk."

He grunted. "Perhaps."

"But the fact that he acted, that fast, to protect you—I think I love him."

"He wields his power—and always has—like a sword and swings it at whatever he pleases, whenever he pleases."

It sounded like an old rehearsed line, as though he'd had the discussion about his father with someone else often. "Your brother and you, you guys used to have these conversations about him, didn't you?"

His gaze met mine. "How did you know?"

"Because you're the solid one, the steady one, second born all the way," I told him. "I bet Cassius was more like your father. He did what he wanted, when he wanted."

"Yes."

"You miss him terribly."

Quick nod.

I stepped into his space, slid my hand around the back of his neck, coaxed his head down onto my shoulder, and held him there, my fingers buried in his hair.

"Much too soft a heart to be the prince's consort," Varic murmured and lifted his head to kiss me deeply.

I melted against him, and he turned and shoved me up against the kitchen wall, jostling pictures. He slipped his hands inside the cardigan he'd given me and under my T-shirt. I wrapped my arms around his neck and held him close, ravaging his mouth, wanting him closer, plastered against me.

He cupped my ass with one hand and squeezed, and I shivered under the domination and possessiveness and how ready my body was to take him in again.

When he broke the kiss seconds later and pulled free, backpedaling to the middle of the room, standing there, panting, and staring at me warily, I was surprised.

"What's wrong?"

"Nothing," he whispered hoarsely. "I just think I should go to the club alone."

It was an out-of-the-blue change that shouldn't have hurt—we weren't attached at the hip, after all—but it felt like a knife in the chest regardless. "Sure," I agreed instead of questioning him, because it was business anyway. I didn't need to go, would have just been sitting there quietly, I was certain, so it was fine.

"You should rest, regain your strength."

I didn't have to be told to take care of myself. I'd been doing it for years.

He swallowed hard and looked unsure, conflicted about whatever was going on in his head before he took a step toward me, stopped, swallowed again, took a breath, and then pivoted and was gone, out of my apartment without a backward glance.

It was surprising that he'd just left, like he was trying to sever the connection between us with the action, but perhaps it was that he had to be in prince mode—leader mode—before he went to see Benny and Niko, and so had to leave me behind. We'd been together a whole minute and a half. I couldn't expect him to know how to compartmentalize his feelings that quickly as well as be able to convey them to me.

Still, it hurt that he walked out. After the intensity that had marked our time together, I was a bit lost.

I was surprised when the door reopened to reveal Tiago and Aziel.

"Hey," I said, forcing a smile.

They walked in. Aziel moved quickly past me to stand where Varic had, at the window in the kitchen, looking down at the street. Tiago gestured for me to follow him into the living room.

"Do not read a lot into him leaving."

"No, of course not. He's a busy man. He can't hang out in bed with me all day just because I haven't been laid in a while." It was nonchalant and crude, but I hardly cared. I'd been caught up in the eye of the tornado that was Varic, and when he left, I was plunged into the actual storm of figuring out how I really fit into his life. It was a wake-up call for me. The romance bubble had popped, leaving me with the reality of the situation.

Tiago coughed softly, taking hold of my bicep. "As strange as this is for you, think about what it must be like for him."

"I'm not following."

"Your space, this apartment, represents a place you could come to leave him. He hates it. Would, in fact, I am sure, love to burn it down."

"What're you—"

"Back in the day, he could have just taken you, kept you, ensconced you in his home in Valletta, confined you to the castle. And that would be your life. He would have you at his beck and call, and if he wanted you with him, you would travel, and if not, you would remain behind. There would be no choices for you."

"It's a bit medieval," I asserted.

"It is the way of things down through the ages. But now he has finally found his consort, and you have your own home, your own life, he has to some-how fit his life around yours and fit you into his."

"And he's scared," I surmised.

"I think terrified."

"It should not be his right," Aziel muttered from the kitchen.

I was going to say something, but Tiago lifted his hand to stop me and turned to Aziel.

"Pardon?" Tiago asked, his voice hard and cold like I'd never heard it before. "Should not be whose right?"

Aziel turned to look at Tiago. "This man has been the prince's consort for mere hours, and already I see our dreaded draugr being led around like a lovesick schoolboy. He's as weak as his father."

I bristled. "Love doesn't make you weak," I argued even though it wasn't love yet, but I couldn't think of a better word to use. What could I say? Lust didn't make you weak? Extreme like? "Love focuses you because once one part of your life is set, you can give your attention to the rest."

"You're wrong," he argued, and I heard the anger in his voice.

"The prince is strong, you know this." Tiago gestured for me to move, to go to the door, to run.

Aziel huffed and rounded on Tiago and me, and it was only then I saw he had his phone in his hand.

"Who did you call?" Tiago wanted to know.

"This is exactly how Rhyton said things would go if the prince saw this man again after the first time," Aziel railed. "He said the prince was acting strange after their initial meeting. He said he thought perhaps he would make him his consort, and that as soon as he did, he'd be weak."

"Rhyton said," Tiago repeated even as he flicked his gaze around the room, possibly looking for other ways out.

He wasn't worried about himself, I knew that. He was a warrior first and had boasted many times of his fighting prowess. It was me he was concerned about... and how to get me safely out of the line of fire.

"He told me to stay close to you, Jason, because there would be a time when the prince wasn't look-ing—and that would be the time to act."

Tiago's laughter surprised me. It was loud, belit-tling, and scornful. "You are listening to a courtier," he mocked. "Are you mad?"

The steps outside the door were too old, too creaky; there was no way to climb them without mak-ing any sound, no matter how light on your feet you were. The men clomping up them now weren't wor-ried about alerting us to their presence.

When the door swung open, I turned and saw the platinum-haired courtier who'd propositioned Varic at Benny's mansion, the vampyr whose presence pushed me to run. He was just as stunning as when he accost-ed me at Garrett's club on Saturday, but this time he held a long, curved dagger in his right hand. The two men behind him were not as beautiful, but what they lacked in appearance they made up for in muscle.

"The king changed the law today for the prince, just as you said he would," Aziel advised. "Everything you said was true, Rhyton."

"I told you," Rhyton said smugly, shifting his weight toward the doorway. "It's only a matter of time before this one makes a slave of your prince."

"I won't have it," Aziel insisted, his eyes flat, dead. "You saved the prince with your actions, Jason Thorpe, so I will make this quick."

"What will you make quick?" Tiago demanded, stepping in front of me, blocking Aziel.

"His death!" Aziel barked. "The prince will be in agony, but I'll have killed those that committed the crime against his beloved."

"And who will you blame?"

"Made vampyrs, of course," Aziel said dismissively. "They're animals. They've killed many."

"As have we. We have killed so very many of them," Tiago told him, gesturing at Rhyton, who was now looking at the frame of the door, as were the others with him, uncertainty washing over their features.

"What dark magic is this?" Rhyton asked Aziel. "Why can't I cross into this room?"

Tiago exhaled as he turned to Aziel, at the same time pulling gloves from each pocket of his suit jacket. They looked like driving gloves, but when he put them on, I saw a metal claw at the tip of each finger.

Aziel scoffed at Tiago's preparation and then looked at me. "You will give them permission, or I will gut this whelp where he stands."

I jolted, reaching out to put a hand on Tiago's shoulder, but he didn't turn to look at me, instead shook his head slightly.

"It is always the same," Tiago said, smiling, stepping sideways, then crouching down, looking like a panther ready to take on a bull as Aziel advanced on him. "Whenever there is change, there are always small-minded fanatics goaded on by those with their own agenda."

Meaning, of course, that Rhyton had worked his charms and rhetoric on the weaker mind that was Aziel's.

"You have no idea what you're talking about," Aziel growled.

Tiago's grin faded. "But I do, and this is sad because I thought you were good and loyal, and I was so very wrong."

"My loyalty is to the prince!" he roared and rushed Tiago.

I kept the baseball bat Ode had given me for my birthday in August in the antique umbrella stand that was well within reach. I shifted to my right, grabbed it, shoved Tiago sideways, and swung.

I'd surprised him—it was the only way I'd managed to knock him off balance.

Aziel grabbed the bat and smiled, as did I before I kicked him in the side of the knee.

"Fuck!" he roared as I yanked the bat free and cracked him on the ear as hard as I could.

"I'll kill you!" he screamed.

I always got that threat after that particular maneuver when I executed the same in the past. You just had to give a guy something to look at first, to block while you used your legs.

He dropped to his good knee, clutching the other, and once he was down, I hit him again in the face, and he went out like a light.

"Jason!"

Turning from the crumpled man, I saw Tiago standing there, fuming.

"What?" I gasped, pulling in air, not because I was winded but because my adrenaline was pumping. "Are you hurt?"

"How could I have been—you could have been killed!" he screeched.

I made a face. "You have lost your mind if you think I'd let you fight my battles for me."

A small statue of Anubis exploded beside Tiago—Rhyton had a gun. Apparently a Glock was not impressed by my barrier.

I tackled Tiago and drove him onto the thick turquoise-and-brown area rug behind my couch and stayed still as he shot at us some more.

Thankfully he was not a good shot, but Tiago kept trying to get me off him—and could have easily—but I was wrapped around him so tight the only way to get me off was to hurt me in the process.

"Jason, move!" he yelled. "I need to subdue Rhyton!"

"Shut up and stay where you are," I warned, pressing him to the floor.

"I will kill you!" Rhyton shrieked. "How dare you put your filthy hands on my prince! He should have nothing to do with something as vile as you!"

"He made me his consort," I yelled. "Not you. Me!"

"When you're dead, everything will go back to the way it was!"

He was so deluded he had no idea that his life was over once I let Tiago up off the floor. The prince's rajan would tear Rhyton's throat out, of that I had no doubt.

"Things will never be the same," I thundered. "And you'll never have him again, not ever."

His scream was loud, pained, and unhinged as he discharged the clip until all he had was empty clicks of the trigger.

I scrambled off Tiago, and he flew across the room toward Rhyton. It happened so fast I could barely follow it, and then they were all gone: the courtier, his goons, and Tiago, as though they'd never been there.

I checked outside and glimpsed Tiago giving chase in the darkness across the rooftops, the men leaping in high arcs, not truly running. Spinning around, I charged over to Aziel, grabbed the phone he'd dropped, used his thumb to unlock it, and scrolled through his contacts until I found Hadrian's number.

It rang three times. His greeting, when he came on the line, sounded harsh. The clipped sound of his voice was a night-and-day difference from how he sounded with me. He sounded nicer when he and I talked and all business when he thought Aziel was calling.

"Hadrian," I said quickly.

"Jason?" he replied. I heard the concern instantly. "Why are you on this phone?"

"Aziel attacked me and Tiago, and that courtier, the blond one, Rhyton, he was here, and he tried to shoot us," I recounted after taking a breath. "Tiago went after them, but there's four of them and just one of him, so you gotta save him."

"Tell the prince there has been an attack!" he shouted at someone, clearly not me. "Get him in the car!"

"Hadrian—"

"I cannot—do you understand that I cannot leave Varic alone, especially now that I have no idea whom to trust!"

His voice fractured, and I understood because I'd faced the same kind of decision during an attack. And though I'd never had to make the choice between love and sworn duty, I'd had to make the one between saving one friend or many others. I knew he had to be breaking inside because leaving Varic was not an option, but neither was abandoning Tiago to his fate.

"There have to be others," I urged, "at least one person you have faith in."

Mere seconds ticked by, but it felt like an eternity.

"Eris," Hadrian yelled, "Duro!"

I didn't remember meeting them, but if he was calling for them now, of all moments, needing them to save his heart, then he had to be sure of them.

"Return to the apartment and chase the scent of the rajan from there!"

I wanted Hadrian to have backup. I was worried about him. I knew he was a badass, but I wasn't sure what the limit of his power was.

"You—" Hadrian huffed a shaky breath. "Was Tiago hurt?"

"Not yet, but tell them to hurry," I implored, not ready to lose Tiago when I just got him back in my life. I was probably scared for no reason, because again, you didn't get to be the rajan if you weren't deadly, but still….

"They are already gone."

Vampyr speed was really something.

"I will inform my prince and have you—"

"Don't worry about me," I impelled, needing him to listen. "Just make sure Varic's safe, and then get to Tiago yourself. He's gonna need you."

"Are you safe there? Is Aziel—"

"He's out, so send whoever here and get him."

"We will go to your home and—"

"Save Tiago!" I yelled. "For fuck's sake, Hadrian, he's the love of your fuckin' long-ass life, isn't he? Stop screwing around and go save your man!"

He hung up on me, which I approved of. It didn't escape my notice, as I bolted to my bedroom to grab clothes, not knowing how long I might need to be out of my apartment, that I didn't have Varic's number to call him. My main concern at the moment was getting out of my place. I didn't want to be there when Aziel woke up to Hadrian's wrath.

Chapter Eleven

THE NIGHT was darker than usual because of
the thunderclouds, and even though rain wasn't coming down anymore, the sidewalks were wet from earlier. Rain on concrete had a smell all its own, not quite
earthy, more like a graveyard scent of stone and de-
caying leaves.

I felt strange, unmoored... caught between a
maybe and something solid.

I couldn't get Varic's choice out of my head.

He made a decision to leave, to walk out on his
own, and yes, space was a good thing, a needed thing,
but so soon after serious, forever words were spoken?
I couldn't reconcile it all in my mind—or in my heart.

I had gotten ahead of myself, wrapped up in something too new too fast. It was actually good he'd taken
a time-out; I needed a moment to myself to breathe.

I stood at the river and looked out over the water, and when gentle drops became a deluge, I darted under an awning and huddled there with a few homeless guys.

Pulling what I had on me out of my back pocket, I offered them the fifteen dollars, got sincere thanks, and then moved on, walking toward Canal Street alongside the aquarium. There weren't many people out in the rain, but when I crossed the street, some lingered in the doorways of clubs, cigar stores, and the ever-present New Orleans souvenir spots.

My phone rang as I walked toward Royal Street. I sat down on a bench outside a closed yogurt store, the rain now barely a mist, and checked the display. The caller ID read Unknown. I was suddenly exhausted, and it didn't even matter.

"Hello?"

"Jason." Varic said my name gruffly.

"Is Tiago all right?"

"Jason, where—"

"Is Tiago all right?" I asked again, insistent, refusing to move beyond that question.

"Yes."

I took a breath. "Oh thank God."

"Jason, where—"

"What about Rhyton?"

He took a sharp breath. "Rhyton is no longer."

That answered that, I didn't need to know the details. "And Aziel?"

"Aziel is gone as well. It seems that Rhyton was poisoning his mind against me for quite some time."

"I'm sorry."

"So am I," he said softly. "I consider the dreki not just my personal guard, but part of my family as well. It hurts to know I was shortsighted."

"At least you always have Tiago and Hadrian."

"Yes. It's a blessing," he replied, tone wooden. "Now where are you?"

"Is Aziel out of my place?"

"He is. I asked Niko to arrange to have people there to dig the bullets out of your walls and clean up," he explained tightly. "I'm so sorry that a past dalliance of mine has infringed on your life in such a way."

"You mean you're sorry one of your fuck buddies tried to kill me," I fired at him, angry, the heat in my words obvious.

"Yes." His reply was quiet, calm, gentle. Everything my words were not.

It struck me that I was being an ass. I blamed him because he'd left me alone and I was attacked. It wasn't fair to him. It wasn't right, and so I took a breath.

"Jason?"

I cleared my throat. "I have a question, if that's all right."

"Please. Ask."

"What happens with the courtiers? How do they come to be at your father's court?"

If he thought the inquiry strange, he didn't voice it. "There are celebrations during the year, one a season, and there's feasting and balls, and everyone is allowed onto the grounds of the castle to meet my father and me."

"Not your mother?"

"She hasn't attended in years."

"Because of your father's courtesans?"

"Yes, but could we talk about where—"

"You said I could ask a question, and this is still the same one," I reminded him firmly. There were answers I wanted, and I refused to be shortchanged. I kept having to pick up pieces of information like bread crumbs in a forest, and instead of that, I wanted a full explanation all at one time.

"You're right, I'm sorry. Please continue."

"I want to know how it all works. What happens after they come to one of the parties at the castle? I'm just trying to get an idea of why you don't just date people. Why courtiers and not just one guy after another after another?"

"Why not a serial dater?"

"Yes."

"Because there's a tradition," he informed me, sighing, being patient with my query. "Back when my father was a prince, all the men and women of a certain age would be presented at court. If any one of them caught the eye of him, or his father, or any member of the nobility, then that individual would be asked if they wanted to remain at court, and if so, then the court took over the entirety of their care."

"Food, clothes, everything?"

"Yes."

"And while they were a courtier, what was expected?"

"Basically what you're thinking," he told me, his voice gaining a slight edge as though he was ready to be done. "Courtiers are sex partners—unless you serve in my mother's court—travel companions, basically entertainment for whomever they serve."

"And what rights, if any, do they have?"

"There are contracts signed that protect both parties," he said, brusque. "It's like a prenuptial agreement where everything is spelled out. The individual they serve provides food and clothing and an allowance for whatever the courtier wants or needs."

"What about if the courtier wants to leave, or you get bored?"

He huffed, a quick, sharp breath that told me he was done talking about the customs of his father's court. "There is normally a generous cash settlement when the courtier leaves, and, upon occasion, property granted."

"Have you had many courtiers?"

"Yes," he answered flatly. "But never a courtesan, as I have no children."

"Then a courtesan is a courtier who has children?"

"That's correct."

Silence stretched between us.

"Thank you for explaining," I said honestly, because I'd needed to know. I wanted to try to understand Rhyton's thinking, what had provoked him, but hearing how much of a nonromantic, almost business deal the whole courtier agreement was, I had no fresh insight into his motivation. "I thought if I understood how an individual became a courtier that it would help me figure something out about what happened."

"It won't," he assured me with steel-hard certainty. I could hear the conviction in his voice. "None of what occurred makes any sense."

"You never got that possessiveness from him before?"

"Absolutely not."

"Well, I thought maybe courtiers were people who were groomed to marry—"

"No," he said, clipping the word. "A courtier has no delusions of becoming a queen, a princess, or a consort. That's never a station they can aspire to."

"Why not?" I asked gently, because even though he was irritated, he was still talking to me, we were having a discussion, and I appreciated that fact. I was trying to understand, and he was taking the time to explain. It boded well for us, for our continued communication. "Can't a prince fall in love with a courtier?" I sighed deeply, content just hearing his voice. "What if I had come to your court as a courtier?"

He didn't answer; he just made a sound, a sumptuous, carnal, decadent sound like he was sitting in bed stroking himself, thinking of me. There was no chance of me stifling the answering moan he dragged out of my chest.

"Where are you?"

"Not far from my place," I said, smiling into the phone. "I like hearing your voice."

"I am quite fond of yours as well."

"Tell me why you left," I asked as I stood up and started walking home, wanting to hear the explanation but no longer hurt that he'd gone. Whatever was going on in his head felt as though it had more to do with him than me, because he wanted me, there was no doubt in my mind about that.

"I'm sorry I left," he said, dark and low. "But in my defense, I've never felt like this, and I've been alive a very long time."

I was walking, beaming like an idiot, probably looking stoned to the people I passed, blissed-out happy with him confessing he was as big a mess as I was.

"There I was, standing in your home, looking around at all your things, at your life, and all I wanted to do was have you pack it all up so it could be shipped home with me."

I stayed quiet, listening, not wanting to do anything that might make him stop sharing what was in his heart.

"I don't want you to have anything that isn't shared with me. I don't want you to have anything alone, and I realized how crazy that sounded in my head, and I could barely breathe."

But he had kick-started my heart just fine.

"It was overwhelming," he croaked, a catch in his voice, a hitch in his tone telling he was having trouble speaking. "I've never—I shouldn't have left, but I felt like I was going to suffocate."

"Wait," I said, because that word, suffocate, gave me pause. "If I'm making you feel like you can't breathe, then—"

"No," he snapped. "It's just that when I came to the city a few days ago, I had no idea that my life could change so thoroughly so very quickly."

Neither did I. "It's fast," I said because it was true. Taking some time apart to think and work through what we were both feeling, without the lure of sex, was probably a really good idea.

"It certainly is," he agreed, breaking into my thoughts as I heard the deep, contented sigh. "But in the very best way. No question about that."

"You know," I broached gently, passing by the Hotel Monteleone on Royal, headed for home, then stepping off the curb to let a family stay together before returning to the sidewalk, "maybe you had a good idea."

"And what is that?"

"Space," I murmured, not sure how I felt at the moment. I wasn't sad, and I wasn't worried about the two of us. It was important to process "us" in context of "we." As in we as individuals. Like how did I fit into his life, how did he fit into mine?

"I don't want to be apart! I want you to come back to the penthouse and sleep with me."

I smiled. Varic was so passionate about his life, about me, about everything, and I found it exhilarating. "But you have business," I prodded. "Remember?"

"I already spoke to Benny and Niko, and while I feel that Niko and I clearly spoke the same language, I think Benny has serious reservations about a truce between the classes."

"I can't say. I don't think he likes me."

"Perhaps he feels that your presence challenges the status quo," Varic offered by way of explanation. "Before you showed up, I suspect that things had been going on a certain way here in the Quarter for quite a long time."

"But I don't think anybody wants to fight," I said. It only made sense. "Why would anyone want things how they were? It wasn't safe. What am I missing?"

"The fact that I want to see you," he said flatly.

"No," I said quickly. "Not about us, about—"

"I know," he retorted, not angry but sharp. "But I don't want to talk about the vampyrs of the Quarter… you are my primary—I just want to see you."

"I do too, but is that the smart thing?" I need-ed time to think and get my head on straight, and I was fairly certain he did as well. "Maybe earlier, you needing to leave wasn't just about you feeling smothered—"

"Suffocated," he corrected me.

I chuckled at his wording, not at him. "Oh, that's so much better."

"Jason—"

"I'm not trying to think for you—I have no right—but what I am suggesting is that we could both do with time to process everything that's happened."

"We just had sex, Jason," he quipped. "What's there to have to delve deeply into?"

I stopped walking. It was like he'd reached through the phone and slapped me. Because yes, we'd had a lot of sex, but I'd never thought for a moment that was all it was, even in the moment, even if we consummated nothing. I couldn't separate my heart from my body; it was how I was made.

"That's not—you know that's not what I—"

"*I* need time alone, then," I croaked out, stress-ing the word, feeling gutted. "Just me. It's how I am. Something happens, and I roll it around in my brain, so I'm gonna do that, and I'll see you tomorrow."

"It already is tomorrow."

I could see on my phone it was after one. "Well, then, I'll call you now that I have your number."

He was quiet for a moment. "How did we go from talking to this?"

"We're fine. Everything's fine," I said. It was true, even if I felt off-center at the moment. "Unless you're not, and if so, tell me."

"No," he whispered, voice hoarse. "But please go home. Everyone is gone. Don't walk the streets like a ghost, thinking I'm haunting your place, because I wouldn't do that."

"Okay," I agreed. "Thank you. I'll talk to you later."

He didn't call back after I hung up.

EVERYTHING WAS the same when I got home. In fact, it was a little cleaner, and someone had opened the windows to air the place out. Between the jasmine and the rain, I could feel myself settle and calm. After I took a long, cool shower, I felt even better, and as I stood on the tiny balcony off my bedroom, drinking a bottle of water, I lifted my face into the breeze and breathed.

The sound of footsteps in the gravel below me drew my attention, and Varic appeared on the other side of the small alley, looking up at me. He stood half-in and half-out of the shadows, and that combined with the curtain billowing beside me gave the whole scene a dreamlike quality that wasn't lost on me, even though my first instinct was not that I was happy to see him.

"You specifically said you wouldn't be here," I said softly since it was after two in the morning, and I was outside and I had neighbors.

"I know," he answered, moving closer so I could look straight down at him. "And now you think I'm not a man of my word."

"Well, you are, in fact, not doing what you said," I pointed out, not sure how I was feeling at the moment, because half of me was thrilled that he couldn't leave me alone, and the other half did think I needed some time away from him, and he was infringing on that. I was torn right down the middle. "Why aren't you back at the penthouse?"

"Because the idea of you being here and me being there when we could be together instead was driving me mad," he confessed, hands in his pockets as he stared up at me. "Could I please come up and speak with you?"

My heart leapt at the suggestion, which basically informed my brain the time away from him I thought I needed was crap. What I wanted was to talk to him. "You can't tell me one thing and do another," I said, needing that clear between us. "If I explain that I need something and you agree to it, I better get it, or you really aren't a man of your word."

"I am, though," he insisted. "I don't threaten idly, and if I make a promise, I follow through. That's simply not what happened in this instance."

I tried not to smile, but he was very charming while trying to explain himself, and both of those things combined cracked open my resolve. "Is that right?"

"Yes," he said gruffly, his smoky growl intoxicating to me. "Because I realized, after I told you that I wouldn't be here, that following through on that action was completely illogical. Therefore, as you can see, I've corrected the error, and here I am."

"And what was the error?"

"Letting you think that anything we've done together hasn't been the highlight of my very long life."

That annihilated me. He was absolutely all I wanted.

"Earlier, for a split second, I was momentarily overwhelmed, as I've already stated. But you can't expect me to stay away from you now—that's insane."

Yes. Yes, it was.

"And I know what you must be thinking," he insisted from directly under my small balcony. "But really, Jason, it's the first mistake of millions. I'm not perfect, just really old."

A laugh tore out of me. He said it so deadpan, without a trace of self-consciousness. Between his humor and his sincerity, I was putty in Varic's hand. That was not to be forgotten. "Come up and talk to me," I said, turning away, heading toward the front door to unlock it for him.

The movement behind me had me checking, and there he was, on the balcony where I'd been seconds before.

"Holy shit," I said, awed.

His sinful grin, with the playfully arched eyebrow thrown in for good measure, made me sigh like the lovesick dork I was. "That's a neat trick."

"You liked that?" he teased as he brushed the curtain away and crossed into the room. "Did it make you hot?"

I nodded, my eyes glued to him as he took off his jacket and draped it over the large wingback chair close to my bed.

"You noticed I was quiet and didn't wake your neighbors."

"It was very considerate of you," I said, putting the water bottle down on the nightstand. "So where's Hadrian and the rest of your guards?" I'd been wondering about that since I first saw him. Had he snuck away, and if so, how much trouble was he in when they found out?

"At times, concessions must be made, as there are even greater concerns than my safety."

"Oh yeah? Like what?"

"Like you," he whispered before he rushed over and cupped my cheek with one hand as he slipped the other over my hip. "I had a moment of trepidation because this—us—has never happened to me before," he said flatly, staring into my eyes. "Thank you for not sending me away, because I honestly do want to talk to you."

Easing from his hands, I walked around my bed, keeping it between us. "I think we need to talk about a lot of things."

"You're right," he agreed, cleared his throat, and gestured at the bed. "But first, tell me, how many men have been in this bed?"

It was very telling, the way he clenched his jaw like he dreaded the number but resigned himself to it at the same time.

"None," I answered, watching his face change as soon as he got the answer. His thick black brows lifted from the crease, his lips parted, followed by a fall of his shoulders. "I told you before we started that it has to mean something to me. I've had enough sex in my life. I'm in it for something more now."

"As am I," he said levelly, and without preamble, sat down on the bed, took off each of his leather lace-ups, and then began to stretch out.

"Comfortable?" I teased, enjoying the way he shifted his long, hard body out on my bed that had never looked better.

"In the bed, yes, with you… not yet," he replied, arms crossed, reclined but not relaxed, instead looking as though he could spring right up off the mattress without a problem. "No one's ever had power over me before, and I find it terrifying."

"What power? What are you talking about?" I asked, trying to focus but really enjoying him in my room. He fit there, he belonged, and I had the urge to climb on top of him, to be close, needing it, craving it, but I remained still instead.

"I want you all the time, and no one's ever held that draw for me. Always I could walk away and not look back."

"So earlier when we were talking about you being in Malta and me here, you didn't like the sound of that any more than I did."

"No."

"And the leaving and not looking back, you could even do that with the courtiers?"

"Especially with them," he explained, and I could hear the contempt in his tone, his complete disregard. "They were at my beck and call, and I had the most beautiful of them travel with me and service me, but I never slept with them, I didn't hold them. We weren't mated."

I nodded. Sleeping in someone's arms could be even more intimate than sex.

"There was no bond," he husked, and I understood these confessions were from his soul, not easy to express. "Do you understand?"

"Yes."

"Then act like you do and come here," he ordered, his voice faltering on the last word.

I stayed where I was. I wanted to hear more, have him put us into a framework I could use.

"You see? That's what I mean. You don't have to do what I want, because I can't make you and still have what I want," he said, sounding wrung-out and miserable.

"And what is that?"

"Your free will."

"Well, there should be no question in your head that I want you," I confessed so he'd know he had me.

"But you see, I *need* you to want me, and that's power that you have that I've given you, and it's so foreign to me that when I kissed you and the hunger rose so fast…. I was blindsided by how changed I am in so little time."

"It's the same for me," I said, easing down onto the bed, then crawling over to him.

The noises he made when I reached him—his sharp gasp, then an almost strangled sound of joy, and finally a deep, up-from-his-soul sigh when I climbed over him and straddled his hips—deeply satisfied me. He wanted to be exactly where he was, and since I wanted the same, we were in perfect alignment.

"I knew leaving was wrong the second I was out of the door. I felt it in my chest."

They were simple words, but just hearing them—because they were exactly how I felt—soothed away the last of the hurt. It was strange when he left, like it didn't fit my narrative, and hearing it was the same for him went a long way.

Curling over him, I kissed him deeply, taking what I'd wanted since he stepped into my bedroom with that wicked, hungry smile of his.

His groan was filthy as he clutched my thighs, holding on, not allowing me to move. When I broke the kiss to sit up, he hooked a hand around the back of my neck and eased me back down for another.

Needing to show him I wanted him just as badly as he seemed to want me, I kissed him breathless, and when I finally lifted my lips from his, he was panting.

"I want you to take for granted that I won't ever leave you."

I nodded quickly and pressed my forehead to his, and we breathed each other's air.

"And for no other reason than I just don't want to."

I smiled before leaning sideways to kiss the side of his neck.

"I'm not too proud to acknowledge your power over me," he whispered urgently. "I wouldn't change it, even if I could."

I kissed behind his ear and felt him jolt under me.

"You asked earlier what I would have done had you come to me as a courtier," he husked, hands sliding up under my T-shirt to my skin. "I would have laid claim the moment I saw you and made you mine... just as you are now."

I sat up, smiling down at him.

"Come back," he grumbled, reaching for my face.

Varic was like a train running through me, annihilating in the best way—as well as the scariest. "I thought, if he leaves, that's okay, I'll be all right," I admitted as he settled his hands back on my thighs, smoothing them up and down over my light cotton sleep shorts. "But I won't be, and you need to know that so you don't think you're the only one having a nervous breakdown here, all right?"

He nodded, sliding his hands under the thin cotton material to my fuzzy legs. "I'm all settled back into my skin now," he told me. "So shall I scare you now, or wait?"

I cleared my throat. "Scare me now."

"You need to come here first," he said, tugging gently on my T-shirt, trying to ease me down into his arms.

Letting myself be moved, I stretched out on top of him, my head under his chin. He sank his fingers into my hair and massaged my scalp.

"Don't fall asleep," he threatened even as the chill from his body combined with the warm breeze filling the room made me shiver. Apparently he had to feed to keep his body temperature the same as mine— it had returned to being several degrees cooler. "And don't do that either."

I smiled languidly, parting my lips against the smooth skin of his throat. "Any more orders?"

"Yes. Many," he muttered, fisting his hand in my hair to tilt my head back. I thought he was going to kiss me, but he pulled something from his pocket instead. "But first I want you to have something."

I didn't need anything. I already had what I desired: Varic in my bed with me, cuddling, talking, closer now because we'd talked and cleared up any misconceptions between us.

"Look at this," he directed.

I sat up, resting my hands on my knees, my legs tucked under me, before Varic passed me a small drawstring pouch. Inside was a red pendant set in gold, hanging from a hammered gold chain. As I held it in the light coming in from the window and slipped my fingertip over the stone, I could tell it was carved with some sort of design.

"This is beautiful," I said, unable to take my eyes off it, feeling the weight and delicacy at the same time. "Let me turn on the light."

Once I flipped the switch of the small lamp on my nightstand, I could see the wolf cut deeply into the stone. It wasn't crude, instead finely done.

"It's my seal," he told me, and I could hear the pride in his voice. "The wolf of Maedoc."

"I thought they called your dreki the wolves of the house of Maedoc."

"They do," he said. "And I lead them."

"So you're the alpha."

"I am," he assured me, sitting up beside me. "Now give it back."

We jostled around, bumping each other, and then he draped the chain—surprisingly heavy for something so thin, over my head and let the pendant fall. It rested almost between my pectorals, under my collarbone.

"Oh, that's perfect," he breathed, and I could tell from how bright his smile was that he was very pleased.

I took the seal in hand and met his gaze. "Tell me what this means."

"This was made for me. It's mine, commissioned by my father for my consort, and you wearing it tells everyone who sees it that I belong to you."

It was a surprise. "I thought I belonged to you."

"You do. Between us, you're mine," he explained, his tone steady and low, somber and serious, and I understood he was making a pledge to me. "But this is my seal. The wolf represents me, and now I'm yours, if you accept me."

What was said before, all my heartfelt confessions, all of his, coalesced into the vow I was making in this one moment. "I do," I said. I slid my fingers over his jaw as I drew him close.

Keeping my hands to myself and not ravishing Varic at any time was going to be an ongoing battle. Because he tasted so good; he was strong and powerful under my hands, and our lips fit together like I'd been kissing him my whole life. And the most amazing part of all was the more I took, the more I licked and bit and sucked, the more he clutched at me—my arms, shoulders—so obviously wanting more and more, not for a moment less. He didn't tell me I was too rough or too desperate or too intense. Instead he let out a hoarse moan when I pressed him down onto the bed. When I reached for his belt buckle, he broke the kiss and stared up at me.

"What?" I gasped, not wanting to stop, needing to reestablish the closeness from earlier.

"Listen," he growled from the back of his throat. "You wear my seal; this is us now. Do you understand? It can't be undone."

"Yes," I said, then recaptured his mouth as I went to work on his belt buckle, needing to claim his body now as I so obviously had claimed his soul.

He let me have my way, allowing the voracious hunger to build between us, and then stopped me, his hands gripping my thighs so tightly they would leave bruises.

"Look at me," he directed, and I heard the thread of steel in his voice. Here was the prince used to having everyone jump at his every command.

I froze over him.

"This is what I want," he said, shucking me forward, and my crease slid over the long line of his hardened shaft under his dress pants. "I want to take you home with me and present you at court to my parents and my extended family as my consort."

I stopped breathing. He wanted everyone to know about me.

About him and me.

About us.

"I want us to stand up together and make vows."

It was terrifying and stunningly romantic at the same time. He was moving at supersonic speed, but I found myself not caring.

I was in love with a vampyr.

No use tiptoeing around the inevitable, trying to convince myself I wasn't falling hard.

Christ.

The facts were indisputable. I fell for him. Past tense. Over and done.

I had leaped without looking and never once checked for a net.

From the first time I saw him, when he didn't know who I was, to last night when I decided denying him anything was just plain stupid… I hadn't wanted to untangle myself. And now we had a lot to discuss and figure out, everything from geography to vows, but I certainly wasn't going to let either of our momentary lapses in judgment derail us. That fast, just imagining my life without Varic in it, made my heart hurt. I'd never get over him, so it was time to start treating him like I'd already given him my heart, because it was an absolute fact.

"Yes, please," I whispered. I was a bit over-whelmed and having trouble pushing air through my lungs, controlling the excited shivers running over my skin, and, of course, speaking. It was hard to talk around the lump in my throat. All of it, every bit, was Varic's fault for telling me what he wanted. And no, we didn't have the words—the three little ones that meant the world—but what we did have were plans, concrete intentions for the future.

"I want other things too," he said, and his face relaxed, like perhaps his words were settling him as well because of their effect on me. I was so happy, I had to be glowing. "But for now, just know that you're never getting rid of me."

I nodded because my voice had not yet returned. I bent and kissed him deeply, letting him feel what I couldn't say before I hugged him.

"You know not everyone's lucky enough to have their destiny walk into a room, light it up, and show them what they've been missing," he said, his voice bottoming out for a moment, clearly as affected as I was.

I couldn't meet his gaze, instead looking down at my own chest. I took the seal in hand to study it.

"In the morning you'll be able to see that it's a carved carnelian. I wish it were a ruby or a diamond or—"

"No, it's perfect," I whispered, clutching it close.

"If you were a vampyr," he said under his breath, "I wouldn't push like this, but you're not, so… I have to hurry. Every second counts, starting now."

I met his eyes. "Because I ain't gonna live as long you, am I right?"

It was meant to be teasing, but I realized as soon as I said it that, so fresh on the heels of making a commitment, my timing was crap.

He didn't say anything, but he gently moved my leg so he could slide out from under me. Before he could stand, I grabbed the pillow he'd been lying on and smacked him on the side of the head. He was sad, and I wasn't going to allow that to continue.

"You hit me!" Varic was indignant, mouth open, eyes wide, the expression of complete and utter astonishment on his face making me laugh.

"Close your mouth, honey, you look like a fish," I baited him.

"How dare—"

I hit him again because any sentence that started like that deserved instant retribution.

He looked just as dumbfounded the second time. "I'm the prince of the noreia!" he advised, all up on his high horse. "Your life is forfeit to me for this grievous offense."

"Oh yeah? Grievous?" I said sarcastically. "Well, before you have me flogged or something, just keep in mind that I don't plan to die tomorrow, and that maybe my mutant gene will let me live a little longer than you're thinking."

His smile fell away as he nodded.

"Just come here and lie down beside me, all right? Because I missed you even for that small amount of time you were gone."

"You did?"

"Of course I did."

Varic grabbed me and had me back down on the bed with my head beside him on the pillow seconds

later. The expression on his face—utterly stricken—
made me lift my hand to touch his cheek.

"What's wrong?"

"You take my breath away."

"I can't tell if that's good or bad from your
expression."

"It's brand-new," he sighed, clutching me tight,
"and terrifying."

"Why?"

"I've never been afraid of losing anyone or anything before," he said as he pressed me closer, sliding
his thigh between mine as we fit into place. "This is
what being human must be like."

"It's wonderful, isn't it?"

"Don't tease me," he rumbled, nuzzling my hair.
"I'm fragile, you know."

And I did know. His heart was a delicate thing because he'd never given it away before, and so it hadn't
hardened. If I let it go, if I dropped it, I had no doubt it
would shatter into a million pieces. It was up to me to be
very careful with its care. "Don't worry. I've got you."

His sigh of contentment was so very good to hear.

Chapter Twelve

I WAS standing at the counter with Ode when Varic came in through the back door, hair tousled, clothes rumpled, one eye open, one eye closed, looking annoyed.

My snort of laughter made him growl. "Morning, sunshine."

"Where were you?" he groused.

I pointed at the clock. "It's after eleven. Some of us actually work for a living."

"It is not eleven," he snapped, squinting at the antique clock on the wall.

"Oh, he is pretty, you were right," Ode agreed, looking Varic up and down, smiling and nodding her approval. "I like him much better than the guy I set you up with."

"Who were you set up with?" Varic asked, furrowing his brows into a dark scowl.

"Nobody," I promised, walking over to him to give him a kiss, which he prolonged, sliding his hand around the back of my neck and up into my hair, holding me tight so I couldn't move. I felt his raw possessiveness, the claiming and the dominance that demanded—even with a simple kiss—my submission.

"Oh… yeah," Ode murmured, "I see the appeal."

He let me go, pleased with himself, smug, and brushed by me to reach Ode, hand out.

She took it fast, holding tight. "Such a great pleasure to meet you."

His smile went lethal that fast. "Did he tell you all about me?"

"He did. And I'm glad to hear that you weren't, in fact, more interested in pretty boys than my man here. I understand that was just a misunderstanding."

"*My* man," he corrected, "and yes, it was."

Her smirk over his correction was adorable. "Promise me you'll take good care of him."

He put his hand over his heart. "You have my solemn word."

She was utterly charmed by him. I saw it in the slight tremble, the pop of her dimples, and her gleaming eyes. "Excellent," she sighed. "And by the way, I love the necklace you gifted him with. Carnelian is such a magical stone."

He stared into her eyes, narrowing his, and she met his gaze and held it. "Tell me about your parents," he said.

Since they were talking, I helped customers and answered the phone, and then a bit later, as Ode gave him the tour, talked to more people who came in. I had to go to the stock room to grab more of our signature scent Spark and Ember candles, and when I returned to the sales floor, Varic was leaning on the counter, smelling pieces of Palo Santo wood arranged in an abalone shell.

"You done flirting with my friend yet?" I teased him.

He chuckled and turned around to face me, then put his hands on my hips. "She's like sunshine in a person."

"Yes, she is," I agreed, inhaling his delicious scent as he leaned me into him, his cheek in my hair. "Nice that you saw that too."

He grunted. "I have to go back to the penthouse, shower, change, and meet with the state leaders this afternoon."

I tried not to smile, but he sounded like he was going to face a firing squad. "Okay."

"I would invite you to sit at my side as I address them," he said, almost groaning. "But that would be mean, and I kind of like you."

I laughed at him, stepping back and poking him in the ribs. "Prince of the noreia, your job is a snoozefest."

"Oh, you have no idea," he agreed, thumb and forefinger in his eye socket as though keeping it open.

I launched myself at him, wrapped my arms around his neck, and held him tight. "You know, with how cute and charming you are, you're making it damn hard not to fall in love with you."

"Well, I should hope so," he whispered against my cheek before wrapping his arms close around me.

ODE WANTED to talk about Varic once he left, but my stomach was growling, and so was hers.

When I stopped at the deli close to the store, I found Leni, sunglasses on, head down, and hand braced against the door of a refrigerator full of cold drinks before she pressed her cheek to the glass. She looked like absolute hell. I cackled over her state, and she flipped me off.

"Maybe you should get into the fridge with the soda, huh?"

"Why are you yelling at me?" she almost cried.

"How do you guys even get drunk?" I asked, interested in the answer, careful not to say the word vampyr in the mixed company of the sandwich shop.

"We digest and metabolize just like you. Think about those shakes people drink to lose weight. Technically that's a liquid protein diet too."

"True."

"We get drunk just as easy as you."

I laughed softly. "Got it. So how late were you out, my darling?"

"What time is it now?"

I chuckled, put an arm around her, and leaned her into me. Her whimpering sigh made me smile. After I bought lunch for me and Ode, and coffee and water for Leni, we headed for the shop. But halfway down the sidewalk, I realized I was by myself. Trotting back to her, I saw her frozen there like a statue.

"You want me to carry you?"

Slowly she eased her sunglasses down her nose to reveal her now-bloodshot turquoise-blue eyes as round as saucers.

"What's wrong with you?"

She pointed at me. "I thought it was something in the store that was freshly baked or—but it wasn't. It was you. Why do you smell like that?"

"Like what?"

"Dessert," she said in a breathless whine. "Candy. Gooey, thick, rich, and yummy."

I grinned wide. "What does gooey smell like?"

"Beignets and sticky buns and cinnamon rolls with extra icing."

"How would you know?"

"I might not eat them, but I smell them, and holy crap, Jase, why do you smell so good?"

"I have no idea," I said, chuckling because it was not a bad thing to smell like sugary goodness. "Maybe I've always smelled like this, and you're just now noticing."

She shook her head gently. "No. This is new. Definitely new."

"Well, it could be that—"

"Jason!"

We turned to see Avery, one of Benny Diallo's guys, in the back seat of a Chevy Suburban, having called to me from his rolled-down window.

I moved to the curb and would have leaned into the window, but Leni took hold of my bicep and held tight.

I turned to look at her. "What's wrong?"

"Nothing, just stay here."

It was weird. I had no idea she even knew Avery—not that I knew everyone she did—but it was strange. She was acting scared. She rarely gave me orders, and when she did, they were never delivered monotone, with her fingers digging into my arm.

"Jason," Avery said to draw my attention from my friend. "Benny sent me to pick you up. He and Niko have a thing they need to discuss."

"Okay, but everyone usually comes to the shop."

"I don't know what to tell you. He just said to come, so I came."

Normally I wouldn't have thought twice about going with him, and I definitely didn't want to do anything to put the arrangement in the Quarter at risk. But Leni was out of sorts, and that gave me pause even though, besides the driver, Avery was the only one in the car.

"Seriously," he snapped, impatient. "Benny is counting on me to bring you instead of Niko having to get Garrett out here, so—could you just fuckin' come with me so I don't look like an asshole?"

"Too late," I said curtly, studying his angry face.

He flipped me off, and I nodded slowly, passing the food to Leni. "Sweetie, do me a favor and take this to Ode, all right? No reason for her to starve just because I will."

"No," she said, tugging on my arm, trying to pull me after her. "Let's go back to the store together. If Benny wants to see you, he can come there."

But it wasn't my place to tell Benny to do anything. I didn't know if there were new rules about listening to me now that I was Varic's consort, but as far as I knew, he hadn't shared that information with anyone outside of his immediate circle. Basically, I put myself at Benny's beck and call because continued peace in the Quarter was something I truly wanted for all the people I cared about. "It's fine," I told her before I lifted my arm free and took hold of the door. "I doubt it'll take long."

"Jason," she pleaded, "stay with me."

When I saw her stricken face, I couldn't say no.

I leaned on the door so I could see Avery better. "You know what, just tell Benny that—"

"I'm afraid I'll have to insist that you come," he said icily, and something—a needle—pricked the side of my neck.

I stared at him, utterly stricken, thunderstruck that he'd attacked me. I was betrayed and hurt, because even though we'd only ever spoken in passing, I'd counted him as a good guy. How could I have been so wrong? First Aziel, and now him. Clearly I was a crappy judge of character.

Leni's scream seemed as long as a train whistle.

I COULDN'T see anything. My body didn't immediately respond when I tried to open my eyes. It was like I was on a delay switch or something.

"There you are."

Blinking rapidly, I could finally make out Garrett and Avery, the two of them standing off to the side with four guys I didn't know—and Niko, and also Cooke, who was tied to a chair, bleeding. I could hear more voices than I could see people, so I had no real head count. I was suspended from the ceiling, my feet barely touching the floor, with my arms curled behind me over a thick metal bar and my neck in a noose I guessed would tighten if I didn't keep my back rigid. Eventually, if I hung there long enough and my muscles got weak, the ropes would bow me backward, tighter and tighter in centimeters, compressing my spine and folding me in half. Either way—my spine snapping or strangling to death—I wasn't long for the world. The kicker was the slight swinging back and forth on the ropes and the tips of my sneakers brushing over the unfinished wood beams. Shards of pain spasmed through my entire body. They didn't call them stress positions for nothing.

"The hell is going on?" I rasped, barely able to pull enough air into my lungs to form words. The menial O2 I did gulp tasted like a rusted copper penny from the floorboards of a dirty pickup, which told me blood was filling up where it shouldn't, adding asphyxiation by bodily fluids to my growing list of impending causes of death.

Niko punched Cooke across the face, and he pitched sideways, chair and all, and sputtered, spitting up blood as he tried to breathe. The sound his face made hitting the hardwood was something akin to a steel mallet pounding out raw meat. His face looked the part, resembling an oozing raw burger, most of his chiseled bone structure crushed to powder from the beating they'd given him.

Three guys clustered around his prone body, and now I could see eight who stepped out of the shadows, Avery and Garrett having moved next to Niko, with another four milling close to me.

I'd been in this situation before. Not exactly, there'd been no ropes, but I'd been tortured, held, bound, beaten, lung punctured, ribs broken, and cut with a knife.

The difference was the torture I'd endured was done specifically for information. In this scenario, I had nothing to tell.

"Niko!" I yelled, my panic rising. "The fuck do you want?"

The vampyr speed put him almost nose to nose with me in seconds.

"You won't die, Jason," he told me. "And you fuckin' need to."

"The hell are you talking about?" I rasped, so confused by the situation, utterly blindsided by his action.

He threw up his hands. "Friday night I had men attack Benny's mansion and try and kill you. I figured everyone would assume whoever was after the prince accidentally caught you in the crossfire, and I even got you to leave so you'd be easy to pick off, but then you didn't go…. What did you do, get lost?"

No. I found Varic and was captivated at first sight. I'd had no idea my new life started at that exact moment.

"And then later when my man got you to chase him from Benny's place, his backup knocked you out instead of putting a bullet in you! Those idiots had one job, and they fucked it up because they got cold feet!" He huffed. "It would have been so easy, but they heard you were special and decided on their own to scare you instead of kill you."

I was thankful they'd had a change of heart. "Did you kill them?"

"No, I did that," Garrett chimed in, taking credit. "They were idiots!"

I had been called that as well that night.

"And then I hired a guy from out of town, completely untraceable, to catch you out. And when I saw you at the club, I made sure that everyone saw me talking to you—and then saw me leave before he killed you—but how the hell did you get away from that guy? He was highly trained."

Clearly Niko's idea of lethal and mine were very different things. I suspected I was the better judge of who was or wasn't capable. "I'm scrappy," I gasped because the pain was intensifying, my body cramping, wanting to stretch out, to relax, and finding no relief.

He nodded and then punched me in the face.

The blow sent shards of pain everywhere at once, and I shouted because I had nothing to prove. I wasn't trying to impress these cowards who tied me and Cooke up.

"The only good thing I can say about the asshole that couldn't get you out of the club is that at least he killed himself before Hadrian could get to him. I've heard he has methods of extracting information that will make you shit your pants, so I suspect that my hitman took the easy way out."

From what I knew of Hadrian, I couldn't imagine him being that scary, but I'd only ever irritated him, not sent him into a rage.

"Why not just shoot me?" I asked, curious and angry, getting madder by the second. Why not just take me out to the bayou and drown me and feed me to the alligators? Why all the in-my-face shit? "I'm only human. Lots of ways to kill me."

"Because it had to look random. Accidental, unplanned," he told me, slapping my cheek lightly, causing more pain than normal because of the earlier punch. "If you go missing, everyone will be looking for you. Everyone will want to know what happened. I'd have the entire community screaming for answers."

I understood. I had made a difference being a matan. Niko and Benny, at the top of the food chain, would have to provide explanations by any means necessary. Benny, especially, would be on a warpath because people would look to him more than Niko. He was older, richer, better connected, and more than anything, the pureblood leader of the city. People would be all over him if I evaporated into the ether, and Benny, being the thorough man he was, would solve the mystery of my disappearance, much to Niko's regret.

On the other hand, if I was killed during the attack at his home or became the victim of some random run-in with a creep at a club—no one would second-guess that. Everyone would see me dead; it would be open and closed.

"You know," Niko continued, squinting at me, "I was going to make another attempt on your life, but then lo and behold, one of the prince's whores and one of his own precious dreki tried to put you in the grave. Imagine my surprise when you and the prince's puppy lived."

"Tiago's not a puppy," I said, defending my friend, the irony not lost on me that, once upon a time, I'd thought of him as a bunny. "He's actually pretty fuckin' deadly."

"He must be," Niko granted, then took hold of my throat and squeezed, cutting off my air. "Because the wolves of the house of Maedoc are nothing to scoff at."

I struggled, which tightened the ropes, but I needed air more than anything and so I squirmed and pitched, fighting for every small gasp of oxygen.

"Niko!" Avery shouted.

My lungs felt like they were going to explode, and the next second, I could breathe again as he released me.

"You can't kill him like that!" Avery yelled. "He has to bleed out, and he has to be alive for that to fuckin' happen!"

"Stick to the plan," Garrett urged, shivering.

"What's with you?"

"Nothing," he snapped. "Let's just get this over with."

Garrett shuddered then. I saw it. Everyone did.

"Are you scared of something?" Niko baited.

"Fuck yeah, I'm scared. The prince is going to ask questions, and when he does, Hadrian does, and that guy scares the fuck out of me."

Niko shook his head dismissively. "No one's going to be the wiser. All we have to do is first kill Cooke—hell, he's half-dead already—slice up Jason and make it look like Cooke did it, and everything is back to the way it was before he got here."

"Okay, I'll bite," I said, not wanting him to go back to working Cooke over. "Why do you hate me?"

He shook his head. "Are you kidding? You've been messing with my livelihood since fuckin' Cooke over there happened into your shop."

"How?" I asked as Garrett and Avery and two others joined us, knives in hand.

"I had a business," Niko informed me. "One that was working well for all of us here."

That's right. I'd seen some of these men with Benny, and others with Niko. They were a mix of pureblood and made vampyrs.

"What business?" I asked, trying to buy time in case Leni was able to make a rescue call. I hoped she was alive. I'd heard her shrieking, but if they hadn't wanted to leave a witness…. "You should at least tell me why I'm dying."

Niko laughed over that. "It's simple, Jason. Rich pureblood vampyrs don't want to worry about their kids every time they step out of the house, so they hire Avery here to protect them. He's the face because I can't very well do it. I'm a made vampyr. They don't trust me, but they do trust one of their own," he said snidely, smacking my face again almost absently. "And now and then, when one of the kids not watched by Avery would get attacked or killed... well, that always got him new people ready to sign on for protection."

"Garrett works the same angle from his side," Avery boasted. "Made vampyrs afraid for their loved ones pay him insurance to watch children, parents, wives, girlfriends, husbands, boyfriends, even their pets. It's an endless supply of revenue." They were being defrauded by the very people they trusted to keep them safe.

It was reprehensible, and I was sick just looking at them. How could they look at people with kids and elderly parents and hurt them? And Jesus... what about the kids who were out and saw Avery or Garrett, and because they thought they were safe with them, went willingly to the slaughter? Adorable little faces snuffed out for greed. It was horrific, and I wasn't surprised when my eyes filled and my heart hurt.

"You all deserve to fuckin' die," I choked out, my voice hoarse from him almost crushing my larynx. "You did this all for greed. You killed kids for greed." Hot tears rolled down my cheeks as I thought about parents holding lifeless bodies and of the last moments of their children, the fear and betrayal and pain. "I hope you hear their screams in your sleep."

"I sleep just fine, Jason," Niko informed me snidely. "But you know, now and then business tapers off even with everyone paying, and so then we have to stir the pot."

"Please," I begged, my mind filled with images of dead kids. "I don't want to—"

"That's when I let anyone who has a grudge or just wants to let off a little steam have their fun. They go out and visit whoever's turned them down for a date, or some pureblood who thinks they're too good for a made vampyr gets what's coming to them."

They didn't just kill; they raped too. "How many?" I asked, my breath ragged, my voice a harsh whisper.

"How many what, Jason?" Niko was patronizing me. "How many have we killed?"

"No," I choked out, furious, barely able to look at him. "How many of you are there? Just you here, or are there more?"

"I think there's more than enough of us," he declared with a snicker. "But yes, I like to keep things small, so we all know our part. I had to hire out for the attack on Benny's house. We needed some humans to help out."

"Not that they lasted long," Avery informed me. "Your kind is a bit delicate."

"And yet we're not hiding what we are," I managed to get out. I looked over at Cooke. His breathing sounded wet. "Why did you hurt him?"

"I told you," Niko explained, pointing at my broken friend. "We have a plan. He kills you, and then we kill him in revenge. It's very tidy."

"No one who knows me or Cooke will ever buy it," I assured them, struggling for breath as all the ropes tightened with my weight pulling on them. "And especially not Benny," I said to Avery. "Your boss is much smarter than that. He'll figure it out."

"Benny will take my word over that girl's," Avery assured me. "And once no one's listening to her…." He leered. "We'll all take good care of her."

My stomach roiled at the thought of them touching Leni, but I swallowed my disgust and fear. "He won't, though. Benny's not like that," I said confidently. The man I knew thought with his head first, heart second. "Even though he'll want to trust you, he'll talk to Leni and he'll figure out that she's the one telling the truth. You know he will."

For the first time I saw a chink in Avery's smug armor as he thought about Benny Diallo. I'd known him for only a short time, but I knew him to be tenacious and methodical. Avery had years with him but had apparently made a conscious decision to believe Niko instead and throw away everything else.

"You're thinking that Niko is smarter, and you're dead wrong."

Niko turned to Garrett, who came forward, grabbed the front of my shirt to keep me still, and punched me hard in the face. I tasted blood, turned my head, and spat.

"The fuck is that?" Garrett growled, stepping back like I'd somehow zapped him with electricity. "Do you smell that now?"

"I thought it was something in here," Avery grumbled, leaning close and inhaling, smelling me. "But it's not. You're right, it's him." He directed his words to Garrett before turning to Niko. "Why the hell does he smell like that?"

I would have asked *Do I smell like beignets and sticky buns?* but since I had to use my air sparingly, because I was panting now, taking short little sips of oxygen, I kept my mouth shut.

It had to be Varic. When he made me his consort, when he changed my blood, it must have altered my smell. I thought when he said it was sweeter, he'd meant to his taste. When he drank from me. I had no idea I'd started smelling like frosted baked goods. I would have to tell Leni when I saw her.

It had to be *when* and not *if*. That's how I'd been trained. It was always when.

"I don't know why he smells like that," Niko admitted, his voice cracking for a moment, leaning in close to inhale my scent, then pressing the tip of the hunting knife in his left hand to the side of my neck. "But I'm going to drain him, so we'll all know the answer."

Cooke whimpered.

"Please," I gasped, terrified, but not for myself. This was only meant to hurt me. And in hurting me, they were hurting Varic… and that was the part gutting me.

It would kill him to know he hadn't been there to protect me. He would carry the failure and the rage and maybe even think he should never have reached out for me to begin with. He would curse the decision to take a frail human consort. And I was guessing I knew enough about him to know most of it was the truth.

"You smell like fear," Niko advised, leaning close, so smug. "I like that scent on you, human."

It was over-the-top and stupid. "You're an idiot," I heaved, choking for air.

It was useless to move, the way they had me trussed up, but I fought anyway, trying to get loose, twisting and straining. They laughed and jeered. The backhand across my face and Garrett cinching the rope sent another scalding lance of pain roaring up my spine.

"I'm going to—"

"Holy shit," Garrett gasped, cutting Niko off, pointing, "what the fuck is that?"

It was difficult to see anything in the darkness filling the edges of the room. Flickering fluorescent lights illuminated us like a spotlight, and even Cooke lay within the circle, strapped to that chair, but beyond that…. I was fairly certain we were in some kind of warehouse. I strained to listen, and I could have sworn there was something in the shadows panting.

It wasn't like I sounded, the light in and out, and it wasn't like a golden retriever ready to slobber on you. It was heavy and rough, and the fact that I could easily hear it now meant it was getting louder. More importantly, to make a sound like that, it had to be big.

Very big.

The vampyrs gathered in the light and clustered together, peering into the darkness. Judging by the way they moved, whatever it was, was circling us.

"Goddammit," the guy beside Garrett whispered, "you said we didn't need guns for this!"

Why would they need guns? This wasn't a movie; I wasn't a rival cartel lord. No one came expecting a shootout. They'd obviously planned to cut me open and let me bleed all over the floor. No one needed a firearm for that.

Now, whatever lurked just beyond the light, they didn't want to cut up. They wanted to shoot. I knew I should have been scared, but for the moment, I wasn't being gutted, so I was thankful for the temporary respite and also strangely curious. I was always the guy who went to look, just as I had the night I heard Tiago scream. I had to know what I was up against, so I wanted it to step into the circle of light.

Cooke began crying softly and then shaking violently. I didn't understand until an enormous fur-covered hand with claws at least four inches long broke into my line of sight and touched the floor right beside Cooke's head.

Several men screamed, others cried out, and three ran. I could do nothing but watch, helpless.

I'd seen vampyrs do amazing things—the speed, the agility, the fighting skill—and it was extraordinary, preternatural, not outside the realm of science.

But I could not make sense of that appendage.

Those who ran drew the creature's interest, as evidenced by the hand... now paw... lifting and retreating into the darkness, followed almost instantly by screams of horror and fear and pain.

A body was flung into the light, cleaved in half, a riot of gore and thick, viscous ooze, no longer a vampyr but instead a mutilated heap. More sounds, wet, like a bucket of water thrown onto a floor, made me thankful for the darkness.

"You want to die here like sheep?" one man yelled, turning on the flashlight on his cell phone, and a few others agreed and yelled their solidarity.

He turned, and a creature's head filled the light: teeth, dripping jaws, and so much blood. If I'd had the air, I would have gasped or yelled or shrieked just like everyone else.

That cell phone hit the ground, landed so the light beamed straight up, enough to show us the bite that severed his head from his shoulders.

Blood splashed as the creature picked up the head and crushed it, muscle, flesh, and pieces of bone dripping from between its claws.

I could feel the bile rising in my stomach and fought hard not to vomit as the creature moved forward, all of it now in the light.

It was a wolf, of a sort, but the muzzle was wrong, distended, deformed, drawn-back, blood-soaked lips that didn't cover teeth, so instead of a furry snout, caustic saliva dripped from long, viperlike fangs that gleamed like Damascus steel. Cruel contempt was etched on its monstrously disfigured visage. The way it was standing, on back legs with front legs elongated like arms, the proportions off, was somehow even more disturbing. A six-foot-something feral nightmare didn't look natural... and if you weren't sure what it was, how could you kill it?

"The fuck is that?" Niko cried, raising the hunting knife meant to gut me.

Flat and straight hair, sticking up at the ends, covered the creature, and its eyes were slits of amber in its enormous skull. It was massive in size and musculature, and the claws it dragged across the unfinished floor, leaving deep grooves in the wood, created a horrible tearing, scratching, that made everyone gasp.

The others, five left in all, counting Garrett and Avery, gathered close to each other as the werewolf—that was all it could be—circled and then leaped.

It flew forward like a locomotive cleaving the darkness and took two men, one in its enormous

piercing grip, the other in its jaws, and dismembered
them in seconds. Avery was next, his head torn from
his body. I watched as it rolled out of the circle of
light. His body was hurled away, discarded like nothing, and when it landed, was still twitching. It pounced
on the next man and ripped him in half—blood, tissue, and flesh falling heavily to the floor in sticky wet
clumps of gore.

Niko screamed. Garrett ran into the darkness toward the door, and his howl of pain echoed, followed
by an audible splash of blood before the creature re-
appeared, its entire face painted a deep purplish claret.

I should have been horrified or scared, but I was
too numb. I was prepared to die, and I was certain it
would be fast. I'd just watched the creature eviscerate
others right in front of me, after all, so I knew I'd only
feel the pain for a split second.

I was surprised when the creature bolted forward,
then stopped, breathed a dew of blood-filled air onto
his face, and then instead of rushing me, closed in
slowly.

It moved its claw faster than I could follow, and I
fell hard to the floor. It winded me, and I was thankful
I fell face-first and not on my back. Had I fallen backward, the snap of both of my arms would certainly
have been my reality. Instead I lay there and gulped
air like a fish on land.

"Oh dear God," Niko whimpered, and I watched
as he dropped to his knees and released the knife so
it clattered to the ground beside his leg. "Is that the
prince's seal?"

The seal worried him? A creature out of nightmare was standing right there in front of us, and

he was freaking out over a token of love Varic had given me?

I would have screamed at him if I'd had the air.

The pendant had slipped from inside my T-shirt and lay on the floor next to my cheek, the hammered gold chain catching the dim light.

"I'm the prince's consort," I rasped as the creature nudged my hip gently with its enormous viscera-covered snout. "Of course I wear his seal."

It had never occurred to me to bargain for my life by announcing who I was to Varic. Honestly, I doubted Niko would have believed me, and even if I had thought to say "I wear the prince's seal," I was pretty sure Niko's plan would have been to kill me anyway. He was in too deep the moment he had Avery grab me. He couldn't have let either me or Cooke go, or everyone would have found out the truth about him. Killing us was his only option.

Niko started to cry as the creature rounded on him, reared back its head, jaw stretched wide, and emitted a guttural growl.

"I can't breathe," I managed.

The creature slipped a single claw under the rope around my neck. The binding sprang off with force, and I gulped air, panting at its feet, its hot breath on my face as it slipped its tongue between those wicked fangs and dragged it down the side of my neck.

"Wolf of Maedoc," I said under my breath, the realization seizing me of what—or more accurately, who—I was looking at. "I understand now."

Niko scrambled back a few feet, and I watched in awe as the beast from hell melted away to morph into a heavily muscled man covered in tattoos and brands, runes and glyphs I would have to remember to ask about later, and then finally, after a few long moments, to the naked form of the man I had been in bed with the night before.

Varic Maedoc, prince of the noreia.

His eyes remained amber as he slid a hand through my hair, and when I sighed, they returned into the deep, dark, primordial forest green I knew.

"You came for me," I sighed, so happy and relieved to see him that I shivered.

"Are you scared now?" he asked, and I could hear the dread in his voice.

"No," I said, smiling because he had to see on my face as well as hear in my tone that I loved him no matter what form he took. "I'm amazed. That's incredible, what you can do. How is that possible?"

"As you said, the wolf of Maedoc." He leaned sideways to grab Niko's knife and started sawing at the ropes. "It's genetic in my father's line."

I glanced at Niko, making sure he wasn't moving, and found that not only was he still, but he'd folded up his arms and legs as tight as he could against his body. He also had his face pressed to the floor, totally submissive and quaking in fear.

"So he can do that too?" I asked, focusing again on Varic.

"He used to," he said, removing the brace from behind my back, which allowed my arms to fall to my sides. "But once the prince is able, the king refrains because the burden of keeping the law lies with the prince, as well as the punishment."

"It's probably present in your blood for wartime as well, right?"

"It is," he said, helping me sit up, then propping me against him as he got the last of the ropes off and then drove the knife down hard into the floor, embedding it there. "It goes back to the berserkers we were talking about before, and the blood frenzy."

"Did your brother change into the wolf before you?"

Quick nod, his brow creasing like it hurt to remember. "He did. He used the middle form for most of his fighting, which was how we lost him. He couldn't—" He coughed, clearing his throat softly. "There's no thinking in either form. It's all adrenaline and rage."

That couldn't be right. I'd seen him calm with my own eyes. He'd reached me and been gentle, the bloodlust gone in moments.

I reached up slowly as the blood rushing back to my arms caused sharp tingles, and cupped his cheek and drew him forward, not caring that his face, body, and hair were streaked and spattered with blood.

He resisted, holding himself back, not allowing the kiss. "No, you—you don't want—"

"I do want," I assured him, using my T-shirt to wipe the blood off his mouth before kissing those delectable lips. He was surprised—I saw it in his face when I eased back to look into his eyes. "I want all of you."

A quick tremble rolled through him. "I should have known that my consort would want me, and see me, the prince, in every form I take and claim all of them—all of me."

"Yes, you should have," I said, taking his face in my hands and kissing him again.

Varic tucked me under his arm as a door opened and more lights illuminated the blood-splattered walls, exposing the many corpses.

Hadrian and Tiago rushed into the room with the rest of the dreki. Tiago checked on Cooke, and Hadrian reached us and draped a blanket around Varic's shoulders before he took hold of mine and checked me over.

"I'm fine," I reassured him.

"Thankfully, or the rampage would have been catastrophic," he said flatly before he turned to Niko, lifted him off the floor, and savagely backhanded him. "You fool. Don't you know you sacrifice your family, your entire line, when you attack the house of Maedoc?"

I was going to correct Hadrian and tell him I wasn't part of the royal family, but as Varic collapsed into my lap, his head in my hands, his strength gone, wanting to be close, needing me exactly where I was, I realized that, ready or not, I belonged to Varic Maedoc, body and soul.

He was right that first night. Loving him was truly not for the faint of heart.

Chapter Thirteen

I SAID no, my place would be fine, but my word apparently meant nothing. Hadrian nodded a lot, but instead of driving Varic and me back to my home, he drove us to the Garden District. The house was in the Central City area on the 1400 block of Fourth Street, and though much smaller than Benny's mansion, it was still enormous by my standards, with its six bedrooms.

"He is the prince," Hadrian reminded me from the front seat. "And he has people who must be with him at all times, including myself and Tiago."

"You weren't with him when I met you the first time," I countered, stroking Varic's hair as he sprawled beside me in the back seat. He was groggy, zapped of his strength, and needed to eat and sleep.

"The prince was home in Malta, with his guard as well as that of the king," Hadrian explained. "I worry not for him when he is there."

Of course he had to go and throw logic at me.

"I need clothes," I groused.

"Tiago is there going through your closet as we speak."

It was not a comforting idea, having the fashion police sifting through my things.

The house, with its wrought iron fence, was beautiful. Each of the three bedrooms on the second floor had a balcony; Corinthian columns stood out front, marble floors and mantels throughout, windows so big you could use them as doors, and a private terrace off the master bedroom that overlooked a wildflower garden.

We put him in the shower. Hadrian held him up as I used the removable showerhead and washed him from head to toe. It took a while for the water to run clear, but once he was clean and dry, he looked better, more like himself, and I kissed him after we put him in the enormous bed.

"Please don't leave the house," he murmured, trying valiantly to keep his eyes open.

"I won't," I whispered, soothing him, and a slight smile curled his lips before he succumbed to sleep.

Darting back to the bathroom, I took a shower as well, needing to wash the day off. Once I was out, I heard a knock on the door before Hadrian leaned in with a pair of pajama bottoms and a T-shirt.

"Thank you."

"If I allowed you to walk about nude or in only a robe, my prince would have my head."

I doubted it was that serious, but I appreciated the clothes.

Back at Varic's bedside, I watched him sleep and then turned to Hadrian when he paused beside me, towel-drying his hair and dressed in a pair of shorts. He'd been covered in as much gore as I had after helping to move all the bodies. "How long will he sleep?" I asked.

"I hope until tomorrow, but we shall see."

I nodded.

Hadrian took hold of my shoulder, turning me to him. "I have never seen him so frightened."

"And I'm sorry I was the cause," I told him, thinking about being snatched off the street and strung up like a piece of meat. "I'm worried that he'll start to think that having a human consort isn't such a great idea."

"Oh no," Hadrian said quietly. Seriousness filled his voice as his cognac-colored eyes met mine. "He changed back so quickly for you. That transformation usually takes hours, but this time, mere moments." He searched my face. "It is unheard of and tells me something extraordinary."

"Oh yeah? What's that?"

He took a breath. "He needed to converse with you, to speak and be heard, and could not as the wolf and so returned to his true form. He loves you."

And I loved him back.

"I thought he wanted you for his consort because you are a matan, and for the power that you give him. I was wrong. He wants you because you are you, because he loves you."

I let the words wash over me, settled, once more, in my skin.

"I am sorry you had to see him like that, though."

"I'm not," I said, needing to feel the sun on my skin, to remind myself I was alive and safe. After climbing off the bed, I crossed to the terrace and walked into the warmth to look down at the garden before leaning forward and folding my arms on the railing. The breeze on my face felt so good, so comforting. "I want to know all of him, not just one part."

"Well, you certainly had a trial by fire," Hadrian grumbled. "Now we shall find you some food. I can hear your stomach growling from over here."

HOURS LATER I was sitting in the shade of the garden when Cooke walked out and joined me, easing himself gently down onto the chaise beside me. I'd insisted he be brought wherever I was going to be so I could watch over him until he healed. No one had argued, and two of Hadrian's men had been careful putting him in the car.

Now, he moved stiffly and looked a bit banged up, but a thousand times better than a handful of hours ago.

"How'd you do that?" I asked him.

"The rajan's blood," he said sheepishly. "That's... amazing stuff."

Shock flooded me. "Tiago let you feed from him?"

The look of horror that came over his face made me laugh. "Are you high? He filled one of the water goblets for me."

"Gotcha."

"Drink from him," he scoffed. "Good God."

"You're right. I can't see Hadrian letting you do that."

"No," he said, widening his eyes for emphasis. "He's very protective of the rajan's space. I can't imagine him letting anyone put fangs in his boyfriend."

Tiago gave Hadrian a scare chasing Rhyton and the others. Hadrian had made that clear when he brought me a meal.

"He will not be allowed to take such chances in the future," he informed me.

"Did you tell him that?"

"I have," he said, standing there all big and scary, scowling at me.

"And, uhm." I snickered. "How'd he take that?"

He rolled his eyes and stormed out of the room. I could only guess I was being ridiculous for asking such a question.

When I was done eating, I'd walked out into the hall, and Tiago startled me by hurling my duffel to the floor in front of me and rounding on Hadrian right behind him. On the one hand, I was happy to have some more clothes, but on the other, his volume was daunting.

"I am not a child!" he thundered, stomping his foot, bristling with fury.

"No, you are not," Hadrian rumbled, taking his chin in hand, forcing Tiago's eyes to meet his. "You are a beautiful, strong man who belongs to me." Tiago trembled in his grip, eyes fluttering for a moment before he regained his composure and met Hadrian's stare. "Yes?"

"Yes," Tiago whispered, then swallowed hard.

"Then," Hadrian said, leaning forward until there was only a hairsbreadth of space between their lips, "allow me to worry."

Tiago closed his eyes as he lifted for the kiss. They were so beautiful together, the contrast simply stunning: one taller, one shorter; one darker, one lighter; one fragile and delicate in appearance, the other carved and muscular. It was hard not to stare, but I turned away to give them their privacy.

"I feel like crap," Cooke complained, returning me to the present. "In case you're wondering."

I grinned, knowing what he meant. We'd been through an ordeal together, and I hoped neither of us would be too scarred up. The outside would heal—the inside was the issue. I still had bad dreams from the war sometimes, not violent with night sweats and screaming, but the kind that jolted me awake and kept me that way. "You might need to see someone and talk that shit out," I told him.

"We'll see," he murmured, closing his eyes for a moment and tipping his face up to the sun. "I'm good right now."

I was glad he felt safe and secure. "So how's your room?"

His eyes popped open as he turned to look at me. "It's the most amazing room I've ever been in in my life."

"Good," I sighed, so comfortable outside in the early afternoon, loving the smell of the flowers, the warm and gentle breeze, the gurgle of the fountain farther out in the yard—just the absolute serenity of all of it together. "I think I love it here."

"Well, yeah, it's a palace."

"I think we have to go to Malta to see a real palace—or castle, as the case may be."

"I'm game," he assured me.

As was I. Whatever Varic wanted, I was up for. He'd saved my life. Leni had run back to the shop, and Ode ordered her to call Varic. Tiago and Hadrian both told me he lost his mind when Leni told him I'd been taken.

"His reaction to her phone call was unprecedented," Tiago said solemnly. "I have never seen him shift so fast."

The vampyr speed was a blessing. Even across rooftops, the draugr would have been spotted if he wasn't moving in a blur, following my scent like a beacon.

"Hadrian said," Cooke started hesitantly, trying out the rekkr's name, but also reminding me I was having a conversation with him, "that I should get my stuff and move in here."

That was kind, thoughtful, and I found it endearing that Hadrian had offered my friend shelter. "Will you?"

"Is, uhm—" He coughed. "—that what you want?"

Hadrian had already invited him, and he was asking me? I had no idea how long I would be there, but whatever the time period, I wanted Cooke close. He'd clearly shown himself to be a man who needed babysitting. "Hell yeah. You know you need a keeper. I don't know anyone who gets into more shit than you."

"Me? Pot, kettle."

I dismissed him with a wave of my hand. "Dude, you're a mess."

He didn't say anything for a second, and when I glanced at him, he was grinning at me. "Okay, then," he said quickly, turning away. "I can hang here for a bit."

Neither of us said anything more.

I WAS glad I had underwear and jeans to change into before Ode and Leni showed up. They arrived right after six and Leni was so relieved to see me—even though she'd been told I was safe—that she collapsed in the middle of the foyer and sobbed. Ode, who hadn't been freaked-out, then *got* freaked-out and started to yell at me for making her worry.

"You promised me you wouldn't do this kinda shit anymore," Ode snapped.

"I'm sorry," I grumbled, scooping up Leni and then depositing her on the couch, where I held her hand and smiled at her. "Sweetie, I'm fine."

"The hell was up with Avery?" she asked sharply, still sounding a bit unhinged. "He scared the crap out of me."

"He wasn't who any of us thought," I told her, sighing deeply. "Thank you for calling the prince. You and Ode saved my life."

"Which shouldn't need saving all the time," Ode growled as she stomped to where I sat and stood over me.

I could see how furious she was. "Why am I in trouble?"

"I don't know! Why do you continually get into trouble?"

Telling her none of it was my fault probably wouldn't fly, so instead I stood up and leaned over to hug her. "I'll stop right this second."

"That's what you said the last time," Ode groused under her breath.

"Yeah, but this time I mean it."

She grunted.

"And now you'll have other people around to give me shit if I screw up."

"Oh?" she said, easing back to look up at me. "And who would that be?"

I was about to tell her Varic was all over taking care of me, but suddenly Duro, one of Hadrian's guys who'd chased after Rhyton, sprinted across the room to reach us, leaving his partner, Eris, a tall willowy woman with a red braid hanging over her shoulder, by the doorway.

Slowly, gently, he took Ode's hand in both of his. She had to tip her head back to see his face—he had to be six five, and she was five eight—but she smiled as she did.

"Don't fear," he said softly, staring down into her eyes. "I won't let anything happen to him or you, my lady. On my life."

"On your life?"

"Yes."

She was deciding as she looked at him. I could tell. I knew when her brain was working, figuring things out. "My name's Ode," she told him after a moment, her voice even more melodic than usual.

His grin made his dark eyes glint. "I'm Duro, and I would be proud to be your champion."

"I never had a champion before."

"And you will need no other," he promised, taking a step closer, the muscles in his jaw tightening as he gazed at her. "Ever."

It was a nice sentiment, very romantic, and I smiled as Hadrian joined me, standing at my right.

"Interesting," he said clinically, peering as though the two of them together was a shocking science experiment.

"What?"

Before I could press him, I felt a touch on my arm. Leni stood beside me, eyes wide, staring at her friend and the massively built man who dwarfed her.

"Uh, isn't he a member of the dreki?" Leni asked, still sniffling as Eris joined us, on the other side of Hadrian, her eyes round as she stared at her fellow guard.

I put an arm around her and tucked her up against my side, giving her a squeeze. "Are you all right now?"

"Yeah, no, I was just worried about you, but… at the moment, I'm more worried about her."

"Why?"

She leaned forward to look around me at Hadrian. "He is one of your men, right?"

He nodded, staring at Duro and Ode.

"And you guys—you mate for life, don't you?"

Another nod from him.

She leaned back into my side. "I think someone better tell Ode about vampyrs right fuckin' now, because he's about a second away from claiming her, and no one gets between a member of the dreki and their mate."

"Is that true?" I asked Hadrian.

He made a noise that was part grunt, part overwhelmed deer caught in a headlight. On the other side of him, Eris was slowly nodding in answer to my question.

Bumping him with my shoulder was like pushing on a brick wall, but he turned his head and regarded me. "Tell me fated mates are not a thing," I said.

"Fated mates are not—" He swallowed hard. "—*supposed* to be real except in regards to the nobility, and certainly not between vampyrs and humans."

"And yet?"

"And yet," he repeated softly, obviously gob-smacked. "He appears quite in earnest."

"Possibly the understatement of the year," Eris huffed.

We watched as Ode slid her hands up the big man's chest, lifting to her toes at the same time as he bent over so their foreheads touched and they shared breath.

"Ode," I called to her. "Honey, we need to talk."

"Okay," she chirped, not listening to me one bit.

"We need to speak to you *right now*," Leni insisted.

"Mmmmm-hmmm," she murmured.

"Let go of the man and come over here so I can talk to you," I said, using my big voice.

Eris snorted, clearly amused by the whole thing.

"In just a minute," Ode sighed, not giving a crap that I was having a nervous breakdown.

"I'm going to drag you away from him," I threatened.

"You have to go through Duro," she sighed, closing her eyes.

"You have to go through me," he echoed, closing his eyes as well as he inhaled her scent and then seemed to settle in his skin.

"Only the rekkr could get through Duro," Eris chimed in. "I wouldn't attempt it."

I turned to Leni, "That's how vampyrs take their mates?"

"Like I would know," she said absently, smiling, then making that noise I normally made when I saw Chihuahua puppies. "Look how cute they are together."

"That is precisely how vampyrs react to finding their mates," Hadrian proclaimed authoritatively, crossing his arms as the studied the couple. "It was the same for me when I first saw Tiago. It was as if everything came to a halt and there was only him, all I could see."

"Well, it's seriously romantic."

"I had no idea it looked like something out of a bad movie," he said, gesturing at them. "Frankly I find it horrifying. Small wonder my entire retinue of guards was laughing at me."

As though on cue, Brenna, another of his guards, snickered from her post at the door, and Hadrian shot her a death glare, which only made her laugh aloud before she schooled her expression and looked up and away innocently.

I smiled. "I bet it was cute."

He did a slow pan to look at me. "Were you not the consort of my prince, I would gut you where you stand."

My snort of laughter did nothing for his mood.

"I'm going to need a different partner for a while," Eris muttered, though she watched Duro and Ode with a small smile.

ODE TOOK the news about vampyrs so much better than I had.

She listened to Leni, to Hadrian, to Cooke, to Tiago—whom she found especially charming—and finally to me. She held Duro's hand as he explained about the law and how it had changed and how much she would love Malta.

"Malta?" she asked. I didn't doubt for a moment she knew where it was. I could only assume Duro's absolute conviction she would be going with him prompted her to look at him in question.

"No member of my family has ever left the prince's dreki, but I would do so if that meant that I was able to remain at your side," he promised.

"We should talk about all of this," she told him, "but first I need to yell at Jason."

Everyone cleared out after that, though Duro didn't go far. He paced on the patio while Ode and I sat farther out, under an ancient magnolia tree in the garden.

"Why didn't you tell me as soon as you knew?" she snapped from her chaise.

"You would have believed in vampyrs?" I asked drolly, one eyebrow lifted. "Really?"

"Not at first, but I would have after I met Cooke."

"Yeah," I agreed with a shrug. "But it's hard to know what to say."

She gazed at nothing, lost in thought, and I had a moment to rejoice over the fact that she was in on the secret. Life would be so much easier now, and I'd watched how relieved Leni was when Ode hugged her and said nothing was changed. She almost started crying a second time.

"Hey."

She turned to look at me.

"I know it's a lot to process. It took me a while."

"Certain things," she said softly, thoughtfully, "make sense now."

"I agree. You'll notice them more and more. I do."

"Well, this is good. Now we have one more thing to bond over and talk about. I think it's helpful when you and your best friend are able to share everything."

I took a quick breath, suddenly lost in memories because of the particular words she'd used.

Best friend.

A lot of baggage there.

She got up, rushed over to me, and took hold of my hands. "Oh, Jase, I'm not trying to take his place," she promised, squeezing tight. "I know you loved Eddie so much, from all the stories you've told me about him, but I think he'd want me to take over until you see him again."

I stared into her bottomless brown eyes.

"And I want the job real bad," she said, bottom lip quivering and tears welling up as her gaze held mine. "I love you so much."

"I love you too," I pledged, prying the words loose, not having said them to anyone outside of my parents, ever. "You know I do."

"I do," she cried, dissolving as I grabbed her and hugged her tight. "And promise me, no more lies or omissions."

"No. No more. Cross my heart."

One other person in the house deserved a confession, and I was kidding myself if I thought it could wait even a moment longer.

"So," she said, wiping under her eyes, sniffling a bit before straightening her button-down shirt, then smoothing her pencil skirt while we got ourselves together. "Tell me, consort of the prince, do you got a spare bedroom in this shack? 'Cause there's a man who needs to talk to me, and then apparently bite me, right fuckin' now."

"You know it might hurt when he bites you."

She tipped her head, pretending to ponder that. "I think it'll depend on what he's doing when he bites me—don't you think?"

She wasn't subtle, my girl, and I was betting Duro was about to be shown what a true goddess looked like when she claimed him as her own.

I told her to talk to Hadrian, and she left to find him as Tiago walked out onto the patio.

"You are surrounded by friends and vampyrs, Jason."

"I think some are both, don't you?"

"Perhaps," he allowed, arching an eyebrow for me. "Everyone has a destiny. Perhaps this was yours all along."

It was hard to argue.

"By the way, we received a message from the king," he said, putting a hand on my bicep. "He wants to formally present you and Varic at court, to the dacian, so you will have to leave for Malta within the next couple of days."

I nodded.

"Is your passport up-to-date?"

"It is."

"Good. Benny Diallo will be in charge of all the vampyrs here in the Quarter until a suitable leader of the made vampyrs can be found."

"Will Benny be good to the made vampyrs? Because after Varic originally talked to him, he didn't think they were on the same page."

"I suspect that I sound as though I am contradicting my prince, but that is only due to the act of betrayal committed by Niko."

Varic wouldn't just be looking to Benny to pick up the slack if Niko had been a good guy. "So now Benny is to be trusted?"

"Apparently he is not a classist and sees no difference between him and them, so perhaps it might not even be needed to find a replacement for Niko. We shall have to see," he mused. "But as you are here, as this is your home, and the prince has taken up residence in this"—he glanced around and shuddered—"abode, I am not worried about anyone stepping out of line."

"Not after Varic showed them what the wolf of Maedoc truly is," I replied, enjoying being in the garden, the attack the furthest thing from my mind. Especially as dusk settled around us, it almost felt like a dream, like something that happened to someone else. Everyone was safe, Ode knew about vampyrs, and the love of my life was sleeping upstairs.

The transformation of the worst Tuesday of my life to the best was profound.

"No, not after that."

I turned to him. "I assume you've seen him change shape like that many times."

He nodded.

"Did it scare you the first time?"

"No," he asserted, smiling. "Like you, I see him in all his forms. My love for him does not wane based on his visage."

"That's good," I sighed, watching the shadows start to steal over the flowers. "Tell me, is Niko dead?"

He took a breath. "Niko, along with his family, has to be taken to court and judged by the king for his trespass against you. It is for him to decide if only Niko dies or his entire line."

"But I thought Varic would—"

Tiago shook his head. "Not when the trespass is against the prince himself... or his consort. The king will decide."

"No, he can't," I breathed, shaken. "Tiago... I won't be responsible for the death of innocent people."

He nodded. "Then I suggest you learn how to plead with a king, because Messina Maedoc is a kind, generous monarch who is utterly devoid of mercy when it comes to threats against his family." He sighed deeply. "I have never heard of a line he did not put to the blade for sedition, but perhaps this will be the first."

"It can't be sedition. I'm not a royal."

"You are the consort of the draugr, and clearly you need to learn your place."

"The hell are you talking about?"

"You are the heart of the prince; you need to realize that your life will never be the same."

I was starting to get that. I had to figure out what a consort was. I knew there would be limits to what I had a say in, and Tiago saying I had to learn my place could mean that. I would be Varic's mate, but perhaps without any rights in his court, if he wasn't with me. It also meant I had sway over Varic, and as his love, I had to be careful not to keep him from his duties. It would be a whole new world, and I had so much to learn. It was daunting to think about, and I didn't want to screw up, but I also didn't want to try to become something I wasn't. It would be a tightrope walk, a balancing act of biblical proportions I was only agreeing to because of Varic.

I had to be with Varic.

But my hopes, fears, and all the in-between was not something to discuss with Tiago. "It's a nice house," I said to change the subject.

"Is it?" he asked, a pained look on his face, grimacing before he started walking away.

He was such a snob. "It's got six bedrooms, you know!" I called after him. "And a kitchen that my apartment could fit into, and a big-ass living room, and, hello, a garden!"

"There are no pools or stables, no servants' quarters, no library…. It is a regrettable space," he commented tersely over his shoulder. "I heard your friend call it a shack, and she is perfectly correct in her assessment."

"She was kidding!"

"I highly doubt that."

"You're such a snob!" I finished, realizing he was completely unaffected by my judgment of his character.

Alone again, I flopped down onto the closest chaise and tried to think of how I was going to save Niko's family.

For a moment I drowned in guilt, terrified about how I would make a vampyr king understand a purely human perspective. And then I had an epiphany.

Varic.

If I could make my mate understand, he would sway the king. My only issue was making him see my side when the man in question had planned to kill me.

I wasn't sure how forgiving Varic would be, but I'd never forgive myself if I didn't try.

I had no other option.

LATE IN the evening, I took another shower, much longer than the first time. It wasn't just about cleaning off blood; it was more about relaxation. I stood under the hot water for what seemed like an hour and utilized all the different angled jets. It was heavenly.

Once I was done, I wiped fog off the mirror and examined myself. I was surprised to find the rope burns on my neck didn't hurt because they had faded already. Apparently when Varic changed my blood so I could feed him, he did something to my healing ability as well. I would have to ask him.

I climbed into bed beside him and opened my iPad, which Tiago had grabbed from my apartment, and I was glad to see an email from Rachel telling me about a nice high school football coach she met when he came into the ER with a broken arm. He was funny, she said, and had a good laugh. I told her I expected to meet him soon, so happy for her. And though I didn't know if, only a year after Eddie's death, she would be ready to fall in love again, just the fact that she could make a new friend was wonderful.

I had an email from my mother as well, letting me know she and my father were taking my sister and her family on a cruise for Christmas. I was invited too, as long as I came alone, the meaning implicit that having me bring someone special would not be appreciated. I sent her a note thanking her and wished her good holidays. From Thanksgiving on through to the New

Year, I would be traveling myself, I told her, and she wouldn't be able to reach me.

As I closed my email, I realized what used to be gut-wrenching pain when it was new had succumbed to time and become, finally, a mild ache. When I came out to my parents, they inexorably withdrew, and the closeness never returned. I grieved that for years, but first Eddie and I became friends, and his family loved me as well, and then I moved to the Quarter and met Ode and Cooke. It all changed my life. I started seeing myself through different eyes. And now—Tiago was right. I was ready to step into a whole new life—with all the ups and downs that came with it—and follow the man I loved.

"Shit," I groaned, smiling as I put my iPad on the nightstand before turning back to Varic, wanting to wrap myself around him. But I froze midmotion, caught in his clear green gaze. "Oh, you're up."

"Why are you swearing?" he asked, reaching for my face.

I laughed softly, leaned into his hand, then let him ease me into his arms.

"Tell me," he demanded, rolling me to my back, settling his body over mine.

"Couple of things."

"I want to know," he said, smiling lazily, staring down at me. "Speak."

"I'm worried about Niko's family," I told him. "I don't want them to pay for his crimes. I couldn't live with it."

"You will live with the will of the king, as he is your sovereign now as much as mine. And as for what punishment Niko's family receives, that will depend on them and what response they give to their king," he explained softly, mildly, no power behind the words, instead tender with me, his voice gravelly, as he'd just woken. "Niko's role in overseeing the extortion of his own people is keenly disturbing, and if any of his family members knew of his crime and either ignored it or participated in it, then they too are culpable and will be disqualified from mercy."

It made sense when he explained it that way.

"However, if they can convince my father that they will never seek retribution on Niko's behalf, and if they don't share in his treachery, they will live. I swear to you. My father is many things, but unmerciful is not one of them. He has devoted his life to the service and defense of our race and will allow no unjust harm to come to any of his people."

He clearly trusted his father, and since I had the same faith in him, I needed to wait and see instead of filling my mind with what-ifs.

"And you have to think: Niko would have cut your throat and left you for dead. If his family is just like him, perhaps allowing them to lead others in this city is not wise."

On the whole, it was a valid argument.

"Ruling isn't easy. There are hard choices to be made, and someday I, too, will have to make them for all," he finished solemnly.

"Yes."

"But unlike my father, I'll be blessed with not having to make those decisions alone."

"Oh?"

"Yes, love. I'll have you at my side during all trials so that you'll be able to advise me from your heart as I use my head."

"Remember I'm a soldier too," I told him. "I can be logical as well."

"I know you can, but you have proven time and time again to have quite a gentle soul, and for the consort of the prince, it's a rare and fine quality."

"That's a nice thing to say."

"Well, I mean it."

"Yeah, I know, that's why it's special."

He bent and kissed me, taking my mouth slowly, seeking entrance with his tongue, which I instantly allowed. I whimpered in the back of my throat, offering, submitting, and he deepened the kiss to a ravenous yearning that became the claiming I craved.

"Such a strong and beautiful and virile man, and yet you yield to me every time," he finished gruffly. His voice had a rough sweetness that raced through my blood and set me on fire. "I can taste the surrender when I kiss you."

"I give in because I want to. Can't you taste that too?"

"Of course."

I took a breath. "I'm the consort. I give and my prince takes. That's the way of it, and it feels right."

He reclaimed my mouth in a mauling kiss that left no doubt that worked for him.

"You're the only one I can be this way with," I admitted. "I trust you."

"And I will always be worthy of my consort's faith."

I knew he would. I'd already seen his heart, and it was like my own filled to bursting all at once. He was so good, so kind, so thoughtful, and so mine. He was absolutely the best man, and I was going to do my damnedest to deserve him.

"Tell me what else is on your mind," he prodded, his smile wicked. He obviously liked us in bed, between the sheets, talking. I understood. It was an intimacy neither of us had before: someone we slept with who we shared our life with as well.

"Your father wants us at court."

"Oh?"

"Yeah," I gasped as he slid his hardening cock over my thickening one. Only the thin layer of my sleep shorts separated us. "We've been summoned."

"Then we had better go," he said, lifting off me to reach into the nightstand for a bottle of lube before rolling sideways.

"Who put that there?" I asked, chuckling, yanking my shorts down and off. "I mean, when did you even have time to buy this house?"

"Tiago placed this here, I'm sure," he answered, lying down on his back and smiling up at me as he waved the bottle. "And I told him to find me a home—not a house—that you could make your own, one that would have room for your friends as well as him and Hadrian and the rest of my men, but still be cozy, still be warm like you."

"This mansion is your idea of cozy?" I teased, crawling over him. I straddled his thighs, took the lube from him, and popped open the cap.

"It's ridiculously small," he explained, sounding just as haughty and put out as Tiago earlier. "We'll all be on top of each other, and soon enough you'll realize that something much bigger will be necessary."

But I wouldn't. "The garden is beautiful," I told him while putting lube in my palm before taking my lover's long, gorgeously thick cock in hand.

He dropped his head back onto the pillow, and a filthy moan came out of those full, dusky lips. He pushed up into my hand, and I squeezed and stroked, loving the feel of his slick skin sliding through my fingers.

"The whole house is beautiful," I told him, lifting up over him. I pressed the wide head of his cock to my hole and slowly seated myself.

"*You* are the most beautiful thing in this house," he groaned, grabbing hold of my thigh with one hand and my shaft with the other. "My consort, my heart… my blood."

What he was doing with his left hand, tugging, pulling, was the perfect counterpoint to his slow push inside of me, the filling and stretching as he made certain, with the iron hold of his right hand, that I could not rush any part of being impaled on his cock.

"Are you ready to show me off?" I asked, finishing the slide down, fully seated, my ass flush with his hips, my hands flat on his chest. I lifted and repeated the motion, gasping as he filled me again. I was utterly lost in the sensation.

"I am ready to have everyone see you at my side," he husked, lifting me off him as I protested, loudly, only to pull me down into his arms and hold me close, spooning, side by side on the bed.

The power in him was breathtaking, and I wasn't a small man, but he moved me effortlessly, seamlessly, to our sides with him at my back. When he put his right hand under my thigh and lifted, spreading me wide to fuck me from the side, his name spilled out of me.

"Oh, yes," he rumbled, his mouth on the side of my neck. He kissed and sucked as he cradled my head in his left arm. "I'm yours."

He held me tight as he thrust every hard inch into me over and over. It was both erotic and grounding. I was ravaged and safe, more care and nurturing there than I had ever experienced with any other lover. He took and gave in equal measure, and as I slipped my hand up into his hair, the words cracked loose, and I was helpless to stop them. "I love you," I confessed. The thrusts became fluid and rolling, pressing deep and pulling back, straddling that razor-thin line between pleasure and pain. But in moments my body suffused with heat, and there was pressure as my balls drew up tight, my cock leaking as he took hold of it and stroked, working my flesh in the same rhythm as he fucked me.

"And I love you," he said darkly, his voice a husky growl before he bit me.

His fangs puncturing my skin brought me to blinding, roaring climax, and I came apart in his hands, the throbbing pleasure utterly consuming for long, endless moments. I checked out to everything but the loud beating of my heart and his cock buried inside me.

My body jolted against him as he ground into me, his thirst endless for my body and my blood.

"I'm all yours," I murmured, and I felt his rhythm falter before he drove to my core and came deep within my body.

He withdrew his fangs from the side of my neck and licked the wound, the last drops on his tongue, and I let my head fall back and took deep breaths, cradled against him.

"I have all that I could ever need here in my arms," he whispered into my ear. "There is no part of me that you don't feed and nourish and love."

When I turned so I could see him, he leaned in and kissed me.

It was a long, wet, thorough kiss, and when I twitched, oversensitized as he eased free of my body, he rolled me over and drew me close again, tucking my face into the hollow of his throat.

He pulled the sheet around us and didn't let me go. "I like you wrapped around me," he said, yawning.

"Well, you'll sleep better on me," I said, shifting around so I had my head on the pillow and his on my chest. We were still finding our spots and where we were most comfortable and how we fit.

"Oh yes," he sighed, draping an arm over my waist, and I felt his weight sink over me. "This is better. You're a very smart man."

"I try," I said, luxuriating in the feel of his skin, his warmth, his closeness, and let the idea that he was actually mine become my reality.

After long minutes of silence where I almost fell asleep, his deep, resonant voice stirred me. "I normally dread returning to Valletta, making my appearance at court, dealing with the different agendas, the gossip and the jealousy, but now…." He sighed. "Now I can't wait to take you with me and show you my home." He finished by lifting his arm from my side to move the seal where he wanted it, right under my collarbone. "I can't wait to show you my world and have you take your place in it at my side."

"I can't either."

"You're my consort, but first, before anything, you're my love."

I couldn't imagine there being anything I'd ever want more.

Read more from Mary Calmes

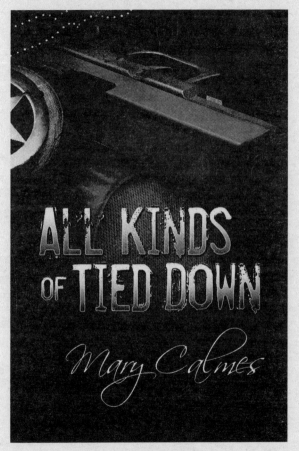

Marshals: Book One

Deputy US Marshal Miro Jones has a reputation for being calm and collected under fire. These traits serve him well with his hotshot partner, Ian Doyle, the kind of guy who can start a fight in an empty room. In the past three years of their life-and-death job, they've gone from strangers to professional coworkers to devoted teammates and best friends. Miro's cultivated blind faith in the man who has his back… faith and something more.

As a marshal and a soldier, Ian's expected to lead. But the power and control that brings Ian success and fulfillment in the field isn't working anywhere else. Ian's always resisted all kinds of tied down, but having no home—and no one to come home to—is slowly eating him up inside. Over time, Ian has grudgingly accepted that going anywhere without his partner simply doesn't work. Now Miro just has to convince him that getting tangled up in heartstrings isn't being tied down at all.

www.dreamspinnerpress.com

Chapter One

RUNNING.

All our interactions with suspects ended the same way. I would say, hey, let's wait for backup or a warrant. I'd mention we didn't have probable cause, and sometimes I would even go so far as to point out we weren't armed because it was our damn day off! Not that he ever listened. The chase was always on seconds after I spoke. The fact that he even stopped to listen to me before acting stunned most people who knew us.

"Please," I would beg him. "Just this once."

And then I'd get the head tip or the shrug or the grin that crinkled his pale blue eyes in half before he'd explode into action, the velocity of movement utterly breathtaking. Watching him run was a treat; I just wished I wasn't always following him into the path of whizzing bullets, speeding cars, or flying fists. Since

I'd become his partner, the number of scars on my body had doubled.

I considered it a win if I got Ian Doyle to put on a Kevlar vest before he kicked down a door or charged headfirst into the unknown. I saw the looks we got from the other marshals when we returned with bloodied suspects, recaptured felons, or secured witnesses, and over the years they had changed from respect for Ian to sympathy for me.

When I was first partnered with him, some of the other marshals were confused about it. Why was the new guy—me—being partnered with the ex-Special Forces soldier, the Green Beret? How did that make sense? I think they thought I got an unfair advantage and that getting him as a partner was like winning the lottery. I was the newest marshal, low man on the totem pole, so how did I rate Captain America?

What everyone missed was that Ian didn't come from a police background like most of us. He came from the military and wasn't versed in proper police procedure or adherence to the letter of the law. As the newest marshal on the team, I was the one who had the book memorized the best, so the supervisory deputy, my boss, assigned me to him. It actually made sense.

Lucky me.

Doyle was a nightmare. And while I wasn't a Boy Scout, in comparison to my "shoot first, ask questions later" partner, I came off as calm and rational.

After the first six months, everyone stopped looking at me with envy and switched to pity. Now, going on three years, marshals in my field office would bring me an ice pack, pass me whatever pharmaceuticals they had in their desks, and even occasionally offer advice. It was always the same.

"For crissakes, Jones, you need to talk to the boss about him."

My boss, Supervisory Deputy Sam Kage, recently called me into his office and asked me flat out if there was any truth to the rumors he was hearing. Did I want a change of partner? The blank stare I gave him hopefully conveyed my confusion. So it was no one's fault but my own that I was running in the slushy melting snow down the forty-seven hundred block of Ninety-Fifth Street in Oak Lawn at ten on a cold Tuesday morning in mid-January.

Arms pumping, Glock 20 in my hand, I saw Ian motion to the left, so I veered off and leaped an overturned garbage can as I headed into an alley. I should have been the one on the street; my partner was better at leaping and running up walls like a ninja. Even though I was younger than his thirty-six by five years, at six two and 185 pounds, he was in much better shape than me. While he was all lean, carved muscle with eight-pack abs and arms that made women itch to touch, I was built heavier at five eleven, with bulky muscle and wide shoulders, more bull than panther. Ian had a sleek, fluid way about him; I was all sharp angles and herky-jerky motion. We were as different as we could be, though people often commented that we had a really similar irritating way of carrying ourselves when together, an unmistakable strut. But I would have known if I was doing that, if I puffed up when I walked beside my partner. No way I swaggered and didn't notice.

The second I emerged from the trash-strewn alley, I was hit by a 250-pound freight train of a man and smashed onto the pavement under him.

"Oh!" I heard my partner yell as my spine splintered and every gasp of air in my body was trounced out of my frame. "Nice block, M!"

The escaped convict tried to lever up off me, but Ian was there, yanking him sideways, driving him down on the sidewalk beside me with a boot on his collarbone. I would have told him not to go overboard with manhandling—I took it upon myself to caution him against all manner of infractions during the course of a normal day—but I had no air, no voice, nothing. All I could do was lie on the cold, clammy cement and wonder how many of my ribs were broken.

"Are you getting up?" Ian asked snidely as he rolled Eddie Madrid to his stomach, pulled his arms behind his back, and cuffed him quickly before moving to squat next to me. "Or are you resting?"

All I could do was stare up at him, noting that he was scowling, as usual. That scowl was permanently etched on his face, and even when he grinned, the creases above and between his eyebrows never smoothed all the way. He was tense, just a little, at all times.

"If I didn't know you were tough, I'd be starting to worry," he said gruffly.

The fact that neither I nor Eddie was moving should have clued him in.

"M?"

I tried to move and pain shot through my left wrist. What was interesting was that the second I winced, his light eyes darkened with concern.

"Did you break your wrist?"

As though I was responsible for my own bones getting snapped. "I didn't break anything," I groaned, a bit of air finally inflating my lungs, enough to give me a hoarse, crackly voice. "But I think your friend over here did."

"Maybe we better get you to the hospital."

"I'll go by myself," I groused. "You take Madrid in."

He opened his mouth to argue.

"Just do what I say," I ordered, annoyed that I was broken. Again. "I'll call you if I can't make picking up Stubbs from lockup."

His scowl deepened as he took my good hand and hauled me to my feet. I went to move around him, but he leaned forward and his prickly dark brown stubble grazed my ear, the sensation making me jolt involuntarily.

"I'm coming with you," he said hoarsely. "Don't be an ass."

I studied him, the face I knew as well as my own—maybe better after looking at it for the past three years, straight on or in profile as he drove. His gaze on the ground, suddenly flicking up, colliding with mine, startled me with its intensity. He was utterly focused; I had every drop of his attention.

"Sorry."

I was stunned, and it must have shown on my face because the furrowed brows, the glower, were instant. "Holy shit," I teased. "It's a little early for spring thaw."

"You're a dick," he flared, turning away.

After grabbing hold of his shoulder, I yanked hard, fisting my hand in the half trench he wore, stepping in close. "No, I'm happy—actually, really happy. Come on. Relax."

He growled at me.

"Take me to the emergency room." I chuckled, holding on to him.

His grunt made me smile, and when I squeezed his shoulder, I saw how pleased he seemed to be. "Let's go."

He heaved Madrid to his feet—which was interesting since our fugitive outweighed him by a good sixty pounds—threw him up against the car, opened the back door, and shoved him in. It took only moments, and then he was back to facing me, stepping forward into my space, so close I could feel the heat rolling off him.

"You should never question that I'm gonna go with you. That's what partners are for."

"Yeah, but—"

"Say okay."

He never demanded things of me. Normally there was browbeating, teasing, derision—but not concern. It was strange. "Yeah, okay."

Nodding quickly, he walked around the side of the 1969 Cadillac deVille we were currently driving. Whatever was seized during drug raids or other criminal activity was what we got. The last ride had been a 2000 Ford Mustang I was crazy about, either driving—which I scarcely ever did—or riding in. It was a sad day when it became the victim of heavy machine-gun fire. The grenade tossed through the window had been the final straw. Ian kept saying it was fixable up until that point.

The *bow-chicka-bow-wow* car we were in now, all whitewall tires and green metallic paint, was a little much for the US Marshals Service. But we were supposed to travel incognito, and cruising through the worst parts of Chicago, no one gave us a second look.

"Get in," he barked.

"Yessir."

And as usual, we were off like a rocket, no gentle merge into traffic. Ian always drove like he was fleeing a bank robbery and I had learned to simply buckle up.

"What the fuck," Eddie Madrid yelled from the backseat, having lurched forward and then been hurled back in a whiplash maneuver. "Someone belt me in."

I started laughing as I turned to my partner, who was swearing at the people sharing the road with them. "Even our prisoner fears for his life."

"Fuck him," he snarled, taking a corner like he was a stunt driver getting ready to jump out.

Eddie slammed into the partial window on the passenger side of the sedan. "Jesus Christ, man!"

I just braced for impact, hoping I'd make it to the hospital in one piece.

"LEMME GET this straight," Ian said that afternoon as he led James "the Cleaver" Pellegrino to our car. "You've got a broken wrist, and you're bitching about your shoes?"

Normally doctors didn't cast broken bones until a few days later due to swelling. But because I had no intention of riding my desk until it mended, and because it was a clean break, the ER doctor had made an exception. He said that if the cast got too loose, I might have to return and have another put on. I didn't care; the important thing was that I could follow Ian back out into the field.

"Yeah," I whined, scrutinizing the plaster cast on my wrist and then, more importantly, my now scuffed-up John Varvatos cap-toe boots. Pellegrino had taken one look at me standing in the doorway when he came up from the basement, and bolted. We had been responding to an anonymous tip and found him at his cousin's house in La Grange. To keep him from making it out the back door, I dived at him. We ended up rolling over concrete before Ian had come flying around the side of the house and landed all over the guy. "They were new last week."

"And they were gonna be trashed by now anyway," Ian commented. "No way around it in the snow."

I glanced up at him. "This is why I wanted to move to Miami with Brent. Snow would be a distant memory."

He snorted out a laugh. "That guy was so not worth moving for."

I arched an eyebrow.

"And besides," he said gruffly, "you weren't gonna leave me anyway."

"I would ditch you in a second, buddy. Don't kid yourself."

He scoffed. "Yeah, right."

Apparently he knew better than to believe such an outright lie.

"You guys want me to leave you alone?" Pellegrino said snidely.

Ian threw him up against the car, and Pellegrino screamed because he landed on his chest, the same place that had recently been in contact with exposed brick.

"Shut up."

"This is police brutality."

"Lucky we're not the police," Ian reminded him, smacking him on the back of the head before his light blue gaze landed on me. "And why do you wear your good stuff to work? I've never understood that."

"Because," I answered, gesturing at him, "Dockers and a button-down and an ugly tie is not what I wanna be seen in every day."

"Well, that's great, but you ruin a ton of shit and then bitch about it."

"Hiking boots do not scream fashion."

"Yeah, but your John-whatever boots are fucked up already, and mine are still good."

"They look like shit," I assured him.

"But still functional," he teased, and the rakish curl of his lip did flip-floppy things to my stomach.

It was bad. So very, very bad. Ian Doyle was my totally straight best friend and partner. I had no right to even be noticing how the half trench coat molded to his shoulders; the roping veins in his forearms; or the way he touched me when he talked to me, sat beside me, or got anywhere in my general vicinity. How he was always in my personal space, as though I had none, was not something he was even aware of, so truthfully, it wasn't right for me to notice. But trying to pretend I didn't was eating me up alive. It was the real reason I should have asked for a change of partner, because I dreamed of being in bed with my current one.

"No snarky comeback?"

I coughed. "No."

He squinted. "How come?"

"You have a point, I guess. I shouldn't wear shoes to work that'll get ruined."

"I can get you a new pair," the Cleaver offered quickly before Ian could form a reply. "Please."

Ian smacked him on the back of the head again, opened the car door, pushed my seat forward, and shoved Pellegrino in.

"You're such an asshole, Doyle!" Pellegrino yelled before Ian slammed the door shut.

"Don't bruise him," I cautioned like I always did.

"Why the fuck not?"

I groaned.

"And for the record," Ian huffed, rounding on me. "You do not go into buildings alone. What did we say about that after Felix Ledesma?"

I mumbled something because my iPhone had buzzed with a text and I was reading.

"Miro!"

"I hear you."

"Look at me."

My head snapped up. "Yeah, fine, okay, shut up."

"No, not fine. Not okay. Every fuckin' time you take off your shirt and I see the scar right above your heart, I—"

"I know," I soothed, leaning close to bump his shoulder with mine.

He growled.

"Oh," I said, noticing the time. "You need to dump me and the Cleaver off so you can make your date with Emma."

The way his whole face tightened was not a good sign, but far be it from me to tell him that his girlfriend, though wonderful, was not for him. It would have been so much easier if she was toxic and I hated her. The truth was, she was sort of perfect. Just not for him.

"What're you gonna do?"

"When?" I was confused. "I'll process our prisoner so you can be on time for once."

He looked uncomfortable. "And then what?"

"Oh, I'm supposed to be playing pool tonight with some guys from my gym."

His face lit up.

"No." I snickered. "Bad. Your girlfriend does not want to play pool with strangers."

His glare was ridiculously hot. "How do you know?"

"That's not a date, Ian."

"Well, you shouldn't go either."

I wondered vaguely if he had any idea how petulant he sounded. "I broke my left wrist, not the right. I can hold a cue just fine."

"You should go home and go to bed," Ian said, glowering as he walked around the car to the driver's door.

"No, man, I gotta work through the pain," I teased before I got in.

"What're you talking about?" he asked irritably after he slammed his door and turned to me. "You broke your fuckin' wrist."

"But isn't that your mantra or some shit? The Green Beret code and all? Screw the pain?"

"Playing pool isn't work. You don't hafta do it."

Throat clearing from the back seat. "You know, you guys could just leave me here," the Cleaver suggested cheerfully. "Then nobody has to do paperwork at all, and maybe you guys could double date."

Ian twisted around in his seat. "I have a better idea. Why don't you shut the fuck up before I get you back out of this car, take off the cuffs, and make you run away so I can shoot you."

"Maybe you'll miss."

Ian scoffed.

"I'll take that deal. What're you carrying, a nine millimeter?"

"Again, not cops. Marshals," Ian explained. "You ever get shot with a forty caliber?"

I couldn't contain my chuckle at how contrite the Cleaver appeared.

"Maybe I'll just stay put."

"And shut up," Ian barked.

"Yeah, okay."

He turned around and gripped the steering wheel, and I realized how tense he was.

"Shooting people is bad," I stressed playfully, poking Ian's bicep.

I got a derisive sound back, but that quickly, he seemed better, the edge gone.

"Move this crate. I need to get this guy processed fast, because I really have to change."

"At least your shoes, huh?" Ian teased, the tip of his head and the eyebrow waggle really annoying.

I did my best to ignore him.

Chapter Two

Granger's was an older pub downtown, close to The Loop. I had fallen in love with it over the many times Ian dragged me there. It had good cheap beer, great hotdogs, and a haphazard floor layout that sort of meandered from room to room, making it feel bigger than it really was. Ian and I normally staked out a spot between the pool tables and the dart boards where we could still see whatever game was on the TV above the bar as well as the door. Checking who came in was always important to law-enforcement types and was something that couldn't be turned off.

So I wasn't thrilled that the table where my gym cronies gathered was toward the back, but I made my way through the crowd to them anyway after stopping at the bar to get an IPA I liked.

"Miro you made it," Eric Graff, my occasional racquetball partner and one-time fuck buddy, greeted me as I reached them.

The other men and women were also pleased to see me, all except Eric's new boyfriend, Kyle, who, I was guessing, didn't love Eric's arm draped around my shoulders. I would have told him not to worry—I never went back for seconds unless either my mind was challenged or there were fireworks in bed. Neither had been the case with Eric.

Giving his arm a quick pat, I extricated myself and moved through the group until I reached Thad Horton, who was more than an acquaintance but not quite a friend.

"Hey," I greeted the pretty man who I had swam laps with many a time. He was a tanned, tweezed, manscaped twink, always quick with a smile and a kind word.

"Miro," he almost squeaked when he saw me, which alerted the gorilla standing beside him.

"Babe?" he asked, checking on Thad before focusing his attention on me. "Who're you?"

"Just a friend from the gym," I said quickly. "You must be Matt. Thad talks about you all the time."

He took my hand, clearly relieved, shaking fast. "Matt Ruben."

"Pleasure."

"Oh, are you the FBI agent?"

"Marshal," I corrected him, watching Thad grimace behind him and mouth the word "*Sorry.*"

Quick shake of my head to let him know it was no big deal.

"That's right. Marshal," Matt went on. "Thad was very impressed."

"It sounds far more glamorous than it is."

"Doubtful," Matt said kindly. "You wanna break, man? We're just starting a new game."

"Yeah, sure."

It was fine, and everyone was nice enough, but I'd made up my mind to leave when the game was over. I was bored, as was the usual with me unless either Ian or one of my very best friends was there. I really was lousy at casual interactions. When my phone buzzed a few minutes later, I leaned back against the exposed brick wall to answer.

"You're on a date," I commented.

"It's actually a group thing, and we're having dim sum."

I snorted out a laugh. Dim sum would not fill Ian up. He loved Chinese food as much as me—but noodles, chicken, and pork in large portions, not small pieces in steamer baskets.

"Fuck you, come meet me."

"Meet you? It's a date. She wants you to get comfortable with her friends."

"I don't care. I feel like hitting a ball."

Whenever he was bored, he thought about going to the batting cages. "Closed until March, buddy," I reminded him. "It's like twenty degrees outside right now, plus snow."

"What about bowling?"

"What about it?" I chuckled.

Silence.

God, I was ridiculous for even considering going. "Where are you?"

My hunger for Ian Doyle's company had gone from casual appreciation and friendship to a craving for the man himself that sat like a cold, hard stone in the pit of my stomach. Not that anyone knew; even the object of my affection would never be allowed to see how famished I was for his touch on my skin, his scent on my sheets, his breath in my ear. I hid the yearning well.

"At Torque in River North."

"That's not a Chinese restaurant."

"Like I don't fuckin' know that."

"Then what're you—"

"I told you, it's stupid."

"Are you sure it's okay?"

"Yeah, I'm sure, just come on."

"All right," I muttered, levering off the wall, "Gimme like—"

"Wait, where are you?"

"I'm at Granger's."

"Oh, I'll come there instead."

"Ian, buddy, you're on a *date*," I emphasized. "You're not supposed to bail."

"I'll just tell them—"

"Just stay put. I'll be right there."

A huff of breath and then he was gone.

I made my excuses to the group, drained my beer, handed off my pool cue, and was on my way to the door when I moved to shift around a woman and she turned.

"Jill," I said, smiling fast.

"Miro." She beamed for a second and then faltered. "Oh, is Ian with you?"

How her whole face fell, like there was nothing worse she could think of than seeing my partner, was sort of sad. "No, he's not. I'm actually going to meet him now."

"Good," she sighed, clearly relieved, and then she visibly realized what she'd said. "Oh, no, I didn't mean it like—"

"It's fine."

She exhaled sharply. "I'm sorry. I know he's your partner, but honestly the only good quality the man has is having you for a best friend."

I smirked. "You don't think that's a little harsh?"

"No, I really don't. You should have a PSA made, Miro. Something like: even though Ian Doyle is drop-dead gorgeous, just walk away, because dating him will be short and disappointing, as he's clearly holding out for someone else."

I nodded, moving to leave. "So you've given this some thought, I see."

"I wasted a month of my life thinking a US marshal would be a fun thing to have," she said, shrugging. "I may be an idiot, but he's the one guilty of false advertising."

"Well, I think—"

"And he's terrible in the sack."

It was my cue to run; it was too bad I couldn't. The crowd was too thick for me to bolt, so I plastered on a smile and pushed through. She caught my hand quickly, squeezing tight, letting me know that we were still good, before I pulled away and she was swallowed.

Outside, I moved to the curb to hail a cab, and my phone rang.

"What?"

"We're on our way to The Velvet Lounge. Meet me there."

I laughed into the phone. "Ian, buddy, I am so not dressed for The Velvet Lounge."

"Me neither."

"You're wearing a suit, aren't you?"

"No. Why?"

Lord. "Let me talk to Emma."

There was some muffled noise and then, "Miro?"

"Hey, Em," I said softly. "Are you guys going to The Velvet Lounge?"

"Yeah, we are, right after we drive Ian by his place so he can change."

I coughed softly. "Em?"

"Yes?"

"Was The Velvet Lounge a last-minute group decision?"

"Well, yeah. I'm doing some PR work for the owner, and he just called to say he put me on the list for tonight. How awesome is that?"

"So great," I agreed weakly. "But would it be okay if I borrowed Ian? My plans fell through, and I don't know if he told you I broke my wrist today, but—"

"No, he—oh, I'm so sorry," she said sympathetically. "But ohmygod, yes. Can I pretty please pawn him off on you?" Her voice had dropped to a whisper. "I swear to God, he's so bored and he's bringing everybody down."

I was certain he was. Ian did not suffer in silence. "Yeah, please. Put him on."

"I'll owe you big time. Thank you."

If she only knew how permanently I wanted to take him off her hands. "No problem."

Again there was the muffled noise of a phone being passed around. "Hey?"

"I'll grab sandwiches at Bruno & Meade. You come over, bring Chickie, and we'll take him for a run after we eat, all right?"

"Yeah?" He sounded so hopeful.

"Yeah, come on. Your woman said you can come play with me."

"I don't need fuckin' permission," he said, instantly defensive.

"Yeah, but you didn't want to hurt her feelings, which was nice," I pacified. "But she's fine, ready to have a fun night, and you're bringing all the hipsters down."

"Like I give a—"

"You'd rather be there?"

No answer.

"E?"

"I'll meet you at home."

"No, at my place, not yours."

"That's what I said."

It *wasn't* what he said unless… but thoughts like that did me no good. "Okay."

"Yeah, so, all right."

Which was his version of thank you and I'm sorry for being a dick and everything else. He was very lucky I spoke Ian. "Don't forget to bring the scoop thing, 'cause I ain't picking up your dog's crap."

He was laughing when I hung up.

WHEN I got home, the lights were on in my small Greystone, so I knew Ian was already inside. I tried really hard not to like the idea of him being there when I walked through the door, because wanting something I couldn't have was a recipe for bitterness. I loved having Ian as a partner, we fit perfectly, each playing off the other's strengths, and I didn't want that feeling to change. So I squashed down the stomach flip over seeing him in my kitchen, drinking a glass of water as he leaned against the counter.

"Just come in, why don't you," I groused.

From around the side of the couch came Ian's creature. Easily a hundred pounds of powerful muscle, Chickie appeared even bigger than he was with all the long black and white hair. I wasn't sure what kind of dog he was, and Ian didn't know either. I had often said maybe timber wolf.

"What are you doing in my house?" I asked the dog, who didn't break stride until he reached me, shoved his wet nose in my palm and danced for me, so very happy to be included.

"Thanks, M," Ian said as he drained his glass and sat it down. "You're the only one he doesn't freak out."

"It's because I know he doesn't really eat people," I said, scratching behind Chickie's ears and under his chin as he wriggled and then pranced after me as I joined Ian in the kitchen. "Maybe we should run him now, before we eat. He seems kinda wound up."

"Yeah, that'd be good," he agreed.

"Lemme change," I said, putting the bag of food down in front of Ian. He was in sweats and a hoodie, so I needed to be dressed the same. "Throw this in the fridge and see if I have any beer glasses in the freezer."

"What's wrong with drinking from the bottle, princess?" He grinned at me.

"Dick."

He started to whistle as I took the stairs to the loft where my bed, closet, and second bathroom were. It wasn't a whole second level, which I liked about the layout.

Once I was in sweats that had "US Marshal" down the side, I came back down and headed toward the front door.

"Why do you wear those?"

He lost me. "What?"

"The work sweats."

"I don't understand the question. We wear these when we train."

"Yeah, I know, so why the hell would you wear them when you're off?"

"They're sweats, Ian. Who the hell cares?"

"They're flashy."

My eyebrows lifted involuntarily. "They're flashy?"

He flipped me off, snapping Chickie's leash on and stalking to the door.

"They're *flashy*," I repeated.

"People are gonna want to see if you're a real marshal, and what if they fuck with you?"

"Yeah, that's true, because, you know, the dog won't deter anyone at all."

Again I was flipped the bird before the three of us went out the front door. Locking it behind me, I leaped off the top step of the small stoop.

"One, two, three—go!" I yelled, and I bolted away from Ian, running down the sidewalk like a crazy man and charging across the street without looking, knowing that in my Lincoln Park neighborhood the only thing I was in danger of being hit by would be a snowplow.

It was dark but the streetlights were on, and the sky was a beautiful deep blue with indigo patches that would soon be lit up with stars—though I might or might not be able to see them for the light pollution. I loved the time of night when people were sitting down to dinner and I could see into their homes for just a moment as I jogged by on my normal run. The houses blurred at the moment, as I raced toward the park with Ian and Chickie close behind.

"Miro!"

I didn't stop, and I heard Ian curse before Chickie was suddenly running beside me. Ian had allowed him to run free off the leash.

Veering right, I ran by one of the poles that kept cars off the gravel path between the field where kids played soccer and the playground with the swings and jungle gym. Chickie caught up with me again, and when I took a different route down toward the jogging path, Ian was there, hand suddenly fisted in the back of my jacket, holding on.

I slowed down, laughing, and he yanked me into him, bumping; his chest pressed into my back. We were both still moving, so he lost his balance when we collided and would have gone down if he hadn't wrapped an arm around my neck for balance.

His hot breath, his lips accidentally brushing against my nape, brought on a shiver I couldn't contain.

"Why'd you run?" he asked, still holding on, his other hand clutching the front of my jacket, his arm over my shoulder, across my chest.

"Just to make sure Chickie had fun," I said, feeling how hard my heart was beating and knowing it had nothing to do with the sprint I'd just led him on.

"Yeah, but you're cold," Ian said, opening one hand, pressing it over my heart for a moment before he stepped away from me.

I was freezing the second he moved. "Yeah, I am," I agreed quickly, patting Chickie, who was nuzzling into my side. "Let's jog back, get the blood pumping. That way we'll get warm."

Ian agreed, and we jogged together along the path, Chickie flying forward, only to come loping back, making sure Ian was where he could see him.

We made a giant loop and made it back home right before we both turned into Popsicles. Since I hadn't seen Chickie relieve himself, I told Ian he should probably walk him around the block once more.

"But I'm hungry," he whined.

"Well, I don't know what to tell you. Your dog did not take a shit, and he needs to."

Ian pivoted to look at his dog. "Chickie!" he yelled.

Chickie took one look at his master and squatted right there on the patch of grass beside the curb. Ian's expression of disgust and disbelief sent me into hysterics.

"You scared the shit outta the dog!"

"That's not funny."

I couldn't even breathe, it was so funny.

As Ian pulled plastic bags from his pocket, I doubled over, and Chickie came barreling up the steps past him—right to me—and licked my face, very pleased with himself.

"Stupid dog," he muttered as I continued to howl. "Stupid partner."

The man was cursed with both of us.

IAN TOOK off his hoodie and pulled on a zippered cardigan of mine before he came into the kitchen and watched me put together our sandwiches. I had picked them up from Bruno & Meade, a deli I loved, and what I liked about it was that it didn't assemble to-go orders. They gave you everything that came on the sandwich, all the ingredients, but the bread was sealed separately so it didn't get hard—or soft, depending on which kind you ordered—and everything else came in Ziploc bags or small plastic containers.

"You realize this is the height of laziness, right?" Ian commented as he put sliced bread and butter pickles into his mouth. "I mean, seriously, you could buy all this crap at the store and do this yourself."

"Oh yeah? The aioli mayonnaise, the chorizo salame, and Ossau you like? Really?" I asked, sliding the plate over to him. "You think I could just pop into a Jewel for that?"

He scowled at me.

"The sourdough that's freshly baked every day?"

Something was muttered under his breath.

"I got the gouda you like, and the marinated olives too."

"Are you still talking?"

"Why, yes." I smirked. "I am."

"Shut up," he muttered, grabbing a bottle of his favorite beer—Three Floyds Gumballhead, which I made sure was always there—from the refrigerator before he turned for the living room.

"And roma tomatoes are your favorite, so I made sure I asked for—"

"Yeah, fine, you're a fuckin' saint and I'm an ungrateful ass."

I cackled as he flopped down onto the couch and turned on the TV. The sounds of football filled the room. After a moment he turned around and looked at me.

"What? Need a napkin?"

"No, I have a—you're not gonna argue?"

"Why would I argue?"

"Ass," he mumbled, turning back to the game.

I joined him on the couch, sitting close like I always did, and he took some potato chips off my plate. "Go get your own," I said, smacking his hand away.

He shoved me with his shoulder and I almost dumped my plate.

"What're you doing?"

"Don't be stupid," he retorted, nudging my knee gently with his and then leaving his leg pressed against mine. "Since when don't I eat off your plate?"

He was right. I would let Ian do whatever he wanted, whenever he wanted. I was his for the taking—as were my potato chips.

MARY CALMES believes in romance, happily ever afters, and the faith it takes for her characters to get there. She bleeds coffee, thinks chocolate should be its own food group, and currently lives in Kentucky with a five-pound furry ninja that protects her from baby birds, spiders, and the neighbor's dogs.

To stay up to date on her ponderings and pandemonium (as well as the adventures of the ninja), follow her on Twitter @MaryCalmes, connect with her on Facebook, and subscribe to her Mary's Mob newsletter.

Timing: Book One

Stefan Joss just can't win. Not only does he have to go to Texas in the middle of summer to be the man of honor in his best friend Charlotte's wedding, but he's expected to negotiate a million-dollar business deal at the same time. Worst of all, he's thrown for a loop when he arrives to see the one man Charlotte promised wouldn't be there: her brother, Rand Holloway.

Stefan and Rand have been mortal enemies since the day they met, so Stefan is shocked when a temporary cease-fire sees the usual hostility replaced by instant chemistry. Though leery of the unexpected feelings, Stefan is swayed by a sincere revelation from Rand, and he decides to give Rand a chance.

But their budding romance is threatened when Stefan's business deal goes wrong: the owner of the last ranch he needs to secure for the company is murdered. Stefan's in for the surprise of his life as he finds himself in danger as well.

www.dreamspinnerpress.com

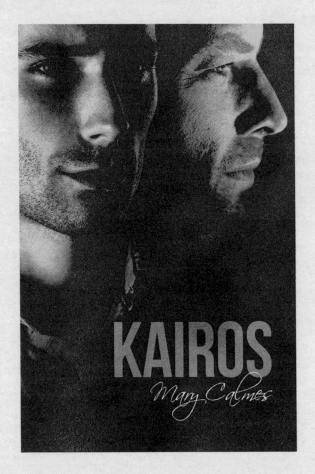

Sometimes the best day of your life is the one you never saw coming.

Joe Cohen has devoted the past two years of his life to one thing: the care and feeding of Kade Bosa. His partner in their PI business, roommate, and best friend, Kade is everything to Joe, even if their relationship falls short of what Joe desires most. But he won't push. Kade has suffered a rough road, and Joe's pretty sure he's the only thing holding Kade together.

Estranged from his own family, Joe knows the value of desperately holding on to someone dear, but he never expected his present and past to collide just as Kade's is doing the same. Now they've stumbled across evidence that could change their lives: the impact of Kade's tragic past, their job partnership, and any future Joe might allow himself to wish for....

www.dreamspinnerpress.com